"It's a buddy tale, a heist caper, a socioeconomic thriller and a steampunk-seasoned fantasia all at once. And it fires beautifully on all cylinders."
Jason Heller for NPR

"Megan O'Keefe's stories are always vivid and compelling."
Tim Powers, author of Declare *and* Three Days to Never

"Megan O'Keefe's prose is so full of fascinating twists and delights, you won't want to put it down. Go ahead, open it up: I dare you!"
David Farland, author of the bestselling Runelords series

"Blend two lovable rogues, a magical doppelganger, and a nasty empire, and you have O'Keefe's Steal the Sky. It's like an epic steampunk Firefly."
Beth Cato, author of The Clockwork Dagger

"Come for the heist, stay for the inventive world building."
Kirkus Reviews

"A fun, page turning debut."
SF Signal

"The tension rises throughout, leading up to an action packed third act, with some characters living up to their full potential. Mysteries keep unfolding, and you never truly learn the whole story, which means that there is now yet another series that I'm eagerly anticipating the follow up to."
Fantasy Faction

"*Steal the Sky* is a fun secondary-world adventure with plenty of exciting action, surprising twists, and wonderful payoffs to small seeds skilfully laid throughout the story."
Lightspeed Magazine

MEGAN E O'KEEFE

Break the Chains

A SCORCHED CONTINENT NOVEL

ANGRY
ROBOT

ANGRY ROBOT
An imprint of Watkins Media Ltd

Lace Market House,
54-56 High Pavement,
Nottingham,
NG1 1HW
UK

angryrobotbooks.com
twitter.com/angryrobotbooks
Busted!

An Angry Robot paperback original 2016
1

A catalogue record for this book is available from the British Library.

ISBN 978 0 85766 492 1
EBook ISBN 978 0 85766 494 5

Set in Meridien by Epub Services.
Printed in the UK by 4edge Ltd.

For Joey.

<3

CHAPTER 1

Cracked Thorn Steading appeared like a festering sore on the horizon. The township's red-painted roofs, crammed into a split in the cliffside, made it look as if the town was bleeding out across the desert sands. Pelkaia stood alongside her first mate, Coss, on the foredeck of the airship which had once been named the *Larkspur*, now rebirthed as the *Mirror*, and watched the township slide into focus. She squinted against the wind and put her eyeglass up, scanning until she found the sandstone jetty the city used to perform its executions.

Figures moved beneath the glaring sun, little more than smudges of silhouettes.

"This'll be a close 'un, captain," Coss said.

Pelkaia nodded and slammed her eyeglass closed against her thigh. Coss didn't need the glass to see what was afoot, that man could see an ant fart at a hundred paces. Although he couldn't move selium gas to save his life, he could see minute selium particles trapped in eddies of air, and how they bent around a body. He was useless for manipulating the selium bladders which gave the airship lift, but he was brilliant as a lookout. And as a spy. Not a day went by Pelkaia didn't bless the stable sands she'd scrounged him up out of Kalisan.

"We'll make it," she insisted.

He shoved his hands into his pockets and slouched

backward, a scowl carved into the granite square of his jaw. "You sure it's worth the risk? Could be a bum report, rumors being what they are. Wouldn't want to kick up a fight with the local watchers over a petty thief."

The *Mirror* caught a draft of good tailwind in its sails and lurched forward, eager to claim the speck of a prize standing on that spear of rock. She stroked the fore rail and gave Coss a tight nod.

"Our mere existence is a risk. If we're wrong, we're wrong. But I won't let them murder a so-called deviant just for breathing if there's a chance I can stop it."

She spun on her heel and pinned her makeshift crew under a critical gaze. Deviants, all of them, each one a selium-sensitive capable of manipulating that precious gas in a way the empire deemed indecent, if not outright illegal. They'd all been destined for a jail cell before Pelkaia came along and scooped them up, though none had been plucked out of a situation quite as dire as this.

Five souls handled the rigging, two hauled at the propeller cranks. Not a one of them was necessary to pilot the ship. If needed, Pelkaia could manipulate the directional force of the vast selium bladders hidden in the ship's hull. But most airships sported one sel-sensitive pilot, if that. A whole ship full was destined to raise a few eyebrows.

Jeffin, her mirrors-man, sat on the deck with his back against the captain's podium, eyes half-closed as he gathered his strength. Between the young man's wind-reddened cheeks and tousled, sandy hair, she could never quite tell when he was truly tired or just suffering the bodily abuses of late adolescence.

Stuck to Jeffin's shadow, as always, was Laella. The young woman had coaxed little Essi into sitting across from her on the top of a barrel. Though Laella's fingers were busy braiding the younger girl's hair, Pelkaia could see clear as a blue sky that the woman's eyes were locked on Jeffin, waiting for him to need her assistance. They were a study in contrasts;

the long-limbed woman born of aristocracy, and her sturdy Scorched counterpart. Try as Pelkaia might to keep an open mind, the simple presence of Laella rankled. Here was the daughter of her oppressor, no matter her deviant sensitivity.

"Laella!" Pelkaia snapped. "Stopped being a damned distraction and let Essi tie the blasted sails up."

She winced and bowed an apology. Essi leapt from the barrel, half-braided hair flapping in the breeze, and darted toward the mainmast.

"Jeffin! Mirrors up! Make us look like a flat-bellied wallower."

The young man leapt to his feet and saluted, then sat right back down and closed his eyes. Laella's shoulders slumped, but Pelkaia ignored her disappointment. The girl came from privilege. She could wait her turn. Pelkaia extended her sel-sense and felt Jeffin draw from the invisible selium ring her crew kept looped around the ship at all times. He sectioned off what he needed and shaped it into mirrors all along the hull. By the time he was done the ship looked like any other dinky imperial cruiser, the distinctive lines of the original *Larkspur* hidden away. She smiled to herself. This was what the empire missed out on, outlawing any sensitive who could do more than just move selium into airships. They'd never see them coming.

"Lotta watchers up there," Coss said, squinting toward the growing township.

"If they've got an illusionist, it'll be worth it." She folded her arms over her coat, a uniform piece stolen from an imperial commodore. The burgundy cloth stank of fresh dye, and the buttons had yet to lose their shine. The woman Pelkaia had snatched it from probably lost her post over the theft, but that wasn't any of Pelkaia's business.

She smiled at the approaching township. *This* was her business.

Coss grinned at her. "Rumor was a firebug."

"Now look who's bending to rumor."

"Oh fah. Can you imagine if it's true?"

She pursed her lips and adjusted her overlarge lapels. "Yes. Yes I can."

Coss's eyes widened and he looked away, pressing his mouth shut so hard his lips went bloodless. She knew the unspoken rule amongst her crew, though no one had ever dared tell it to her outright: *Don't speak of the Honding.* It'd been a year since she'd seen that firebug-scoundrel, and still the shadow of their meeting dogged her. She clenched her fists, and called out to those up on deck.

"To arms, all of you lazy scabs! Those bastards mean to send one of ours to the endless night today. And what do we have to say to that?"

"Get fucked!" the chorus went up.

She laughed, and strode toward her cabin. "Prepare yourselves. I need to put my face on."

Within her cabin, warm wax and raw oak permeated the air. She settled herself onto the padded seat of her new vanity, and unlatched the cap on her private sel bladder. While she worked, she ignored the gentle sway of the ship, the clatter of her crew, and the lack of her old bed behind her. The one her son had made.

In Aransa, she had used one of her bed's four high posts as a guide. Now, she had only the seams in the wall's planks to line up with. Guiding the selium to lay across her face in a fine, thin mask, she extended her senses and shifted the gas's color and texture.

She shaped a simple face, an approximation of the drink-sodden commodore she had liberated the coat from. It needn't be a perfect match, it was doubtful anyone would recognize a commodore of an inconsequential mercantile barge, but still Pelkaia found it advantageous to do her work beneath a mask. It left her true countenance unknowable; wanted posters difficult to print.

And it was always easier to put on an act while wearing

someone else's face.

It'd be a lovely thing, if the deviant they were looking to save now was also an illusionist. Having a twin in ability would make Pelkaia's work that much easier.

Coss's patterned knock rattled her door and she polished off her new visage. It was quick work, and wouldn't hold up under tight scrutiny, but she didn't expect the ruse to last. Despite Coss's reservations about a fight, the lads and ladies of the *Mirror* needed to start testing their teeth if they were ever going to strike back against Valathea's oppressive rule.

"Lookin' lovely," Coss said with a little smirk. "Do something with your hair, did you?"

"Nothing ever gets by you."

"We're almost in visual range for you blindies. Time for our esteemed commodore to make an appearance, eh?"

"Lead the way."

The *Mirror* slewed to a halt alongside the jetty, looking for all the world like an imperial patroller. While the ship settled she scanned the scene, taking in the half dozen watchers and the bound-and-bagged man in their charge. He stood barefooted on the hard stone, his breeches scarcely reaching past his knees and his shirt smeared with filth. Some over-puffed watcher in a faded blue uniform had been encouraging him toward the edge with the point of a cutlass, but now that Pelkaia's ship had arrived, his attention wavered. Pelkaia prayed to the sweet skies that the condemned man wouldn't take the distraction as an opportunity to end his own life.

"Ho, watchers," she called as she slung herself over the *Mirror*'s rail and onto solid land. "What's the meaning of this?"

Coss scrambled over after her and circled those gathered, edging toward the captive man. Pelkaia forced herself to keep her gaze on the watchers. Coss knew his business.

A watcher sheathed his cutlass and stomped toward her. The crust of a grey beard ensconced his sagging chin, and he had a few more bars stitched to his shoulder than the rest. As he moved, the other watchers turned their gazes after him, intent.

"Got ourselves a damned deviant, commodore." He cut a tight bow and gestured toward the waiting prisoner. "Care to do the honors yourself?"

She glanced at Coss, who held the captured man's bound wrists. Good, the condemned wouldn't do anything too stupid with Coss there to anchor him. Her crew dropped over the rail and fanned out around her, hands held easy at their sides. The watch-captain flicked narrowed eyes from one to the next, and rested his hand on the grip of his cutlass. Pelkaia sighed.

"What was his crime?" she asked.

"Pardon?"

"You heard me, what did this man *do*?"

He hawked and spat. "Crime of being a viper-kissed deviant, is what he did."

"Really," she drawled. "And did anyone happen to see him perform these deviant abilities?"

"Uh." One of the younger watchers stepped forward. "I did, commodore, begging your pardon. Saw him myself. Mercer Trag has... er, had... this pin, you see. Pretty thing you stick on your coat, real fancy. Was bragging about it, showed how there was a little ball of sel inside it, and it was nice, I'll grant you, and then this man–" he pointed to the convict, "–says how he'll, ah, give the Mercer something pretty to choke on, and poof, the thing burst into flames."

"I see, a smart-lipped firebug. Of course. And did he do anything else? Is anyone dead or grievously injured due to this man's behavior?"

"No, commodore, but–"

"And is the penalty for petty destruction of property in Cracked Thorn death?"

The watch-captain's lip curled in disgust. "Being deviant is crime enough."

"I will hear what this man has to say for himself. Coss, bring him."

The watch-captain's cheeks grew red with the effort of containing his anger. "Now wait a moment, commodore–"

She held up a hand and snapped it into a fist, cutting him off. "Do you mean to contradict the order of a commodore?"

"No, but–"

"Then be silent."

Her crew moved around her, shifting their positions to make it clear weapons were easy to hand. The watchers, to their credit, stood stiff-backed and allowed their hands to creep toward their own weapons. Pelkaia resisted an urge to sigh again. If only they knew her appropriation had nothing to do with petty jurisdiction politics.

Coss dragged the prisoner over and ripped the bag off his head.

Pelkaia stared.

"Detan. Honding."

Deep sun lines creased the corners of his eyes, and his hair stuck up in all directions. The sharpness of his chin and cheeks gave away a certain lack of consideration for proper nourishment. He grinned at her. That same, stupid grin he'd given her the first time she'd seen him.

"Pelly, old girl, I do love the way you say my name."

"Coss, throw him off," she said.

"Don't throw me. But do throw that bag off. It stank."

Coss stood where he was, baffled, looking like he was about to pinch the Honding to see if he were real. For his part, Detan appeared nonplussed. Irritation raked over her spine, raising gooseprickles. She opened her fists with the sudden desire to choke the mad bastard.

"You two *know* each other?" The watch-captain freed his cutlass, triggering his men to do likewise. Each blade was a fine piece of work, unblemished steel with the gleam of regular oil. They were probably the best kept things in the whole of this tumble-down town. Pelkaia snapped her fingers low and to the side. Coss nodded, and began to cut Detan free.

CHAPTER 2

Knives came out all around him, looking rather pointy, and Detan took an involuntary step backward. The sturdy man with the too-clean hair holding him by the ropes stopped Detan's retreat and leaned down to whisper, "Got a weapon?"

Detan blinked. "Gosh, me? I'm really more a master of the art of running away."

Pelkaia's man scowled at him, and he beamed right back, biting the insides of his cheeks in frustration. This was taking longer than he'd hoped.

The man cut his ropes and the blood rushed back, tingling his fingertips. Detan sighed with relief and rubbed the life back into his hands. It would've been embarrassing to lose a finger due to lack of circulation.

He clapped. A big, echoing crack that slammed the ears, courtesy of the mighty strange acoustics caused by Cracked Thorn's placement. All eyes turned to him, bright as the metal in their hands. For a heartbeat, he hesitated. What could he say to these wound-up vultures to keep them from plucking each other's eyes out?

Pelkaia's man pushed the grip of a knife into his palm. Poor bastard probably thought Detan knew how to use it. He hoped it wasn't the only one the man'd brought. Detan tested its weight, as he'd seen many knife-carriers do, and found it lighter than it should have been. Hesitantly, he extended his sel-sense. The thing had sel in its handle, making it as light as it was sharp. Detan frowned at it, something like an idea coming to him. A bad idea, more than likely, but he'd never been picky with a plan when the alternative was being stabbed. Clearing his throat, he reseated an affable grin.

"Commodore! There is no need for arguments, these men have proven well how ardent they are in carrying out the good laws of Valathea. Why, they were so damnably thorough I didn't even have a moment to explain that they had passed the test before we all ended up out here."

Pelkaia's eyes narrowed beneath the mask of her borrowed face, and he forced himself to stride forward without care, surreptitiously unscrewing the ball at end of the dagger's grip. A few tiny sel beads leaked out, struggling to rise. He centered himself, pushing aside any hint of fear or anger, as he held the sel in his mind.

This was his element, he was *good* at this. He would not lose control. Not again.

"A test?" The watch-captain grunted in disgust. "My man saw you work the deviant power with his own bald eyes. You sayin' that was staged somehow? Mercer Trag's pin catching fire like that?"

Detan chuckled as he sauntered forward, walking the border between the two sets of blades. Their points followed him as he passed. He itched to sprint away, to throw himself over the edge and trust to luck, but he forced himself to stand tall. To slip a pinch of sel between thumb and forefinger.

"Deviant power, me? What nonsense! Though I am flattered to hear you found the display convincing, it was just a harmless parlor trick. See? Smoke powder."

He stood in the center of the gulf between the two forces and faced the watchers, his body a wall between his hands and Pelkaia's crew. He held up a hand and snapped his fingers, feeding a sliver of anger into the sel. A bright, hot spark ignited. Detan cut off his connection to the spark, but it snaked out in all directions anyway. It lashed the air with the frantic motions of a beheaded snake, growing bright enough to send the watchers squealing and scampering.

He grimaced. Lost control. Again.

"Oops. Time to go!" He sang as he spun on his heel and grabbed the sleeve of the nearest scrubber-of-the-deck. The grubby man shook off his grip, but he followed Detan all the same. Indignant the man may be, but he had his survival instincts intact. Pelkaia gave the command to retreat and they fled as one, leaping the thick rail of the *Larkspur*'s deck.

With his sore, bare feet safely aboard the *Larkspur*'s silk-smooth deck he spun around and crowded the fore rail, hooting as the watchers recovered and dashed after them. Pelkaia vaulted the rail and stood beside him, her alien face grim. When all souls were back on board, he felt her extend her sel-sense. The massive presence of selium tucked away in the hull jerked to the side. The ship scuttled sideways, dancing out of the pursuing watchers' reach.

Detan cursed and hugged the rail to keep from falling. Out on the spire the watchers rallied – damnably efficient folk – and scampered towards their own flier, the craft that'd brought them up to the jetty so that Detan could kiss the sands from the skies.

Not a quick ship, not compared to the sleek beauty of the *Larkspur*, but quick enough to get them into arrow-firing range. Detan had long ago learned never to trust his luck, nor his skin, to poor aim. Pressed against the rail, he shifted his weight back and forth in a shuffling little dance, waiting for the crew to do something. Anything.

They didn't.

"Begging your pardon, Pelly old girl, but some sel wouldn't go amiss right about now."

Pelkaia raised her hand, and for one mad moment he

thought she would slap him. He cringed back, and she rolled her eyes. She ripped her false face off and flung it toward the watchers. Detan scrambled to extend his much clumsier sel-sense and grab the sel, then float it over to the stone arch between the jetty's edge and the flier's dock. The watchers were drawing close.

Sweating something fierce, he forced the fistful of incandescent gas against the arch's keystone and opened himself to it, venting his frustration.

For just a breath, the siren call of the sel surrounding him – more than the gas in the buoyancy sacks below – threatened to overwhelm him. A ring of sel orbited the ship, shifted to a mirror shine, a great swollen hoop ripe and ready for him to explode. A flutter of panic itched up his arm and he cut off his senses, digging his fingers into the rail so hard his nails bent backward.

Stone groaned, men cried out, and the whole thing went to the pits in a puff of dust and the flailing of blue coats running to clear the avalanche. He slumped, giving up his weight to the rail in exhaustion, too terrified to look back and see how large his conflagration had grown.

A cheer went up from the crew behind him, a good rousing tally-ho of the spirit, and he forced himself to plaster a smile back on his sweat-slick face and whirl around to take a bow. He liked to tell himself his knees didn't wobble and his arms didn't shake. If they did, the others were too polite to bring it up.

"With me, clown." Talon-like fingers dug into his shoulder. Pelkaia marched him forward in a neat line, the crew's eyes stuck to them like wool to a fine-toothed cactus. He smiled at them, and managed a few little waves, but each time he did, Pelkaia dug her nails in deeper. By the time they made it to the confines of her cabin – a space that was once *his* cabin – he thought his shoulder would be crushed to bits.

Though the unstable nature of ships didn't allow for a lot of decorative leeway, Pelkaia'd done her room up in full Catari style all the same. Indigo prayer mats embroidered with crisp white stars hung from the walls, strings of beads carved from all the rock types the Scorched had to offer looped her bed rail. It seemed Pelly didn't mind discovery of her bloodline anymore, no matter its outlawed status with Valathea. Detan wasn't sure if that was good for his schemes or not.

He kept his trap shut, tamping down the urge to make a smart remark about being dragged straight to the bedroom, and tried to look contrite. "I am so glad you got my message!"

Her sun-bleached brows shoved together. "Your message...? Oh, oh gods above and below, the rumors–"

"Tibs is such a little gossiper." The moment she closed her eyes in annoyance he flit his gaze around the cramped room to see if there was anything he could use to convince her to help him in his schemes. Too soon her eyes snapped back open, and he shrugged, palms out as if in offering.

"And what were you going to do if I hadn't received your so-called message?"

"Die of shock, more than likely. You've created a few choice rumors of your own, you know. Stories of a black ship snaking through the night, picking up any sel-sensitives with the tiniest deviation of ability. You're damned near a folk legend, Pelly. Say, I wonder if anyone's written a song about you? Something stompy, with a banjo. Oh! I bet–"

"Shut up."

He did.

"What do you want, Honding?"

"A long, fulfilling life. Possibly a chilled drink and one of those pastries with cactus pear jelly in the center. Do you have any?"

"Honding!"

He ducked his head to fake being chagrinned and ran one hand through his dusty, greasy hair. He had to get the contrition just right to win her to his cause. Had to measure the subtle shift of his weight to one side, as if uncertain, the soft blush of rising embarrassment, the catch of emotion in his throat. It was a real good thing Tibs had made him practice so many cursed times.

"I need your help, Pelkaia. Ripka and New Chum, they're in trouble."

Her eyes narrowed, but she leaned forward, interested. "What's happened?"

"We were up in Kalisan... Sightseeing."

"Sure you were."

"Well, Ripka caught a rumor from some old watcher buddies that Kalisan's warden was preparing to make a move on some local deviants. He'd planned on wrapping them up with a bow and handing them over to the whitecoats for a favor. Wasn't any way we could get in touch with these deviants, understand, so we poked around a bit. Found out the old warden was right particular about a certain notebook. Ripka went for it – took New Chum with her – without telling me or Tibs and got caught.

"Rumor is, she managed to hide the book somewhere before she got brought in, but no one knows where. She and New Chum got shipped off to the Remnant prison to sweat out their worries and consider how much smoother things might be if they give the crusty old warden back his intel. We tried to intervene during the transport, but missed the chance, so, you see–"

Pelkaia held up a silencing hand. "You expect me to believe Ripka would make a move like that without assistance?"

"A lot's changed since you skirted off with my ship," he snapped, not needing to fake indignity. "And Ripka is her own woman. Just because she's taken berth on my flier doesn't mean she tells me every cursed thing."

"If you recall, you were contracted to steal this ship for me." She laid a hand against the smooth wood of her cabin wall. "It was never meant for you."

Detan snorted. "More the fool you were, thinking I'd intended to just hand it over."

"And yet you did just hand it over."

"Only because you'd drugged the others! What was I supposed to do? Fight you off with my back crisped like I'd taken a nap on a firepit? Pits below, Pelkaia, you've never given us – never given *me* – any choice in your games. Everyone bends to your demented agenda, or you break them. Sometimes I wonder why I didn't leave you to rot in that cursed hole of a city. Why I didn't let Thratia run you through."

"Everyone always bends to *my* agenda?" She rose up, shoulders straightening, chin lifting, fury sparking bright in her eyes. Detan took a hesitant step back, trying to get a leash on his temper. Tibs would kick his teeth clean out if he blew this chance over a squabble.

"Pelkaia, look, I don't want to–"

"I don't care what you want," she growled, fists clenched at her sides. "You come onto my ship, ask me for help, and then insult me? Maybe Ripka and New Chum got themselves arrested to relieve themselves of your company."

"No matter what you think of me, those two deserve–"

"Deserve a better friend than you."

A heavy tattoo pounded on the door before it was wrenched open. The sturdy man who'd freed his wrists stuck his head in and raised both brows.

"Hate to interrupt the domestics," he said, "but it appears someone is trying to board us. Rinky little flier. Got *Happy Birthday Virra!* painted on the side."

"Tibs!" Ignoring Pelkaia's scowl, Detan pushed past the first mate and spilled out onto the deck, casting around for the flier's familiar silhouette. It bobbed in the air off the starboard side, a collection of rather large spring-loaded harpoons pointed at it by the stable hands of the *Larkspur*'s crew.

"Stand down!" Detan ordered, and received nothing but

blank stares and a few light chuckles. Right. Likc they'd listen
to him. Plastering on a fake smile, Detan sidled up as close
as he could to the rail and squinted against the silvery light
glinting off nearby clouds.

Tibs stood on the flier's deck, cutting a rather obvious
target, one hand cranking the wheel that powered their rear
propeller while the other hand kept his hat stuck to his head.
Poor sod must be wearing himself out, fighting a headwind
while trying to keep up with the much larger – and faster –
Larkspur.

"Stand down," Pelkaia said, voice raw with irritation
but modulated with the tones of easy command. Her crew
shrugged and swung their weapons aside, lounging against
the harpoon stands as if they did this sort of thing every day.
Detan swallowed. Maybe they did. Maybe Pelkaia had grown
far more militant than he'd guessed.

"Wave the boarding flag, Coss."

The first mate scrambled to a canvas sack tacked against
the cabin's exterior wall and pulled out two bright red flags
on stubby sticks. He flashed the semaphore for safe-to-board,
and Tibs eased the flier toward the *Larkspur*'s sleek hull.

Pelkaia's crew hopped to work. Although their expressions
were bright with curiosity, they didn't say a word. Their
shoulders were hunched, each move made with mechanical
precision. Someone threw a tie-rope across and Tibs anchored
it, wiry shoulders slumping with relief now that he didn't
have to keep pace with the speedier ship.

Once secured, Tibs hauled himself up a rope ladder. The
first mate and another man helped him to crest the high rail.
Tibs dusted his breeches with one hand and tipped his hat
brim to Pelkaia.

"Much obliged, captain."

"A pleasure to see *you*, Tibal," she said, then jerked her
head to the first mate. "Show these gentlemen to a cabin,
Coss. And lock the door."

"Wait just a sands-cursed moment..." Detan began.

"We'll drop them in Petrastad." She turned her back on Detan while she spoke with Coss. "They can find their own way from there."

With a sheepish grin, Coss grabbed Detan and Tibs by the upper arms and steered them midship. He opened a door to a small sleeping cabin, and shoved them inside.

"Sorry 'bout this," Coss said, and locked the door anyway.

Tibs caught Detan's eye and tipped his hat back. "Conversation went well, then?"

Detan grimaced. "Beautifully."

CHAPTER 3

The Remnant's newest inmates arrayed themselves in a snaking line, each and every one shivering from the cold in their thin linen jumpsuits but doing their damnedest to hide it. Ripka stood with New Chum to her right and an unknown woman to her left, squinting against the salt-laden wind that whipped her hair across her face. She'd been on the Remnant's island for less than a day, and already she hated it.

Though the sun was just as bright as it was over the Scorched, the Endless Sea sucked up the warm rays and held them, making the beach waters balmy but the air crisp and unforgiving. For Ripka, who was used to wearing her heavy coat all over Aransa's sun-bleached streets, the exposure to the cold made her teeth chatter.

She curled her toes in her boots, an old watcher trick to warm her feet. A little chill wasn't going to deter her from her mission. She would find Nouli Bern. She would get him to Hond Steading before Thratia's invading army knocked on that vulnerable city's doors. With his engineering genius on their side, with his inside knowledge of Thratia's methods, they could not lose. Or so she told herself.

Ripka had lost one city to Thratia's thorny hands. Had watched as Thratia spun the city into fear and traded its residents into slavery in exchange for weapons. She would not lose another.

They waited on a balcony overlooking the rec yard, their backs to a building that was used for all the bureaucratic minutiae that went along with running a prison. Three identical buildings hemmed in the rec yard, narrow balconies banding the five stories of each.

The captain sauntered along the line of new intakes, somehow managing to peer down at every inmate, even those who were taller.

"Welcome to the Remnant," he said when he'd made a complete pass and returned to the center. "My name is Captain Lankal, and I'll be your director for the duration of your stay."

Nervous chuckles all around. The only way off the Remnant was to be recalled by a Valathean court to fight for the Fleet and your freedom. That, or take a swim with the sharks surrounding the island. Both options had an equal chance of survival.

"You stand in the bird's nest," he continued, gesturing to the stone beneath their feet. "A balcony which all must pass through to enter, or exit, the docks that harbor airships to and from the mainland. For many of you, this will be the last time you stand upon these stones. But if you behave yourselves, and are kind to your fellow inmates and guards, you may just see this view again."

A sober silence spread throughout those gathered, one the captain let percolate. His warnings held no sway over Ripka – she planned to quit this place before the month was out and the monsoon season came – and so she took the opportunity to glance over his shoulder to the rec yard below.

There, the prison's population mingled. As the Remnant was never at capacity, men and women were allowed the common areas together, and the privacy of personal cells to retreat to during the night. These inmates were, it was said, the vilest scrapings of the Scorched's bootheels. The most ruthless cutthroats, traffickers, and political prisoners. The empire's general opinion on the matter was that if you were tough enough to deserve a sentence here, you were tough enough to weather the presence of your fellows' company.

If Nouli really was down there amongst those monsters, then how he had survived here so long was a mystery she was itching to solve. Nouli was a genius, a renowned polymath, not a murderer or a raconteur. Though he had served the empress by engineering her machines of war, as far as Ripka knew he hadn't seen a lick of real violence in his life. He wasn't equipped to survive in a place like this. If he had gone mad, or died, before Ripka had the chance to whisk him to Hond Steading then this whole scheme could be for naught.

Thratia's forces were preparing to march. She needed Nouli to be here. To be safe, and hale of mind, so that he could lend Hond Steading his insight.

Ripka peeked at New Chum, whose freshly dyed jumpsuit named him Enard Harwit. He'd claimed the first name was his own, but had said nothing about the family moniker. He observed Captain Lankal with the calm assurance she'd come to admire in him, his hands at ease and his face relaxed. His simple, steady presence reassured her. If anyone could help her rescue Nouli Bern, it was Enard.

The captain interrupted her thoughts, "You've all been assigned your bunks, your toiletries."

Her "welcoming kit" weighed down her pocket. A cloth wrapped around a tooth stick, a lumpy brick of soap, a scrap of washcloth and a chit with her cell number painted on it. She'd lucked out and gotten a cell next to Enard. The guards didn't much care about friends sticking close together. They searched the cells often enough to make sure no one was up to any sort of shenanigans.

"But you're going to have to wait to freshen up. It's midday meal time, and I expect every last one of you to file down there, get your plates, and sit your asses down without a word. No fights, no jostling. Play it real nice, and don't no one try and out-tough one another, understand? That sort of behavior gets you a swift trip to the bottom of the well to think about what you've done."

They walked down a narrow stairway, just wide enough for a single person to manage without bumping their elbows – a good point to bottleneck in case of a riot. The woman behind Ripka, a slender thing with scraggly blonde hair and sunken eyes in a sun-darkened face, was breathing hard by the time they reached the bottom.

"You all right?" she whispered over her shoulder.

"Quiet!" a guard midway down the line barked.

The woman narrowed citrine eyes and spat her displeasure. Wonderful. Ripka suppressed a sigh and an urge to ball up her fists. She needed to keep on being bland, indifferent. She couldn't let her conscience get in the way.

This wasn't the watch, and this wasn't her stationhouse. The prisoners' health should be none of her concern. She slowed her pace down the steps, pretending to take extra care on the slick, grey stone, so that the woman behind her wouldn't have to move so fast to keep up.

As they filed out into the rec yard, Ripka surveyed the inmates gathered there, looking for anyone who might be Nouli. Detan had described the engineer as a lean man of middle years, his short, tightly curled hair already gone to grey, and topaz eyes forever hidden behind wide spectacles.

Scanning the crowd, she couldn't imagine a man like that here. Couldn't make her mental image of a wizened, learned man shove gruel down his gullet while growling at his neighbors to stay back. Not that any of the prisoners behaved quite so gruffly – though she could have sworn she saw one man snarl at their line.

They were given bowls of beige porridge, pocked with what Ripka hoped was dates, and directed to an empty trestle table. The bench was hard, cold, and the splintered tabletop marked over with a half dozen stains she didn't even attempt to recognize. Someone had carved a stick figure of a woman bent over a barrel onto the tabletop. Charming.

In the divot of the rec yard, the wind was not so bad. The sun bathed her shoulders, warmed her through the jumpsuit, and the knots in her back muscles relaxed.

Beside her, the slender woman coughed and coughed, each whooping exhalation like a crane's complaint.

"Would you shutthefuckup!" a woman seated across from them hissed, using an arm to shield her porridge from the ill woman's coughs.

Ripka tensed. The guards drifted away, giving the prisoners a wide berth. Was this a part of their initiation to the Remnant? To see how they handled emergent problems on their own?

The coughing woman stiffened. Ripka peeked sideways at her jumpsuit, read the name stained in dark dye there – Junie. Ripka glanced around as covertly as she could. Everyone except her and Enard studied their gruel with a strange intensity.

Ripka's belly soured as Junie leaned back and drew herself up, preparing to launch a forceful cough right at the woman who had told her off.

"Junie, there's no need to–"

Ripka was cut off by an explosive cough. Spittle dampened the hardwood tabletop with wet freckles. The other woman – Henta, her jumpsuit said – screeched and threw her bowl at Junie's head, dousing her in pale sludge. Ripka jerked sideways, bumping Enard as she scrambled to get out of the way.

Whoops and jeers exploded all around. The man sitting next to Henta burst out into a fit of laughter.

Junie wasn't laughing. The slender woman screeched with rage and leapt forward, the bowl that'd bounced off her breastbone raised like a club. Henta, grinning, sprung up to meet her halfway. Before Ripka could finish blinking they tangled together on the tabletop, hollering and kicking and bashing each other with any random piece of cookware that came to hand.

A strange, stunned stillness filled the air – and then chaos broke loose. The shouting of the guards was drowned out by the delighted cries of the inmates. A great brass bell rang somewhere above, signaling a riot. Those seated at the table the two women squabbled on jumped to their feet and cheered on one woman or another.

"Enough!" Ripka barked before she could stop herself, all her training as a watch-captain bubbling to the surface. Her instinct to restore order overrode her desire not to make a spectacle of herself.

Enard blurted something she couldn't quite hear. Didn't care to hear. Blood thrummed in her ears as her heart pounded, preparing her muscles for action. She leapt onto the table and stood above the wrestling pair. They whacked one another on the head and back with gruel-smeared bowls, yelling expletives all the while.

She saw an opening in the melee and seized it, grabbing Junie by the back of her jumpsuit. With a grunt she heaved the smaller woman back and the pair broke apart. Junie flailed, overbalanced Ripka, and she staggered – her foot hit empty air over the table's edge. With a yelp she and Junie crashed backwards, sprawling onto the gruel and dust-spattered floor. Laughter roiled up from the spectators, but Ripka's focus wasn't on the bruise spreading on her hip nor her pride – it was on getting this pit-cursed woman under control.

Grunting with the effort, Ripka wrenched Junie around and pinned her chest-down on the dirt, twisting her arms behind her in a classic restraint hold. She heard scuffling all around, the crunch of boots approaching, and looked up, ready to explain herself.

It wasn't a guard.

Some big bruiser from the general population stomped her way, veins sticking out on the sides of his neck, fists raised in preparation to strike. Cold fear coiled in her belly. The man's almond-dark skin was covered by the same dreary jumpsuit they all wore, but he'd gone to the trouble of ripping open a shoulder seam to reveal the snake tattoo of the Glasseaters.

Now that she'd gotten Junie pinned to the ground, she saw the same tattoo peeking out from a ragged tear in the woman's new jumpsuit. Wonderful.

Stomping down her pride, she let Junie go and popped to her feet, backing up a step to put the fallen woman's body between her and the advancing bruiser. His scarred lips twisted in a grotesque smile.

And then he stopped short, the smile fading from his rage-blushed face.

Enard stepped beside Ripka, hands held easy and open at his sides, narrow head tilted as he watched the bruiser approach. She frowned, not understanding the big bastard's hesitation. Surely two unaffiliated newbies didn't threaten him? Was there a guard nearby?

"Tender?" the big man asked.

Enard shrugged a little, saying nothing.

Guards swarmed them, breaking apart the knot of prisoners and carting off the injured. Ripka let her wrists be bound behind her back, let herself be dragged away, mind whirling. As she was herded toward her cell, she caught Enard's eye, and mouthed, "Tender?"

"Later," he said, and winked once before they were shoved into their respective cells with empty bellies and fresh bruises to nurse until the morning.

CHAPTER 4

Three bunks were bolted to one wall, a scraggly rug nailed to the center of the floor. The bunks sported the barest of linens, and not so much as a trunk for clothing cluttered the empty room. Tibs tugged his hat down, no doubt to hide an insufferable smirk, and sat on the middle bunk. His long legs dangled, bootheels hooked on the bottom bunk's rail, and he stretched spindly arms up to rest against the top bunk. In effect, cutting Detan off from any of the sparse cabin's small comforts.

"And just what do you suppose we'll do if we can't win Pelkaia to our cause?" Tibs asked.

"Bah, she'll come around. You know how old Pelly can be. Fickle as her face, that woman is."

"As you say, sirra."

Detan frowned. Tibs only called him sirra when he thought Detan was being particularly idiotic. He couldn't think of a thing he'd done in the last few marks that was worse than usual by his persnickety companion's estimation.

"Who put sand in your trousers?" he asked, and turned to examine the door that held them. The *Larkspur* had been constructed to the rigorous specifications of its previous – and intended – owner, the exiled commodore Thratia Ganal.

Ruthless woman that she was, Thratia was more inclined to cut throats than corners with construction. Unfortunately for Detan, it seemed Pelkaia kept up with the commodore's maintenance schedule. The hinges were well-oiled, the ever-shifting gaps between the boards filled with waxen mortar.

"You'll pardon my sour mood if I find it a touch worrisome we're sitting above all this–" Tibs stomped a boot on the annoyingly well-cared-for floor, "–and you seem pleased as punch to make things go boom."

Detan hid a grimace by giving the door another close examination. "It wasn't my intention to make use of my sel-sense, but Pelly put me rather in a spot. If I refused, she'd realize how unpredictable my talent has grown, and then where would we be? If she doesn't think she can use me, she won't help, and if she won't help, then Ripka and New Chum will have to get real cozy out at the Remnant, because our trusty ole flier sure as shit isn't going to fare well crossing the Endless Sea. Not to mention pass for anything like an official vessel once we get there."

"Making the lady's face go up, I understand. But that stunt with the knife?"

Detan fiddled with the hem of his sleeve. "Saw that, did you? Err. Ah. Well, I mean, it was such a *small* amount."

"And did you mean for that demonstration to be quite so large?"

"Not exactly, of course, but..."

Tibs sighed, low and ragged, and the sound was like raking a bed of nails over Detan's conscience.

"Look," Detan said, turning to look Tibs in the eye. "It's getting better. I'm regaining control."

Tibs pursed his lips like a fish's kiss, exhibiting his whole opinion in one bitter expression. The ship shifted, changing course with a sudden jerk, and Detan grew aware of the vast selium stores beneath his feet.

All that sel, and all it would take from him was one flare-up. One tiny spark of rage to set the whole contraption ablaze. His stomach sank. This cabin wasn't so different from the one he'd been held in, near on a year ago now. The bunks were new – the rug a nice touch of homeliness – but the warm scent of the wood, the subtle tinge of leather and iron in the air, dragged at him. Pushed at barriers he'd long since held in mind.

Little ribbons of pain drew his attention. He'd been scratching at the interior of his elbow, at the ruby-red scar that Callia's needle had left behind.

It'd been year, sure. A year since that whitecoat, Callia, had strapped him to a table in a room on another airship. A year since she'd experimented upon him on behalf of the empire, dug around in his flesh and his blood to see what made his destructive sel-sense tick. Funny how that single event haunted him more than the first time he'd been a guest of the whitecoats.

That first time, he'd been locked away in the Bone Tower like a proper prisoner. He'd had the scent of char from accidentally exploding his selium pipeline – and his fellow sel-sensitives – fresh in his nostrils. He'd given up then. Given himself over to whatever harsh end the empire had planned for him in their quest to dig the truth of his deviant sensitivity out of him.

But he had escaped. He'd tasted clean air, open air. Found his way back to the Scorched and found a friend in Tibs, too. And that's why it'd hurt so much, that second time, a year ago. Brief though Callia's experiments upon him had been, not even the invasive prodding of the Bone Tower had left him so hollowed out inside. So unsure of the nature of himself and his ability. And Tibs had been there for him through both returns from the whitecoats' clutches. He owed Tibs so much. More than he could ever find the words to say.

Detan dragged his hands through his hair and stared at his feet.

"Sorry."

Tibs shrugged, a slow roll of the shoulders that dismissed their whole argument, and pushed his hat back. "Think she really will come 'round?"

Detan settled cross-legged on the floor and rubbed the rough side of his cheek. They'd been a week in Cracked Thorn before opportunity had arisen to get himself arrested, and his chin hadn't seen the slick side of a blade since. He wiggled his bare toes.

"Don't know, truth be told. I figured the bait of the deviant list would be enough to tempt her along, but she didn't seem half so interested as I'd hoped."

"Oh, the list that doesn't exist?"

Detan scowled and shushed him. "Keep it quiet, lest you want her to tip us over the side."

"Had you considered, by any chance, telling her the truth?"

He stood and paced, irritated by the tight confines and lack of control. Wasn't right to keep him cooped up like this, not when he hadn't done Pelkaia any direct harm. It was downright inhospitable, come to think on it.

"Think she'd let us keep Nouli, if she knew what kind of knowledge he holds?"

"We can only keep him if they can find him."

"They will. He's there. If anyone can suss that wily rat out of hiding, it's Ripka Leshe."

"Wish I could say I shared your faith. Not that the lady's skills are in question – I'm sure she'll find him, if he's there to be found – but what kind of man will he be? You think he couldn't have gotten out on his own, if he wanted it?"

Tibs plucked a deck of cards from his breast pocket and flicked out a hand. Detan stopped pacing and crouched down to gather up the fallen cards. Having something in his hands, something to *do*, kept his mind moving along smoothly.

"There's got to be a reason he's stuck around. Maybe he fears the empire's reach – or Thratia's. Nouli served the empress a long time, and often on Thratia's ships. Thratia knows he's got an inside peek at her methods. Could be she wants him for herself, or wants him dead. This is Thratia Ganal we're talking about. The woman they call General Throatslitter, and she smiles about it. The woman who the empire exiled for being too power-hungry. The woman who... Who killed an innocent woman, let her bleed out at our feet, just to make a point. Who sold deviant sensitives into slavery, not because she didn't think it was wrong, but because she found doing so expedient to her plans. If I were Nouli, I'd hide behind the Remnant's walls too.

"But no matter his reasons, it's got to be tried. Hond Steading has always relied on its legacy and its size to keep itself safe. The monsoon season will slow Thratia's troops, but it won't be long now. She wants Hond Steading. Valathea wants it, too. And my dear old auntie's going to get caught in the crossfire. We need a strategist with inside knowledge."

"Putting a lot of faith in this man, considering who we're up against. Putting a whole city in his hands, and you haven't even said hello yet."

"Auntie Honding's got a lot of things at her fingertips. Got watchers, sel-sensitives, loyalists, and every old thing you'd need to hold a city being besieged. But what she needs to win – to push back those forces and not just waste away until she's rolled over by hunger – is a trump card." He flicked out a card. Tibs snatched it up. "An upper hand Thratia won't see coming. Nouli's that. Even just knowing we have him will give her pause. Maybe make her be a little too slow, a little too cautious."

"Know what else might slow her down?"

"Getting a look at your mug?"

"Discovering the Lord Honding has returned home, trained, and is ready for her."

The cards in his hand rustled as he stifled a tremble. "We're asking a lot of miracles of the world already. Wouldn't want to push our luck."

"There's no luck in asking for help."

"Depends on who you're asking."

Tibs's wizened little eyes swiveled to the door.

"You've got to be kidding. Ask Pelkaia to train me? Black skies, Tibs, she nearly pitched me off the cliff the moment she saw me. We're already asking her to help us get the gang out of the clink. Talk about pushing our luck – she'll push back."

"Doesn't have to be her. Could be your ownself."

Detan froze with a card held halfway out. "I don't have the temperament for it."

"Yet you've refused to give up the possibility."

"What in the pits is that supposed to mean?"

Tibs closed the fan of his cards and pressed them facedown against his thigh. "I get why you won't go back to Hond Steading. I do. But for all your running away from that city – you still bear its brand. You still count yourself its heir. What do you think's going to happen when Dame Honding dies, and you're the only sack of flesh drifting around the Scorched with a proper heir brand on his neck? Think the city's just going to sit quietly and wait for you to get yourself together? Think your abandonment won't cause upheaval? Won't hurt people?

"You could relinquish it. Could cross it out and demand Dame Honding burn some other sod with the burden. But you don't. You're still responsible for that city in your heart – so you're going to have to take control of yourself real quick. Nouli can't do that for you."

"Five," Detan said.

"Excuse me?"

He rubbed the back of his neck, where his family's crest had been branded into his skin at the age of twelve. He'd wanted it, then. He'd never really stopped wanting it. Never stopped knowing what it meant. It wasn't the power, not really, though most would see it that way. It was stewardship, his mother had told him while her jaw creaked from the bonewither eating her alive. It was a promise from Detan to Hond Steading. A promise that he'd do his best to care for the city for the rest of his life. A chance to do something right.

"Five lives. Last time I was there. Last time I took responsibility for the city. I stood with a group of five miners moving sel and lost control. That little demonstration landed me in the Bone Tower, guest of Callia's bastard colleagues, and I'll be damned if I ever get myself anywhere near a situation like that again. I do what I can for Hond Steading. I just do it from a distance."

"And is it the whitecoats that keep you up at night, or fear of failing your responsibility to Hond Steading?"

"That was three years ago. You think I wouldn't do worse now, pushed just right? Staying away is the best thing I can do for them. Finding Nouli and sending him there is the second best."

Tibs pressed his lips together and laid out a pair of cards. The ship slalomed sideways. Detan nearly lost his balance as it bumped up against something firm and unforgiving. A soft squeal reached his ears, the complaint of wood and metal rubbing shoulders. He was grateful for the distraction. Detan popped back to his feet and slipped his cards into his pocket.

"Are we under attack?" he asked the air, staring at the iron-bound door and wishing he could see what was happening.

Tibs chuckled. "Under attack by a dock? Sure."

Before he could muster a response the huge door swung open. Coss leaned against the doorframe, brows raised in amusement. Detan flicked his collar to straighten it and tried to look confident, unconcerned. Coss smirked.

"Pack your things, lads, you've arrived."

"I'll have you know, I arrived ages ago," Detan said.

Coss rolled his eyes. "Cute. Now heave-to-it." He stepped aside, leaving the doorway wide open for them to pass through. Detan peered at that sliver of freedom, suspicious.

"I'd hoped to bend your captain's ear a little while longer," he ventured.

"Hope all you want, Honding, she ain't interested. Am I going to have to grab some boys to help you on your way out?"

"No need for that," Tibs said. He levered himself out of his sprawl over the bunks.

"And may I ask which lovely establishment of the Scorched you're dumping our sorry hides in?" Detan asked.

"See for yourself." Coss gestured toward the side of the ship with one arm.

Detan peered over the ship's rail. A city of brownstone and twisted wood splayed below him, the square buildings tall and wide, their roofs peppered with airship moorings and outdoor sleeping quarters. The city was tucked into the curve of a frothing bay, the angry splash of the Endless Sea adding some rare greenery to the shoreline. Beyond the sprawl of buildings and streets, cactus and pricklegrain farms sprouted, their plots mirroring the city's square towers.

In the far distance, little more than a black smudge on the sea against the horizon, he could make out the first of the Remnant Isles. Somewhere beyond that blurred dot, Ripka and New Chum awaited. Hopefully with Nouli in hand. Detan swallowed.

"Petrastad," he said.

"Very good!" Coss clapped him on the back. "I see you paid attention in geography."

"Does this mean Pelkaia intends to help us?" he asked, sharing a sideways glance with Tibs as the lanky man slipped up to the rail alongside him.

"Haven't a clue what you're on about. Captain wants us to put in here for her own reasons. Said to see you off, nice and quick, so if you don't mind...?"

Coss pointed toward the gangplank that sloped down to the roof of one of the large, square, brownstone buildings.

The rest of the crew jostled back and forth across the ship, seeing to their tasks. Pelkaia had vanished.

"Hold on now," Detan said as Coss grabbed the cloth at the back of his neck and shoved him forward. "I demand to speak with your captain for being so rudely manhandled."

"I'm sure your treatment will break her heart." Coss kept on herding Detan along, Tibs loping beside them with his hands stuffed in his pockets. "You'll find your flier has been safely stowed at this fine dock, though how you'll pay to get her back is your problem."

"This is absurd," Detan protested, digging his heels in to slow the stocky man down. "Never mind Pelkaia's thrice-cursed pride. I'm offering her real benefit, a trade of skill."

Coss hesitated, his grip loosened a touch. "Not my decision," he said, and Detan suppressed a grin. Maybe it wasn't Coss's decision outright, but he'd bet his shoeless feet that the first mate had a healthy say in the dealings of the *Larkspur*.

"Not to mention the–" He cut himself off, faking a nervous glance around for eavesdroppers, and whispered, "the list."

"What list?" Coss asked, voice pitched low though he kept on pushing Detan toward the slanted gangplank.

"Of deviants, of course. Ones the empire's got a sideways eye stuck on."

"You have this list?"

"Personally? No. But I need Pelkaia's help to free the woman who does."

Coss mulled that over, sucking on his teeth so hard his cheeks grew sunken. "Orders are orders," he eventually said, but there was a hesitance there that gave Detan a small tingle. He doubted Pelkaia would get much peace from her first mate tonight.

As they reached the gangplank, Coss gave him a final shove. Detan stumbled and nearly lost his footing on the rough slip of wood. With the plank groaning under their combined weight, Detan and Tibs hurried down to the dust-coated rooftop.

A chill breeze washed over them, smelling of brine and something deeper, something loamy. Heat rose across his scarred back, the crew's gazes boring into him as he disembarked. He spun around before taking the last step and saw them there, scattered across the deck and the rigging, not bothering to obscure their stares.

Pelkaia stood at the helm, her long back straight as a mast pole, her hard stare pointed his direction. Ripka's posture, he mused, and wondered how much of the watch-captain's habits Pelkaia couldn't shake from all that time she'd spent imitating her in Aransa. He gave her a cheery wave.

"See you soon, Pelly!" he called, high and bright as he could, and was rewarded with a few nervous chuckles from her crew. And a certain finger raised in salute from Pelkaia.

"Lovely," Tibs muttered as they hopped down onto the roof.

"Oh, pah. She'll come around. I doubt that first mate of hers will give her much choice."

"And if she doesn't?"

Detan shrugged, surveying their new surroundings. The flier was tied up alongside the *Larkspur*, its rectangular deck and tubular buoyancy sack rather dinky in the shadow of the greater ship's sleek hull. Detan looked twice at the *Larkspur*. The ship he knew he'd flown in on looked nothing like the ship he'd stolen in Aransa. Sure, the masts were the same, and the bowsprit featuring an angry air-serpent looked mighty familiar, but its body had changed. It looked flattened, plain. Like nothing more than an overgrown Valathean transport vessel.

He whistled low in appreciation. When the ship had come rushing in to pluck him off the cliff's edge, he hadn't gotten a solid look at it, and he certainly hadn't been able to see much better locked up in one of the cabins. Whoever Pelkaia had on board making the ship look boring, they were doing a mighty fine job. Clever, he thought, filing that trick away for later.

Over the edge of the building, the streets bustled with locals going about their daily chores. Across the narrow lane, about three stories up, Detan spied an open window with a sign pinned above that read: *Lotti's Cards and Pleasures.* Beige curtains had been pulled back to let the air in, and they twisted in the sea breeze. Loud whoops sounded from within, glasses clinked, and a handful of men in the crisp white shirts of the Valathean Fleet sat hunched around a table with fans of cards in their hands.

"I think," Detan said, slinging an arm around Tibs's shoulders to point him toward the window, "we should go make some new friends, seek some new pleasures. What do you say?"

Tibs eyed Detan's bare feet and torn trousers. "I say we'd better get you dressed, first." He wrinkled his nose. "And a bath wouldn't go amiss."

CHAPTER 5

Pelkaia leaned against the cabin's exterior wall, watching Detan and Tibs make their way to a ladder at the roof's edge, and breathed easy. She'd never been so relieved to be free of a passenger before. She caught herself drumming her fingers against her thigh and stopped. No matter what stories he told – possibly especially because of the stories he told – Detan wasn't a soul she could trust, not like the rest of her well-vetted crew.

Jeffin slunk up alongside her, the lanky man's face sallow in the seashore sun. A tiara of sweat gleamed across his forehead, and the crescents beneath his eyes looked bruised and sunken. "Begging your pardon, captain, but should we shove off? I'm, ah, getting rather tired."

Glancing at the sun's angle, Pelkaia clapped him on the back and nodded. "We're going to put in here for the night. As soon as it gets full dark, drop your mirrors. In fact, you can try and pass them onto Laella, if you think she's up for it."

A frown flitted across Jeffin's already drawn face. He crossed his heart with the old Catari constellation for strength. His lineage was nearly as tangled in Catari blood as Pelkaia's, though he seemed to harbor a deeper loyalty than she did. The man still said prayers to the stars every night, while

Pelkaia was lucky if she remembered to cross her heart with the constellations once a week, no matter her full-blooded body.

No matter her childhood in the dusty oases, hiding like stonerabbits in the badlands from the advance of the Valathean Fleet.

"I'll show her how," Jeffin said. His voice sounded like it was tumbling out over hard stones. Forced as his helpfulness was, she was grateful for it, and she gave his shoulder a small squeeze. Valathean, Catari. They were all deviant selium sensitives. They were all outcasts, in their own way. She and Jeffin would just have to get used to the Valathean girl's presence.

Coss approached her, his slate-grey eyes bright and a strange tension in the tendons of his jaw.

"Ho, captain," he said, but there wasn't as much affection in it as usual. Jeffin tucked his head to the first mate and, sensing Coss's agitation as surely as Pelkaia did, scampered off in a rush to find Laella.

"Ho, mate," she said, drawing out the word "mate". Coss rewarded her with a soft flush and shifted his weight.

"May we talk in quarters?" he asked.

Pelkaia surveyed her ship. Essi was up the ropes, getting a lesson from Old Ulder on proper knot-tying, and Jeffin had disappeared into the cabins to find Laella. The others lounged about, trading stories and drinks in Petrastad's sea breeze. Watching them now, she could not help but imagine her son, Kel, amongst them. He had been a simple sel-sensitive, the kind the empire approved of. But even that had not been enough to keep him safe from the power struggles between Valathea and their once-commodore, Thratia. He'd died in Aransa for being a witness to Thratia's treachery. Someday, with the help of this crew, she would balance those scales.

The crew did not need her now, and so she nodded to Coss. "Spending time with the Honding that bad?"

"Something like that," Coss said and took off toward Pelkaia's cabin.

She followed, checking on her ship with every step, but scarcely seeing a thing. What had gotten Coss so wound up? The man was a rock. Cheeky, sure, but stable in all weather. Seeing him tense as a harpoon spring made her heart ramp its pace.

In the privacy of her cabin, with the door shut and the thick black curtains drawn against the light, he dropped all pretense of affability. He would never question her in front of the crew – they'd agreed to that – but she'd given him permission to be open with her in private. From the way his expression darkened, she wished she'd rethought that plan. Criticisms were always worse from Coss. Due to his deviation, he was the only one in the whole of the world who could see her true face hidden beneath her selium mask.

"Why in the black skies didn't you tell me Detan has access to a list of deviants?" he demanded.

"Captain's decision," she said, knowing as soon as the words left her lips that they were the wrong thing to say.

"Really? The fate of a whole fistful of deviants, and it's just you who gets to decide? Thought we were all important on this ship. Thought *we were* partners." He stepped forward as he said "we," his body canting toward her, his tannic breath gusting against her cheek. She shifted backward, putting distance between them. Long ago, she'd decided neither one of them could afford to be distracted by the sly glances they stole at one another – nor by the comfort she took in knowing he was near.

"This is exactly why I didn't tell you. You've never worked with Honding before. He'll play you, even as you're playing him. Maybe there is a list, maybe there isn't, but he wants something from me – from *us* – that I can't see yet, and I'm not chasing his tail without a clearer picture of where we're going."

"So you *are* considering it."

"I didn't put down in Petrastad for the food. I docked us

here to see what he does next, to see how desperate he is to get out to those isles."

"What isles?" he asked, quick enough to make Pelkaia snort a laugh. Of course Detan wouldn't have explained the dangerous aspects of his supposed plan.

"Didn't he tell you the whole story while he turned you against me? I'm shocked he wasn't more forthright. The woman with the whereabouts of that mythic list is a prisoner at the Remnant, as is her friend, and Detan expects me to swish on over there in the *Mirror* and pluck them out."

Coss folded his arms over his ribs and slouched, wary. "What'd this woman do to get locked up in a place like that?"

"If Detan's to be believed, she got caught stealing the list and hid it somewhere before being apprehended."

"She a deviant?"

"Ripka Leshe, a deviant?" Pelkaia shook her head. "She'd knock you cold to hear you say it. That woman's as banal as they come – and as straightlaced, too. That's the only real believable part of Detan's story. If Ripka was going to get herself locked up for anything, it'd be a good cause."

"And you're willing to let a woman like that rot?"

"Let? Clear skies, Coss, there's little all I can do. This is the Remnant we're talking about, the most secure prison in the whole Scorched. I wouldn't know where to begin plucking her free, even if I wanted to. And regardless, it's not me who got her locked up there."

"Real nice." He snorted. "So just because it's not your fault means it's not your problem?"

Her back stiffened and she picked her chin up. "What's so wrong about that?"

"What's *good* about it?" He threw his hands in the air, grasping as if he could wring an answer from the emptiness. "I thought we were trying to change things – thought this crew was meant for bigger things than snatching sands-cursed deviants away from death at the final moment."

"And you think breaking someone out of the Remnant is worth risking this crew? You think trusting a thing Honding has to say is wise? Even if the list is real, there's no telling what became of those on it. They could be captured already. We could be wasting a lot of time for nothing."

"Regardless of the list, I think saving a good woman from a wretched end is worth it, yes. And I think the crew would agree with me. Pits below, maybe you should ask the crew what they want to do about it. For once, give them a say in matters. They aren't children. Well, all except Essi anyway, and she's no innocent. And if that list *is* real, then there's a chance–"

"Stop." She pinched the bridge of her nose between two fingers. "I agree with you, it's just that..."

"Pell." Coss settled a hand against her upper arm and the warmth of him spread through her sleeve. She pushed his hand away. "You're afraid to risk the crew."

"It's not the crew I'm worried about. He's stolen this ship once before. I wouldn't put it past him to try again."

Coss shoved his hands in his pockets. "Stole it because you tricked him into it, unless there's a piece of that story you're not sharing. There are sixteen of us, and one of him. Two if you count Tibal. I think we can do it. I think we should at least *try*."

"We're not ready for something like this. We're not even properly armed if it comes to a fight."

An impish grin curled its way over Coss's lips and he cocked his head to the side. "This is Petrastad, captain. We'll put a watch on Honding, see what he does, and if his story checks out – well then. There are weapons to be had aplenty in this salty hole, and a man with his particular talent is well suited for recovering them."

Pelkaia picked her head up and met his eyes. A smile worked its way across her tired features. "You mean to rob the imperial weapons vault."

"I do. And what better man for the job than Detan Honding?"

CHAPTER 6

The cell door slammed open, startling Ripka out of a fretful doze. She jerked upright and squinted against the sunlight's intrusion, her eyes watering. A flat-faced guard loomed in her doorway, tapping his foot.

"Midday meal. Get up and get out, or don't eat."

Though her joints were stiff, she forced herself to straighten and hurry to the opened door – but not too fast. The last thing she needed was another bruise to nurse.

Apparently she hadn't been alone in isolation throughout the morning meal. Her neighbors were being hauled out of their beds and shoved into an unsteady line along the balcony. Most sported hair mussed from too long abed and wrinkled jumpsuits. Newbies, all of them, their eyes wide and their postures uncertain and guarded.

Enard – or Tender, as that man called him – faced straight out to the rec yard below, dark eyes squinted against the sun's glare. She endeavored to catch his eye, but he ignored her existence. Blasted man owed her an explanation for his familiarity with the Remnant's rougher crowd, and she was determined to wring it from him as soon as she could.

The guards arrayed themselves at opposite ends of the balconies, with an additional guard in the center of each line.

Ripka's rude awakener was her row's centerpoint, and she supposed his broad shoulders and twice-broken nose had something to do with that. Sticking the biggest, meanest-looking guard where everyone had an equal chance to get a good, long look at him was exactly what she'd do if she were in charge.

Her chest surged with a twang of regret. No one would ever let her run a single jail cell, let alone a whole prison, ever again.

"Turn right," the big guard ordered without so much as a glance down the row.

They turned and shuffled forward as one unit. The guard's shadow projected over her shoulder, and he shifted his crossbow to keep it pointed at their backs. Lazy, she thought. Worse yet – dangerous. If the stupid man so much as stubbed his toe he risked accidentally discharging his weapon into his wards' backs.

More importantly, into *her* back.

Sea mist left the stone balcony sticky beneath her thin shoes, the air chilled enough to rake goosebumps over her arms. They were ushered out into the rec yard, the narrow tables on which they'd had yesterday's meal already laid out with plates, troughs, and mugs filled with cold, fresh water. No time for a gruel line today.

On the other side of the rec yard smaller tables hosted the established residents. Most gave the new arrivals a wary eye. As Ripka's row marched by a lopsided table seating three women, every last one watched the procession. She nearly jumped out of her skin when the woman nearest her – a lean thing with a mess of dark pecan hair – let out a shrill whistle.

"Hey, Hessan," she crooned, wriggling a finger at the big man who'd opened Ripka's door. "Bring the lil' one in front of you over here. The fighty one."

Ripka's skin itched, but she bit her tongue. The guard paused, letting a gap grow in the line, and leaned his crossbow against his shoulder, pointing it up at the sky. At least that was an improvement.

"I don't know, Clink. Still a sparrow, after all."

"Aww, c'mon, we'll treat the lil' bird real nice. And look, Kisser is out with the shits, we're gonna need the extra hand today. Might as well get the girl acquainted, neh?"

The guard let loose the long-suffering sigh of a man who'd had this argument before, and remembered just where it'd gotten him last time.

"You rats rope her into any nasty business, and I'll punch new holes in you." He pat the crossbow. "Understand?"

"You'd like that, wouldn't you? New holes?" Clink leered.

Hessan actually blushed. A seed of anger hardened in Ripka's chest. Whoever managed training here was a nightmare. Prisoners shouldn't be able to fluster a guard so easily. Shouldn't be able to *ask* to have the rules broken, and be given what they wanted. If she had command of the Remnant, then Hessan would be out on his ass so fast—

"Go on." Hessan shoved her toward the women's table. "Eat your meal. Don't cause no trouble."

Ripka stumbled but caught herself, dropping into a grappling stance on instinct. She caught Enard's gaze over Hessan's shoulder, and though his eyes were wide with interest, he didn't seem worried. He shrugged and mouthed, "Later."

Easy for him to say, he was already acquainted with one of the biggest bastards in the place.

Setting aside her desire to dress down Hessan and extract the truth from Enard, she ducked her head and took the seat Clink offered. Cold bit through her jumpsuit's backside, and she hissed between her teeth. If she regretted anything about this mad scheme of theirs, it was the cursed cold. What she wouldn't give for a lazy afternoon laying out on the flier's deck, a pulped cactus drink in her hand.

She eyed the scrubbed-down wooden tabletop. At least

the accommodations here were cleaner than on Detan's flier. Then again, most things were cleaner than anything that man came into contact with.

"Don't worry, takes all sparrows a while to adjust to the cold," the woman to Ripka's left whispered. She was a petite creature, with close-cropped blonde curls framing a rounded face, the corners of her eyes wrinkled deep as an old raisin. She sat with her shoulders hunched, a small, forced smile on her mouth. Ripka wondered what such a shy woman had done to get herself locked up in here.

"More like your ass goes permanently numb," Clink said, shoveling a chunk of old bread into her mouth. She spoke while she chewed, somehow managing not to choke on the dry crust. "You know my name, now, what's yours, little birdie?"

"Enkel," she said, gesturing to the fresh-dyed name on her jumpsuit. Clink's name had been smeared, or stained, into oblivion. "Ripka Enkel."

Her first name was common enough, and she wasn't practiced at responding to fake names, so she'd decided her safest bet was to keep it. Detan had insisted she assume a false last name – an insistence she was grateful for now. Chances were good not a soul on this hunk of rock would have heard of her work in Aransa, but there was always a slim possibility someone she'd crossed once might recognize her. With a false last name emblazoned across her chest, anyone who looked twice at her would assume themselves mistaken. She hoped.

Clink tossed her hair and laughed. "You think my mama named me Clink right out the womb? Come on, girl, what's your *name*. Not a lot formal manners to go by here, understand?"

Ripka licked her lips, glancing at the hard faces watching her, and feigned embarrassment to cover the frantic line of her thoughts.

"Who did name you Clink, then?" she asked, giving herself

time to think. It had to be something easy, something she'd know to answer to on instinct. An idea hit, and she let herself smile.

Clink pawed through the communal plate for another thick crust. "Never said no one gave it to me, did I?"

"Right," Ripka said. "None of my business."

"You're damned right it ain't. Now, what do we call you?"

"Captain," she said without hesitation.

The woman beside Clink leaned forward, dark eyes wide with interest. The curtain of her black hair swung across her cheeks. "You captain a ship or something?"

"Something," she said, recalling Detan's admonishment that she was a terrible liar, and to stick to half-truths if at all possible. "Thought that was none of your business?"

They laughed, Clink elbowing her neighbor goodnaturedly in the side, and Ripka relaxed. She reached for a crust of bread and mug of water, and nobody stopped her.

"What're you in for?" Clink pushed a plate of suspicious cheese toward her.

Ripka snuck a glance at the other women. They were relaxed, eating their meal with as much gusto as one could muster for stale bread and moldy cheese. They paid attention to her, but tension had eased from their faces and bodies. The posturing was over, for now.

"Theft," Ripka said, which was true enough.

They looked at her as one unit, and a spark of worry wormed through her.

"Don't get put in a place like this for theft," the blonde woman said, her voice a whisper. Ripka realized from the soft rasp straining her words that she couldn't raise her voice any higher.

Ripka shrugged. "You do when you steal information."

"Ah," Clink leaned back and pinned Ripka with a narrowed gaze. "Got ourselves a spy, girls."

"I–"

Clink closed a fist in the air between them, cutting off Ripka's rejoinder. With a shallow breath, she forced herself to calm. To wait for whatever their ringleader had to say.

"None of my business, but it explains a lot. 'S why I grabbed you over here, truth be told. You never been in a place like this before, neh?"

Ripka gave a slight shake of her head. "City jails. Nothing lasting."

"Mmmhmm." She eyed her girls. Each one gave her a nod of assent. "Explains why you were stupid enough to attack a songbird."

"A what?" Ripka shook visions of punching a lark from her mind. "That fight yesterday? I just broke it up."

"Sure you did. But you embarrassed that songbird real good when you wrestled her down, and mark me, she'll hold that against you."

Ripka caught herself clenching her jaw and loosened it. "What, exactly, is a songbird?"

Clink smirked. "A girl who gets herself sent to prison to be with her man. Comes to sing behind the bars, if you catch my meaning. Naive little shits, mostly. Some of 'em don't even do the crime that gets them sent here, they just take the fall for it. Last a month or two, till they realize their beloved has had a few on the side since they've been away. Then it's all screeching and tears."

"It's one to a cell. How do they even... you know what? I can guess. Never mind."

The dark-haired woman chuckled. "She gets it."

"Pits below, the guards here are *terrible*."

"True," Clink said slowly. "Overworked and understaffed, but that's fine by me. If I'm going to spend the rest of my days rotting here, might as well have a little leeway, neh? But I ain't called you over here to talk about the Remnant's staff problems. Called you over to talk about your problems, miss Captain."

"I don't even know where you'd begin."

"I got a place. That songbird you ruffled is paired up with Oiler. Nasty piece, that one. Runs with the Glasseaters, and not low on the pole by any stretch. His birdie is going to be puffed up with a queenie complex for a while, most of 'em are, and she'll point her bony finger right at you."

"Great," Ripka drawled. "So I watch myself. Planned on it anyway, you know."

Clink dragged her fingers halfway through her hair, then shook it out like she was trying to kick loose a flea infestation. "Look, girl. No one's a lone shark here. I like the way you moved on the songbird – no hesitation, nothing sloppy in it. Don't know what you stole – none of my business – but you got pro skills. Me, Forge, Honey, and Kisser–" she nodded to each in turn; the raspy woman was Honey, the raven-haired woman Forge, the empty seat Kisser, "–we could use someone like that around.

"We're not looking to start fights. Ain't no one wants to avail themselves of the Remnant's apothik services. But having people around who can handle a fight has a way of deterring them. Understand? And regardless, girl, you're going to need a work detail, and you're not going to want to go that alone. They split us lads and ladies up for that, neh? So you and tall, dark, and scrawny won't have each other's backs out there. You get hooked up with the songbird and her cronies, and you won't see the inside of a week here."

A shrill whistle cut through the air, jerking Ripka's head up and cutting off Clink. Only the newbies – the sparrows – looked around wide-eyed and confused. The rest were busy grabbing leftover food as fast as they could chew it or stuff it into their pockets. Ripka took the cue and chugged a gulp of water while reaching for what was left of the bread.

"That's the work detail warning, next whistle we gotta be up and ready to do our part," Forge said.

"What's it gonna be, then? You running with us?" Clink pressed.

Ripka chewed bread as quickly as she could, swallowed hard and gulped water again. She couldn't seem anxious for their protection, but there wasn't much choice. If she was going to spend any time here – and it looked like it, with Nouli failing to show himself – then she'd need allies. It couldn't hurt to have friends in her corner who had some level of control over the guards. And she couldn't very well count on Enard's strange past to keep her sheltered for the rest of her stay.

"I'm in."

The work whistle trilled again, and the women of her newfound coterie stood as one. Ripka followed a little later, scanning the rec yard curiously as the guards urged every last inmate to their feet. Nothing had been explained to her about how life in the prison worked. She'd just been chucked on an airship with the rest, heaped together like moldy grain sacks, and hauled out here to the middle of the sea. Captain Lankal's orientation on the sparrow's nest the day before was the only information she had to work with, and that was slim pickings.

Despite her boasts to Tibs and Detan, she was beginning to realize she couldn't rely on her experience as a watch-captain to muddle her way through. A ten-cell jail meant to hold a prisoner no longer than a few weeks was one thing. This monstrous building, this layer upon layer of cells shoved off to hide the darkest fringe of the empire's denizens, was something else altogether.

It had seemed so simple, working through the scheme on the deck of the flier with freedom all around them as far as the eye could see. They had a plan.

She wondered if that plan was strong enough to stand up to an institution like this.

CHAPTER 7

"We don't serve shitheads like you," the big bruiser said, startlingly hazel eyes ringed by the smoke wafting out from the ajar door behind him.

Detan held out both hands, palms pointed to the sweet skies in contrition, and tried on a polite smile. It just made the craggy man's frown dig deeper.

"You don't serve shitheads with the grains to pay?" He turned his hand over, gamboling a copper grain across his knuckles in a glittering dance. The bruiser's bloodshot gaze followed the sparkling coinage. The spherical granule rolled smooth as silk over Detan's roughed skin.

"This ain't a copper bit kind of establishment."

"Oh? Is that copper? I say!" With twist of his wrist he switched out the copper for a silver, and rolled that across his knuckles once before bouncing it over to the knuckles of his other hand. "Ah, now, that's more like it, isn't it?"

The bruiser's eyes remained narrowed, but he held out one meaty hand. Detan deposited the grain into the man's palm with a flourish and took a bow. The big man hawked and spat on the already stained hallway floor.

"Go on in then," he rumbled. "Run out of coin, or start trouble, and it's out the window with you, understand?"

"Perfectly, my good man, I am well acquainted with the particulars of defenestration." Detan snatched Tibs's hat and donned it. Tibs grabbed it back with a grunt, and they sidled their way through the narrow crack the bruiser allowed. Detan did his best not to comment on the bouncer's unique aroma.

The room was hazy with smoke and other noxious fumes. He couldn't figure out which smell dominated: the cigarettes, cheap alcohol, incense burners, or the fetor of the patrons. Detan's nose was so overwhelmed it simply gave up, a deprivation he was grateful for. From the twist of Tibs's face, his olfactory system hadn't done him the same favor.

Square tables dotted a squeaking, wooden floor that had been hastily covered with threadbare rugs. The window from which Detan had spotted the festivities, it seemed, was singular. Which rather explained the hazy atmosphere.

Marking the table nearest that breezy view, Detan strolled over and dragged a chair up to an empty side. It gave a rather alarming creak as he sat.

"What's the game, gentlemen?" he asked the guards arrayed at either end. They wore the simple white linen shirts assigned to all enlistees of the empire's many branches. The smoky grey coats that marked them as Fleet guards hung from pegs next to the nearby door. Though their attire was identical, one was large about the shoulders with dark mutton chops marring his firm jaw line, the other shorter, his rectangular head topped by a tangle of curls like a brushweed. They gave him a look, each in turn, then glanced at one another and shrugged.

"Rabbit," said the one hogging the window seat – the beefy man with the impressive muttonchops.

"That the menu, or the game?" Detan asked, shooting a bewildered glance towards Tibs – who had scarpered off and found another table, leaving Detan raising his eyebrows at the empty air.

Muttonchops chuckled. "Never played rabbit before, eh? Sure you want to put a wager down?"

Detan felt the weight of the grains in his pocket, considering. He had scarce little to lose, and these louts were no doubt testing him to see if he'd buy into their probably-made-up rules. But they were guards. Remnant guards, if the black patches sewn on their sleeves held any truth, and he needed information. Better, he needed buddies on that island – and the best way to turn a target into a friend, Detan had long since discovered, was to lose a whole lotta grains to them.

"I'll have you know I'm a man anxious for knowledge, thirsty for new experiences. I'll play your rabbit – and roast it too."

The guards laughed, comfortable with what they were certain was a sure win. "Suit yourself," muttonchops said as he dealt out a fan of face-down cards before each of them. "I'm Garlt, and this here's Yisson. Buy-in's a copper."

"Is that all?" Detan winked at Garlt to let him know he was being facetious. Willing as he was to part with grain for friendship, there were limits, and he didn't want this man thinking he had much more to burn. With a flick of his wrist he rolled a grain out of his sleeve and back across his knuckles, then plunked it down in the pale chalk circle in the center of the table.

"None o' that sleight of hand nonsense, Mister...?"

"Wenton's the name, Wenton Dakfert. And I promise you, that's the only trick I've got up my ratty sleeves. Took me nigh on a year to learn that bit of nonsense, so I show it off every chance I get."

As he scooped up his hand, he let one card drop and fall face-up to the table. Mustering a blush, he pretended to fumble and snatch it up quick as could be, slapping his palm down over it in an effort to hide the face, but not fast enough. Detan let loose with a nervous chuckle.

"Ah, see? I'd say I had butterfingers, if I could afford butter."

Garlt guffawed and thumped the table with his fist hard enough to slosh his cup of suspiciously yellow brew, no doubt trying to make Detan drop another card or two. He refrained. Just because he'd planned on losing to these two knuckleheads didn't mean he was going to make it *that* easy for them.

"What is it you do, Wenton, that you can't afford some butter for your bread?"

"Who said I could afford bread?"

Yisson snorted and tossed a card face-up onto the three antes. "Match house or color, toss it down the rabbit hole," he said, not bothering to explain any of the finer points. Or any of the coarser points, really. "And you..." He snapped his fingers at a harried serving girl. "Bring Wenton here a beer, will you? I take it you can afford beer?"

"I would rather spend my grains on beer than bread, it's true." Detan pitched in a matching color of low house. Garlt's brows shot up. Low houses were good, then.

"You so hard up, whatcha doing in this stinkhole?" Garlt asked, flicking down a high house.

"Ah, so you denizens had noticed the local... flavor. I was beginning to think I was hallucinating."

"Can't hallucinate with your nose, can ya?" Yisson slapped down a matching color and grinned. Detan had no idea what to make of that.

"If the odor is strong enough, certain visuals might become involved."

"Would explain your card playing," Garlt said, getting a chuckle out of his friend.

"Har-dee-har," Detan drawled as he watched Yisson open a fan of a different house on the table and receive replacements from Garlt. Yisson scowled at his new hand and waved for Detan to play. He frowned. No one bothered to explain that move to him.

"Truth is, lads, I'm a prospector."

Garlt worked up the nerve to ask the pertinent question, and Detan marked him as the aggressive player of the two. "Of what?"

"Metals, gems, whatever I can scrounge up out of this cracked dustbowl. What?" He smirked, laying down a random card. "You two think I might be some kind of sensitive?"

Garlt shrugged. "Lotta rumors of those lately, what with the empire losing its hold on Aransa. That shitty city lost a lot of sensitives the day Thratia took over. Fleeing being associated with anyone anti-Valathea, I'd wager. Some o' em went to other mining cities to work, but some went rogue, too. Trying to find tiny caches they can siphon up and sell on the black market."

Garlt snorted and took a deep drink of his pale libation as the serving girl appeared with the drink's match. Detan paused, pretending to pursue his cards with care, as he tried to keep his expression from giving away his thoughts. He hadn't heard that Thratia'd lost sensitives in her takeover. He'd assumed that, with half the city wearing her uniform, they'd been more than happy to see the old guard out and the new warden warming the seat.

But sel-sensitive refugees, scattered across the Scorched? If some sought employment at other mining cities he had no doubt they'd flock to his aunt's city, Hond Steading. Why hadn't she mentioned it in her last letter? She couldn't be *that* cross with him.

"Wish I had a talent like that, sensing sel. Would mean I'd always have work, eh?" Detan said, watching Garlt's expression over his hand of cards.

"I wouldn't want it, that's fer damned sure."

"Right you are," Yisson said. "At least when you sign on for the Fleet, you get good pay and the right to quit if you ever wanna. Those sorry sacks of sel-sniffers are stuck tight. Empire needs 'em to keep the Fleet afloat, and sure as the pits doesn't want them falling into anyone else's hands. Harsh punishment for those who get caught running, too."

Yisson glanced at Garlt, who was too busy chugging ale to see the question in Yisson's eyes. The big man thumped his drink down on the table and belched. "The Remnant's no pretty place, but it's better than a hanging."

Detan's heart kicked up its beat, and he didn't bother looking at whatever card he lay down. Yisson chuckled and clucked his tongue, but Detan didn't pay him any mind. So the Remnant housed rogue sel-sensitives. A nice, juicy bit of bait to stick on the end of the lure he wanted to lead out to Pelkaia.

"Sounds like a sweet gig, minding the ole bars," Detan said. "The Fleet hiring?"

"For the island?" Garlt grunted. "Wish they would. Way it works now, we only get one day o' leave time. Can't get far from the Remnant in just a day, it's Petrastad or one o' those little fishing villages."

"Pah," Yisson tossed down a card. "They call 'emselves fishing villages but we all know they're smugglers. Pearls, mostly, I think. Dunno why the empire doesn't shut 'em down."

"Probably because they like the cheap pearls and aren't keen on doing the labor 'emselves."

"When are they ever?" Detan interjected, winning a laugh and a thump on the back from Garlt that was, he suspected, designed to make him lose his grip on his cards again. He clung on, just to spite.

"You're all right, Wenton."

He took a swig of ale and grimaced. "Mind pointing me towards the bathroom?"

"Gotten to you already, has it?"

"Through me like piss through cheesecloth. Tastes like it, too."

"Hah, that it does. Bathroom's down the hall, but I warn you, the reason it's called a bathroom is because the only thing you'll want after visiting it is a bath."

"A boiling one," Yisson added.

Detan rose, effecting a sway, and left his cards face down on the table with full knowledge they'd peek at them the moment he was out of sight. He pretended an orientating glance, making it look as if he was searching for the door. Spotting Tibs in the corner of the room, he paused long enough to let him feel his gaze probing his back, then swaggered out into the hall.

He used the bathroom. Yisson was, it turned out, being kind.

When he returned to the hall the bouncer ducked into the card room, drawn by the sound of raised voices. Tibs waited, one dead-caterpillar eyebrow arched in question. "Win anything?"

"Pits, no. In fact, we better scuttle before they come out here looking to see if they can squeeze any more out of me."

"Thought we didn't have grain to lose?"

"Bah." Detan slung an arm around Tibs's shoulder, wiping a sticky substance he'd acquired from the bathroom off his hand onto Tibs's coat. "Your short-sighted, pocket-pinching ways never fail to distress me, old friend. It was not the proliferation of grains I was after, but the information."

"Really. And did you manage to lose some information, too?"

"You wound me." He stepped aside as a broad-shouldered man spilled out of the card room's doorway into the hall with them. The man staggered, obviously having stomached more ale than Detan could manage, and rammed his shoulder straight into Detan's chest. With a grunt and a forced laugh, Detan nudged the man upright and steadied him.

"You all right, mister...?"

"Buncha cheats in there," the drunken man muttered and tugged at his rumpled collar. He pat Detan's chest with one sticky hand. "You're all right, though."

The man dragged his hand free of Detan's shirt, turning to struggle his way down the stairs, and the harsh rip of fabric tearing filled the hallway. Everyone froze, staring at the spill of cards that Tibs had dealt Detan to keep his hands busy while they were locked in a cabin on the *Larkspur*, splayed out across the stained hallway floor.

"Err," Detan said.

"Cheater!" the drunken man roared, and grabbed Detan's rumpled shirt in both meaty fists.

Detan attempted a protest, but with his feet dangling off the ground and his collar ratcheted up tight around his throat all he managed was a pale imitation of a dunkeet squawk. His back struck the wall and dust rained down upon him, filling his eyes with grit and tears. On instinct he kicked out – more of a flail, if he was being honest with himself – and struck the man hard in, what he was disturbed to realize, was the man's crotch.

Wheezing and grunting, the drunken man dropped Detan with a thud and staggered back, folding up upon himself like flaccid sail. Detan wanted to harangue the man for his uncalled for assault, but Tibs grabbed him by the sleeve and jerked him toward the stairs.

Shouts sounded from inside the card room. The big man's cries of cheater must have been overheard. Which was really unfair, considering this had been one of the few times Detan hadn't had any intention of cheating.

With a weary groan he scurried after Tibs, tromping down the creaky steps and out into the strange streets of Petrastad. A fine mist ensconced the city, bitter cold and obscuring, as night crept in across the waves.

"I blame you for that." Detan propped his hands against his knees, huffing the chilly air. Tibs rolled his eyes.

"Blame me all you like, you still owe me a new deck of cards."

"Preposterous! I could not have foreseen that brute's–"

"There they are!" The singular window of Lotti's Cards sprouted two heads. One of them hurled a lantern. The glass shattered and splashed burning oil a mere few paces from where Detan hunched. He yelped and jumped aside.

"Now that was uncalled for!"

"Come *on*." Tibs took off down a side street, and with a muffled curse Detan sprinted after him, boots slipping on the mist-slick cobblestones.

"Why," Tibs demanded through harsh breaths, "didn't you change your shirt?"

"It was clean enough! Do you have any idea where you're going?"

"Away from them seems the best course," Tibs replied as he twisted down yet another street. Detan jogged along, beginning to notice a disturbing pattern. This city, just like its rectangular buildings, was laid out in grids. Nice, wide, easy to follow grids. Not a simple city to hide in, not at all. And it didn't help matters much that their boots smeared mud with every step they took.

Detan sighed. "I hate this city."

"Didn't take you long," Tibs called back over his shoulder.

"Never does."

Shouts sounded somewhere behind them, echoing off the neat, straight stone walls, and Detan forced his legs to pump a little faster. He told himself it could be worse. It could be the local watchers hard on his heels, but the thought didn't much soothe when his knees ached and the damned mist was clogging up his eyes.

"Fucking Petrastad," he said to no one in particular.

CHAPTER 8

As the shrill whistle tolled, the guards grouped the sparrows for work details. Ripka caught sight of Enard over by the trestle table they'd taken their first meal on, lumped together with a handful of other male sparrows. They held wire brushes for deep cleaning, and were being handed rusty wrenches. Despite her uneasiness with Clink, she was glad she wasn't in that group.

"This way," Clink said, waving an arm toward the edge of the rec yard.

Ripka followed, hesitant but with her head up, waiting for the guards to yell at their little party for moving without permission. To let loose with those too-casual crossbows. Not a one so much as twitched an eyebrow their direction.

Clink stopped at a doorway leading into the dormitory on the western edge of the rec yard. It was huge and arched, thick planks of darkwood banded with iron kissed by rust. She pounded twice on the door with her fist and, after a moment, it swung open. Another guard stood framed by a long hallway, eyes bloodshot from lack of sleep, her shirt half tucked and a deep scowl on her lips.

"Didn't you hear the whistles?" Clink asked, a little too firmly for Ripka's liking. If Clink had been a prisoner in her jail, she'd be scolded for that. Of course, Ripka doubted a scolding would do much good against a woman like Clink, but at least an attempt at decorum would have been made.

"Aren't you an industrious little bee?" The guard sneered and stepped aside, gesturing them through the door.

"We don't farm, we don't eat." Clink eyed the guard. "And we wouldn't last long if we were forced to eat the local wildlife. They're all so *spindly*."

The guard snorted and pointed to the wall. Hanging from the grey, unfinished stone were five buckets stuffed with hand spades, claw rakes, pruning shears, and leather gloves. Ripka stared, dumbstruck. Every last piece of equipment could be fashioned into a deadly weapon.

"Grab a bucket," Honey whispered, nudging her forward. The pale-haired woman hugged her bucket against her midsection with one arm, a spade clutched in the other hand. She brought the spade up to her cheek and brushed the cool steel against her skin. All the while smiling with those big, doe, eyes at Ripka.

Ripka cleared her throat. "They let us use this stuff?"

The guard said, "Only to do your work. Cause any trouble out there and you get thrown in the well. Try and sneak anything back in, you get thrown in the well. Sneak anything back in and *use* it, you get thrown to the sharks. Clear?"

"As the skies," Ripka said as she took a bucket from a hook.

"Now hold still." The rumpled guard jerked a patch from her pocket, spilling a few more to the floor, and kicked the fallen ones aside. Thick stalks of grain were embroidered in the middle of the patch, a gleaming bucket alongside them. Her face pinched with concentration, the guard pressed the patch against Ripka's arm. She tugged a folded card from her pocket and flipped it open to reveal a set of pre-threaded needles. Tongue sticking out of the corner of her mouth, the guard leaned over the patch and Ripka held her breath as the woman drew a few sloppy stitches through, then broke the thread and tied off a knot.

"There. You're official. Don't fucking lose it."

Ripka pulled on the leather gloves she found in the bottom of the bucket. Once the guard's small group was prepared, she ushered them out into the sun. The bright glare was nothing compared to Aransa's oppressive heat, but Ripka took a moment to stand still, soaking in the warm rays. The warmth also did a fine job of spreading a rotten-sweet stench.

Shoved up against the Remnant's exterior wall, a gaping pit wafted vile clouds into the air. She cringed away, turning her head so that she wouldn't have to breathe in the moldering heap.

Clink laughed and chucked her in the shoulder. "Better get used to it. That's our midden heap. Come fertilizing day you'll get real acquainted."

"Oh good, something to look forward to." She sighed, glancing back at the mound of refuse. A narrow pipe poked through the stone wall above it, something slimy and unctuous dribbling into the pile. She shivered and trudged onward.

Outside of the grey confines of the prison, the island was, she grudgingly admitted, quite beautiful. It offered nothing of the brutal beauty of the desert or the scrublands, but its rocky ground and patchwork gardens gleamed beneath the soft kiss of the sun. While the daylight was high, the sea breeze didn't feel quite so bone-biting. The salty tang in the air mingled with a darker, earthy aroma was almost refreshing.

A packed dirt path lead them away from the stone arms of the prison, winding through patches of vegetable gardens. A gravel path would have made much more sense at a prison, then the guards could more easily hear footsteps, but Ripka was beginning to expect incompetence, or at the very least laziness, from her surroundings.

She followed the sinuous line of another, thicker path through the plots with her eye. It twisted toward the shore, then looped back toward the prison. At the apex of that twist, she thought she could see a smaller building – right in the center of a field she'd been certain was empty from her vantage in the bird's nest.

The building was low and squat, its flat roof gleaming with a faint sheen under the sunlight. Something seemed... off, about it. Something with the shadows, or the wideness. She couldn't quite tell. Even the color of the walls looked wrong. They were yellowstone, the same rock that made up most of Aransa's buildings, but there wasn't a quarry for that stone anywhere near the Remnant, so far as she could recall.

"Got sap in your boots?" Forge hissed in her ear, giving her a shove.

Hiding a flush by turning her face back to the track, Ripka hurried to close the small gap that had opened between her and Clink. At least the guard didn't seem half so annoyed as Forge did.

They passed a triangular plot of land dotted with a few dozen beetlenut trees. Half the inmates assigned to work the trees had climbed them, and were busy shaking the branches to drop nuts onto blankets held out by those waiting below. One of the climbers nearest the road shook his grey hair to clear it of leaves and sucked deep on a rolled cigarette. The cloud he exhaled was sweet, acrid. Like nothing Ripka'd smelled before.

"The guards let us smoke?" she asked, not bothering to hide her incredulous tone.

"Not exactly," Forge said, eyeing the grey-haired man. "But he's puffing mudleaf. Keeps you calm, you know? Normally they'd make you snuff it if you were smoking out in the open, but that's Sasan. He's been here thirty years, and will stay until the day he dies. If the older lifers need a little extra to take the edge off, everyone looks the other way."

"Contraband is really that easy to come by around here?"

Forge grinned. "You'd be surprised."

Her heart gave a kick of anticipation as they turned down the path toward the strange building, but she kept her steps steady. Just short of the start of the curve that would bring them to the building, the guard ordered them to disperse into a field of grains. The plants glimmered as the sea breeze stroked them, reminding Ripka of a silvery-backed locust swarm.

The women were tasked to weeding the ground between the rows, and spread out. Ripka hesitated, spade in hand. Apparently no one doubted that she knew how to weed a garden. She supposed it shouldn't be too hard – just pluck anything that wasn't obviously grain and toss it in her bucket.

Honey leaned close and whispered, "Just a quick jab." She demonstrated with the spade. "And a little twist. They pop right out. Sometimes you get lucky and can feel the roots break." She gave Ripka what was probably meant to be a reassuring pat on the shoulder and stepped up to a row. With a vigorous jab, she speared the ground near a green-leafed weed and twisted. A delighted smile lit up her features, and she began to hum softly. Ripka forgotten, Honey disappeared down her row in search of more prey for her spade.

Left to her own devices, Ripka wandered down the row assigned to her, feeling the sunlight on her back in earnest. Just jab and twist, as Honey had said. Should be easy enough. A small trickle of sweat began across her neck, her shoulders, tickling her sun-tired skin. She wondered if they'd bring water out here for them before the work was through.

She also wondered how close they were watching her.

Covering her reconnaissance by pretending to be on sharp lookout for pesky weeds, she advanced down the row, drawing closer to the strange building with every step she took.

When she reached the end of the line, her bucket half-filled with bruised green plants and her eyes stinging against the sweat that'd rolled into them, she glanced round. No one was watching. She spent a long moment crouched there, marking the rotation of guards across the dormitory roof, and found their timing conveniently regular. Slowly, as to not rustle the deadfall scattering the ground, she crept forward, drawing closer to the house.

She could make out the faintest details of the building now and, sidling up near the bent trunk of a spineneedle tree, she shaded her eyes with her hand. The door didn't look very secure. In fact, it appeared quite small and ordinary.

A laugh burbled up from the grains and she flinched, glancing back toward the small plot. No one came her way. She breathed out, shoulders easing.

"Just what do you think you're doing?"

A woman in a guard's uniform stepped from beside the tree. Ripka jumped, nearly lost her bucket, and caught herself halfway through raising her spade to strike. The guard was slender, narrow boned and narrow waisted, her dark head shorn of hair, even the eyebrows. The guard glanced down at the raised spade and let out a small whistle through the gap between her two front teeth.

"Wouldn't bother with that. Attacking a guard'll get you dumped in the well."

"What's this well everyone keeps talking about?" Ripka said, trying to hide the adrenaline tremor in her voice as she straightened from a fighting stance and put the spade back in the bucket.

"Best you don't find out." The woman smiled a gap-toothed smile and gestured toward the field with the butt of her spear. "Get back to work. Wouldn't want to lose the grain harvest to a missed weed, now would we?"

Ripka jerked her chin toward the smaller building. "What is that place?"

The guard pursed her lips together and angled her body to cover Ripka's view of the compound. "None of your business, sparrow."

"Misol." The surly guard who had herded them out to their work duty emerged from the end of a row. "What's this? The sparrow trying to fly off?"

Misol eyed Ripka, rolled something around in her mouth and then spat black fluid on the grey rocks. "Naw. Just wanted to have a chat with the new bird. You can have her back, now."

"Well la-tee-da, aren't you generous. This is real work these gophers are doing, you know. Puts food on your plate, too."

"Calm your shit," Misol said, her knuckles going pale as paper against the grip of her spear.

"Want me to tell Warden Radu you've been chatting with the scruff when they should be working?"

"Go ahead. Tell him." Misol smirked at the guard's flustered expression, winked once at Ripka, and then strolled off back toward the building.

"What a bitch," the guard muttered.

"I finished my row," Ripka said, hoping a little good news might ease her captor's mood.

"Congratulations. Now you got fifty more to do."

"Fifty? There aren't even that many in this field."

"Ain't the only field on the island, is it? Line back up with the others, no dallying."

Ripka rolled her shoulders to ease their ache, then glanced back toward the tree Misol had appeared from behind. Wasn't much to hide behind, there. It was a glorified stick, no wider around than Ripka's thigh. Misol had been a skinny thing, sure, but not even she could blend so completely with the landscape. Ripka should have noticed her.

"Hurry up!" the guard yelled. Ripka trudged back to work, mind a mess of possibilities.

CHAPTER 9

Detan was beginning to think that he'd grown too old for this kind of nonsense, when he rounded a corner and confirmed the fact. Sitting smack in the middle of the lane, cross-legged and drooping with boredom, was a girl of about thirteen. Her round face puckered upon sighting them, as if they were expected. Detan grabbed a hold of Tibs's coat to keep him from trampling the little thing. Sometimes Detan suspected Tibs's legs were too long for the man to see the ground.

"Finally," the girl said. The word was cut in twain by a yawn large enough to make a rockcat jealous. "Thought I'd be here all night, waiting for you two idiots to turn the right way."

"Begging your pardon, miss," he stammered between panting breaths, "but we are in a spot of a hurry."

Shouts echoed behind them, entirely too close.

"And doing a poor job of evasion." The girl stood in one fluid movement and flexed her bare feet against the stone road. Her sandy hair was a mess of wind-tousled curls, her cheeks puckered with the redness of too long spent in the wind. Trousers, bare feet, running amok in the city in the middle of the night looking like she'd swooped in out of the sky. Pieces clicked into place in Detan's overheated mind.

"You're one of Pelkaia's."

She gave him a slow, sarcastic round of applause. "They warned me you were clever. Now hurry, before that big brain of yours gets staved in by your new friends."

"Cheeky kid."

"You do bring out the best in people," Tibs said.

The girl took off without another word, slipping along the streets as if she'd been born to them. With a synchronized roll of the shoulders they ran after her, throwing their fate in her small hands and hoping Pelkaia didn't have it out for them too badly. He recalled how long and hard Pelkaia could hold a grudge, and amended his thoughts. Best not to trust – best to have an eye out for another opening, if that woman was in the mix.

After running what felt like half the night away, but was probably only a mere quarter-mark, the shouts behind them disappeared into the usual mutter and bustle of a city at night. Detan had no idea where they'd ended up – every building in this sea-spit city looked the same – but he didn't rightly care as long as he wasn't in imminent danger of a beating.

They staggered to a stop. Tibs and Detan panted while the girl crossed her arms and eyed them, bored now that the threat had passed.

"You two geezers having heart attacks?"

Detan mock-gasped and clutched his chest. "Oh, the cruelty of the young and snot-nosed wounds me so."

"Ugh," she said, with all the indignity a teenager was capable of mustering. "You do think you're clever. Pity." The girl rose to her toes to peer over his shoulder, and frowned. "More pity, looks like we really did lose them."

Detan's brows shot up. "You wanted a fight?"

She shrugged. "Just a little one."

"Who in the black skies are you?"

She rolled her eyes, turned down a side lane, and vanished in a cloud of mist.

"What in the..."

He scurried after her. The mist felt cool to his skin, sticky with the brine of the sea. He waved his hands through it, tangling his fingers in the smoky wisps. A tingle begged for attention at the edge of his senses. Sel. He scratched the inside crook of his elbow.

She'd made sel look like smoke and melded it with the mist to cover her escape. He stood silent, trying to ignore the pounding of his heart in his ears, but couldn't hear her footsteps pattering anywhere nearby.

"Creepy kid," he muttered.

"One of Pelkaia's, what'd you expect? Now what'd you go and lose our grains for?"

"Ever the miser. Come along, I think I see the *Larkspur's* new facade over yonder, which means the flier is close by."

Detan explained what he'd learned as they plodded along the mist-slick street toward the dock. A fretful wind rolled in off the sea, kicking up dirt and detritus in equal measure. When they drew within sight of the dock's building, they sought shelter in the leeway of a nondescript brown building to talk through their next steps. Tibs rested his back against the alley wall to look over Detan's shoulder while Detan watched over Tibs's. Just because they'd left their pursuers behind didn't mean they weren't likely to stumble across someone who'd recognized them.

Detan had made that mistake before. He hunched his shoulders, flipping up his collar to hide the house sigil seared into the flesh at the back of his neck. His hair was long enough to hide it now, but in this wind he didn't trust to that particular method.

"I suppose you got something good after all," Tibs admitted when Detan had finished relaying the information he'd squeezed from the guards.

"A little more faith from you, I think, is in order." He grinned as Tibs rolled his eyes so hard all he could see were the whites of them. "Though the news that the Remnant's been housing rogue sensitives is a worry."

"Could be a hook for Pelkaia."

Detan grimaced. "Could be a hindrance, too. Sauntering in to break out three souls is a bit different than liberating a whole wing of high-priority prisoners." A stray gust carried the scent of seared fish marinated in some sort of citrus. The hollow in Detan's belly, alleviated by only a few sips of that nasty ale, rumbled.

"Did *you* happen to win any grains?" he asked. "I could use a bite or ten. I can't believe Pelkaia didn't even treat us to tea. Quite rude of her, after we'd gone to all that trouble to arrange a visit."

"She never struck me as one inclined to hospitality."

"Dangers of living your life under a shifting sea of faces, you never know where your manners will come from."

"Don't think it works that way."

"I'm afraid I'm too starved to think straight on the matter." Detan scowled at the empty alley, all its heaps and piles of rubbish looking decidedly inedible. He kicked the ground, dislodging a pebble, just to show the city how annoyed he was with its shameful lack of provisions.

"There's food on the flier," Tibs said.

"Of course, but I haven't a clue how much berthage that posh dock Pelkaia dropped us at costs, and I doubt the lady paid our fare – no, I'm sure she didn't. We got lucky sneaking on the first time to grab my shoes, I doubt we'll be so lucky again. I suppose we could scout another card house, play some local roughs for real gain."

"Or," Tibs drawled, reaching into his rumpled grey coat, "we could bribe the dock porter. Did some digging of my own. Turns out his favorite brew is Rinton Red."

From within the voluminous confines of his coat Tibs produced a dark green bottle two hands tall, with a smudged brown label proclaiming the aforementioned vintage.

Detan stared, open-mouthed, until the dust on the wind demonstrated the benefits of keeping his mouth closed. "What... I mean... When? How? When did you get that? Never saw you leave, and I sure as the pits know you weren't toting it around with you before."

Tibs waved a hand through the air and pushed off from the wall, ambling toward the docks with a nonchalant stroll. "I'm not the only one who can lose at cards."

"What does that even mean? How'd you get it, Tibs? Come on, spill!"

"Nope."

"Nope? Nope? You can't answer a question like that with *nope*. We're partners. Fess up."

"Man's gotta have his secrets." Tibs tugged the brim of his singed grey hat lower. "Keep an air of mystery about himself."

"Mystery? You? You're the straightest nail I've never bent. Why, I remember when we first met–"

Tibs shushed him with a wave of the hand as they mounted the steps back to the docks. Detan forced himself to bite his tongue, focusing on the narrow wooden stairs attached to the side of the building. He wondered what the interior held. More taverns and places of business, like the one across the street, or apartments? All the narrow windows had their curtains pulled tight, their shutters locked against sea winds. The air inside had to be vile – stuffy and damp. How people could live like that, all stacked up one atop the other, he couldn't begin to understand.

As they crested the rooftop, Tibs strolled ahead to have a talk with the porter. Detan gave him a few moments of privacy before sidling up to them, an affable smile plastered on his face.

The porter had the bottle in his hands and turned it over with strange tenderness as he licked pillowy lips. "Which one you say was yours?" he asked Tibs.

"The flier, over there." Tibs jerked his thumb at their bird, looking mighty rickety next to the reduced grandeur of the *Larkspur*. *Happy Birthday Virra!* was painted in pristine purple paint on the side of the buoyancy sack. They'd taken turns refreshing the color every other moonturn.

The porter raised both eyebrows. "And which one of you is Virra, then?"

"He is," they said in unison.

With a world-weary sigh the porter stuffed the bottle into an oversized pocket and hooked his thumbs in the loops of his trousers. "I suppose berth for such a small vessel won't amount to much. You in for a day or two?"

"Two, maybe more. We overstay our welcome, another gift'll be in order," Tibs said.

The porter chewed this around, cheeks bulging as he poked his tongue against the interior of them, then nodded, subconsciously giving his bottle a pat. "Go on then. And don't cause no trouble."

"Wouldn't dream of it," Detan said with a chipper wink.

Tibs grabbed his sleeve and tugged him away from the narrowing eyes of the porter. They scrambled aboard in silence, checked the deck for stowaways, then exchanged a questioning glance. It was time to go below.

With an exaggerated yawn and catlike stretch for anyone who might have been watching, Detan entered the cabin sticking up dead center of the flier's deck, Tibs close on his heels. With a practiced flick of the wrist Tibs threw the lock on the door behind him, and they stood a moment in silence, listening.

Nothing but the wind.

Whistling a chipper tune, Detan dragged one of the limp mattresses they kept for show to the side of the cabin and flipped up the disguised wooden latch on the trapdoor hidden beneath. He hauled it up, grabbed a lantern for light, and shimmied down the narrow ladder.

While the deck and cabin of the flier were modest in their

accoutrements, Tibs and Detan had shoved everything they owned of value down into the smuggler's hold in the keel of their flat-bellied ship. Barrels of booze, a stash of false grain making equipment, luxurious mattresses, all their clothes.

And, apparently, Pelkaia.

She sat on the edge of Detan's mattress, his favorite silken pillow resting on her knees, a knife that was most certainly not his resting on top of that. She wore her own face, and the dune-smooth lines of her Catari heritage unsettled him. She was of the people his family had inadvertently uprooted, all those years ago when they'd sailed on ancient sea ships in search of better farming and had discovered the Scorched – and the selium – instead.

The simple fact that a people already called this sun-blasted continent home had not stopped the Valathean advance. In some ways, he suspected it'd encouraged them. Valatheans had always been keen on a fight.

"Coulda just knocked," he said, stepping aside so that Tibs could drop down from the ladder beside him.

"I'm here to offer you assistance, Honding."

"Ah, well, I hope it's not with redecorating..."

He cringed as she tossed the pillow to the floor. Fine silk like that shouldn't be abused so. As she stood, he watched the way she held her knife, low but loose, not preparing for a fight. Her open stance and pursed lips eased the tension between his shoulder blades. Her pointed glance toward the curtained-off section Ripka had used to sleep in brought the tension right back.

"I will help you recover Watch-captain Leshe and your wayward friend. But first..." Pelkaia glanced to the knife in her hand, and he had no idea what to make of the decisive nod she gave herself.

"You're going to have to help me with a little side project."

Detan swallowed. "I'm listening."

CHAPTER 10

By the time the dinner bell rolled around, Ripka was ready to eat her own arm – or the raw grain growing around her. The midday meal had been little more than stale water and staler bread, eaten under the paltry shade of a knobby old tree. Her newfound crew trudged back down the path to the prison, rendered silent by exhaustion. Ripka was perversely glad she wasn't the only one hurting. She'd always counted herself in good shape – she'd had to be to maintain her post as the watch-captain of Aransa – but this was too much. Hours spent bent over, scraping dirt in the sun, was enough to break the spirit of anyone.

Which was precisely why the guards made the inmates do it. Despite her aches, she saw the cleverness in their system. Good behavior got you out where you could taste a hint of freedom, but it also got you so worn down you couldn't start a fight even if you were itching to pop off. It kept people in line, too, that their food source was tied directly to their work. Ripka held no illusions as to who would be fed first if the island crops failed and the monsoons kept airship delivery at bay. It was, she realized, the only system on the Remnant she'd been impressed by.

They were pat down before they were allowed back in the

hallway, pat down again after they'd deposited their buckets stuffed with tools, and then let loose. They wandered in a droopy clump toward the long tables where stale rolls and fruit-pocked mush were being handed out.

"By the blue skies, if I weren't so cursed hungry I'd swear off eating bread ever again," Clink said.

"I hear ya." Forge brushed sweat-plastered strands of hair off her forehead. "But if we swear off every flavor of crop we work on we'd never eat again."

Ripka blinked. "You mean we switch crops?"

"Every day," Clink affirmed. "Warden don't want us getting too familiar with any one piece of land. They switch up the type of crop, the task, and the order in which we go to the crops. Anything to keep us off-balance."

"Inefficient," Ripka said.

"We're free labor," Honey murmured. "Warden doesn't care how long it takes to get done, so long as it does."

"Fair point." Ripka tried on a smile in her direction. Honey stared at her.

Unsettled, Ripka glanced around the yard and spotted Enard in the same seat he'd taken the night before. Luckily his neighbors had changed. His shoulders were hunched, his hands busy shoveling food into his mouth. She could only imagine what sort of day he'd had, what sort of work they'd found for him. Regardless of his, or her, exhaustion, she had to tell him what she'd found. Of the strange compound, and the guard who could disappear behind trees. And he owed her more than a handful of answers.

"Hey, Clink," she said, turning to their de facto leader. "I'm going to–"

"Go on." She waved her hand in expansive dismissal. "Go see your man. You know our table. We'll see you at it in the morning. Clear?"

"He's not my–"

"Just *go*."

Ripka peeled away from the group, awareness of her isolation growing with every step she took. Knots of prisoners dotted the rec yard. Some ate, some played games and socialized. Anytime she drew within ten steps of any one of them, they hushed and looked up as one, watching her pass with wary eyes.

Any of those groups could contain the songbird. Any one of them could be an ally of that woman or her man. And there Ripka was, striking out alone across the massive courtyard.

Breathe, she told herself. You're no sparrow, you're a thrice-cursed hawk, and you've handled shadier bastards than this lot. She kept her chin up, let her gaze roam, but not flick, not allowing a sliver of nervousness into her expression. By the time she sat down next to Enard she'd worked herself up enough to fight every last soul in the whole building.

"Good evening, cap... miss."

"Captain suits me fine, here."

He startled and raised his brows at her. She shrugged. "They asked my *other* name, figured that one was suitable."

"Bold choice." He pushed a plate of bread and half-bruised fruit toward her.

"I'm not likely to forget it, at least."

"True." He stirred the mush on his plate with a wooden spoon, lost in thought.

She picked out a few pieces of better looking fruit and popped them into her mouth, savoring the over-ripe sweetness, the rush of flavor across her parched tongue. They'd brought her water in the fields, sure, but it'd been stale and warm, good for little more than keeping her alive.

At least they'd gone to the trouble of keeping her alive.

When he'd been quiet long enough she feared they'd have their dinner broken up before being able to discuss anything, she lowered her voice and asked, "So, 'Tender', is it?"

"Ah. That."

He laid his bread back down on his plate, sat up straight as he could on the wobbly bench and brushed crumbs from his fingers. Every last move was precise, dignified, the same old Enard she'd come to know over the last year trolling around on Detan's flier. But there was something else to him now – a darker current, an edge of danger. How she hadn't seen it before, she couldn't say for certain. Maybe he hadn't wanted her to. Probably she hadn't wanted to.

"You recall I was a steward at the Salt Baths in Aransa, of course. But that was not my only experience with such work. I come from a family of particular valets."

"Valets?" She leaned closer as his voice lowered to keep those nearby from overhearing.

"Yes. Personal stewards, of a sort. My family's specialty was... clandestine. We were valets for the Glasseater bosses. First in Valathea, then the Scorched when they expanded. We did odd jobs for them. Private work, you understand. I received my name when I was assigned a post at a boss's tavern. I tended bar – and kept an eye out for a certain amount of misbehavior from his compatriots."

"I see. And so they called you Tender, for your work."

"And for how I left those I found misbehaving."

Ripka felt her world shift. Patient, kind, affable Enard had been a crime boss's right-hand. A knee buster. An assassin, quite probably, if it came to it. Certainly not the gentle, well-mannered young man Detan thought he'd picked up looking for an adventure in the Baths. This was a man with a reputation. A reputation dark enough to frighten that big bruiser. She paused until the knot in her throat smoothed away and she could speak without a hitch in her voice.

"Not a job someone leaves lightly."

He stared at his hands, folded with care on the rough tabletop. The muscles of his jaw jumped. He swallowed before he spoke.

"No. It isn't. My reasons are personal, though I think you would agree with them. There was a certain woman who I felt was undeserving of my work."

"And so you left."

"And so I fled."

"Ah." She closed her eyes, rubbed her temples to keep from grinding her teeth. If they were looking for him still, and she had no reason to doubt that they were, then being recognized here was dangerous for them both. His reputation settled between them, heavy and cold.

"Did the others know? Detan and Tibal, have you told them?"

"They knew I left the Glasseaters, nothing more. They asked no further questions."

"Of course they didn't. Denial is Detan's greatest talent."

She closed her eyes, imagining wringing Detan's neck for the position his willful ignorance had put her in. Enard could out her if he chose, reveal her as Aransa's ex-watch-captain to all these bitter souls. Might have to do it as a bargaining chip to save his own ass from the wrath he brought chasing him. Isolation ensconced her once more. She blew out the breath she was holding, and looked at him long and hard.

"What will you do?" she asked.

"I'm here to get Nouli out. To get him to Hond Steading where he can do some good. That's all."

"Right," she said, "as am I." She had no choice but to believe him, and no desire to do otherwise. Whatever he'd been, he was her friend now. If she couldn't rely on him, she might as well throw herself to the sharks and be done with it all.

"Is that all?"

She stiffened, not liking his sudden change of topic. It was a tactic she'd used herself many times in interrogation rooms. "What do you mean?"

He picked up his spoon and pushed gruel across the plate once more. "Seems a lot of trouble to go to, to help out one city that you've never even stepped foot in. I grant you, protecting Hond Steading from Commodore Ganal is a noble goal, but I had wondered... If you might have another motive. Some unfinished business here, from your time as a watcher."

Ripka twisted her spoon between her fingers. There was no sense in lying to him. If she did so now, she might break the fragile trust they'd re-established. He knew that, of course. It was why he'd chosen now to ask his question, when he'd had ample time before they'd ever arrived in the Remnant. "I won't lose another city to Thratia Ganal."

"Ah. It's atonement for you, then."

"It's the right thing to do," she snapped and pointed the spoon at him. A bit of gruel dripped off the end.

"Forgive me. It's just that, it had occurred to me, that you could easily serve Hond Steading's bid for freedom by enlisting yourself in their watch. Bringing your expertise to their planning."

She pulled the spoon back and slumped over her meal, poking at it. "Forgive me, if I've lost a great deal of faith in the systems of the watch. Now. Will you help me find Nouli? Are we committed to this plan together?"

A sly grin overrode the consternation that'd been building on his features, and he glanced pointedly at the prison walls. "I think we had better be."

She choked on a laugh. "In that case..." She told him about the strangeness she'd seen around the compound, the way Misol had stepped out of the empty sky alongside the tree. He listened, nodding slowly, polishing off the last of his food as she spoke.

"We'll have to get a closer look at that building," he said. "I accepted the work detail I thought would be most appealing to Nouli, maintaining the water systems. The infrastructure is shockingly well cared for. I suspect he must have had a hand in its maintenance, and yet I haven't seen a sign of him. When I asked the other lads if they'd heard of a man too

smart for his own good being brought in, a man with a mind
for machines who didn't look like he belonged here, they all
get tight-lipped. Like it's a ghost we're talking about and if
anyone says his name he'll come screaming out of the dark."

"So they know something."

"But they're not telling me. And it may be a good while
yet before I have their trust enough to get them to talk. Men
like these, they don't play loose with information. Even if it's
just what color the sky was that morning, they'll clam up and
tell you they don't know – ain't never seen no sky, nor no
colors." He finished with a drawling flourish, and she had to
stuff bread in her mouth to stifle her chuckle.

Despite Clink's objection to the grains, Ripka found she had
no trouble at all devouring the bread. Whole loaves like this
were a rarity in the inland cities of the Scorched. And, she
felt a little more personal about it now. Like she'd earned it.

"We don't have time for them to loosen up. Detan and Tibs
said they'd come for us before the monsoon season starts up,
after that no one sails for the Remnant for months."

"So we'd better work quick."

Ripka watched him trace his finger over the plate's edge
in thought, round and round. A kernel of an idea solidified.
"You still got your waterworks patch?"

He turned so she could see the pipe and wrench motif
whip-stitched to his sleeve. "I suspected that, although my
initial inquiries were fruitless, it would be a good idea to keep
it up for a while. I can't imagine Nouli taking an interest in
any of the other work details."

"Farming could use an efficient touch," she muttered, then
snatched up his plate.

"Pardon, captain, but what are you doing?"

She reached across the table and gathered up a few half-
chewed crusts left by other inmates, a couple of soggy fruit
cores, and any other food detritus she could get her hands on,
piling them on both of their plates.

"Help me get these loaded," she said. "I have an idea."

For the first time since their arrival, she saw Enard grin.

"Happy to be of service, captain."

I'm sure you are, she thought, then pushed the bitterness aside. They had work yet to do. Together.

CHAPTER 11

A donkey stood braying on the deck of the *Larkspur*, and if it shat itself before they'd gotten it off the ship Pelkaia was going to toss whoever caused the delay over the rail. Even if it was Coss. Maybe especially if it was Coss.

"I don't see why it has to be just the two of us," he said.

"Because eventually it will be the four of us, and that's a large enough party to raise a few eyebrows."

She tugged a waxed tarp taut across the empty bed of the two-wheeled cart hitched to the donkey. On the other side of the cart, Laella fussed with one of the thin ropes meant to hold that side of the tarp in place. Pelkaia bit her tongue as Laella's delicate fingers fumbled through the simple loops of a slip knot. The only way that pampered young woman would learn any practical skills at all was by figuring them out for herself.

"The weapons will be heavy," Coss insisted.

"That's what the donkey's for."

"Essi could obscure our escape."

"And risk revealing us all as deviants."

"Oi." Essi stomped her small bare foot and waved a hand in the air. "Don't talk about me like I'm not here. And, cap'n, I just got back from saving Honding and Tibs's butts. Used my power, and no one noticed. Well, I'm sure *they* did, but who cares? I could help."

"You're not coming with us."

"But I *just—*"

"And you shouldn't have. Stars above." Pelkaia tipped her head back to glare at the clouds building in the sky. "Am I not the captain of this ship? Aren't my orders law on these decks?"

"Well, sure, but we'll be leaving the deck. And I'm real good with donkeys."

"I'm better with 'em," Jeffin said. "My parents had a whole mess of 'em when I was growing up. Let me lead the cart, I practically speak donkey."

Essi smirked. "Explains your ears."

Embarrassment rashed Jeffin's cheeks and his shoulders hunched forward. Laella stifled a chuckle behind an upraised palm, fudging her knots in the process. Jeffin erupted in spluttering insults, setting off a chain reaction of chatter from Essi and Laella.

Pelkaia slammed her fists against the cart's rail, frightening everyone into silence. The donkey brayed.

"That's enough. I didn't pull you all out of death's reach so you could bicker like children on my ship, understand? I command the *Mirror*, and that means its crew too. Unless any of you would like to disembark and make a fresh start in Petrastad?"

Silence met her hard glare. Essi fidgeted with the ragged ends of her sleeves while Jeffin and Laella stared at the deck boards, shame-faced. Without a word, Coss handed her one of the two crossbows still in working order. She jammed it under the tarp. Laella scrambled to finish her knots while Pelkaia slung the donkey's leads down from around its harness, giving the poor creature a stiff jerk. It snorted, but followed her to the gangplank all the same. At least the donkey was obedient.

Laella scurried a few steps after them. "I'll relieve Jeffin on the mirrors while you're gone."

Pelkaia eyed the half-flopping knot Laella had tied on the tarp, and shook her head. "No. Don't care how good you are with sel, girl, you're still too Valathean. Jeffin will keep the mirrors up."

Laella's mouth dropped open. "But earlier Jeffin said you said—"

"I. Said. No."

Her throat bobbed as she swallowed, but she held her palms up toward the sky and bowed over them stiffly, the most formal of Valathean agreements, then turned tight on her heel and strode back toward the cabins. Pelkaia sighed. She never should have picked up a daughter of wealth and privilege. Laella was far too soft for the work they needed to do.

"Jeffin," she said, and he snapped a salute so quick he nearly took off an eyebrow. "I know it's been a long day, and you're tired, but hold those mirrors out a little longer. And if Detan Honding comes anywhere near my ship while I'm gone, you've my permission to hang him from the mast by his balls."

"Yes, captain."

"And you." She pointed a finger at Essi, who stood stalk straight at the attention. "You keep both those feet on this ship, understand?"

"Yes, captain."

She puffed out her cheeks and nodded. "Good. Keep your heads down, all of you. We'll be back as soon as we can."

She gave the donkey's reins another tug and the animal ambled down the gangplank onto the roof. The patient beast cared not a whit for the yawning open space on either side of the plank, and Pelkaia found herself admiring the animal's calm. Or maybe it was just too stupid to know the danger. Something the beast more than likely had in common with most of her crew.

After they'd lead the animal down a series of switch-backing ramps and into the city streets, Coss swung up into the driver's seat and Pelkaia settled into the back of the cart, her crossbow close to hand. Coss snapped the reins, urging the donkey onward, his shoulders hunched up as he studiously surveyed the streets. He hadn't said a word to her since they'd stepped off the ship.

"What is it?" she asked.

"Coulda used their help," he said.

"They'd get in the way. You know that."

"Would they?" He snorted as he guided the donkey down a side street. "You're itching to turn them into an army, Pelkaia, but you won't let them take any real risks. I know Essi's young, but she's clever, and that Laella is champing to prove how useful she can be. Every last soul we picked up – even the weakest of them – has spent most of their lives hiding their power just to stay alive. They're not going to forget all of those skills just because they've found some safety."

"They're all too soft to handle off-ship missions. Once we get them some training with these weapons–"

"Soft? We found Essi picking pockets in Tanasa and Jeffin running dice scams in Kalisan. These aren't calm cities, and those aren't pleasant professions. They may not have spilt a warden's blood like you, but they've got teeth. You just have to let them get used to the idea. Let them pull a few jobs, maybe rescue a few deviants on their own instead of you and me always swooping in on point."

"Essi and Jeffin are close, sure, but Laella? Or old Ulder? Sharpest thing Laella ever held was a sewing needle, and Ulder's half-blind."

"Yet he's the best at running the sails up. And Laella's the strongest sensitive we've got, though you seem in denial about it. Jeffin may have come along first, but that's a matter of chance, and you're running him to dust trying to keep her from contributing. You should have given her mirror duty tonight."

"They're not ready. None of them are."

"And what, exactly, does ready mean to you? A week ago you were running on about how they were ready to start weapons training. Now they can't even tag along on a simple grab-and-dash."

"That was before Honding entered the mix. I played him once, Coss. But it was a near thing. I'm not sure I can do it again. I don't even know what he really wants from us."

Coss sighed and shook his head. "I don't know why that man's got you so spooked."

"You haven't seen him work, you don't know what he's capable of."

He flicked the reins and the cart shuddered as it turned down a narrow street. "I'm about to find out."

CHAPTER 12

"This is a terrible idea." Tibs slouched, hiding his whole body in the shadow of his hat.

"So you've expressed. But it seems we are committed for the time being, and as such must make the best of it."

"I believe the best of it, in this instance, would be to run away and never look back."

Detan scoffed, but couldn't shake a suspicion that Tibs was right. They crouched in the shadow of an awning, pretending to be just another couple of drunks out in the cold night of Petrastad, chatting off their buzz or working out where to get another.

Petrastad's nightlife pulsed around them – subdued, but not insubstantial. Unlike the inland cities of the Scorched, Petrastad didn't have to wait until the harsh sun had set to get its vices out of its system, and as such the nightlife was quieter than most cities of the scrubland. Which was too bad, because Detan suspected that he and Tibs could use the extra cover of a rowdy crowd.

From within the unsettlingly tall building Detan rested his back against, soft music burbled forth. Some sort of rhythmic drum-and-pipe affair, and by the sounds of the hoots and whistles accompanying it there was at least one under-clothed person involved.

Truth be told, he'd much rather join them – even if it meant he'd be the one stripping to his smallclothes – than undertake this foolish plan. But these were Pelkaia's terms for loaning him the use of the *Larkspur* to collect Ripka and New Chum and, with the monsoon season fast approaching, he couldn't allow them to wait much longer. Ripka would no doubt hang Detan by his tonsils if he left her rotting in the Remnant any longer than required.

He tried to put Ripka out of his mind, though he imagined he could feel her narrow, almond eyes boring holes into the back of his neck. New Chum, at least, would have the decency to ask him which body part he wanted to be hung from.

Down the street a little ways the road widened, emptying out into a bulb-shaped courtyard. In the center a tiered fountain tooted dual jets of water, a gross display of Petrastad's overabundance in that particular resource. A planter ringed the fountain, thick with flowers rare to the Scorched. The whole courtyard was dotted with trees and benches meant to shade weary citizens.

Detan eyed those trees, suspicious. Birds probably roosted in them, ready to shit on any unsuspecting shade-partaker. Not to mention the bugs. A tree like that could host an army of the crawling bastards. He'd much rather take his rest under the shade of a nice, wide awning. Or the shelter of a lovely woman's shared parasol.

At the blunt end of the courtyard, a building hunkered. Its front portico was low and single-stepped, lined with fluted columns of grey stone that looked distinctly out of place amongst the muted browns and reds the Scorched usually had to offer. The sigil of the Imperial Fleet was carved in thick grooves above the building's wide, double doors, the grooves themselves stained with black ink. The whole affair very nearly screamed municipal.

A single guard lounged outside the door. He leaned against

the wall and smoked a rolled cigarillo, his shoulders hunched against the sea breeze. Detan could sympathize. The man's job wasn't an exciting one. The building he watched over was a Fleet administration office – containing records, maps, payment boxes for Fleeties too far afield to be given their pay directly.

And weapons. Lots and lots of weapons.

No one in their right mind would try breaking into a place like that. Unfortunately for Detan, Pelkaia had never seemed particularly in a healthy mental state of being. And he really, really needed the use of her airship.

"I could just steal the *Larkspur* again," he muttered.

"That worked so well last time."

A gust of wind snapped across his cheek, stinging it cold, as if the weather itself were urging him to hurry on. Ripka and New Chum were waiting.

"Shall we check round back, then?" Detan asked, shaking out his legs to get some warmth back into them. After all of this was done, he'd be finished with coastal cities for the rest of his life.

"I don't know, shall we?" Tibs said, his voice raised with a mocking edge. Detan scowled at him and stalked off, wending his way to the back of the Fleet building without making the path look too direct.

Sneaking, misdirection. These were things he could do. Had done a hundred times a hundred over. They strolled up alongside a residential building. All the shutters were drawn and thin cracks of light leaked out like tears along the rough walls. A broad road separated the back of the Fleet building from the residential block, its face worn through with countless crisscrossing wheel ruts. A heavy, metal set of double doors faced them, a single guard looking as bored as the first lingering beside them. The door's hinges were large, but supported by wood framing. A weak point. If he could wedge some sel in there he could blow them wide. Just as

Pelkaia had said.

Trouble was, he didn't trust himself to *just* blow the hinges, let alone the doors, and with the guards involved... He wasn't a fighting man, and he'd never been one to bloody a nose that didn't earn it. Maybe they could distract the guard, draw him away before the fireworks started.

"Tibs, could you—"

"No."

"You didn't even let me finish."

Tibs yanked his hat down to hide his eyes. "Don't need to. I know what you're thinking. I go cause a ruckus off on some side street and that guard, bored as he is, figures he better go check it out. And then you shift a little sel over there, blow the hinges, run in and... what? You don't know what's on the other side. Could be nothing. Could be a person. Could be the weapons are behind another locked door and you'll have to blow that, too. And then you've used the power *twice* and I pitsdamned know how hard it is for you to keep it under wraps once. And the guards will come running at the noise – and then what? Going to blow your way free of them, too? And how are you going to get the weapons out, just on your lonesome? Even if they're conveniently loaded on a cart, you got arms like toothpicks and legs to match. You're not haulin' 'em anywhere on your own."

Detan gripped the air, as if he could grasp an idea out of the chilly night. "Pelkaia said this was the way – that her people would come at the sound of the explosion and load it all out. We don't do this, we don't get the ship, and Ripka—"

"Ripka would take your eyes out through your mouth for what you're planning on." Tibs jabbed Detan's forehead with his finger and scowled. "You spent years keeping that sands-cursed power of yours under wraps, and just because Pelkaia told you to use it you're going to hop to it? When you're at your most unstable? She said get the weapons. Said her people would come when they heard a blast to help load 'em out. That is what you have to work with, and *this* plan ain't what we do. So you best figure out another way, because I'm mighty thin of patience."

Detan's temper flared, rage bubbling up through his veins like a kettle ready to blow its lid and hiss at the world at large. He became acutely aware of the pouch of selium Pelkaia had given him to do the work with. The shape of it, the bloated cloud contained within a thin leather sack tied to his belt and the inside of his jacket to keep it from floating off or wrenching his clothes askew.

Maybe it was his imagination – he hoped it was – but the substance called to him, luring, siren in its possibilities. Its potentiality. It would be so easy to give up his anger, to shunt it aside into that cloud of gas and watch it tear itself apart. The impending satisfaction of that moment thrilled through him, tingling him straight down to his toes.

He wouldn't be able to control it. It would rend both he and Tibs – and the whole of the apartment building behind them – to dust and ashes.

Tibs flicked him between the eyes.

"Right..." He breathed out the word, relaxing his fists. Awareness of the bladder of selium faded. "Right."

"Good." Tibs stepped back, folding his arms. "So, what's it going to be?"

"Tibs, my old chum." Detan slung an arm around the dusty man's shoulders. "We're going to need some new coats, and I know just the place."

Their new uniforms stank of stale ale and some pungent smokable that appeared to be all the rage amongst the Remnant guards. Detan hoped it would at least add an air of authenticity to their costumes, because it wasn't doing anything at all to help the air in general.

"You reek," Tibs said, plucking at Detan's sleeve with a grotesque curl to his lip.

"*You* reek."

"I think you reek enough for the both of us." Tibs shoved his hands in his pockets. His expression twisted. Slowly, he drew one hand out and held it up to the faint streetlight. His fingers were coated in something brown and sticky, twisted filaments sticking up in all directions. A distinct aroma clouded around his fingers, mimicking the char-and-smoke scent that already clung to the coats. The source of the guards' new smokable.

Slowly, deliberately, he wiped his fingers off on the hem of his coat. Detan's lunch threatened to revolt.

"Ugh," he said.

"Well," Tibs drawled, "now we know what it looks like in the raw."

"Wish we didn't."

"Me too. Me too."

They'd been lucky on their return visit to Lotti's card room. The late mark meant all the regulars were already deep in their cups. The crowd was split between those desperate to win back what they'd lost, and those manic with success. No one had an eye for the pegs the coats were dangling from, and even the bouncer had been off on some other errand. Probably kicking someone who'd taken losing a little too close to heart out of the building.

They were, however, not quite as lucky with the guards at the Fleet's weapon cache.

The man guarding the back door had drifted off to sleep – making him an unlikely mark. Detan'd often found it was a might more difficult to convince a man of your good intentions when you'd roused him from a nap.

The other, who was meant to be minding the front door, was much more interested in the young woman who'd come to pay him a visit. They stood with their bodies angled close together, the woman's clothing and face hidden by a long, dark cloak. Probably she'd slipped out from under the eye of a maid, or a mother, to make this rendezvous. From the way they were carrying on, Detan was quite sure she wasn't supposed to be out. No one took *that* much delight in a midnight conversation unless it were a forbidden one.

"What do you think, Tibs? Shall we interrupt new love, or a nice rest?"

Tibs *hmmed* to himself. They'd returned to the awning down the street from the courtyard, letting the shadows do half the work of making them invisible, their uniforms doing the other half. No one bothered Fleet guards in Petrastad. Not so close to Remnant, where any enemy of the empire could be chucked at a moment's notice.

"Love, I think," Tibs said. "Give the young man a chance to show off how important he is."

Detan grinned. "Now that, I like."

He tugged the collar of his new coat straight and took off down the street with a military swagger, careful not to let his hands drift too near his pockets. The guard's attention was riveted upon his lady; he did not so much as glance at the two men walking straight toward him. Detan grimaced. The last thing he needed was to surprise the lad and put him on edge.

He whistled a soft, merry tune, and when the man picked his head up and looked his way Detan smiled and waved as if delighted to see an old friend.

"Ho there!" Detan called as he jumped up the short, low step with Tibs fast on his heels. The woman sidled sideways, quick as a rockcat, to put the young man between them. She had a small face, making her eyes look unnaturally large and expressive. That was the gaze of a frightened woman. No – wait – this woman was excited. Thrilled, even, by the prospect of danger. Detan could work with that.

"Are you in charge of things tonight?" Detan asked the young guard. He was a good half-hand shorter than Detan, so Detan worked up a slouch to make him feel taller, more in control. Uneven stubble sprouted across the lad's cheek and jaw, and he pushed his chest forward as he gave them a curt nod.

"I am. I am Captain Allat. What can I do for you...?" He raised his brows, leaving an opening for Detan to supply a name.

He didn't have one. His go-to alias, Dakfert, he'd already used with the guard whose coat he might be currently wearing. Didn't do to use the same alias twice with the same set of people, not unless he wanted them to start making connections – and he certainly didn't.

Keeping his affable smile plastered on, he searched his surroundings for inspiration. Pillars, some awnings, a shrubbery...

"Pilawshru–" Tibs elbowed him in the ribs. He grunted, coughed, and offered up a sheepish grin. "Name's Step Pilawshru." He stomped one foot on the step for emphasis. "Like the real thing. And this here's, uh, Brownie Pilawshru. We're brothers."

He slung an arm around Tibs's shoulders and squeezed him close, cutting off another of the man's jabs to the ribs.

The woman narrowed those large eyes at him. "Odd names," she said.

"Ruma, that's unkind." Allat's protest was a lame one; he clearly agreed.

"Ah, well," Detan smiled so hard he hurt his cheeks. "Mom was a bit, you know," he twirled a finger through the air by his temple. "Special. Yeah?"

"My apologies, Step, Brownie." Allat bowed his head. Such a formal young lad.

"Worry not, brother-at-arms! My mother's disposition is no fault of yours. Now." Detan released Tibs and clapped his hands together, rubbing them. "Maybe you can help us out. Ole rockbrain here–" he thumped Tibs lightly on the back of the head, "–has gone and lost his baton. We're due to report for the ship-out to the big 'R' in the morning, and the captain is sure to wring Brownie's scrawny little neck if he doesn't have his poker."

Allat squinted, no doubt trying to wend his way through Detan's barrage of half-comprehensible jargon. Detan may not have known much about guarding, well, anything, but he knew full well that anyone in a Fleet uniform was likely to use some sort of mystical vocabulary that only half-sounded like Valathean.

It worked.

"I'd love to help you out, but the vault's locked down. Business hours, and all that."

Detan whistled low and punched Tibs in the shoulder. "Tole you you were doomed."

Allat shifted his weight. "If you come back in the morning..."

"No time for that, I'm afraid. Gotta be lined up before the sun's pissing the sky yellow. Begging your pardon, miss." He pretended to look abashed and tipped his head to Ruma. "Soldiery talk is hard to abandon, you understand."

Ruma reached out one small, blessed hand and squeezed Allat's upper arm. "Oh, do help them. He can't help it he lost his baton, why I'd lose my own hair if it weren't attached. Can't you let them in? You do have the keys, don't you?"

The noble captain shifted his weight again, pursing his lips, a furrow worming its way between his brows. Detan knew what the man must be thinking – *What could go wrong? It's just a baton. These are fellow guards. And Ruma is watching...*

His hand drifted toward his pocket, where the curved line of a keyring pressed against his imperial-issue trousers. Detan stifled a smirk. Too easy.

"We'll make it quick," Allat said, almost to himself, as he slipped the key into the great door's lock and clicked it over.

"Quick as lightning!" Detan agreed, crowding up behind him as the door began its ponderous swing inward.

And that was when the screaming from the back door began.

CHAPTER 13

Enard walked in front of her, his narrow back stiff with apprehension. She wanted to tell him to relax, that being so anxious was a sure sign of their deceit, then changed her mind. Every sparrow on the Remnant was tense. Confidence was the only thing that truly stood out here. No doubt that was why she had drawn so much attention with her first scuffle.

They shuffled down the line to the trash chute, overfull plates of foodscrap in hand. A single guard minded the line, but he seemed far more concerned with cleaning his nails than paying attention to what the inmates were doing. Complacency, lack of training. These were weaknesses Ripka had learned to spot in her staff, because they could be easily exploited by the right mind set on doing so.

Checking to be sure the guard wasn't looking, Enard dumped his scraps, then wedged the clay plate into the chute sideways. He strolled away, keeping his steps slow, and rubbed the back of his neck as if he couldn't wait to seek his bed. Probably that was true, but Ripka had other plans for their evening.

She tossed her scraps down the chute and swore as a goodly portion of them splashed back out at her. She kicked food filth from her shoes as those behind her in line chuckled.

"What's the problem?" the guard said, feigning interest.

"Blasted pipe is clogged."

He shrugged. "Not my purview. I mind the dish cleaners." He tipped his chin to the stack of soiled clay plates on a wheeled cart beside him. "Better get someone from waterworks up to fix it."

"You can't do anything?" She gestured to the pile on the floor, to her shoes. "This is a mess, I'm not waiting around with my feet in filth... Hey!" She whirled, pretending to get a good look at Enard for the first time. "You're waterworks. Get over here and fix this."

"I'll fix your pipes, girl," someone from the back of the line called. A chorus of chuckles went up. Ripka clenched her jaw, but otherwise didn't react. Any reaction would escalate the taunts.

Enard let out a big, heavy sigh. "What's wrong with it?" he asked, slinking back over to the pipe.

"How am I supposed to know?" She tapped her farm badge. "This is your job."

He rolled his eyes so hard Ripka feared they'd never come back around.

"Fine," he said, and gave the blockage a few ineffectual prods. "It's clogged, all right, but I can't see the blockage from here. Going to have to weed it out from the other side."

"Oh no," the guard said. "I'm not letting you out there without an escort."

"Suit yourself. But if that pipe doesn't get cleared, then you're going to have one pits cursed time cleaning all the food-covered plates tonight, not to mention the floor here."

"I can't believe this shit." The guard waved down another guard passing through a nearby row of tables on his rounds. "Hey, get your ass over here and watch the line. I gotta run this waterworks grunt out to clear a blockage."

"Excellent," Enard rubbed his hands together. "I'll need

an extra set of hands for this, I'm sure. Good thing you'll be
along to help. Got gloves on you?"

The guard blanched. "No way am I sticking my hands in
that heap. You–" He jerked a thumb at Ripka, who had made
certain she was lingering conveniently close by, trying to
scrape the garbage off her shoe against the wall. She looked
up at his summons, feigning confusion.

"What?"

"Come on, farm girl. You're the one who made a stink
about the problem, you can help waterworks here muck it
out."

She screwed up her face as if she'd never heard a more
disgusting proposition in her life. Silently, she thanked Detan
for teaching her to let her expressions over-react to cover any
unconvincing note to her words. "You kidding me? I already
got garbage all over my shoes."

"Then more won't hurt."

She grunted and shuffled forward to take up position
alongside Enard as the guard fumbled with his keyring
and heaved open yet another heavy, iron-banded door. In
his haste, the guard didn't bother to pat them down as he
shuffled them through and locked the door behind him.
Ripka struggled to hide a scowl of distaste. What in the blue
skies was the warden of this cage thinking, keeping such lazy
sods on staff?

The hallway was much like the one she'd passed through
to go out to her farming duties. Knapsacks of equipment lined
one wall, and three doors studded the other. Enard grabbed
a bag without hesitation and slung it over his shoulder. He
snatched up another and held it out to her.

"Best take one of these, might need the extra set."

She eyed it. "I don't know what to do with half that stuff."

"Just listen to my direction, all right?"

"Hurry it up," the guard growled. The exterior door already
stood halfway open.

Sighing as if put upon, she took the bag and hoisted it over her shoulder. Its weight, and the heavy metal clanking of the tools within, jarred her. Whatever waterworks needed, it was a lot more substantial than the small kit given to the gardening crews. So far. She supposed there was time enough to have heavier work foisted upon the gardeners – they hadn't gotten to harvest yet, or planting season. She hoped to be long gone by the time that happened.

The guard herded them down a packed dirt path the mirror of the one she'd shuffled along that morning. Her hard-soled leather shoes made not a sound against the dirt, even as she scuffed to test how loud she could make them. She allowed herself a small smile, face turned toward the ground so that the guard wouldn't see. It was going to be easier than she'd hoped to sneak around the island, as long as she could shake the guard's attention.

Dark burgeoned, the sun little more than a red smear against the horizon, a chill breeze rolling in off the sea to wash the day's heat away. They hurried down the path toward the open mouth of the pipe and the heaping pile of compost at the foot of it.

Up close, Ripka could better see the hollow dug into the ground alongside the wall of the prison proper. The thick grey wall extended all the way down to at least the bottom of the pit, and no doubt deeper. There would be no digging to freedom for the inmates, even if they could find a secretive place in which to do so.

The refuse pile mounded toward the mouth of the chute, slumping at the edge farthest from the wall. Metal ladders had been screwed into the wall on both sides of the pipe, presumably for maintenance access. A set of stairs slashed the ground on the opposite side so that the farmers could get to the refuse with ease even when the pit wasn't full.

But what truly made the clearest impression upon Ripka, was the stench.

"Ugh," she said, not having to pretend disgust.

The air was redolent with the fecal-sweet aroma of rotting plant material, heavy with the pungent scent of decay. It was far worse up close than it had been that morning.

"I think something might have died down there," Enard said.

"Could be a dead rat blocking the pipe."

"Or a rat king."

"Sweet skies," the guard said, bringing his hand up to cover his mouth and nose. "Get this over with, will you?"

"Go on down the stairs at the other end," Enard said. "I'll tell you what to do from there."

Ripka nodded, a little queasy, and skirted the pit to the steps. The heap wasn't small by any stretch of the imagination, but it had yet to completely collapse at the base, making it a high, narrow pyramid wide enough to hide two widths of her body. She climbed down the steps while Enard swung up the ladder on the opposite side. He was in full view of the guard, but the heap did well to hide her.

"Right, now," Enard said loud enough for the guard to hear. "Take your wrench and pry open the first bolt on the clog trap – no, no, the other one."

Ripka hadn't done anything, didn't have any intention to, but Enard kept on talking and giving direction like she were throwing herself to the task. With care she hung her bag from the lowest rung of the ladder and twisted the strap around so that it would unwind itself and clank against a nearby metal flap. She then crept up the stairs on hands and knees.

Her hands sunk into the dirt on the lower steps, the soil there slightly muddy from having been covered in midden at one point or another, and suppressed a shudder. There'd be plenty of time to wash in her cell, later. At least they didn't need to be stingy with water on this skies-cursed island.

When she crested the top of the steps – the time she was most vulnerable to view – Enard banged on the pipe with his wrench, swearing at it, doing everything he could to draw attention to himself. Breath held, she scurried forward into a nearby stand of scrub, concealing herself behind a thick pricklebrush.

The thorns grabbed at her jumpsuit, raked across her cheeks, but she held firm, waiting to hear a cry of alarm. Nothing but Enard's mutterings met her ears.

She took a deep breath to calm herself and crept forward, away from the midden heap, angling toward the path that led out to the grain plot she'd worked. The path would be dangerous, she'd be visible from the top of the prison's walls every second she walked there, but it was the fastest way – and time was of the essence. Enard could only keep up his antics for so long, and Ripka *had* to know what was amiss with that building. Its hunkering form was a lodestone lodged in the back of her mind.

If Nouli were within it, they'd have to figure out how to get themselves sent over there as quickly as possible.

She paused at the path's edge to catch her breath and listened, turning her head slowly, scanning for any sign of another person nearby. She saw no one, could even make out the silhouette of a guard at the top of the wall turn toward the rec yard, his eyes on the largest congregation of prisoners. They apparently didn't bother looking outside the walls too often on a night with no work details set.

She waited, counting, to see how long it took him to glance toward the fields, then turn back to the courtyard. Two minutes. She'd have plenty of time.

The second he turned away she burst onto the path, sprinting down the hard soil on silent feet, air burning in her throat as adrenaline kicked in, all the while counting down the seconds until he'd turn back toward the outdoors.

She leapt sideways, hit the ground between rows of grain at full speed and tucked, rolling across the dirt. She'd be filthy by the time she got back to the midden heap, but she suspected the guard wouldn't find anything amiss in that. He probably wouldn't bother getting close enough to see if she smelled as foul as she looked.

Hidden by the bowing rows of grain, she ran to the end of the plot and peered at the building. No one was about. Not even a warm light dotted the cracks around the shuttered windows. Smoke curled from the narrow mouth of a chimney, smearing the sky with a grey haze. The ground between her and the building was rocky, uneven. Pocked with twisted brush and gnarled trees. Not good ground for running on, not in the growing dark.

Moving as fast as she dared across the uneven terrain, she slipped up close to the building, pressed her back against the wall perpendicular to any line of sight from the prison's walls, and crept toward one of the shuttered windows. Heart hammering in her ears, she reached up, ran a finger along the underside of one of the shutters, searching for a latch. Maybe it was her nerves, or the light playing tricks in the gathering dusk, but she could have sworn she felt a slight tingle, saw a faint shimmer halo her fingertip. Then it was gone.

"You." The voice was so close beside her that Ripka jumped, dropped into a defensive crouch and reached for a weapon she didn't have.

Misol, the guard who had appeared from behind the tree, stood a bare two paces away, her dark face expressing more amusement than anger. Her bald pate gleamed in the fading light, but not as bright as the steel-tipped spear she cradled in one arm. Ripka straightened, slowly, brushing dust from her jumpsuit but finding she only ground the grime in deeper.

"Aren't you interesting," Misol said, pursing her plush lips in thought. "Most the time, I find someone creeping around the island after work hours, they're looking for a way out – a way off the island. But not you. You're looking for a way in, aren't you?"

"What is this place?" Ripka asked, forcing her voice to calm.

Misol had shattered her concentration. She'd lost her count of the guard's rotation, and that bothered her. More than likely, she wouldn't need it now, but the way this woman unsettled her... It was off. Wrong. Not even the most depraved of souls she'd thrown behind bars or led to the axemen had disturbed her in this fashion. Her skin crawled to be close to Misol, a familiar sensation she couldn't quite pin down.

"What I don't understand, is, why do you want to know, hmm? Most sparrows, they come in wanting to do their time, keep their heads down, and get off this rock if they can. But you – you're poking around like the Remnant's a puzzle to be solved. You're looking for someone, aren't you? You a songbird who can't find her nest-mate?"

Her jaw clenched. "I'm no songbird. And you didn't answer my question."

"Thing is, lil' sparrow, I don't have to. Pity you won't share your reasons with me. Makes you my own puzzle then, doesn't it? But, if you won't share, then I gotta do my job."

Misol paused, giving Ripka a chance to reveal her intentions. The very idea rankled. Maybe Misol could be of some help – certainly she held the key to the secret of the yellowstone building – but Ripka could not be certain. And the more Misol danced around telling her the truth, the more Ripka suspected it must be holding the very thing she sought. Nouli may have been disgraced, but he was still a genius. They wouldn't leave him to rot without protection in the Remnant.

Possibly they were even slaving him to tasks they needed done.

"I guess you gotta, then," Ripka said.

Misol sighed her disappointment. "Have it your way–" she squinted at Ripka's dyed name, "–Enkel. Keep your hands where I can see 'em, now. We're going to go visit the warden, and see what he wants to do about you, little wanderer."

CHAPTER 14

Within a heartbeat of meeting him, Ripka knew that Radu Baset was everything she hated in a watch-captain, let alone a prison's warden.

Misol had led her back to Enard, where she'd ordered the baffled guard who'd escorted them out to the midden heap to bind their wrists. A sour party they made, tromping through the labyrinthine tunnels of the Remnant's hallways. Ripka'd occupied herself by trying to keep track of the twists and turns.

It hadn't helped. A nervousness grew within her stomach, a gaping black maw of regret. She should have waited. Should have played things a little tighter, a little closer. She'd been too anxious to find Nouli, too used to her old authority. Her life as a watch-captain had made her too proud, too sure-footed, and she'd gone and gotten Enard tangled up in her iron-headed determination.

By the time they reached the warden's office, she was ready to hate someone. She'd thought it'd be herself, but Warden Radu Baset had gone ahead and claimed that honor for himself.

He was a big man, a full head taller than her, with more meat on him than a Valathean black bear. She wondered if he had the fur to match under his uniform. Pale hair spattered his wide head, clinging to the forward slope of his scalp, and his nose had the scorpion-red bloom of alcoholism.

Didn't need his countenance to prove his addiction, his breath did enough to give that vice away. It smelled like he'd licked a tavern floor. Ripka couldn't even see the wood of his desk under haphazard piles of paper and splotches of spilt ink. Three wide, red velvet couches filled the office, and every last one had a warden-shaped dent in it. No wonder his staff was so poorly trained. The man spent more time sleeping and drinking than most of the gutter-fillers of Aransa.

Radu looked up at Misol from his slouched seat behind his desk, one eye squinted.

"Wha's all this then?" he stammered. Though he looked strong enough to wrestle half the Remnant's populace to the ground single-handed he had a high, rasping voice. The product of a throat worn raw from too much drink.

"Caught these two sparrows trying to get kicked out of their nest. Trouble is," Misol half-turned, her strange eyes focusing hard on Ripka. "They haven't learned how to fly yet."

"What?" Radu repeated, making a halfhearted attempt to straighten his collar.

"It's my fault, warden." Their escort guard stepped forward, wringing his hands together. "The midden chute was clogged, you see, and–"

Radu seemed to see Ripka for the first time. His dark gaze narrowed, the pouches beneath them scrunching up so high they swallowed his eyes. He cleared his throat and, when he spoke again, he'd ground away most of the drunken slur. Ripka repressed a sigh. So he'd had a lot of practice being drunk on the job. No surprise there.

"Of course it's your fault. I'm amazed every morning when you manage to put your coat on the right way. Misol, I assume it was you who caught these two?"

She inclined her head. "The woman was the one

wandering, the man was a distraction. I caught her down by the yellowhouse, trying to peek in a window."

The knot of Radu's throat bobbed as he swallowed. He reached for a bottle half-buried by papers on his desk, thought better of it, and went to ladle himself a cup of water from a bucket and mug left on the windowsill to absorb the night chill.

"I see," he said once he'd drunk his fill. He tipped his head to the guard. "Get out."

"But I—"

"You're not in trouble, rat. Now scurry."

The guard obeyed. It was the most disciplined thing Ripka had yet seen on the island. When the heavy, iron-bound door thunked shut behind the guard, Radu leaned back in his chair, fingers laced behind his head, and squinted at Misol.

"How nosy was our little sparrow, then?"

Misol shifted her weight and rested her spear against her shoulder with intent. An implicit threat? Why would a simple guard hold sway over the warden?

"The sparrow saw only the fine craftsmanship of our window shutters. I will tell her as much, when I report this incident."

A sour purse came to Radu's lips. Ripka couldn't tell if it were annoyance or indigestion. "Good enough." He sucked his teeth and leaned forward, looming over his desk as if he could threaten his paperwork into organizing itself. "Go file your report, then."

Misol's back went stiff and her chin shot up. "Are you dismissing me?"

"I am."

Ripka shared a look with Enard, curiosity pushing all fear of punishment from her mind. What power dynamic was at play, here? Was the yellowhouse, as Misol had called it, beyond the control of the warden, and if so, why? If Nouli were indeed behind those sunny walls, then Ripka would have to win herself over to Misol's side. Maybe, she thought regretfully, she should have given up a smidgen of information to Misol when she had the chance, told her the barebones of what she was seeking. Now... Now it may be too late.

She tried to catch the woman's eye, tried to pass some understanding between them, but Misol was intent upon Radu, her eyes bright with something akin to anger. Ripka wished she could place the sentiment – Misol was too difficult for her to read.

"I will make my report, then." Misol snapped the warden an overly formal salute and stalked toward the door. Ripka could not capture her eye, could not even see her face, before the door clicked shut behind her.

"Captain," Radu said, bringing her head around with a start. Cold dread filtered through her, freezing her in place like a rabbit in a hawk's shadow. He could not have learned her nickname so quickly. He was a lout, a drunkard, incapable of disciplining his staff into any meaningful force. He was not so aware of his new intakes that he already knew the made-up nickname of a woman who'd been in his care less than two full turns of the sun.

She looked him in the eye, tried to keep her expression calm and mildly confused despite the runaway pounding of her heart. The confusion she didn't need to fake, it was only the fear she had to mask. "Miss Enkel suits me fine," she ventured. "I'm no kind of captain."

"No, no." He sneered as he leaned forward, yellowed teeth looking even more tarnished in the ruddy light of the oil lamps scattered around the room. "Fine woman like yourself is deserving of the title. You earned it fair, even if it was stripped from you under dubious circumstances. "

Pits below, but she wanted to bolt. To tip any one of those merrily burning lanterns into his rat's nest of a desk and flee while the flames made a meal of his neglect. She willed herself to be calm, to stand with her shoulders slouched and her hips cocked to one side – not rigid and petrified, as she actually was. What would the woman she was pretending to be do, if accused of being a disgraced watch-captain?

She forced a smirk and puffed hair from her eyes. "Lovely that you think so highly of me, warden, but the only blues I've been near have been hauling me off in chains."

He chuckled. "Nice try. Been practicing that, have you? Might have worked on another man. Trouble for you is, you don't remember me, but I remember you. I know you, captain. I traveled with Faud out of the Brown Wash same as you, though he didn't end up elevating me to such a lofty position."

Radu snorted, hawked, and spat. Right on the floor. Ripka felt a little faint. Squinting at him, she might see how his face could be familiar. If it were younger, maybe. More hair and less jowl. But she couldn't remember a stitch about him. There'd been a whole handful of mercenaries protecting Faud's vanguard as he crossed the Scorched to settle in Aransa. Most of them had moved on to whatever job was willing to pay as soon as they'd spent the grains Faud had given them in the city. She'd been the only one to stick around, and Faud had rewarded her loyalty by recommending her to the watch.

"I..." she began, but he held up a hand to cut her off. It was well enough, she'd had no idea what she was going to say next.

"I don't begrudge you the post you were given. Truth be told, you were the only member of our band of miscreant do-gooders who actually gave a shit about doing the job right. Now. Why are you here?"

"Theft of classified imperial information," she said automatically, her lips numb from shock.

"Hah. You? The sun would fly down from the sky and kiss the empress's ass before that happened. There's not a body on the Scorched straighter than yours – morals and hips." He smirked, but she swallowed a sharp retort. Years dealing with the bootscrapings of Aransa had left her hard to such harassment.

Enard, however, hadn't experienced the case-hardening she had.

He took a quick step forward, faster than Ripka could follow, his body moving with all the sinuous grace of a snake as he scooped up a lantern. He held it above the mountain range of paperwork upon Radu's desk, tipped precariously.

"Insult the captain once more, and I will see to it that certain parts of your anatomy never stand straight again. Sir."

The calmness with which Enard spoke chilled her. She was tempted to intervene, but she knew that to do so would reveal fear of reprisal. And so she waited, jaw clenched, struggling not to grind her teeth.

Genuine fear flickered across Radu's face, but it was only in passing. He held up his other hand, revealing a small bell cradled in his palm, chained to a ring on one thick finger. He ran his thumb over its shiny brass edge, caressing.

"Everyone plays nice, or I call my friends waiting outside, understand? I ring this, they come and cut you down without a second thought. You willing to start *that* fire?"

Enard's smile was wistful. "Sometimes, I wish I would."

He set the lantern down with exaggerated care and stepped away, his body angled so that he could come between Ripka and Radu if the need arose. It rankled to be protected so, but she reminded herself that, to Enard, this was his duty. His life's calling. He'd agreed to help her find Nouli, and he couldn't do that if she were dead.

"Now that the cockfighting's out of the way." Radu closed his hand around the bell to keep it silenced. "We can move on. Why are you here? A woman like you doesn't stumble across the yellowhouse without forethought."

She pressed her lips together, drawing them into a thin, hard line.

"Fine." He dragged his fingers through his hair. "Keep your

cursed secrets. I know you. You can't be planning anything *bad* for my charges. But here's the deal. A person with your skillset has value, value I can't afford to let go unused. Not now, at any rate. You're poking around my island, so I might as well get some use out of you. Lately, we've had a new source of extracurricular experience appear here. Understand?"

"Drugs?" she asked before she could stop herself, professional curiosity overriding her instinct to conceal any interest.

"Aye. Nasty stuff. Makes the inmates minds move faster, makes them restless for more. We've had three breakout attempts since it showed, and one nasty riot. They're calling it clearsky, but no one knows where it's coming from."

Ripka scoffed. "Surely you have informants within the population."

He grinned, as if he'd scored a point by drawing her into using the terminology of a watch-captain. "I do, I do. But they look after my addition to the population. Good stuff, keeps them sleepy-headed and amenable. This new junk, clearsky? Not one of my people can figure out its source."

"*Your* addition? You're leaking drugs to your own prison?"

Radu waved his hand through the air as if brushing away a mildly irritating insect. "I don't force it on anyone, and it keeps them docile."

Ripka stared, open-mouthed, recalling the elderly inmate she'd seen smoking along the path that morning. "You're the mudleaf source? You're encouraging a black market within your own walls. Once those channels open up, they're impossible to close."

"Bah. My people have tight rein on–"

"Then where's the clearsky coming from?"

He clenched his fists so hard she wondered if he'd warp the shape of his emergency bell. "You're going to find that out for me, captain."

She swallowed around a dry throat. It didn't take wild

speculation for her to discern a possible source for the drug. If it were new, that meant someone was bringing it in from off-island – so that someone had to leave periodically and be able to return. Based on what she'd seen of the Remnant's guards, imagining one or more of them slipping in a new poison wasn't much of a stretch. Some of them might even be pretending incompetence and laziness to deflect suspicion.

But she wasn't about to tell Radu that. The fact that he hadn't come to the same conclusion himself meant he was either stupid, or blind arrogant in assuming his guards would never betray his trust. The way Misol had stiffened when he'd dismissed her... That told Ripka all she needed to know about the so-called warden's relationship with his staff.

"And if I refuse to clean up this mess for you?"

"Why, captain, I might let it slip who you really are."

She took a startled half-step back without meaning too, panic tightening her chest. It didn't take firsthand knowledge to know what inmates did to a watcher sharing their incarceration. What they'd do to a full-blown captain, who'd already ruffled the feathers of a songbird? A crawling sensation stole over her skin, and she fought down a shiver.

"You would allow me to be torn apart by your charges, just because I won't play your game?"

"One less mouth to feed." He eyed Enard. "Two, probably."

She tried to breathe deep, but only managed a shallow rasp. Squaring her shoulders, she lifted her chin. Time was slim. She needed all the advantage she could finagle. "If you want my help, warden, I need something in return."

"The integrity of your own skin isn't good enough?"

"Not for this." She stepped forward, angling around Enard, and pressed both palms on the mess of his desk. He went perfectly still. "I want to look in the yellowhouse."

He snorted. Foul breath gusted hair off her cheek. "Nothing in there you'll find pleasant, captain. I suggest you give that little curiosity up."

"Don't care how pleasant it is. I want a look."

His eyes narrowed. "Why?"

She smiled, but said nothing.

"We'll see. Find me the clearsky, and if I have further use of you, I might see the need of trade. Otherwise..." He flicked a dismissive hand. "Fetch me my dealer, or I start spreading nasty little rumors."

"I suppose it wouldn't hurt to ask around," she said, hating herself for her acquiescence.

"I supposed it wouldn't." He smirked as he gestured toward the door. "Go on now, guards will see you to your cells. Sweet dreams, captain."

She resisted an urge to tip over a lantern on her way out.

CHAPTER 15

"Go!" Detan shouted, giving the wide-eyed captain Allat a shove between the shoulder blades. "I'll look after the vault and the lady. Do your duty, man."

The captain glanced to Detan, then to the wide, terrified gaze of his lady, and then to the half-opened door to the Fleet's building. He couldn't leave it standing open with no one to keep an eye on it, they all knew this, but no more did he want to run off after strange screams in the dark. He swallowed, twisting the keyring in his hand.

Detan snatched it from him and rattled them in his face. "Brownie and I will arm ourselves and meet you there. Quick, man!"

Allat nodded, relieved to have a clear plan of action, and sprinted off, his baton already in hand. A needle of worry slivered its way under Detan's skin as he heard the heady twang of a crossbow bolt fill the air, followed by an unintelligible shout, but he steeled his nerves. Whatever was going on back there had given him one skies-blessed opportunity, and he was not about to squander it.

"This way, my lady," he said, doffing the courtly mannerisms his aunt had drilled into him all those years ago. "I would not want you out in the open during a fight."

Ruma narrowed her eyes and glanced over her shoulder in the direction her lover had run. "Shouldn't you help him?"

"Brownie here has lost his baton, remember? And I do not carry mine about on midnight errands. Please, hurry inside so that we may arm ourselves and get to your captain's side with all haste."

The smooth reasonableness of his tone wore away the jagged edges of her suspicion. She gave him a tight nod before slipping inside the Fleet offices. Detan shared a look with Tibs, brows raised in question – *do you think the fight is Pelkaia's doing?* – but Tibs just shrugged. They'd find out soon enough.

Inside the Fleet office, a single candle guttered in a candelabra by the wall, the yellowed light doing little to illuminate the building. Someone must have forgotten to douse it before leaving for the day. Detan thanked the skies for government workers. He pulled the door shut behind them, cutting off the moonlight, and Ruma let out a yelp of surprise.

"Peace," he urged as he scurried over to the candle and took it from its post, then used it to light the other candles and passed one to Tibs. "I know it is a dreadful bore, miss, but please wait here in the lobby. The back rooms are for Fleet personnel only, and the heavy front door should keep out any unwanted intruders."

She stood dead center in the middle of the foyer, hands clasped before her in a tight knot, expression hard and smooth, save for a few worry wrinkles around her eyes. She was so still, so bottled up with unshed emotion, that Detan half expected her to turn on him – to fling a candelabra his way, or force some other attack. The rigid bearing of her body communicated quite clearly that she felt something was amiss, but Detan suspected she couldn't precisely put her finger on the source. She was too polite to make accusations without being certain.

Ah, manners. He could always count on courtly politeness

to shield him from uncomfortable questions. After a too-long pause, she nodded.

He bowed to her. Overkill, no doubt, but he'd learned a long time ago that overdoing flattery made those he flattered less likely to question him. "Let's go, Brownie."

Tibs snorted and strode forward, taking the lead. Though Detan had done his time working for the empire, he'd never been a part of the Fleet. But Tibs had kept the Fleet's propellers purring while they'd rained fire from the sky during the Catari war, and that was knowledge hard to forget. The wrinkled bastard may not like to think on it, or discuss it, or even acknowledge it'd happened, but he knew his way around a Fleet building.

One of the best things about Valathea, Detan had long ago decided, was that they liked to do things the same way no matter where they went. Buildings were laid out in identical patterns, protocols and procedures predictable. It made it easier for the empire to reach further, faster.

Made it easier for him to kick them in the teeth, too.

The foyer of the office was a cavernous, high-ceilinged room dotted with tables and chairs for Fleeties seeking private consultation with Fleet administration. Detan had seen similar layouts in the entrance halls of every watch station-house he'd had the misfortune of treading through. The empire may have had great imagination when it came to the expansion of its borders, but it was decidedly stolid when it came to municipal decor. An unmarked hall bore a hole through the center of the back wall, wide enough for two guards to stand across from each other. Tibs veered straight toward it. Detan trailed in his wake with his lips bitten shut to keep from making a comment. Last thing he needed was to accidentally annoy Tibs when they were so close to their prize.

The hallway widened. A huge set of wooden double doors banded at every handwidth with thick iron loomed to his left. It was his height plus half, the knob surrounded by an elaborate lock as big as his head. The hall was wide enough for a donkey cart to ride into, and it terminated in a smaller, simpler door that Detan recognized as the backdoor Pelkaia had expected him to blow.

Sounds of a scuffle filtered through from outside, startled shouts and harsh whistles filling the night. The watch had been called. Marvelous.

"What now?" Tibs asked.

"Working on it," Detan sang, pacing irritably up and down the width of the hallway. Even if Pelkaia's people were on the other side of the door, there was no making off with the weapons now – not with the watch pounding their way towards the ruckus.

He looked at the keys in his hand. There were only three. The one the captain had used to open the front door, another very much like it, and a third that sported an elaborate flourish on its crown. Good old Valathea. They never could keep from enjoying their own ostentation. It was just a good thing for him they'd cheaped out on the lighting and brought in candles instead of oil lamps.

"Give me your candle."

Tibs handed it over without comment, keeping a wary eye on the door to the outside. Dropping to a crouch, Detan snuffed his candle and set it on the ground. He ran Tibs's lit end along it until the wax was soft enough to shape between his fingers. Shutting out the sounds of battle outside the hallway, he split the softened candle into two parts and wadded each into a ball, discarding the wick. Brushing Tibs's flame over each to keep them pliable, he smooshed the elaborate key into one glob, then counted down from ten, giving the wax time to harden around the metal. Once it was set, he peeled it carefully away and repeated the process with the other side of the key in the other ball of wax.

"Sirra..." Tibs said, a warning note in his voice as something clanged against the door to the outside. Detan grimaced, keeping his hands as still as possible while the wax set.

Three... Two...

He gently lifted the key out of the hardened wax and stuck the two halves of his new mold in his pocket. The pounding on the door grew louder, the wood shaking and the metal fixtures clattering. Detan gave the key one last check to make sure that no waxy residue had been left behind, then strode toward the door. He yanked it open, and stood face to face with a woman he'd never seen before.

And yet he knew her.

"Hullo," he said, slapping on a disarming grin. Pelkaia wore black from head to toe, a rookie mistake, as far as Detan was concerned. Who went thieving looking like a thief? Though she'd rearranged her face – a wider nose, a rounder chin – her accusatory glare was all too familiar.

Before she could say anything, Allat called out, "Arrest that woman!"

Detan blinked, hesitating, but the shrill call of watcher whistles decided him. Blue-coated watchers streamed down the street, nearly a dozen of them, encircling the wagon Pelkaia and Coss had brought to haul off the goods.

If he got caught up in this, he'd never make it to the Remnant in time. He needed to wriggle his way free, and fast. Trouble was, Pelkaia had a cutlass already in hand, and he was all too familiar with her willingness to use it. Unless he could diffuse matters, he might arrive at the Remnant on a prisoner transport ship instead of the *Larkspur*.

"Drop your weapon!" he barked, shaking the key ring at her to distract her with the noise – and possibly to clue her into what he was up to.

She stepped back, startled. "What are you doing, you stupid–"

"Weapons down, all of you!" a watcher cried out, and his voice was, Detan noted grudgingly, much more convincing than his own.

Metal clattered against stone as Pelkaia dropped her cutlass and raised her hands to the air. Detan peered over her shoulder. Coss sat on the driver's seat of the cart, a crossbow fallen to the ground beside him. They'd brought no one else that he could see, unless their other members had already fled into the city.

The guard who had been napping sat on the ground, holding his thigh and moaning. A black shaft stuck up from his leg, a pool of blood coalescing beneath him. Allat stood a few paces in front of him, his baton abandoned for a cutlass, his eyes wild and his hair a sweaty mess.

A brass whistle dangled from around Allat's neck. Detan grimaced. Poor luck. If he'd noticed the lad had means of calling the watch, he'd have offered to go around back himself and sent the lad through to open the back door.

"On your knees!" the watcher yelled.

Pelkaia did not break eye contact with Detan as she knelt, folding her hands behind her head. Detan stared back, impassive. He'd been playacting too long to allow himself to be moved by scorn in such a delicate situation.

"Allat," Tibs called, getting the Fleet guard's attention as the watchers moved in to take command of Pelkaia and Coss. Detan forced himself to turn away from her, to follow Tibs to Allat's side. He could not break character, not now, and a Fleetie's first priority was to his fellows. He'd forgotten that – if not for Tibs's redirection of his attention, he would have dived right in to help the watchers, and nothing looked more suspicious than a Fleetie lending a hand to the local municipality without complaint.

"He all right?" Tibs asked as he knelt alongside the bleeding guard. Detan lingered nearby, trying to keep an eye on the arrest process without being too conspicuous. Pelkaia and Coss had their hands tied and were herded toward the watchers' waiting cart, a sad little donkey ready to pull them along.

"I'll be fine," the bleeding man hissed. "Missed the artery, thank the skies."

Detan tried to pay attention to Tibs's conversation with the guards, but he was stuck on the watchers. With Pelkaia and Coss secured, the watchers started work on Pelkaia's cart, checking it for smuggled goods. As they worked, another watcher took up the donkey driver's seat and flicked the reins – guiding it, and their fresh prisoners, away.

Away to pits knew where. Detan didn't know a thing about this city aside from it was cold and partial to a fish stew. He couldn't trail them, he'd be too obvious, and by the time he managed to slip away from his "fellow" Fleeties they'd be long gone. He didn't have a plan, but he could stall better than a sel-less ship in a storm.

"Wait!" he yelled, holding up a hand to forestall the donkey-driver. The man didn't so much as glance his way, but one of the watchers going over Pelkaia's cart did.

"What's the problem?" he asked, hooking a finger in his belt loop. This watcher was a younger man, slim of frame with well-trimmed hair and a chin bald as a baby's ass. Still paid attention to protocol, then. Not yet jaded by his authority.

Detan's mind raced. What could he say? The injured guard groaned as Tibs and Allat tended to him, sparking an idea. "Those two injured a Fleet guard! They're our prisoners!"

"Hah," the watcher said. "This is our city. You're going to have to take it up with the captain."

"Fine," he scowled. "Where are you taking them?"

"You must be new here." The watcher jerked his thumb toward a slim, round building that towered above all the others of the city. It was crafted of the same boring, brown stone as the rest, unique from its neighbors only by nature of its height and its circular construction. A beacon shone from its top, a radiant glass globe fueled by gaslight. Figured the watchers would see to it they got the most phallic building in the city all to themselves. "They'll go in the Tower, same as everyone else arrested in Petrastad. Make your appeals for control of them there."

The watcher turned back to his work, dismissing Detan with his back. Of course. It had to be a tower. Only one he'd ever stepped foot in before was the whitecoats' Bone Tower, and it hadn't exactly been a welcoming experience. Forcing himself to calm, Detan reached down and clapped a hand on Tibs's shoulder.

"Come along, brother. Let's go see if we can find a late night apothik to tend to our comrade here, eh?"

Tibs tied a strip of cloth around the wounded man's leg, slowing the flow but not cutting it off completely. Reluctantly, he nodded and stood, wiping his hands on the hem of his coat. One more stain to add to the collection.

"Right you are," Tibs said. "Allat, keep pressure on that wound, understand? We'll send someone over quick as we can."

The young guard looked up at them, his face almost as pale as the moon's. "Ruma? Where...?"

"She's safe in the office, we left her locked up in the lobby. Here." Detan handed the keyring over and pat the young man on the shoulder. "I'm sure she'll be pleased as sunshine to see you again and hear all about your heroics. Come along, Brownie."

Detan hooked his arm in Tibs's and forcibly steered him away from the bleeding man. He picked a direction that he hoped veered toward some sort of market and sped his steps.

"Thank you, Step!" Allat yelled after him. Detan lifted a hand to give a cheery wave, and then they turned, disappearing from Allat's line of sight down a side street.

"We are so fucked," Detan said.

"You, admitting defeat?"

"Pah, no, it's just–" He felt the wax mold in his pocket, eyed the slender tower where the watchers kept themselves and their prisoners. Monsoon season was coming quick. The rising pressure of it prickled his skin, the tingle of moisture in the air hinted at more than proximity to the sea. He didn't have time to muck about in Petrastad breaking Pelkaia and her pits cursed first mate out of the clink. Ripka and New Chum wouldn't keep in the Remnant much longer, he was sure of that. They needed him to pick them free before the monsoons trapped them for a full season.

And surely the watch wouldn't execute a couple of failed thieves, even if one had shot a guardsman of the Fleet. He bit both lips, sealing his mouth shut.

"What are you thinking?" Tibs prompted after they'd been walking awhile in silence.

"I think... I think we'd better return to the *Larkspur*."

"To let Pelkaia's crew know what happened?"

Detan grimaced. "Not exactly."

"Ah... I see. In either case, I suggest we find an apothik to send to that guard. He lost a surprising amount of blood, and I fear Allat is no nursemaid."

"Fine," Detan said with an exaggerated sigh, hiding a smile. "You're always such a goodie, Tibs ole chum."

"One of us has to be."

Detan flinched. There was no hint of joking in Tibs's voice.

CHAPTER 16

Ripka dragged herself into the rec yard after a restless night, her limbs so stiff from overwork she feared they'd have to roll her down the stairs like a barrel. She'd only been at the Remnant two days, but already she felt the heavy claws of prolonged routine sink into her. This time around, the guard ushered them into the rec yard in one big clump, not bothering to line them up for the trestle table that was used to feed the sparrows who hadn't found other groups yet.

After one full day in the Remnant, the guards had decided the new intakes were on their own.

The table she'd occupied with Clink and her girls had a new member. A round-faced woman with lips that looked like she'd gotten them stuck in a bottle sat on yesterday's empty seat. Must be Kisser, the ill woman whose manpower they'd pretended to be replacing when they took Ripka from the guard. For a moment Ripka feared she'd been replaced, that they really had only wanted her for her extra set of hands, but as she drew near, Forge's head picked up and some quick words were exchanged amongst the group. Honey reached over and dragged a fresh chair across, giving her a little smile as she pat the seat.

Ripka smiled back, and regretted it. She couldn't let herself get too close to these women. She'd be gone soon, if all went well. And worse, she was going to have to use them to get what she was after. Going to have to probe them to see if they could lead her toward the source of Radu's clearsky dealer.

"You look like shit," Clink announced as she shoved a bowl already topped off with morning gruel toward her.

"Aren't you a ray of sunshine," Ripka drawled as she shoveled the bland food into her mouth. Though she'd never been one for a home-cooked meal, she'd much rather have a bun off a streetcart and a ladle of thick milk tea than this flavorless mush. But, from the way her body ached, she knew she'd be a fool to scorn it for its taste.

"You hear the rumor?" The new woman, Kisser asked, her voice a low murmur as she leaned over the table, bread dangling from her fingertips. Bits of porridge dripped off its soggy edge.

"We get all our rumors from you," Clink said. "Spill it."

Ripka ate her gruel quietly, conscientiously, wondering how Kisser would have come by any rumors if she'd spent the day spewing in her cell as the others had claimed.

"Some sparrow tried to make a break for it last night. Faked something wrong with waterworks and as soon as they got outside ran for the damned sea."

An unground grain caught in Ripka's throat and she coughed. Honey passed her a clay cup of water without comment. All eyes were riveted to Kisser, which was well enough as far as Ripka was concerned.

"What a moron," Clink pronounced. "What would they do if they made it to the beach? *Swim* for Petrastad? That water's bone cold, and shark infested to top it off. They'd be chow or frozen solid before they were even tired out from the backstroke."

Kisser spread her arms expansively, as if gathering in the whole of human folly. "Desperation, no doubt. What drove them here might very well be what's driving them away.

What about you, Captain? You considering taking a dip?"

Ripka blinked at Kisser's use of her false criminal name. It made sense that the others would warn her of the new addition, but Kisser smiled at her as if they'd been friends for ages. After her encounter with Radu, any hint of familiarity made her twitchy.

"I'm from the Scorched. You think I can swim?" she said, getting a laugh.

"It's true, though," Kisser pressed, waving a spoon through the air. "The only way off this rock is up, in an airship. Sea's too rough to try a raft, even if you did know how to build one."

"Not to mention the sharks," Honey said.

"She *already* mentioned the sharks," Forge said, grinning as Honey blushed.

"I like the sharks," Honey murmured.

"You considered building a raft?" Ripka asked, trying to keep the girls focused on the mechanics of the Remnant. The more she could glean about what went on here, the better.

Meanwhile, as long as they were talking to her, they were looking at her, and she took the opportunity to shift her body language. She may not be a practiced con like Tibal or Detan, but she'd seen a few addicts on their come-down in her day. Hunched shoulders, slouched posture, gripping an elbow with one hand while the other scratched lightly at the opposite bicep. Not to mention the teeth clenching. She already had that nasty habit, she just had to do it hard enough for them to notice.

"Me, build a raft?" Kisser snorted and shared a look Ripka couldn't read with Clink. "Naw, but I've heard of people who've tried – stories, you know, nothing recent. More like fairy tales the inmates tell themselves. Evil, determined bastards slipping off in the night on rafts made of old, wax-fortified coats and sticks whittled together from our spoons. It's all nonsense. Just wait your time, work hard, and don't piss too many people off. You'll get out eventually."

"Anyone in particular I should avoid pissing off?"

Clink smirked. "You've already put your foot in it. Got the Glasseaters irritated with you, and the guards who had to break up that fight to match. I'm surprised no one's pissed in your washbucket yet."

"Wonderful." Ripka groaned and stirred her porridge with a wooden spoon of legend, listless, pretending disinterest in food. Forge and Clink exchanged a look.

"Hey, Captain," Clink said, her voice lower than usual. "You hurtin'?"

Ripka pressed her lips together hard to keep from smiling. Didn't matter where you went in the world, those who dealt in illicit trades always made up their own language to obfuscate what they were really up to. She figured the language of Aransa's dark trade would translate just as well here. Radu had insinuated that the drug he wanted rooted out was an upper, and those usually had an acerbic taste from which they took their slang.

"Yeah. Not much time to get used to going without. I got tossed straight on the transport. Anything bitter growing on this rock?"

"Hmmm," Forge said, drumming her nails on the table. "Not much like that around here. Guards keep it pretty tight, but there's..."

Clink cleared her throat and shot Forge a hard look. "I'll ask around. See if I can scrounge up something to help."

Ripka swallowed her disappointment. Either the girls knew something and were keeping the information close, or she'd attached herself to the wrong group. Pits below, she shouldn't have to bother with this bullshit. She should focus on Nouli, on getting close to that yellowhouse. But the thought of being outed... She glanced sideways at Honey, at the hard planes of muscle hidden behind her jumpsuit. They weren't likely to be so friendly with her if they knew where her "name" came from.

"I'd be grateful," she said, forcing a tight smile but not trying too hard to hide her disappointment. They'd expect as much.

"We look out for each other, that's the deal." Clink didn't need to explain what she meant, Ripka could hear between the words easily enough. She'd be called upon someday to repay the favor of their protection, their company, and their drug supplier if it came to that.

A little worm of guilt crawled under her skin as she realized she wouldn't be around long enough to settle the debt Clink had offered her in good faith. But was it good faith, truly? Ripka hadn't the slimmest idea what Clink, or the others, had done to get themselves tossed in the Remnant. Wasn't anything petty, she could count on that. The empire didn't go to the trouble of shipping you out to this sea-slapped rock if you hadn't gone out of your way to earn the dubious honor. It had to be worse than petty theft, but not so nasty they'd lob your head off and be done with it.

Not much was a capital offense in the eyes of the empire, especially not on the Scorched. Planned murder would get you chopped, or being a deviant sel-sensitive – but with the sensitives, they just wanted them out of the breeding pool. In being sent to the Remnant, the empire thought they might be able to squeeze some use out of you someday. Rehabilitation was the lip service they gave it, but in truth this nest of vipers was a place of waiting.

Waiting for the next war, the next selium-rush. Whatever the empire'd need dirty hands for. Hands they didn't mind chopping off.

"Your sweetums is making friends," Honey said in her soft, whispery voice.

Ripka suppressed a scowl at the thought of Enard as anything more than a friend, and followed Honey's gaze. Enard had set himself up at the trestle table again. The population there had thinned, many of the new intakes having broken off to join smaller, more insular groups. Some of them had even formed their own clumps of human protection. But not Enard.

He sat straight-backed, methodically spooning gruel into his mouth, a ratty napkin folded across his lap with angles so crisp Ripka wondered how he'd managed to beat the rumpled material flat, let alone straight. Give the man a change of clothes and you could plop him down in any high society dining hall and no one would be the wiser.

He'd attracted flies. At least, that's what they looked like to Ripka. Three men made a crescent around Enard – one at either side, one at his back – leaning forward with expressions so intense Ripka couldn't tell if they wanted to kill him or fuck him. Maybe both.

That songbird who'd started the fracas stood on the other side of the table, arms crossed, a smug look tugging up her still-swollen lips.

"Trouble," Ripka said, automatically keeping her voice soft.

"Just another day on the Remnant," Clink mused.

"Hope they don't mess up those lovely cheekbones of his," Forge added.

Ripka's fist tightened around her spoon. They were criminals, these new friends of hers. Not her watchers, trained to fall into action by her words, by the subtle shift in her voice. She'd moved on the chair, unconsciously swung her legs around to the other side so that she faced Enard. Her hands curled in her lap, one still holding the wooden spoon. A paltry weapon, that. She'd give anything to have her baton, her crossbow, or her cutlass. Would give so much more to have her old sergeant, Banch, backing her up.

Pits below, she'd even welcome Detan's idiotic face right about now.

"You gon' fight, Captain?" Honey asked.

"Best not, unless you wanna spend a night in the well," Kisser said.

One of the three men was talking, hunched over real close

so Enard couldn't miss a word he said, but Enard kept on eating, bringing that spoon up and down to his own internal rhythm. Maybe they just had harsh words to share. Maybe...

A small hand lighted on her shoulder and she snapped around to face the owner faster than she'd intended. Honey smiled at her, her little hand with its too-short fingers tugging on the cloth by her shoulder.

"Gimme your spoon, mine's broken," she said.

"Honey..." There was a warning note in Clink's voice that Ripka couldn't parse. Was Honey simpleminded? To be worried about cutlery at a time like this was so disjointed from reality that Ripka wasn't sure whether to laugh or yell. She handed the spoon over without comment, acutely aware of the conversation going on at the table while her back was turned.

Honey snatched the spoon with glee and shoved one of her short, thick thumbnails into the end of its handle. Sticking her tongue out with concentration, she twisted her nail around until the wood began to splinter, then upended her plate and fitted the notched end of the handle against its narrow edge. With a few deft taps, she split the spoon in half against the plate and peeled a few splinters off one half. She tested the handle's new point for sharpness, nodded to herself, and handed it back, beaming with triumph.

"For you."

Ripka stared, dumbfounded. In a few heartbeats, Honey'd crafted a serviceable shiv.

"Thank you..." Ripka said, hesitantly, as she took the makeshift weapon and stashed it in her pocket.

"Be careful, there's an awful lot of them."

"I don't think—"

Shouts echoed across the courtyard, cutting her off. The man who had been speaking to Enard grabbed his collar and jerked him from his seat, shoving him toward the ground. Enard twisted expertly, wrenching his shirt away from the man's grasp, and got a hand down to brace himself.

There he perched, his thighs on the bench, a single hand holding him off the ground. Silence wove throughout the moment, the entire rec yard holding its breath to see which way things would swing next.

The man standing behind Enard, his jumpsuit dyed over the shoulders in a scale pattern, kicked Enard's elbow. He crashed to the ground. The yard exploded in whoops and cheers.

Ripka couldn't see Enard after he went down – the three men converged upon him – but she was on her feet before she could think. She sprinted, elbowing aside the crowd that swelled about the nucleus that was Enard.

Enard's head popped up – taller than the rest, dark hair flattened with sweat. A trickle of blood snaked from his nose to his lip. The three tightened the noose, pressing him back against the bench so he'd be off balance. Ripka saw Enard's eyes narrow, his shoulders set, his fists come up, and then she was in.

The crowd broke around her and she grabbed the first man she could reach by the scruff of his jumpsuit, yanked him back with one hand as she drove her other fist into his kidney. He barked in pain, tried to twist around to come at her but she held fast to his collar and kicked the back of his knee. Fabric twisted in her grip, rubbed her knuckles raw as he staggered sideways and wrenched away from her.

"The fuck–" he spat, but before he could get another word out she stepped into him, swung a jab into his liver as he threw his arms out to catch his balance and followed it up with a hook to that nice little sweet spot on his temple. He crumpled.

One down. Someone grabbed her hair and she swore as her head jerked back, chin pointing skywards and vision fuzzed around the edges for a heartbeat. She crouched, the movement just confusing enough for her attacker to think he'd knocked her down. The man let go of her hair and she spun, brought her leg up in a heavy kick aimed at stomach-height and connected with a woman she'd never seen before.

The woman toppled, taken by surprise. Ripka scanned the crowd closing in tight around the brawl. Pockets of fights broke out among the masses, twisted knots pushing and shoving against those who wanted to watch the show. Things were getting out of hand, a riot was about to start.

There – Enard had kicked the bench under the table and had his back against it, facing the two men who circled him. His stance was tight, squared off, his head ducked down while he protected his middle. Ripka grimaced. Decent form for a ring, but he wouldn't last long like that against two determined bastards with his back against a figurative wall.

"Hey!" she yelled and grabbed a fallen clay plate, then hurled it at the back of the man standing closest to her. It shattered in a satisfying puff. "Hey, fuckface!"

He flinched as the plate slammed into his back and took a hit to his chest from Enard while distracted. With an enraged bellow he spun around, seeking his attacker. Ripka forced herself to stand still and smirk at him. He was much, much larger than she had originally thought. This was going to hurt.

If he could catch her.

She kicked up a cup into her hands and chucked it at the man. His lips curled in a snarl as he turned into it, taking the hit on the shoulder. She blew a kiss at him, winked, and spun to elbow her way back through the crowd.

No need to elbow, she realized. The big man chasing her scattered the other inmates like chaff. She sprinted along the edge of the table, threw a glance back over her shoulder to make sure he followed. Yep, still enraged and pointed right at her. She wasn't sure whether to be happy about that or not. It was what she'd wanted, but... Still.

As she glanced back, she caught sight of Enard laying the other man out flat with a heavy blow to the jaw. At least he was safe.

She almost barreled into a cluster of smirking men before she noticed they weren't moving, and she didn't have time to shove them aside. She stumbled, arresting her course, saw one of them reach for her and realized they must be the big bastard's friends, willing to hold her in place while he caught up.

Twisting away, she flung herself atop the trestle table and rolled to her feet, facing the man dashing toward her. The men crowded her side of the table, grins leering up at her. She swung her gaze along the other side of the table and found more of the same. Wonderful. If she could make it back to Enard, then at least she'd have an ally.

Taking a breath to steady her nerves, she sprinted, legs pumping hard enough to shake the table with every step, cutlery and cookware clattering as she stormed down the length of the table. Her heel hit spilled porridge, and she nearly lost her footing. Skidding, cursing, she righted herself and saw… blackness as the world swung above her head.

She hit the table with a grunt, air whooshing free of her lungs, shoulder burning as it took the brunt of her fall. Knowing only she needed to get moving again, she twisted, attempted to kick herself up. Someone had her ankle gripped tight. The songbird.

That cursed woman leaned over the bench on the other side of the table, spindly fingers digging in tight to Ripka's ankle, a satisfied grin twisting up her sunken features. Ripka kicked out with her free foot, aiming for the woman's head, and then the sun went away.

She blinked, understood the darkness as the eclipsing figure of the big man. He towered above her, brought back his arm as if to swing. Ripka threw her arms up, forearms pressed together, to shield her face. But he wasn't interested in hitting her. His massive hand curled around her throat.

Squeezed.

Gasping for air she tried to shove her thumbs under his

fingers. No use, the man was attached to her like a sandtick.

Her vision blurred out at the edges. Her need for air burned in her throat, her chest, her mind. Couldn't think, couldn't work out what to do. Her mind was one big scream of *breathe!*

A strange fuzziness filled her, making the world distant and slowed, the pain somehow less – it'd end soon, one way or another. A tickle of a memory called to her. She felt the hard lump in her pocket, Honey's gift. As her fingers closed around the warm wooden handle she heard Warden Faud's words, from all those years ago, before she'd even been a watch-captain. When he was teaching her to control a fight without killing.

Never go for a death blow, if it can be helped. Find the path to the quickest, safest end, and when you find it, do not hesitate.

On the edges of her awareness voices were raised, the big brass bells of the Remnant's alarm beating along with the fading stutter of her heart. Guards were coming. Would be here soon. Not soon enough.

She shanked the big man in the hollow of his elbow. Drove the point up and in so hard splinters bit her palm and she felt the elastic give and snap of his tendon under the shiv's point. Saw the severed tendon curl up under his skin like a gnarled root.

Maybe I am a farmer, she thought, delirium ebbing away as she sucked in great mouthfuls of sea-salted air. She coughed, retching stomach waters on herself, the table, anywhere at all. Hands closed around her shoulders and shoved her upright.

She heard the big man scream in pain, but she didn't care. He'd made a mistake, looking to kill her.

"Where'd you get that?" Captain Lankal's face loomed into hers, and she laughed, because it seemed such a stupid question. She opened her mouth to answer and tasted fire again, fell into another coughing fit.

"Fine." He snapped as she was dragged off the table by too many hands to count. "You want to start fights, missy? Want to draw blood? I've had enough of your shit. You're going in the well."

As they bound her wrists and marched her out of the rec yard, she caught sight of Honey, watching her from behind the table where her new friends sat, hunger bright as a bonfire in her dark amber eyes. More than hunger. Reverence.

CHAPTER 17

After a few irritating wrong turns, Detan stood on the roof of the building to which both the *Larkspur* and the *Happy Birthday Virra!* were docked. He eyed the long tongue of a gangplank that reached from the *Larkspur*'s deck to the stubby pier which extended from the roof. He didn't have a lot of confidence in that pier. It was a slapdash job of old boards, greyed from the sea winds, supported by equally sorry looking bracing. He liked the look of the gangplank even less. One good kick from either end would send the traverser plummeting to the hard, stone streets below. There wasn't even a decent awning to break his fall.

"Second thoughts?" Tibs asked.

Detan cleared his throat and snapped his coat lapels forward, stretching his neck right to left to work out the kinks nerves had given him. Finding oneself in the middle of a heist gone wrong was a sure way to get the body out of whack.

"Scarcely looks like the old bird, does it?" he said. He was stalling, sure, but he meant what he'd said nonetheless. If he hadn't walked off the *Larkspur*'s deck that morning, he wouldn't recognize the ship for the one he snatched out from under Thratia's nose. Detan just couldn't get his head around the new name painted on its hull – the *Mirror*. Probably

someone thought they were cheeky, but Detan found it
pretentious.

"Gonna stand here and admire their handiwork until the
monsoons roll in and Pelkaia rots to death in that tower?"

"Psh, you're always in such a rush, Tibs."

"Maybe 'cause you always got your heels stuck in the mud,
sirra."

Detan snorted and charged ahead, propelling himself
forward on sheer determination that Tibs not see him
shrink from the task at hand. The moment his boots hit
the gangplank a narrow man with a mighty mop of tousled
sand-red hair appeared at the other end, his own brown boot
planted firmly on the ship's end of the gangplank.

"Ho there, young sir. I come bearing news from your
valorous captain. Permission to board?"

The mop-headed man plucked a wooden pick from
between his lips and squinted down the plank at Detan and
Tibs. Behind him, figures Detan couldn't quite make out
popped up, peering at him over the high rail of the *Larkspur*'s
main deck.

"Name's Jeffin," the scrawny lad said. "And the thing is,
my *valorous* cap'in tole me not to let your 'skies-cursed hide'
anywhere on this ship unless she was with you. She with
you?"

Tibs chuckled behind him, the traitor.

"Not, ah, not at the present, Jeffin. You see, she sent me
ahead to tell you that—"

"Hmm, no."

"No?"

Jeffin shook his head, slow and ponderous. "No. Not
buying what you're selling, Honding. Cap'n warned me you
were shifty as a summer wind, and not to believe a word
coming out of your mouth unless she had a knife to your
balls making you sing."

"That's some, uh, interesting imagery. However—"

"That the Honding?" The girl who'd escorted them through the alleys of Petrastad poked her head over the rail to peer down at him, her small face wrinkled by squinting.

"'Fraid so," Jeffin said.

"The captain with him?"

"She sent me ahead—" Detan began again.

"Naw," Jeffin said, "she's not there."

"Oh. Did you kill her?"

"No!" Detan barked, genuinely taken aback. "I would never do such a thing."

"Aren't you trying to nick her ship?" the girl said. "I mean, that's what I would do if I were trying to steal someone's ship."

"I am *not* trying to steal the *Larkspur*." He allowed himself a grin. "I've already done that."

"Really? Doesn't look like it from this side of the rail." The girl smirked. Detan found himself wondering if anyone would notice if he tipped her over the edge.

"Don't mind lil' Essi, she's a practical spirit." Jeffin reached over and ruffled the girl's hair. She scowled at him, but said nothing.

"Now," Jeffin continued, "you go on back into Petrastad and get the cap'n, if you want aboard. Won't be letting you take a step further otherwise, understand?" He nudged the gangplank with his foot to punctuate his point. Detan's stomach lurched at the implicit threat. Tibs cleared his throat and retreated back to the roof, leaving Detan alone on the treacherous stretch of wood. He couldn't blame him. He'd be right beside him if he thought he could retreat and still convince Jeffin to do what he wanted.

"Retrieving your captain at this juncture is, I'm afraid, impossible."

"At this what now?"

Detan clenched his fists, forced himself to keep on smiling. "At this moment. You see, things went... not quite as planned.

She is indisposed, and will be for quite some time."

Essi's eyes went so wide they competed with the fat, red moon. "You *did* kill her!"

"No! I... Pits*damnit*, this is going nowhere. Listen," he said, taking a step forward, his hands held out imploringly. Jeffin gave the plank a warning nudge. He froze. With one great sigh, he gave up on his plan to weasel them to the Remnant without Pelkaia. Tibs probably would have skinned him alive for trying, anyway.

"Pelly has been arrested."

"Who?" Essi said.

"How?" Jeffin said.

"The usual way, with threats of violence for non-compliance and bonds for her wrists, but the point is she's not coming back to this ship of yours unless we go and get her."

Jeffin's eyes narrowed. Detan could almost hear the gears of the man's mind clicking over as he thought. He suppressed a sigh. If only Pelkaia had left Coss in control of the ship, then they might not have to waste so much time circling one another. That man had seemed like he knew what he was doing – no doubt why Pelkaia had chosen him for her first mate.

"How can I be sure you're not lying?" Jeffin finally asked.

Detan held both his hands out, palms facing the sweet skies, and shrugged. "You can't. You can sit around and wait for her to appear, which won't happen, or you can trust me and help me retrieve her. Those are your only options."

Jeffin chewed his lip, mulling Detan's words over, then looked down at little Essi. "What do you think?"

"I dunno. But if the captain's in jail we'd be waiting a real long time to find out about it. Ain't no one from the watch going to come tell us."

Jeffin turned back to Detan. "And how do you plan on getting her an' Coss back, if I do let you aboard?"

Detan beamed up at them, covering his relief with

exuberance. If Jeffin was at all interested in his plan, then Detan'd hooked him. Soon he'd back aboard the *Larkspur*, night air fresh in his lungs, all the sky splayed out before him. It was just too bad he had to use the opportunity to save Pelkaia's scaly hide.

"I distinctly remember Pelkaia wearing a commodore's coat when she first welcomed me aboard. Still got it?"

"Yes," Jeffin said, wary, drawing out the word. "Whyfor?"

"For adventure, my good man!" Detan took Jeffin's hesitance in hand and strode up the gangplank before he could push it back, arms thrown wide and his face split with the craziest, most delighted grin he could muster. Before Jeffin could mutter a protest, Detan slung an arm around his shoulders and turned him to face the narrow tower that was the watchers' station-house. Its beacon illuminated the gathering clouds in glorious golden light.

"Tibs and I have set the stage," Detan said, tugging on his stolen Fleetie coat for emphasis. "Now, all we need is a fearsome, determined commodore to help us reclaim our stolen prisoner from those cursed, over-reaching watchers!" He shook a fist at the watchtower, and Essi clapped, giggling.

"Where you gon' find a commodore to help you?" Jeffin asked.

"Why, right here." Detan freed Jeffin's shoulders and spun the man around, holding him at arm's length while he looked him over, letting a satisfied smile spread across his features. He was reassured to hear the steady tromp of Tibs's boots coming up the gangplank behind him.

"Tell me," Detan asked Jeffin, "have you ever taken part in the theater?"

CHAPTER 18

After a cursory pat-down to make certain she wasn't hiding any more improvised weapons, Ripka was marched out of the sheltering walls of the prison. Though it was only mid-morning, a darkness crept across the sky, thick clouds casting shadows over the island's cracked and patchwork landscape. Ripka shivered as she was hounded along, one guard and Captain Lankal prodding her down a winding dirt path. A creeping wind wormed its way beneath her jumpsuit.

"How long?" she asked, scanning this new path, trying to fit it in her mental map of the prison's island. They were on the opposite side of the prison from the yellowhouse, as far as she could tell. Here the ground was scattered with fruit-bearing trees and cracked stone beaches plunging down to the frothing shore.

"First offense is eight marks," Lankal said. "Gruel will be handed down to you once every six hours. You'll be given your water for the day when we put you in. Ration it wisely, you won't get more."

The path sloped down a hill, angling for the beach, and through the trees she began to see small cottages in various states of disrepair. Not a single stream of smoke curled from their half-crumbled chimneys.

"People lived out here?"

Lankal snorted. "Used to be the guards brought their families out with them. Now we leave 'em back in Petrastad. Where it's safer." He eyed her, his grip momentarily tightening on her elbow. "Never could be sure what people like you'd do to 'em."

Nothing, she thought. Or at least, I wouldn't. But she bit her tongue to hold back the words. She'd stabbed a man in the elbow, possibly dooming him to a lame arm for life. She doubted Lankal would believe she wouldn't harm an innocent, even if she had been acting in defense of her own life.

He tugged her arm, turning her down a side path, and she nearly stumbled. Her breath felt too-hot in her throat, her voice scratchy and raw. The chill in the air aggravated each breath. Thick-leaved trees lined the path, and at the top of a knoll, she saw it – the well.

It was about three paces in diameter, its walls crafted of native grey stone and its winch and bucket system well cared for – the rope looked unfrayed, the wood recently oiled. A gabled roof covered the top of the well, no doubt meant to keep leaf and other debris from fouling the water. Nothing about it gave her any reason to believe it was anything more than a simple, if large, well.

Unconsciously, she dug her heels in. The other guard jerked on her arm, forcing her forward. "Come on, no stalling."

"That's... That's a real well." Her cheeks went hot with embarrassment as Lankal chuckled.

"What'd you expect?" he asked.

"Something purpose built, like a narrow pit."

"It is a narrow pit, isn't it?" Lankal directed her to the wall around the well. She peered into the hole, and could see nothing but abyssal blackness.

"Up you go." He patted the top of the wall. "Stick your arms out so we can get the sling on you."

At least they weren't going to try to lower her in the bucket. Ripka sat on the cold edge and swung her legs over the rim, feet dangling into the dark. She forced herself to breathe slowly as the guards took straps from the bucket and fitted them with surprising care around her chest and arms. She tried very hard not to think of what waited for her down there in the dark. Forced images of skittering, crawling insects from her mind.

"Is..." She cleared her already sore throat and tried again. "Is there much water left?"

"No more than a dribble, and that's just seep. This well dried up a long time ago." Lankal gave the straps two firm tugs, jerking Ripka forward. She gasped as her center of gravity teetered on the edge of the wall and shot her hands down to grip the hard stone. The other guard snorted. She soothed herself with images of shoving *him* face-first down the well.

A gust of wind pushed at her, taunting. A heavy, dark cloud slid across the sun, making the well look even deeper.

"If it rains?" she asked, visions of the well filling with fresh water rose unbidden to her mind. She swallowed dry air. She hadn't been kidding when she'd said she couldn't swim.

"Someone will come along and pluck you out if it gets too bad. But you'll have to make up the time when the weather clears."

Lankal hesitated, lips pressed together as if he were trying to hold in what he wanted to say. After a moment, he shook his head and puffed out a breath. "Look, Ripka. I know adjustment to the Remnant can be difficult, but you've got to put in the effort." He held up a hand to forestall her response. "I saw why you fought. I watch the yard from the nest. I saw everything. You've got a hard sense of justice, and I can respect that. But you've got to let it go. I looked up your file after that first night. You're a thief, not a killer. Yeah, you got some moves. But we've got nasty pieces of work on this island you seem determined to piss off. There aren't many come through these walls I think can be rehabilitated, but you're one of them. Don't get yourself murdered before you get the chance."

Stunned, it took her a moment to find a response. "I'll do my best. Captain."

That seemed to please him. He nodded, and held out the rope he'd wrapped tightly around his elbow and hand so that she could see it, and then gestured to the pulley system above. "I got you. Go on now."

Clenching her jaw against rising panic, she turned around so that she faced out of the well, then began to ease down, fingers gripping the top of the well's lip so hard that her stubby nails bent back. Stone scratched her chest as she wormed her way over the edge, walking herself down the wall. When she hit a depth as low as her arms would go without dropping and still hadn't touched ground, she froze, squeezing her eyes shut as if internal darkness was somehow safer than the unknown darkness below. Rope slack piled between her shoulder blades.

"Let go," Lankal said.

"I don't—"

The other guard pried her fingers from the wall and she plunged down, the harness snapping tight against her chest. A little cry of shock escaped her as the straps dug into her and she spun, slowly, in the empty air in the well's center. She cracked her eyes open to glare at the grey sky above. The other guard chuckled. Bastard.

Her dangling feet found purchase on moss-slick ground, and she heaved a sigh of relief as her weight was taken off the straps. Rolling her shoulders, she peered at her new place of confinement as best she could in the dark.

As her eyes had not yet adjusted, she saw only gloomy walls of deep grey, reaching up to the equally dismal sky above. The ground was slick with mud and lichens. She trailed her fingers along the hard stone, feeling the shallow gashes made by those who'd come before her. As she brushed deep gouges, spaced evenly as fingernails, she shivered and jerked her hand away.

Tension let out in the rope, and it slid down her back until it looped back up near her hips. "Hey!" she called. The words echoed back at her, slamming against the well's walls. "What do I do about the harness?"

Lankal stuck his head over the wall, she recognized him only by the silhouette of his shaggy hair. "Don't take it off, and if you try to climb out the winch is set to release all the rope. You'll be stuck down there until we can be bothered to get a new rope out to you."

"That happened before?"

"More often than you'd think. And sometimes we have to wait for a shipment to come in from Petrastad. Step to the right."

She did so without thought. His voice carried the air of command she'd grown used to following before she'd risen up to become the watch-captain. Something slammed into the ground alongside her. She knelt, feeling along until she found it. A water bladder, holding maybe a half a bucket's worth. Not enough to sustain her if she'd spent the day in the field, but enough to keep her hydrated while she waited to return to the world above.

"Thanks!" she called, but they had already gone.

That realization, that cold hard truth, that they had left her so easily – and that, in doing so, she was truly alone in this dark hole – bit into her. No more answers to her questions. No more gentle assurances that this was all a part of protocol and would be over soon. No, she was on her own, left to wait out her time until she'd considered what she'd done and decided it wasn't worth this particular flavor of punishment.

But she didn't agree with that. If she hadn't stabbed that man he'd have throttled her to death. *He* should have been the one shoved in this yawning grave, not her. Lankal seemed to agree with her actions. She wasn't even a real criminal, not really. Skies above, she'd been a watch-captain most of her adult life, and a watcher before that. They couldn't know about her past as a prize fighter and, even if they did, everything she'd done then had been above board. Clean. Legal. They couldn't punish her for that.

Couldn't leave her to rot for it.

She caught herself pacing, her steps small and controlled, her hands gesticulating to the empty air as she worked through these thoughts. With a slow, deep, breath she consciously released the tension that had knotted her whole body. Forced herself to relax, concentrated on the thunder of her heart until it'd calmed to a reasonable rate.

She'd only been alone a few moments, and yet the isolation had clutched her fears tight. Didn't help that she'd never been a fan of small spaces.

Rubbing her hands together to hide their tremble, she sat with her back against the wall, head tipped up so she could see what little there was of the sky. A storm was blowing in, she was sure of it. Maybe they'd pull her out early. But they'd have to put her back in later, and it was those first few moments that'd been the worst. That she hoped would continue to be the worst.

She forced herself to think of her tasks. Of finding Radu's competition, of flushing out Nouli before Detan arrived. With the storm threatening, she had no doubt he'd be along soon. No one wanted to get caught out over the Endless Sea when monsoon season struck.

Sometime, during the rambling of her thoughts, her exhausted body gave up, and she sunk into a deep, well-needed rest.

A rock struck her on the head, waking her up.

"Hey," a soft woman's voice whispered from above. "You up?"

Ripka groaned and dragged her hands through her hair, blinking at the renewed vision of the prison walling her in. She wished, deeply, that whoever had woken her had left her alone to rest. Unless they were hauling her up because rain was coming.

The very thought jolted Ripka to her feet. She glared at the sky, fearing blackened clouds and the first brush of droplets, but saw only a clear stretch of pale blue with the silhouette of a woman's head outlined against it. By the poof and curl of the woman's hair, it was either Honey or Kisser. Unless someone else with similar looks had decided to pay her a visit.

"Who's there?"

A snort-laugh. "Kisser, obviously. Came to see how our sparrow was doing in her new nest."

"It's a little drab. Could do with some curtains, or a flower arrangement."

"Didn't peg you as the decorating type."

"I'm not."

"Ah. Jokes to stay sane. I can understand that. You got enough water? Sometimes they short the bag."

Ripka swallowed, the paper-dry rasp of her throat stinging from the motion. How long had she been asleep? Her neck felt swollen, pudgy. She gave the side of it an experimental poke and winced. Not a good idea. Groggy from her nap, she fumbled around on the mossy ground until she found the waterskin. Popping the cap off, she gave it an exploratory sniff. Didn't seem spoiled, or drugged, and that was all she could ask for, really. Carefully, she doled out a few drops onto her tongue and swallowed. It burned going down, but she knew her body needed it.

"Should last me. How long have I been down here?"

"Three or four marks, I should think. Pulling your hair out and screaming at the sky yet?"

Ripka laughed, and regretted the sting in her throat. "Truth be told, Kisser, you woke me up."

"Damn, girl," she whistled low. "Heart of stone in you. Not many can take a catnap in the well."

Now that her eyes had adjusted to the dim light, she could make out the scratch marks along the walls in detail. Most were marks of time, and many stick figure sex scenes, but some... Some were pleas for help. Mad ramblings. And there were those claw marks, like some poor soul had tried to dig their way out. She wondered how many of the insane were stuck down here, simply because the guards didn't know what to do with their outbursts.

Dark stains smeared the grey stone around her. Many looked like palm smears. She tipped her head up and focused on Kisser's eclipsing face instead.

"Not many are as exhausted as I am by the time they get down here. What are you doing over here, anyway? Isn't it work detail?"

The dark shadow of Kisser's hand blurred over the blue sky like a streaking bird as she brushed away Ripka's question. "They're burning lime for fertilizer, and I've got sensitive lungs." She coughed, and Ripka shook her head at the fakeness of the sound. "So they sent me to do my daily wander about the island. Good for my lungs, all that light exercise, you understand."

Ripka pursed her lips. She wasn't fool enough to complain about the lack of oversight from the guards, but their incompetence niggled at her. She'd been in Kisser's company a sum of two marks, being generous, and already she'd determined the woman was faking illness to be let off the prison's leash.

"You got a lot of freedom," she ventured.

"My parents are silk mercers, all the way back in Valathea. I'm no flight risk – everyone here knows I've come to keep my head down, do my time, and get back home to the family business."

"Lotta money in silk," Ripka said, unable to hide the bitter tang to her words. She carried no doubt that Kisser's family was bribing the officials here to allow their child special freedoms. If Ripka'd been warden, she'd have dumped any guard caught taking such a bribe in this blasted well.

Kisser laughed. "True enough. But that's not why I came to see you."

"I'd wondered. For someone interested in keeping her head down, you're sure willing to get tangled up with a troublesome new intake."

"I know what I'm about," Kisser snapped. Ripka tensed, wondering if she'd pushed her too far. After a few beats of strained silence, Kisser said, "Anyway. I know you're hurting. Can't do anything for you now, but once you're out, I can take you to see Uncle. He's curious about you, and your handsome friend."

"Uncle?"

"The man who can get you what you need, understand?"

"Yes... I think I do. Thank you." Ripka's mind was awhirl with possibilities, strategies. If this man were the connection to the outside smuggling, then she'd have to walk a fine line. She'd have to pretend progress to Radu while keeping him off the scent that she'd discovered the source. She couldn't blow her contacts with Kisser and the other girls so soon. A betrayal now, before she found Nouli and was certain of Detan's impending rescue, could leave her without any allies to leverage. Or worse, completely exposed if the whim struck Radu.

"Good. And no need for thanks, we look after our own." Which meant Ripka would owe Kisser one pits-deep favor. Kisser's head disappeared from above the well and she slapped her hand on the top of the wall, the meaty thump echoing around Ripka. "Oh, and Captain?"

"Yes?"

"I asked around about that man of yours. I don't know what you know, but... He's trouble, missy. Watch him close."

Ripka clenched her fists in frustration. "What do you mean?"

"Glasseaters don't just leave."

Kisser's boots crunched away over tree deadfall, leaving Ripka alone with her plans and her worries. With a heavy, exhausted sigh, she sank back down to the loamy ground, praying to the sweet skies that sleep would carry her through the rest of her isolation.

It began to rain.

CHAPTER 19

Stuffed into Pelkaia's stolen commodore coat, Jeffin looked like a young lad playing dress-up in his daddy's wardrobe. Detan fussed with the lay of the boy's lapels to see if he could coax the shape of the coat into giving him some dignity.

"No use," Tibs said.

"What's the matter?" Jeffin asked, turning himself this way and that before a long mirror they'd found tacked up in one of the larger cabins.

"You don't exactly strike a commodorial figure, my dear lad." Detan tried to muster a grin. Catching himself in the mirror, he realized it was more of a grimace.

"More commode-ial," Tibs added.

"Not. Helping."

Detan eyed the girl, Essi, sitting on the costume trunk from which they'd pulled the commodore's coat. Her surly face, her rigid shoulders, her ruthless nature. She'd make the perfect commodore, if only she were a decade older. Essi caught him staring and sniffed, flipping hair from her eyes.

"Won't work," she said.

"I know." He sighed and dragged his fingers through his hair, giving it a good shake. No better ideas came to him. "Anyone you'd recommend?"

"Sure," she said.

"No," Jeffin snapped, perking Detan's interest with his obvious hatred.

"Who?" Detan spun, abandoning Jeffin to address Essi.

"Laella, of course. Not a drop of Catari in her. She may be a deviant, but she's purebred Valathean, and she knows it."

"Rude?" Detan asked. "Impervious to criticism?"

"That's her," Essi agreed.

"Annoying as the day is long," Jeffin grumbled.

"Perfect. Bring her here."

"If you want." Essi dropped down off the trunk and stretched long and hard before making for the cabin's slim door. "Stay here," she said, "I'll be right back."

Detan paced the small cabin while they waited, ignoring the admonishing glares of both Tibs and Jeffin. Neither of them could contribute what he needed now, for what he needed was a picture-perfect authority figure, capable of withstanding even the tightest of scrutiny from the watchers. Detan would play the role himself – he'd been raised to it – but the watchers had already seen him in the role of Step, average Fleetie, and the sudden promotion would give them pause. And might give him a noose to contend with.

"I don't see what's wrong with my appearance," Jeffin protested.

Detan sighed. "A certain strength of chin is lacking, amongst–"

The door banged open. Essi lead a stiff-backed Valathean girl into the cabin. If she'd been a Scorched girl, he'd guess her to be to be somewhere in her early twenties, but the Valathean blood ran so boldly through her veins that Detan guessed her older – late twenties, at least, possibly early-to-mid thirties. Her skin was dark as obsidian, her eyes wide set and amber of hue, her posture firm an elegant. She wore the long, flowing robes imperials favored, accentuating her slight frame, her black hair in tight braids bound against her head.

Upon sighting Detan, she quirked perfectly arched brows and smiled, cautiously. "Lord Honding?"

"I am Detan."

"May the blue skies bless our meeting, my lord." She laced her fingers together and held them up to the sky as she bowed over them, the most formal of Valathean greetings. Detan returned the gesture on instinct. His form may be lacking after years without practice, but his aunt had spent a great many years drilling such courtesies into him.

"Skies keep you, lady, but there is no need for such formality with me. I'm just Detan."

"But a Honding in truth?"

"I am that," he said, rubbing the back of his neck where his family brand puckered his flesh. "But I prefer Detan, if you wouldn't mind."

Her full lips pursed, but she nodded her assent. "If you wish. Now, you have asked for me?"

Detan eyed the girl from head to toe. She was willowy, as was the common body type of Valathean women, tall and narrow of every limb. Her slim face regarded him with care, brows pushed together in mild consternation, every line of her body radiating controlled calm. He shared a look with Tibs, who gave him a nod of agreement.

"And what is your odd little talent?" he asked.

Laella's gaze flitted to lock with Jeffin's. Something venomous passed between them in that moment. Jeffin's brows pulled so far down in annoyance that Detan half expected his face to scrunch up so that his eyebrows became his moustache. It was only a heartbeat's time, but the exchange gave him pause. Things were not so sunny aboard Pelkaia's ship after all.

"I am a mirror-worker, like Jeffin."

"I see." Detan sensed he was treading dangerous waters, but he had scant time for diplomacy. If they were going to fiddle about wasting marks getting Pelkaia and her first mate out of the clink, then it needed to be quick. The longer he waited, the closer monsoon season crept.

"And would you be able to accompany us on an excursion?"

"You're not allowed to leave the ship," Jeffin said. "Captain's orders."

"Captain ain't here, lad," Tibs said in his slow, easy drawl. "And this lady might be able to help us get her back."

Jeffin's lip curled in a subconscious sneer as Tibs said the word "lady." Detan grimaced, knowing what was coming next. Before he could interject, the lad thrust a finger at Laella. "She cannot be trusted."

Detan sighed. Well, there might be something to the boy's anger. Might as well dig up the root of it. "Why are you ordered to stay on the ship, Laella?"

"I am the captain's latest rescue, before yourself, of course. She likes to keep us all aboard until we have proven to her the extent of our abilities, and the quality of our control."

"And how is the quality of your control?"

Essi said, "She bested Jeffin when the captain put them through their paces."

"That true?"

A tiny, modest smile flitted across Laella's lips. "Some think I was given easier tasks. But yes, it is true."

"You *were* given easier tasks!" Jeffin took a step toward Laella. The woman's only response was to lift her chin. "And I say your joining us was far, far too convenient. If you're not an imperial spy, then I'm a bumbling idiot."

"You're a bumbling idiot," Detan said. Laella had the grace to cover her laugh with her fingertips.

Jeffin whirled on him, still shaking that finger, cheeks near as red as his hair. Detan stared in detached wonderment. Was this what Pelkaia allowed to run amok on her ship? Rivalries? Classism? If he'd known ahead of time what divisive lines had been drawn between her crew, he might have tried another angle.

Now, though... now he was tired of it all. And frustrated, and anxious to get their plans swung into full motion. But before he could move on, he'd have to try and mend what Pelkaia had let fester.

"I don't understand," Jeffin's voice was scarcely controlled, his lips flecked with spittle. "How you can trust that... that... that *Valathean*. She's not Scorched! Not like us!"

For just a breath, Detan went very, very still. Of all the petty bullshit he'd encountered over the years, this self-imposed division of allegiance speared deepest. Who in the fiery pits was Jeffin – wretched, weak-willed Jeffin – to denigrate this woman for her blood? She was deviant. End of fucking story.

For the first time in a long, long while, a cold stone of rage metamorphosed in his heart, in his belly. More than just the little ticks of annoyance and impatience he'd been so easily shunting aside. The icy fingers of it extend out from his core, threaded through him, steeled him for what was to come.

Voice like gravel, he said, "She's not like us?"

"No!" Jeffin barked, too tied up in his own anger to sense Detan's burgeoning rage. "She's a pits-cursed monster!"

Detan heard, as if from a great distance, Tibs take a sharp breath. And then his focus narrowed, encompassing only the inflamed face of the man before him, the tipping point of all his frustrations.

"Am I a monster?" he asked, voice smooth as silk, though it sounded far away to him. Dreamy.

Jeffin's hand dropped, his pale brows pushed together in confusion. "No, that's... You're Scorched! Like the rest of us."

He stepped forward. Jeffin stepped back. A woman's voice murmured, but all Detan could hear was Tibs say *hush*.

"Scorched, am I?" He held up his hands between them, turning them over so Jeffin could get a good, long look at his heritage-darkened skin, his Valathean-long fingers. "Who the *fuck* do you think I am? I am, by *blood*, an honest-to-skies lord of your hated empire. That make me a monster?"

"No! I said you were—"

Detan surged forward, grabbed Jeffin by the lapels of his false commodore's coat and rammed his back against the cabin's wall so hard the mirror jumped. A woman screamed, someone clapped with glee, and somewhere in the distance he heard Tibs yell *sirra!* but he didn't care. He was going to squeeze some pits-cursed sense out of this grubby lout Pelkaia had scavenged up.

Jeffin squawked, a wheeze of air squeezed from his throat. Detan lifted him, lifted him so that his stupid little brown boots could no longer touch the floor. With his forearm bracing Jeffin against the wall, he slammed his free fist into the wall beside the lad's head. Grinned as he squealed with fright. Grinned at the satisfying crack of the wood.

"Listen to me, you dripping shit. Purebred Valatheans ain't the only monsters roaming this sun-slapped continent, understand? Weren't Valatheans who turned me over to the whitecoats, weren't just Valatheans who jeered at Aransa's walls while deviants were forced to walk the killing heat of the Black Wash. The empire sets the rules, but it ain't imperial blood that enforces them, it's superstition and hate and fear. We deviant sensitives got enough people to call us monsters without doing it to ourselves."

"I never meant—"

Detan squeezed.

"I know what you meant. You meant she was different. Meant she hadn't grown up chasing sandrats for supper, or crushing palm leaves for a drink."

His vision narrowed, seeing only Jeffin's red face, growing redder from fear and lack of air. Saw the sweat on his brow, the frantic twitching of his gaze as he searched for someone to save him. Jeffin wasn't sorry about what he'd said. Was only sorry it'd bit him in the ass. Even if he did apologize to Laella, he'd never mean it. Not really.

A tremble began beneath Detan's skin, a tingle like the

wind before the crack of lightning. He went rigid. White stars crept to the edges of his vision as his barriers broke, as his sense of the world expanded – came to encompass the great swathes of sel wreathing the ship, hiding it. Keeping all aboard it safe.

There was so much. And it would be so easy.

If Jeffin wouldn't atone, then...

"I'll show you a monster."

A woman gasped. "We're losing the mirrors! The sel's just... It's disappearing!"

Running outside the cabin. Shouts. It didn't matter. Punishing Jeffin – that mattered.

"Detan, no!" Tibs yelled.

Not *sirra*, not *Honding*. Tibs had called him *Detan*. Had sounded afraid when he said it.

With a pained growl Detan tore away from Jeffin, let him fall to the hard ground without a care. He pivoted, yanked the cabin door open and bolted out onto the deck, elbowing aside startled deviants who came running at the shouts.

He ran until his chest hit the *Larkspur*'s rail and gripped it so hard the wood groaned, his bones creaked. He gasped cold night air, sucked it down to drive back the heat of his anger, trying to submerge the rage.

No use.

Whirlwinds of sel thrashed around him, sparkling and flashing, ribbons like lashes speeding faster and faster, attracted by his anger. Craving his destruction.

Shouts echoed to him – Tibs keeping the startled crew back – but the words were little more than a low fizz below the roar of the winds the sel-storm kicked up. He could not hold.

Could not take them all out with him.

Roaring defiance, he threw his hands toward the sky and called upon every ounce of skill he'd used as a selium miner, utilizing the motion of his body combined with his will, to direct where he wanted to the sel to flow. It carved up, damned near leapt with joy, spiraling into the cloud-strewn sky.

He could not wait any longer, could only pray he'd pushed what he'd gathered far enough away. Anger poured through him, boiled through his veins, arced along his extended sel-sense until it reached the whipping strands of selium and then rended them, tore the effervescent gas apart molecule by molecule.

The sky burst with flame. Clouds ignited in shades of blood and gold. Heat washed over him, kissed the top sail. Someone screamed *fire* and he heard the scramble of the crew as they went for the water buckets, the smothering tarps. He didn't look. Couldn't turn away until it'd all burned out and the sky returned to the dark-ash of the night.

He'd contained it, somehow. Kept it away from the buoyancy sacks in the belly of the ship. Kept maybe half the mirror-ring safe. That'd have to be enough.

When his rage had burned through he turned, arms shaky, forehead crested with sweat. The crew stared at him, the only movement a lazy tendril of smoke winding up from the top mast where a fire had gotten started and been promptly squashed. Eyes he did not know, wide with fear and awe and, just maybe, something like respect, pinned him down. Demanded answers.

He never had any.

"Laella." He pointed to the woman, her face slack with shock. He had no time to assuage her worries. They needed to get out of here before watchers showed up to investigate his conflagration. "Get that coat off Jeffin and practice your best commodore impersonation. The rest of you, get this ship looking like something a Fleetie would be proud of. We're going to go break your captain out, and then we're going to rescue my friends. Understand?"

Nervous nods all around.

"Go!" he yelled, and they scattered like dropped grains.

Tibs slipped up beside him, pressed a water cup into his hand. "Not the method I would have chosen."

Detan's laughter was frantic, shuddering. He only stayed on his feet because Tibs held the back of his upper arm, propping him up so that no one could see how badly he needed the support. So much for not being a monster.

CHAPTER 20

After freeing her from her damp prison, the guards had hustled Ripka, dripping, into the stony shelter of her cell and left her without so much as a word. She'd paced, anxious, wondering if her sentence was fulfilled or if they'd come for her once the clouds had wrung themselves dry. None of the guards had given her an answer. Even Lankal had gone mute.

As if someone had ordered them to silence.

Though she had no light to see by, she knew the dinner hour had passed in the rec yard by the stomping of boots and the whoops of the inmates as they went about their scant social time.

Ripka was left to stew. To pace. When the muttering of the inmates in the yard lost its initial fervor, a shallow tray of gruel accompanied by a few oily pieces of cheese was shoved through the narrow slot in her cell door. After a moment's pause, a roll stuffed with limp greens followed, looking very much like it had been sat upon.

She stared at that lump of leavened bread – its smooshed round face, the greenish ooze seeping from a strained side-seam. A temptation to kick it, to crush it beneath her heel and grind it against the floor, thrummed through her.

Ripka took a breath. Consciously loosened her clenched

jaw. Disgusting as it was, her body would need the scant nutrients stuffed in the crusty roll. Bread had been a rare treat in Aransa. She told herself she shouldn't be sick of it so quickly, but it was hard to ignore the panging in her stomach.

She sat cross-legged, facing the door, and dragged the tray within easy reach. Methodically, she forced herself to bite, chew, and swallow every last drop they'd given her. By the time she was finished, she'd gone through half her water supply just to wash the stodgy mess of nutrients down.

Stomach like a lead weight, she flopped backward onto the hard floor, splaying her arms above her head to stretch. She closed her eyes against the faint light of her single candle, focusing on the slow draw of her breath, ignoring the wet strands of hair sticking to her forehead and neck. Though she'd been granted a change of jumpsuits, there was little she could do for her rain-soaked head.

With eyes closed, she allowed her mind to drift along the twisting paths of her possible futures. Kisser had promised her a rendezvous with a clearsky dealer – Uncle, she'd called him – and that put her one step closer to shucking Radu's yoke. With her task for the warden out of the way, she could then turn her focus to discovering Nouli's whereabouts – which meant, she was certain, gaining access to the yellowhouse. Perhaps she could leverage Uncle to discover Nouli. Perhaps Nouli was being put to use by Uncle. For a man with Nouli's brilliance, the creation of such a drug wouldn't be too much of a stretch.

A thrill of a thought sparked in her mind – perhaps Uncle *was* in the yellowhouse. He might even be Nouli himself.

The timeline was tight, she needed all the advantage she could get. *Needed* to get close to the yellowhouse. The sticky, warm rains of the advance monsoon had proven that much to her. If she did not have Nouli in hand by the time Detan came for her, then this whole sordid adventure might be for naught. At least she'd learned a thing or two about running a prison.

She snorted, choking back a laugh. Not that she'd ever need the knowledge. One future she was quite sure was dead to her was that of advancing through the ranks of the watchers. She'd turned her back on the empire, worn her traitor brand with pride. Too bad, really. The Remnant could use a steady, clever hand instead of the garish fumbling of Radu Baset.

She dozed on the hard floor, the exhaustion deep within her bones quick to claim any moment of rest.

The crack of wood against stone awoke her. Ripka jerked awake, reached for a baton she no longer carried. Her fingers tingled from numbness, the frantic patter of her heart rushed blood to the sleeping limb so quickly it felt as if her whole hand burned.

Her cell door stood ajar, Kisser's curved frame filling it. "I know the beds are rough," she drawled, "but surely they're better than the floor?"

"Better than the well." She drew her knees to her chest to stretch them before rising.

"You really can sleep anywhere."

"Lots of practice." Ripka squinted at the man hovering behind Kisser's shoulder, trying to make out which guard Kisser had coaxed into opening Ripka's cell. She didn't recognize him, but she recognized the man standing next to the guard.

"Enard, nice to see you standing."

He rubbed at a dark purple splotch spreading across his chin and cheek. "Thanks to you, I am."

"Save it for later, lovebirds. Uncle's on a tight schedule and our lovely escort isn't even assigned to this block." She hooked her fingers in the guard's collar and steered the blushing man down the hallway. "Chop chop."

Ripka fell into step alongside Kisser, letting the guard lead the way. She swallowed an urge to whisper to Enard, to ask him if he'd found anything out during his second waterworks shift. If he'd caught scent of Nouli, then they might be able to use Kisser's abusive freedoms to find the man. To talk to him alone.

She eyed Enard's narrow back, Kisser's words from above the well floating back to her. *Glasseaters don't just leave.* She'd spent a year with Enard skirting the skies of the Scorched on Detan's flier, working and laughing alongside one another. She'd felt she'd come to know him, to trust him, to understand his motives.

But then, she'd never known his working name, Tender. Never imagined those careful, delicate hands were renown amongst the Glasseaters for the harm they dealt.

Their path shifted. The guard used one of his many keys to open a door leading toward the staff's quarters. Her heart sank. Unless he was about to show her a network of secret tunnels, they weren't headed anywhere near the yellowhouse. She'd have to find another way out there.

The guard heaved up a heavy beam that barred yet another door, standing aside so that Kisser could enter first. Ripka blinked in the faint haze that filled the large workroom.

Oil lamps dotted the walls, casting unctuous light over a long table – obviously stolen from the rec yard – on which a collection of strange glass and metal instruments stood. A small brazier licked flames over the bottom of an amberglass flask. The fumes from the bottle had been angled so that they'd leave the room through a silver grating, about the height where a window would be. The scent of mudleaf clung to the air – not the acrid bite of the smoke, but the sweet scent of the raw plant, green but cloying.

A sleeping cot huddled against the far wall, neglected with lumps of twisted blankets. Dog-eared notebooks scattered the ground like fallen leaves. At the far end of the table, a man – she supposed he was Uncle – bent over a notebook, graphite scribbling furiously, his ash-grey hair stuck up all askew. Kisser cleared her throat.

Uncle looked up, a pleased smile deepening the crevasses

of his features. Ripka's heart skipped a beat. She knew that face. Had studied drawings of it for months.

Nouli Bern.

"Ah, my dear girl," Nouli said as he came around the table, wizened hands outstretched toward Kisser. "Who have you brought me?"

Kisser clasped the man's hands and kissed his cheeks, then pointed her chin at Ripka. "This is Cap—"

Ripka shushed her with a shake of her head, heart pounding in her ears loud enough to wake the dead, and stepped forward. Enard went still, silent, his lips parted in a little "O" of surprise.

This was it. Their chance. She could no longer fear Kisser learning too much about her motives for being within the Remnant. Ripka lifted her palms before her, open toward the skies, to show her respect.

"Well met under blue skies, Nouli Bern. My name is Ripka Leshe. I have come on behalf of the city of Hond Steading to beg your help."

"Oh," Nouli said, "oh my."

Kisser's wide hand fell upon Nouli's shoulder.

"Where," she said firmly, "did you learn *that* name?"

CHAPTER 21

The combined talents of all the deviants aboard did a splendid job of making the *Larkspur* look like a standard Fleet cruiser once more. And they'd been polite enough not to comment on the amount of sel they were missing due to Detan's outburst. Despite the resource's depletion, the remaining selium wrapped around the ship made Detan's skin itch, and not only because it was a fortune's worth of the material.

If he were to lose his temper again, he'd take half of Petrastad with him. The thought froze him to the spot, arrested his steps as he marched down the gangplank toward the grand double-doors of the watchtower. The *Larkspur* loomed behind him, its presence oppressive. So high above the city, the sea winds bit beneath the shelter of his stolen coat, but the chill wasn't near enough to shake the fear from him.

Tibs gave him a gentle nudge in the shoulder. Right. Tibs was here. He'd never let Detan lose control like that. It was their deal – the cornerstone of their relationship. They balanced one another with jokes and barbs, skirted around the short-leashed tempers in both their hearts.

Detan dropped his voice to a whisper. "We're going to save a damsel in distress from a tower, just like in fairy tales."

"Don't let Pelkaia hear you say that, she'll pop your eyes out and throw 'em in a stew."

"Oh, have a little fun. Has it occurred to you that we're breaking a woman out of jail, to break a woman out of jail?"

"Thought had crossed my mind."

"Once this is through, I don't want to see another set of bars for a year. Not so much as a sharpening rod."

"Rather thought you were enjoying yourself."

Detan stifled a grin. "Shut up, Tibs."

"As you say, sirra."

A few long strides ahead of them Laella paused, sized them up with a wary eye, and snapped her fingers. "Hurry up, louts. We have two prisoners to take custody of. Prisoners you idiots let go."

She spun on her heel, the long commodore's coat flying out behind her like a standard of arms, and strode toward the unsuspecting lobby of the watchtower. Detan suppressed a whistle of appreciation. Essl'd been right, picking Laella for this job. The girl had her uppercrust act down pat. Probably because she'd grown up as one, just as Detan had.

The watchers' dock was a two-tier affair, and as they ambled along Detan peered down to get a better look at their neighbors. Only one of the watcher ships was currently manned. A short-bodied barge with a three large buoyancy sacks netted above it, the craft was packed with a handful of watchers. At least three, Detan realized with a start, were sensitives. They appeared to be doing maintenance on the ship – holding sel in place while workers patched the buoyancy sacks. Their presence made him nervous. If they were strong enough to sense the sel hiding the *Larkspur*'s shape, this whole plan might come apart at the seams.

One of the watchtower doors lurched open, the tall pane of lantern light from within casting Laella in silhouette. In flat black outline, her chin high and her stride certain, coat making her figure mast pole-straight, she looked disturbingly like a whitecoat. Detan suppressed a shudder.

"It is the middle of the sands-cursed night," a watcher, in a much fancier coat than the ones who'd come to cart Pelkaia away, said. It was a style of coat he'd come to think of as Ripka's coat. Seeing it on another watcher's shoulders made him scowl. The sturdy man strode out to meet Laella, his back near as straight as hers despite the grey in his beard. "Can you not wait until morning, commodore? At this hour my staff is thin enough. We cannot spare the distraction."

Laella paused, letting the watch-captain close the remaining distance between them. A power move, that. Detan couldn't help but wonder how far the girl had advanced in her courtly etiquette training before Pelkaia had whisked her away to the safety of the sky.

Detan and Tibs stood at ease, flanking Laella a half-step behind her on either side, their hands laid over the grips of cutlasses neither of them knew how to use. The blades had been loaners from Pelkaia's costume trunk, just like Laella's coat.

"I have come to relieve your staff of some of their burden." She modulated her voice downward to lend it carrying power and propped one hand on her hip, admiring the nailbeds of her other hand. The watch-captain frowned at this. Poor move. The staunch old man wasn't likely to take kindly to a bored, disaffected noble. Even if she was in a commodore's coat.

"If it's prisoners you're after, come back in the morning. They'll keep in their cells until the light."

She jerked a thumb over her shoulder toward the clouds, switching from bored to controlled anger so fast it made Detan's head spin. "Do you not see the storm approaching? A half-mark ago the sky was filled with the strangest lightning I've ever seen. Monsoon season comes. I'll have my prisoners back now so that I can see them securely to the Remnant."

Detan flinched as the watch-captain eyed the blackened

sky, wary. Either he'd seen Detan's little firestorm, or he'd heard rumors of it already. To Detan's senses, the very air held the soft, charred aroma of ash.

One of the watchers who had taken Pelkaia away in the goat-cart appeared over the watch-captain's shoulder, a sheaf of papers tucked under one arm and a sour expression on his drooping, exhausted face. Before the watch-captain could give his answer, Detan pointed at the young watcher.

"There! That's the man who took our prisoners." The watcher's head jerked up as he looked for his accuser. Upon sighting Tibs and Detan, his shoulders heaved with a tired sigh.

"You!" Laella approached the man, shouldering the watch-captain aside. Detan followed, giving the captain an apologetic pat on the shoulder as he passed. "You are the man who commandeered Fleet prisoners from my men?"

"Uh," the watcher muttered, glancing from the advancing gale that was Laella to his captain and back again. "They were our prisoners, commodore."

"Really." She stopped an arm's length away from the poor sod and jabbed a finger into his chest. "Was that before, or after, they shot a Fleetman in the leg with an arrow?"

"Crossbow," Detan whispered.

"Even worse!" Laella threw her hands toward the skies in frustration.

"They may have shot a Fleetie," the watcher said.

"A *what*?"

"A, uh, Fleetman, but they did it in Petrastad. Means they're ours."

"He's right." The watch-captain crossed the lobby and stood beside his watcher, thumbs hooked in his belt loops and back slouched with ease. Detan silently cursed himself. He shouldn't have let them retreat to the safety of their tower walls. They should have stayed out on the dock, where the shadow of the so-called commodore's cruiser could loom over them.

"Those two did their crime on Petrastad's soil. They're ours," the captain continued, jutting his chin out as if punctuating his point.

Laella drew her head back, squared off her shoulders, and curled her lip in the most vicious snarl Detan'd ever seen. He was suddenly quite happy she was on their side. If it weren't for her deviant abilities, she'd have been the perfect cog in Valathea's imperial machine.

"Do you think the Fleet cares about your petty soil? We guard the skies, captain, and everything below them. I will take those prisoners now. Bring me to them."

The captain shared a look with the watcher, weighing the value of winning this argument against getting to bed at a decent hour. "All right, commodore. You can have your shooter, but I'm keeping the other."

"I think not. The other is an accomplice. They are both guilty of violations against the very sky we of the Fleet patrol. I'll have them both, or I'll have you both."

Detan stiffened as he and Tibs became the subject of the watch-captain's scrutiny. He wanted to twist Laella's ear for putting them on display. They were no fighting men, they couldn't hold the old watch-captain and the watcher if they'd wanted to. He forced himself to stand straight, yet easy, forced his fingertips to play over the grip of his cutlass as if he knew what to do with it. He could only hope it looked good enough.

The watch-captain sighed. "Two lousy thieves are not worth all this bickering. I assume you two are capable of overseeing the transport?"

"Aye, sir," Tibs said.

"Good, follow me."

The captain waved the other watcher back to his business and led their motley party across the lobby. He paused at a large desk, a horseshoe of a thing taking up half the room, and rifled through a stack of folders until he found the one he wanted.

"Your name please, commodore?" He blotted a pen and poised it above a sheet of paper.

"Laella Eradin."

Detan blanched. Her real name. Unless the family name was faked, but he had no reason to doubt that the impervious girl was a member of the Mercer Eradin family. His stomach churned in panic as the captain's hoary brows rose. Throwing out a heavily Valathean name like that would work in any backwater town, like Cracked Thorn, but here? In the largest port on the southern coast? Detan held his breath.

"I see. And your ship?"

"The *Mirror*," Laella said, not the slightest hitch of hesitation in her voice. At least she hadn't said *Larkspur*.

"Never heard of it," the captain said, eyeing her. He had yet to write any of this information down.

"I do not see how your ignorance is my problem. Hurry up, I do not wish to lose the wind."

Detan cringed. Never sound impatient when you've roused a mark's suspicions, he thought, but it was far too late to teach the girl that now.

To Detan's immense relief, the captain shrugged, scribbled in his notes, and left the folder open on the counter to dry. Spinning a ring of keys around his finger, he bade them follow him down a wide corridor, growing narrower with every step. The labeled doors of watcher offices gave way to blank wooden planks and then, after a short jaunt up a flight of steps, row upon row of heavily iron-banded doors. There was far too much wood being used for construction in this city. He missed the old stone methods of the Scorched's interior, where trees were rarer than a woman willing to smile at him.

Lanterns hung between each door, but still the hall felt dark, oppressive. Just like every other jail cell he'd ever had the misfortune of visiting. Even if he never planned on staying long, something about that gloom always clung to him, weighed him down. Detan fidgeted with the handle of the cutlass he didn't know how to use, anxious to be back out under the sky.

Midway down the hall a guard sat astride a tall stool, his coat unbuttoned and crumpled at a sloppy angle. Detan smirked a little. Ripka would never allow one of her watchers to nap while on guard, let alone dress so poorly. Aransa had lost itself one blasted fine watch-captain when Thratia had made Ripka walk the Black Wash.

"Pedar!" The captain sped his stride. "Wake up, you oaf. We have Fleet visitors!"

He grabbed the man's skewed lapels, and the guard's head lolled to the side. A trickle of blood rolled down from the corner of his lips. "Pits below!" He pressed his fingers against the guard's neck to check his pulse.

"Is he all right?" Detan blurted, taking a half step forward. Laella threw a sharp eye on him – a Fleetie would never take excess action without direct orders from their commodore.

"I don't blasted know! Go call for a cursed apothik."

They hesitated, not wanting to break up their group without a plan in place. "How should I know where to get an apothik?" Detan asked. "I've never been in your tower before."

"Go," Laella said to the captain. She stepped forward and slipped her hand beneath the injured guard's neck to support his head. "I'll look after the man – we'd take too long finding our way."

The captain nodded and eased the guard's weight into Laella's hold. For a man easily twice Detan's age, he certainly hustled as he ran down the hall the way they'd come, calling a name Detan couldn't quite make out. When he disappeared down the steps, Detan rushed over to the guard and claimed his keyring.

"If Pelkaia started the party without me, I swear to the pits..." he muttered, keeping his voice low in case Pedar could overhear.

"What do you mean?" Laella asked, poking at the man's sallow cheeks.

"Whose handiwork do you think that is?" Tibs waved a hand toward the guard.

Laella paled. "Oh..."

"Which one?" Detan asked Tibs.

"Third to your left for Pelkaia, then two down again for Coss."

"How in the clear skies do you know that?" Laella demanded.

"Got a look at the release forms." Tibs shrugged.

"We've been doing..." Detan waved a hand through the air as if to encompass the whole world as he strode off toward the first cell Tibs indicated "...*this* for a while. You get used to it. You learn where to look."

He jammed the skeleton key in its slot and twisted, then flung the door open. Empty. Swearing himself blue, he hustled down to Coss's supposed cell and flung it open, too.

Empty.

"Thrice-cursed woman." He slapped the wall with an open palm and winced. His anger hadn't all boiled off yet. He needed to calm down, and chasing Pelly through a damp city wasn't helping matters much.

"Hurry on now," Tibs urged. Detan glanced his way – Tibs was busy pulling Laella away from the injured man. "He'll be fine, help's on the way, and Pelkaia'll be making her way back to the ship – we gotta beat her back before–"

"What in the pits are you doing?" the watch-captain yelled down the hall, his wizened face red with anger and exertion, and probably a touch of fear. Two apothiks trailed him, the women's white aprons threatening to bring up some mighty uncomfortable memories.

Detan swallowed his past, abandoned his plans, and strode toward the captain, shaking the keys to distract the man from Laella's stunned expression.

"You idiot watchers! The prisoners have escaped!"

"What?" The captain stopped mid-stride, aghast.

"Bloody empty!" Tibs jerked his thumb at the opened cells. One of the apothiks gasped.

The captain recovered his composure with admirable speed. Pointing at the apothik who had gasped, he said, "You, go ring the alarm."

"Y-yes, sir!" She whirled and sprinted down the stairs while her compatriot advanced upon the injured guard.

Detan turned to make eye contact with Tibs, hoping the wiry old bastard would have something in mind. Tibs raised his brows at him in question.

The great brass bells of the watchtower began to ring, the boom of them thundering straight through to his heart.

CHAPTER 22

Coss threw her a stink eye through the shadow of the alcove in which they hid, pressed up hard against the cold stone as they waited for footsteps to dwindle down the hall.

"Will you please take that stupid face off?" he whispered.

Pelkaia grinned, twisting up the borrowed visage of the watcher who had arrested them. "What? Don't you want to kiss me like this?" She leaned forward, smacking the borrowed lips.

He hid a laugh behind his hand and gave her a shove. "Ugh. Stop it. We're *trying* to be quiet. Although," his voice dropped low, "it is good to see you laugh again."

She brushed him off, setting aside the temporary intimacy. Adrenaline thrummed through her veins, making her loose and silly. The mania that seized her whenever she spilt blood burgeoned within her chest, pushing her to do more. To take risks. She needed to focus, find her core of control. It wouldn't be long until the guard she'd tricked into releasing her by wearing his colleague's face was discovered, and their empty cells shortly after that.

Curse Petrastad for building everything so tall. If they were in any other station house in any other Scorched city, they could have climbed out of a window by now. Or at the very least discovered the blasted front door. The footsteps that had urged them to hide petered off into the distance, and her shoulders slumped with relief. Even with her bone-braces, her body ached if she forced it to hold one position for too long.

"Which way?" Coss asked, sticking his head back out into the hall. She had no idea – it all looked the same to her, endless wood paneling and naked stone – but she was his captain. He relied on her to guide them to freedom.

And once free, they'd pummel Honding for his failures together. The very thought gave her cheer. Pelkaia tore off down the western arm of the hall, away from the footsteps, and hoped she had picked true.

"Slow down," Coss said. He pressed a hand against the back of her arm. "Running will just draw attention. The ship will be there when we get back."

He gave her his sweet, lopsided smile. She slowed. "Don't count on it. The longer we leave Detan without supervision, the more likely we are to discover everything's gone to the pits while we were away. That man..." She clenched her fists and paused, peering left and right down a forked hallway. More wood paneling, more doors marked with numbers that might as well have been in an alien language. No staircase. Except... There was a little well of darkness to the left where the lantern light could not quite penetrate all the way to the floor. Promising.

"The very fact he went off-script at the vault indicates he's up to something."

"It was my fault the guardsmen grew suspicious of us," Coss insisted. "You can't blame him for that. And, well, I didn't mean to start a fight, but..."

She bit her lip to keep from reminding him that he was not yet as practiced at violence as she – that he'd been so wound up and itching to brawl that the guard couldn't help but notice and take an interest in them. He'd learn, and grow comfortable with it, or he wouldn't and she'd leave him behind next time. But that wasn't an argument she was willing to have now, with the watchers of Petrastad breathing down their necks.

"Hurry, we must reach the ship before Detan does."

Coss scoffed. "You don't really think he could win the *Mirror* away from the crew in your absence? Jeffin wouldn't let him so much as touch the deck."

They reached the spot of darkness and found a spiral set of hard, stone stairs descending into the black. Dust coated the steps, and unlit lanterns hung from iron hooks. This was access for cleaning staff, or goods transport. Not the warm, rug-run flight of stairs she and Coss had been escorted up. The servants were bound to have easier access to the outdoors, and set away from prying eyes at that. It felt good to have solid, raw stone beneath her feet again, even if the hardness of the stone jarred her aging joints.

"I pray you're right," she said as she doubled back to snatch a lit lantern from the hallway and plunged down the first flight of steps. It was colder in the stairwell. They must be close to the edge of the building now, away from the insulated and fire-warmed interior. "Though I find myself wishing you had thrown him off that jetty in Cracked Thorn."

Halfway down the next level, bells pealed out the alarm. The deep, throaty vibrations reached through the hard stone to vibrate her tired bones. She glanced back, up the steps, and saw Coss's eyes wide and white-rimmed in the faint light of her lantern. The thunder of the bell echoed, hammering her ears.

"Run," Coss mouthed.

Pelkaia took off at a sprint, Coss's boots thudding behind her in rhythm with the bells, the lantern swinging crazily in her hand, throwing shadows in all directions.

How they'd discovered their absence so quickly, she could not figure out. The watcher who'd slammed the door on them had told her they'd missed the dinner hour, and handed them each a crumpled roll and jug of stale water to last until the morning meal. She'd thought they'd have time – maybe even all night – to find their way out of this maze of a tower.

Pelkaia's foot hit a floor landing, and the door beside her swung open. A maid, clutching a basket of laundry to her belly, screamed and dropped her burden. Linens twin to those from her cell spilled across the landing, tangling the maid's feet, though these smelled considerably fresher than the sheets Pelkaia had been stuck with.

"Mallie!" a voice called from behind the maid. "Are you all right?"

Mallie opened her mouth to scream again, but Pelkaia grabbed the woman's arm and yanked her onto the stair landing. Her screech became a breathless squeak as Pelkaia whirled her around and grabbed her tight.

"Don't scream," Coss hissed, racing forward to shut the door halfway so that they could not be seen from the hall behind it. "Call to your friend, tell her you're well and no harm will befall you."

Pelkaia watched the young woman's gaze flick side to side, watched her lick her lips as she considered her options. A brave heart, this one. Pelkaia jabbed two knuckles into her back, above her kidney. She had no weapon, but the maid didn't know that.

"I'm fine!" Mallie called, voice cracking. "Saw a rat!"

"Ugh!" Footsteps stomped away, difficult to hear over the clamor of the alarm bells. Coss crept forward after a pause, peered around the door, then dragged the laundry onto the stair's landing and shut the door the rest of the way.

"Speak softly," Pelkaia whispered to the maid. "And tell us the way out of this nightmarish place."

"Y-you must go down to the third level, miss. That's the closest. Then down the hall, all the way. There'll be a door, it opens up to a walkway that crosses to the washers' house.

Can you let me go now, please? I won't tell anyone, I swear it."

"Sorry, Mallie. You're coming with us as far as the washers' house. If you don't make a peep, you'll be fine. Understand?"

She trembled, but nodded, not so much as murmuring agreement. Quick learner. Dragging Mallie along with them slowed them, and though Pelkaia could see the frustration writ clear in Coss's anxious steps she was soothed by the maid's presence. They knew where they were going. No amount of fleeing at speed could have outpaced that knowledge.

Down one level. Two. Three. Sweat beaded on her brow, dripped into her eyes and blurred her vision with her own stinging salt. Splitting her concentration between holding the selium against her face, escorting the maid, and being mindful of her steps was taking its toll. Her slopped-together mask must look grotesque, but she was loathe to give up the anonymity it offered her.

"I'll take her," Coss said, reaching out to gather the maid in his thicker arm.

The maid squirmed, clearly irritated at being shoved around so. Her pinched gaze fell upon Pelkaia's hands. Saw the lack of weapon in them. Her eyes widened, her lips pressed together in anger. Her head reared back, smacking Coss in the nose. Pelkaia lunged forward, but the maid twisted away.

"He-elp!" she screamed, cupping one hand around her mouth while she hiked her skirts with the other and bolted swift as a monsoon wind down the steps. Her first cry was drowned out by the great clash of the alarm bells, but Pelkaia could see her gather her breath for another roar.

"By the pits," Coss growled, covering his nose with one hand. A thin, bloody trickle rolled over his lips.

"Help!" Mallie screeched high enough to make Pelkaia cringe. The maid was already a great many flights below them, her voice echoing up through the shaft of spiraling stone steps.

"Forget her," Pelkaia said as she grabbed Coss's arm and urged him forward. "We can't be far, and we must be quick."

He grunted, smeared the blood from his nose across the back of his wrist, and followed her at a sprint down the steps. Pelkaia leaned forward into her gait, urging her tired body to fly down the stones.

"Here!" Coss grabbed her arm, thick fingers digging into her flesh as she jerked to a halt. Not bothering to explain, he lunged for the next door and flung it open – Pelkaia caught only a brief glimpse of the number three carved into the old wood – and dragged her through.

The hallway was narrow, the runner-rug thin and the air redolent with warm soap smells. A single door stood at the end of it, painted a sunny yellow. Waiting.

They surged forward. Pelkaia's breath burned over her lips, down her throat, doing little to ease the ache in her chest. Coss flung the door open and they barreled through. The walkway was narrow, but sturdy. It lead to a dark building, to a twin yellow door. Despite the angry lash of the sea winds, the laundry building radiated the faint scent of grit soap and lilacs. Shouts sounded behind them, distant, but growing near.

Pelkaia stumbled, boot catching on a board, and twisted just in time to land hard on her side instead of pitching over the three-story drop to the road below. She gasped as the jar of the fall shuddered through her, enhancing the ache of her already tired body. Her bone-braces could do little against a fall at full speed. Coss's hands were already upon her, lifting, searching for breaks.

As she staggered to her feet she looked back, glancing at the sky instinctively. Her heart missed a beat.

"Pell, what is it?" Concern and fear mingled on his dirt-smudged face. He followed her eye-line, saw the familiar – if obscured – shape of their ship docked against the watchtower.

"What the..." He rubbed his cheeks as if he could massage away the sight.

Pelkaia let out a strangled laugh. "That's what I get, working with Honding. He's here. That daft-headed man came for us. Come on. Let's go get ourselves arrested again."

She wiped the sweat from her face with the bottom of her shirt, then rearranged her mask to the one she had worn when they had been arrested. Through all their fleeing, she had lost a few bits of the mask. It lay thin and patchy against her skin. Fine for fooling an overworked watcher, but no good for close scrutiny.

"Coss, I hate to ask, but..."

He took one look at her face and grimaced. "I see the problem. Give me a moment."

Steadying himself with the handrail, he stared straight at a piece of empty air between them. Her skin tingled as he accessed his sel-sense, focused on the very rawest edge of his sensitivity. While he could see the minute particles of sel drifting in the air at all times, he could also, when matters were desperate, reach out and wrench some of those bits and pieces together – force them to gel into something large enough for another, less fine-tuned, sensitive to use.

He grunted. A little pearl shimmered between them and began to rise. Pelkaia snapped out her senses and captured the new glob of sel, adding it to the thin parts of her mask, trying to ignore the paleness in Coss's cheeks, the slight shiver in the muscles of his arms.

"How is it?"

Coss gave her a tight nod, too tired to waste breath on speech. It would do. He brushed the hair from her forehead, securing it behind her ear, and she ignored the warmth of his touch as she turned back to the station-house. She could not afford to be distracted. Not when Detan Honding waited for her on the other side of that garish, yellow door.

CHAPTER 23

The watch-captain proved fleeter on his feet than Detan had imagined. Panting, he half ran, half stumbled down the stairs after the man. Laella and Tibs pulled ahead to nip at the watch-captain's heels, drawing a glare from Detan. Rude of them to leave him behind. Short bursts from the captain's whistle echoed throughout the stairwell, bouncing off the wooden paneling and piercing his ears. Combined with the steady clang of the alarm bells, Detan feared his head would explode.

"Is that really necessary?" he yelled.

A toot of whistles answered the watch-captain's call from down below. Detan grimaced, understanding. There was no other way for the watchers to communicate amongst themselves as long as those infernal bells thumped along.

"They've been spotted in the service stairs!" the captain cried, and Detan rolled his eyes. Of course that's the way they'd gone – he'd insisted as much before the captain had gone tearing off down the main stairwell. Bloody incompetent lot, these Petrastad watchers. Too simple in their thinking. What he wouldn't give for Ripka to be the watch-captain here, today. At least she was a pleasure to fence with. This cockerel posturing was going to drain his patience, fast.

Blasted Pelkaia. Should have lounged around waiting for rescue, brushing her hair and singing to little birds, or whatever it was damsels in distress did while the knights got run off their feet in the old stories.

The captain wrenched a door open and they jumbled out after him, zigzagging through the maze of corridors that made up the watchtower. There was a certain freedom in having no idea where you were or where you were going. He figured that, at the very least, no one could blame him if they took a wrong turn, and that was fine by him. Detan was getting right sick of shouldering the blame around here.

They reached a darkened alcove, and the captain paused to wrench a lantern from the wall. While they waited for him to wick the light up, Detan grabbed Tibs's arm and pulled him close to whisper.

"New plan; talk over Laella if you have to. Blasted girl is too honest."

"You have a *plan*?"

"I will by the time we find 'em."

Tibs cracked a grin and pulled away, tearing off after the hustling captain. Detan groaned. If Pelkaia didn't have the facilities aboard the *Larkspur* to give him a long, hot bath after this, he was going to insist they turn right back around and drop him at the Salt Baths in Aransa. To the pits with Thratia and her bastard army. The pain in his knees was worse than her trying to kill him.

Cursing under his breath with every thudding step, he forced himself to hurry along, counting on the others to do any finding that needed to be done. He let his mind wander, seeking ahead of their current predicament, trying to see his way through to how in the pits he was going to wiggle Pelkaia and her first mate away from the watchers' hands now that she'd gone and embarrassed them by escaping.

Shouldn't be too hard. He could twist their escape around, make it look like the watchers weren't capable of holding onto a high-value prisoner. It'd be a risk to insult the captain, sure, but Laella'd already gone ahead and stuck her foot down that muddy path, so he might as well roll along with it.

At least Pelkaia'd owe him big after this. He was looking forward to that prize.

The bells sounded duller in the service stairs, muffled by thick stone. While the alarm hadn't ceased, the big thumps came further and further apart – not relinquishing the emergency, but allowing the watchers space to better communicate. Through a break in the bells, a woman's cries echoed up from below. He couldn't tell if the voice was Pelkaia's, and added speed to his struggling steps. When had he grown so achy? He'd never felt so old before. So bone-weary.

A maid crashed into the captain, fleeing up the steps. He grunted, but steadied them both. Detan woofed down air as they caught their balance and their breath.

"Are you all right, miss? Have you seen the escapees?"

"Third floor!" she gasped the words out, pointing back up to the level they'd just passed. "Going for the laundry building!"

"Are you injured?" the captain asked, but Detan was already scurrying ahead. Having fallen behind the others, he was first back up to the third floor. He found the door unlatched and hurried through, closing it enough to give the captain pause. He hoped he could get eyes on Pelkaia before the others arrived and communicate to her somehow to stand down.

No luck. The hall beyond the door was empty, save for a half-opened yellow door at the opposite end. Laella barged in after him, flinging the door wide, and Detan stifled a sigh. He'd have to teach the girl some of the more subtle tricks of his craft if they all made it out of this.

He jogged to the yellow door, grateful for what little padding the thin rug offered, and tugged it all the way open.

Pelkaia stood directly before him, her stranger's face on

despite the sweat glistening across her chest. Her mouth dropped open in shock. For a heartbeat, Detan was tempted to grab her and flee, but he knew that those left on board the ship wouldn't figure out they needed to leave the watchtower right up until a bunch of watchers crawled over their deck.

Shit. What would a Fleetie guard say in this situation? Shoulda let old Tibs go ahead, he'd know what to do.

"Uh," he blathered. "Stand down!"

That was a thing military types said, wasn't it? Judging by the way Pelkaia rolled her eyes, he guessed he missed his mark. She took a half step back, hesitant, glancing down the rope bridge to Detan and back.

He realized her problem. If she were escaping, she'd punch him and run. But she'd cottoned on to the game, and she didn't want to get into a scuffle with him. It'd be too obvious that she'd have to fake losing – he'd never been deft in a fight.

"My face!" Coss yelled from behind Pelkaia, making them both jump. The sturdy lad fell to the floor so hard he rocked the bridge, nearly pitching Pelkaia over. Pelkaia dropped to her knees to steady her groaning first mate, and Detan peered over her shoulder, surprised to find the man's face was indeed smeared with blood. Huh.

"What's happening here?" the captain called. Detan glanced over his shoulder in time to see the blue-coated bastard shove his way past Laella and Tibs. Detan had the good sense to shake his hand out as if he'd dealt Coss a mighty blow and was aching from it.

"Found 'em, captain. Have your lads wrap 'em up so we can get off this cursed rock before the storm sets in."

"Good work." The captain clapped Detan on the shoulder as he shoved him aside to get to Pelkaia and Coss. "One of the apothiks can get you a salve for that hand."

The captain gave his whistle a rhythmic series of high blasts, and soon the hall was so deep with blue coats Detan began to feel he'd been set adrift at sea. Being surrounded by so much authority made him decidedly queasy. He feigned an ache in his hand and slithered to the back of the hall, keeping an eye on things while Pelkaia and Coss were trussed up good and tight. He grinned a little. They weren't being gentle this time 'round. Despite the gaggle of watchers, not a one was willing to let their recaptured prisoners get even the tiniest bit loose.

"I thank you for your assistance," Laella said to the captain. Detan's head jerked up and he tried to spot Tibs in the crowd. Tibs had gotten himself in with the prisoner escort and had a hand squarely on the ropes wrapped around Pelkaia's wrists. Too far away to intervene if Laella began to lose the plot. Trying to make it look casual, he waited for her to pass him by and fell in step beside her, joining the little blue procession back up the watchtower – and hopefully to the deck of the *Larkspur*.

"Assistance?" The captain wiped sweat from his brow to the back of his sleeve. "That wasn't for you, commodore. Those two bastards knocked one of my men clear out. You know how bad that can be for a mind? He'd been out awhile, too. If he suffers any permanent damage..." He trailed off, rubbing one fist around and around in the palm of his other hand as he imagined all the nasty he things he might do to Pelkaia and Coss.

Detan suppressed a sigh. And it had all been going so well... Up until the alarm bells and empty cells, at any rate.

Laella straightened a few strands of hair that had flown free during the chase and squared her shoulders. "I will personally see to it that they work hard labor on the Remnant."

"Remnant?" The captain cast her a sidelong glance. "I think not. They assaulted a watcher, they will serve their time under a watcher roof, penned in by watcher walls."

"Are you mad?" Laella scoffed and tossed her head. Detan winced at her overacting. "They *shot* a Fleetman! They are mine to do with as I please, and I will take them to the cold care of the Remnant."

"Begging your pardon, commodore, but you have no jurisdiction–"

Detan rubbed his temples to smooth out the pounding their bickering brought on. They were over halfway back up the tower, if the ache in Detan's legs was any marker to go by. He had to get the captain's mind turned around quick. It was time to yank the rockcat's tail.

"Pardon me, watch-captain," he interjected, laying on as much scorn as he could muster. "But we can hardly trust you to keep *anything* under a watcher roof. These two failed thieves were under your care scarcely more than a mark and already they'd run off halfway to the laundry hut. You're incapable of containing them. Unless, of course, you *want* them running free...?"

"How dare you!" The captain's cheeks flared red and his eyes bugged out as he whirled upon Detan. "This is the most secure facility in all of Petrastad!"

Detan mustered up a wide yawn. "Really? How quaint. Then I suppose we cannot leave them here, if this is the best you've to offer."

The captain punched him. Detan's head jerked and he exaggerated a sideways stumble, just managing to catch himself on the stairwell banister. Bright, stinging pain exploded across his face, followed by a cold, numbing sensation and then a dull, aching warmth. A trickle of blood strolled down his lip. Though it stung like fire ants, he was glad for the dramatic flair of a spot of blood.

The sea of watchers stilled, fell silent. Detan rubbed his cheek and genuinely flinched. Tibs caught his eye, and there was so much anger in that gaze Detan half expected him to rip the watch-captain's head clear off. Detan gave a slight shake of the head, and reminded himself to be more careful. Tibs's temper wasn't as quick to boil as his own, but it was dangerous all the same. He may not be a dab hand in a fight, but that didn't mean Tibs was unable of exacting some punishment when he felt the need. Detan turned, slowly, to regard the captain. He was staring at his hand as if it'd betrayed him.

"I... I apologize, Fleetman...?" He stumbled over his words, realizing he did not even know Detan's name.

Laella stepped close to the captain and dropped her voice to a low hiss. "I will forgive this trespass against the Fleet, if you relinquish the prisoners to my control."

The knot of his throat bobbed twice in quick succession. He nodded. "They are yours."

Laella turned sharp on her heel, skies bless her, and strode up the stone steps like she owned them. The stunned watchers shifted aside to let her pass, then reluctantly fell into step once more, herding their prisoners back up toward the lobby. Detan was chagrined to spot a wide, delighted smile on Pelkaia's borrowed face.

They passed the rest of the way up the steps in tense silence, save for the labored breathing of a few – Detan included – who'd rather overdone it in all the excitement. His face ached, making deep breaths an uncomfortable arrangement, but he figured a little sting was easier to deal with than convincing that captain to give up his charges willingly.

Wasn't the first time he'd riled a man into punching him, and it wouldn't be the last.

While Laella and the captain filled out the necessary transfer paperwork – all forged on Laella's end, of course – Detan slunk over to Tibs, Pelkaia, and Coss. He didn't dare say a word, but it felt good to have the thing – or people – he'd come to filch close by. Made him confident he'd win through. And had the added benefit of hiding him from view of the cursed apothik roaming around the lobby, checking the watchers for injury. Last thing he needed right now was a sour memory of whitecoats and cold potions setting off his fear – and his anger. He was already a might uncomfortable with the selium plastered to Pelkaia's face.

"If that will be all...?" Laella said, letting her tone make it clear as a blue sky that had *better* be all.

"Yes, of course," the captain said, his voice subdued now that he'd screwed himself out of his quarry. Detan couldn't blame the man. He knew what it was like to lose your temper, to lash out without thought and ruin damned near everything. "Gag 'em up for transport," he added.

Detan blinked as the meaning settled over him. He turned, caught Pelkaia's eyes growing wide with panic. "That's not necessary," he rushed over the words, reaching out to stop her watcher.

Too late. The watcher wrapped a clean, white linen gag around Pelkaia's mouth, tugged it tight against her cheeks. Against her false, selium-crafted cheeks, Pelkaia was good, but she couldn't shift the sel that fast. No one could.

Her flesh shimmered in the tell-tale hues only sel could produce.

"Doppel!" the watcher who'd gagged her cried and leapt back as if his fingers had been burned.

A roar of outrage waved through the gathered sea of blue. Detan looked to Tibs, to Pelkaia, to Coss and to Laella. All wore baffled faces.

There was no conning their way out of this. Doppels were put to death. Always.

"Run!" he yelled, kicking the legs out from under the watcher standing between him and Pelkaia. The dock wasn't far. They could make it. They had to.

CHAPTER 24

"Nouli's name?" Ripka asked, taking a half-step backward.

The muscles of Kisser's neck jumped and she closed the distance Ripka had put between them. "Yes. Tell me how you know of my uncle."

Ripka licked her lips, resisting an urge to glance to Enard for guidance. She knew Detan's story of Nouli's exploits as well as he did. "Detan Honding told me of his inventions. Of his time spent in Valathea, and with Thratia Ganal when she took over the Saldive Isles."

A soft sound escaped Nouli's lips, something between a moan and a curse, and he shuffled away from them, covering half his face with one hand as he eased himself onto a bench with the other. He knocked piles of clothes to the ground, and didn't seem to notice. Ripka's stomach fell. This was the great Nouli Bern?

Kisser stepped to Ripka's side and dropped her voice, nearly pressing her lips against Ripka's ear as she whispered, "Do you have any idea what you're doing to him?"

Ripka's back stiffened at the insinuation that she meant Nouli harm. Enard placed his hand on Kisser's arm and turned her, gently, toward him, his voice soft as silk. "Tell us."

She snorted and shook him off. "Why would I talk to you,

Glasseater?" She shooed them away. "Get out. Leave him in peace."

Ripka locked her gaze on Nouli, on every deep line of his wizened face, trying to judge what he'd say, what he'd do. She wished Detan were here. He was better at reading people and adjusting schemes on the fly than she was.

Skies above, until a year ago she'd never needed to have schemes outside of the petty politics of the watch.

"We don't mean any harm," she said.

"It's all right," Nouli spoke to Kisser without looking at her. His shock had faded, his face slack. He appeared calm to her now, though she couldn't tell if it was his strength or his panic that had fled him. "Let her speak her piece."

Kisser huffed and crossed her arms. It was as much permission as Ripka could ever hope to get. Stifling an urge to shove Kisser aside and drop to her knees before Nouli, she cleared her throat and said, "I know you've been here a long time, Master Bern. Have you heard of Thratia Ganal's seizure of Aransa?"

He wiped his hands on a clean cloth thrown over his shoulder and glanced at Kisser.

"Tell her what you want, Uncle, you're the one who wanted to hear what she has to say."

With a sigh he stood, shaky, and settled onto a stool behind the table, making a shield of his instruments. He gestured to a few crates scattered nearby. "Please, sit. I suspect this conversation will take longer than anticipated. Yes, I am aware of Ganal's dictatorship in Aransa. What does it matter to you?"

"Aransa was my city... my home. Though I knew her rule would be with a firm hand, I had not guessed that she would go so far as to buck all imperial influence. She's created a city-state for herself, independent of the governance of Valathea."

"So she thinks," Kisser scoffed.

"Hush," Nouli said. "Please continue, Miss...?"

"Leshe," she reminded him. Ripka took the proffered seat on an old crate, and Enard dragged over its twin to sit beside her.

Enard cleared his throat. "Forgive me, Master Bern, but before we continue it would be a comfort to know your mindset in regards to the exiled commodore. Were you friends?"

Nouli snorted. "Your comfort does not concern me. I will hear what you have to say, and I make no other consolations."

Ripka narrowed her eyes upon the aging engineer. His fingers drummed incessantly on the top of his table, their movement blurring the hint of a tremble in his long limbs. His spectacles had slid down his nose, the tip of which was quite red, the vessels all around it burst near the surface. His swinging emotional state – his physical presentation – she'd seen those symptoms many times before. Kisser hovered close to him, fidgeting as if unsure what to do with her hands.

"Are you well?" Ripka asked.

"If I am ill, it is because I am *sick* of having my time wasted."

The clearsky. The air heavy with mudleaf. Ripka couldn't help but press. "I see. Perhaps you should be more careful in the sampling of your own wares?"

His eyes bulged. "Enough! My health is not for you to remark upon. Tell me why you've come or I will have Kisser toss you back in the well."

Kisser flinched, a minute movement, but enough to cement Ripka's suspicions. "You're not really prisoners, are you?" She stood and leaned toward them, falling into her old role as investigator as easily as slipping on a favorite glove. "Both of you." She tipped her head toward Kisser. "Your special privileges, your fear of real names." She pointed to Nouli. "Your workshop, tucked away amongst the guards' quarters and yet hidden from them still. This grating–" she gestured toward the metal mesh laid over the place where a window should be, a multitude of pipe mouths angling toward it to vent their fumes to the outdoors, "–it's camouflaged on the outside, isn't it? Not all the guards know you're here – Warden Baset certainly doesn't. So how? Who's sheltering you, Nouli? Who's funding your sordid concoctions? And why are you making them here?"

He'd gone pale as chalk dust. Even the red marring his nose had faded.

"That's enough." Kisser grabbed her arm. Ripka let the woman's fingers bite down into the muscle beneath her flesh, but planted her feet when Kisser started to drag her toward the door. "Back to your cell, *captain*, and I better not see you at my breakfast table, understand?"

"The others don't know, do they? Forge and Honey and Clink – pits below, I'd thought Clink was your ringleader. But they're puppets for you, aren't they? You're jerking their strings to provide you protection, to shield you from suspicion. I wonder what they'd say, if they knew their leader wasn't even a convict?"

Kisser struck her, a burning streak of pain lancing across her jaw. Ripka jerked back, twisted her arm free, and brought her hands up to shield her face from further attack. Enard slipped to his feet, falling in alongside her, his presence a silent threat. Kisser's chest heaved with angry breaths, hair hiding half her face.

"Tell her," Nouli said.

"No."

"She's gotten this far." Nouli rubbed his cheeks with both hands, as if he could massage the blood back into them. "You'll either have to tell her, or kill her, and I for one could use another ally. Especially one as observant as Miss Leshe."

Ripka watched in morbid fascination as Kisser mulled over the decision, subconsciously rolling her shoulders to loosen them for a fight if it came to that. After a breathless pause, Kisser's posture deflated.

"If I'd known what trouble you'd be, I'd have encouraged

that songbird to shank you. Sit." Kisser pointed to the crate.
Ripka obliged. The woman was ready to talk, and she wasn't
about to be quarrelsome until she'd heard what she'd had to
say. Enard settled in alongside her.

Nouli said, "Allow me to explain. I am the one insisting,
after all."

"Go on then, you fool old man." Kisser crossed her arms
and slouched with her back against the wall, angling herself
to keep all three of them in her line of sight.

"If you are here to ask my help, then I assume you know
of my... reputation."

Ripka inclined her head. "The Century Gates."

His eyes closed, a brief fluttering, as if recalling the name
brought the image so strongly to the forefront of his mind that
he could not resist basking in it for a moment. "Yes. My Gates.
Great soaring walls of granite filled in with weaker stone,
buttressed so high the tops of them scraped the empress's
floating palace. I built them to keep Valathea's inner heart
strong and safe for a hundred years, sheltered from monsoon
winds and invasion alike. Until that skies-cursed Honding
blew a hole in the side of one, precisely where a key support
leaned its weight."

Conversations she'd had with Detan, late at night when
maybe the liquor had flowed a little too freely, came to mind.
How he'd described his escape from the Bone Tower. How
he'd run in blind fear, full of nothing but animal panic to
escape. He hadn't found out until much later that the wall
he'd destroyed was a part of the famous Century Gates.
Hadn't found out until later that innocents had died in that
conflagration. She knew what was coming. Tried to keep her
face neutral as he pressed on.

His fingers curled into fists upon his lap, his lips drew
thin. "A large section of the wall came down, crushing noble
houses that had been built too close for my liking. Hundreds
died. I'd seen the firebombs we used in war, of course, had

designed many myself, and the Gates had been constructed to withstand them, but the rending strength of that explosion... I saw pieces of the rubble, later. Twisted. The very grain of the rock metamorphose into some other stone. I could never have planned for such a force. And yet I was responsible for it."

"It was not your fault—" Kisser began, but Nouli held up a hand, silencing her.

"Maybe. But it was my fault I could not see how to rebuild it."

Kisser looked away, bunching the loose cloth of her jumpsuit in both fists. Nouli's gaze drifted, snagged on the tools spread across his desk as if he hadn't seen them before.

"Your age..." Ripka murmured. He only nodded.

"I see. But the walls were rebuilt—"

"Yes," he reached out and pat Kisser's arm. "She was always my finest apprentice."

"I'm no engineer." Kisser shook her head. "My specialty is chemistry."

"You give yourself too little credit," Nouli said. "After the wall was repaired, rumors of my absence from the project spread. The empress grew worried. How could she publicly hire a man with a reputation for failure? How could she hire a man when her courtiers whispered that his mind had been demolished along with his finest creation? It helped not at all that I began forgetting names publicly. And so she ignored me."

"Until she sent you away to rot."

"Kanaea, please—"

Kisser's rounded cheeks flamed red. "No names!"

Nouli waved a dismissive hand. "Calm yourself, girl, we are beyond such concerns now."

"He is your real uncle?" Ripka asked, weathering Kisser's glare.

"I am that." Nouli rose from his seat and fussed with the

instruments strewn across his table. "My empress sent Kanaea with me into exile to keep an eye on me, and to assist me in my efforts to cure my mind. And to remind me that she could do anything at all she liked with my family."

"I insisted," Kisser retorted.

"My dear, she expected you to."

She snorted and turned away from him, crossing her arms so tightly the force dragged taut lines into the material of her jumpsuit. Ripka wondered at her intentions – at her need for both independence for herself, and to look after her uncle. Ripka could not even recall the names of her aunts and uncles, so brief her time living near her family had been. What life had led Kisser – Kanaea – into such loyalty for her family? Ripka decided she'd do well to try and keep the woman on her good side. They might need her expertise.

"And so all of this," Ripka prompted, extending her arm to encompass the accoutrements scattered over the table, "is the result of your research? But why distribute the clearsky? What does the empress want with a petty street-drug? Aside from annoying Radu Baset, which is an endeavor I heartily approve of."

Nouli grunted a laugh. "Baset is a gnat, not worth the wave of my hand. This... keeps me lucid, for a while, a step toward clarity. And the empress believes it will help her deal with the Scorched problem."

Ripka exchanged an anxious glance with Enard. "And just what problem would that be?"

"Can you not guess? The empress is tired of her colonies acting up. The loss of Aransa's selium mines annoyed her greatly, and she fears the other cities of the Scorched may take Thratia's cue. She cares little for the middling cities, of course, but to lose control of the selium-producing cities? She won't have it. Selium is the trade-blood of Valathea. A few uppity city states will not stand in her way."

Ripka swallowed, the dryness in her throat as rough as

sand. "And how does this substance of yours fit into this?"

Nouli passed his hand over the air above his contraption, as if caressing a lover's back. "Imagine a Fleetman who needs half the sleep of a normal man. A Fleetman with sight keen beyond normal reckoning, and energy that never fails when he calls upon it. That's clearsky. That is the future of all of this."

"You're experimenting. On the prisoners." Her skin grew cold and clammy. Visions of Detan's sparse tales from his time spent in the Bone Tower danced behind her eyes.

"Nothing as heinous as all that." He brushed aside her concerns with a wave of his hand. "These people *ask* for my formulations. They come here without having had the chance to properly come down from their previous preferred methods of... deterring reality, I suppose you could say. Certainly some of them find solace in that mind-numbing barbarism Baset peddles, but I offer them a better alternative. I mean no harm, Miss Leshe. I mean only to enhance their minds and bodies."

Despite herself, her lip curled in disgust. "At the risk of addiction. At the risk of... of skies know what. You say it grants clarity of mind, but how long does that last? What is the down slope like? I've scraped many a man off the street twitching and drooling, scratching themselves raw because they can't afford another hit of whatever back alley apothik got them hooked in the first place."

Enard squeezed her arm, hard. She cut herself off, swallowing anger.

"Have you now?" Kisser said, her round eyes locked upon Ripka.

"Have I what?"

"Scraped many an addicted man off the street."

"I cared for Aransa. I helped where I could," she said, hoping her anger would cover her anxiety. She'd given them her name, she was not yet sure she wanted to offer up her old profession as well.

"Such a good little citizen." Kisser tapped her lips with one finger, thinking. "I wonder what it was you stole to end up here, hmm?"

"You said no details."

"Hah," Nouli cut it, his hoary brows lifted with curiosity. "I think we've been pretty free with details thus far. You know our business. What did an upstanding woman like yourself do to get locked in with the likes of us?"

"Or are *you* really a prisoner?" Kisser's hand dropped to her hip, an instinctual grab for a weapon she no longer carried.

"Tell them," Enard said, his voice strangely resigned.

"Shipment details," she admitted, glancing down as she spoke, the way Detan had taught her to hide any tension that might creep across her face. What she was telling them now was only a half-truth, and she knew from long experience that she was poor at disguising her expression. "An imperial manifest for a Fleet cargo vessel – the precise locations and nature of that cargo."

"The manifest alone?" Nouli asked, leaning toward her. "To what purpose? I suppose you must have passed it along to some of those men you swept out of gutters to do the real thieving work."

"The cargo was people, Master Bern. Selium sensitives of deviant abilities, being kidnapped and shipped off to Valathea to undergo experimentation at the empress's behest. Think what you will of me, but my actions are not petty. I passed this information along to those who might be able to do something about it before I was captured. I pray to the sweet skies they found a way."

"Such a noble soul." Kisser rolled her eyes and slumped back against the wall. "If your story can be believed."

She spread her palms in supplication to the sky. "Believe it or not, but I did get myself sent to the Remnant with a purpose."

"We had planned on capture," Enard said. "I am familiar

with the workings of these things. The stealing of the list
was for good, yes, but also to be sure Valathea would wish to
punish us dearly – without execution being a legal option."

"Clever," Nouli mused.

"Short-sighted," Kisser said. "You came here to find my
uncle, well, you've done so. Now what?"

Ripka hesitated, not wishing to lay too much of her true
plans at their feet. But she could not remain coy much longer
– Kisser was liable to drop them both in the well at any
moment.

"Tell me, Master Bern, what is your goal at the empress's
behest? What would she use such soldiers for?"

He shrugged as if the empress's end designs mattered not a
whit in all the world to him. "The re-taking of the Scorched,
the crushing of Thratia, the bringing to heel of Hond Steading.
She believes she's let the Scorched's native cities go to seed
too long. They need to be reined in, their courses righted.
Their heads of state replaced with her chosen, their flimsy
democracies cut down in place of heartier stock."

"And you'd experiment upon the prisoners to fulfill your
goals?" she asked, unable to hide her disgust, despite her
better judgment screaming at her not to antagonize the very
man whose assistance she'd come to beg. But what benefit
would he provide, if he were no better than the whitecoats?
She had to ask. Had to know what his intentions were – what
he was willing to break to achieve his goals.

"My preferences are not in play here. Though I have small
freedoms other inmates do not, you can see my hands are
tied. I do as my empire bids me."

"As do their whitecoats. And I've seen the gleam of passion
in their eyes. Do you not love your work as they do, no matter
the form it takes?"

"Do not compare me to those perversions!" He slapped
a hand against his desk. "Do I love to practice science? Yes,
of course. I am full of questions only experimentation may

answer. But science is neutral – it does nothing but raise questions. How one goes about collecting those answers is a function only of human folly and evil. Or, in my case, imperial threat. You should know something of the business of asking difficult questions, Miss Leshe. Or were your efforts to steal information always humane?"

She winced. "Once, to save a great many people..."

"Then you know the nature of this burden. If I were given freedom to investigate these questions of mental alacrity as I saw fit, then I would use only free and informed volunteers, not addicts desperate for their next fix. But the empire binds me. And even still, I have caught and accidentally murdered a great many rats to be certain I was not poisoning anyone."

"I am offering you that freedom, Nouli. Will you take it?"

Nouli looked up from his work, a sheen of hunger in his eyes so profound it made Ripka jerk back in her seat. "My dear, I will take anything that gets me off this cursed rock. The empress has promised me release upon my success. If you have come bearing a better offer, I suggest you make it now."

Was this worth the risk? If Nouli turned on them now, much more would be lost than a chance to out-strategize Thratia. He and Kanaea could twist their connections to keep Ripka and Enard on the Remnant indefinitely. Could even prepare to capture Detan, when he came for them. Could hand any information Nouli managed to weasel out of them straight to the empress.

But they'd come this far, and had been lucky enough to find the old engineer somewhat sound of mind, if drifting in moral compass.

"If you agree to assist Dame Honding in defense of her city, I can return you to the Scorched before the monsoons come."

Nouli sucked his teeth; Kisser let out a low hiss.

"You can't be serious," Kisser said.

"I am. Arrangements have been made. I will share no more

information, for obvious reasons. Know that I am serious. That I have implanted myself within these walls for the singular purpose of extricating you. Hond Steading requires your expertise. Will you give it?"

He licked his lips, a fresh gleam in his eye – something beyond hunger to be free, something so profound it brought dampness to his eyes, filling his slightly rheumy orbs with a soft, glimmering sheen. "If you can free me, Miss Leshe, I will be forever in your debt. Yours and your friend's, if he is indeed involved."

"He is."

"But monsoon season is coming now." Kisser cocked her head to one side as if she could smell the approaching rains. "How can you promise this?"

"No details." Ripka allowed herself a small smile at Kisser's scowl over hearing her words thrown back at her. "Just be ready to flee at any moment, to jump when I say so and ask no questions. And–" she swallowed, knowing she took a risk pushing her luck, "–be prepared to leave this nonsense behind." She jerked her chin to the clearsky distillation system.

Nouli wrung his hands in the towel slung over his shoulder, gaze darting between his work and the metal mesh over his window – that sliver of freedom. "You will have work for me in Hond Steading? I will not be left idle?"

"Better work, more suited to your talents. Not this twisted dabbling."

"My mind..." he protested.

"You will be allowed to continue pursuit of a cure, and to make what you need to keep yourself lucid in the meantime. But only for yourself."

"That is acceptable," he said, nodding slowly.

"Uncle, please, we cannot trust her."

"Hush, girl. You require only that I be prepared to flee when the time comes? There is no other task of me? Nothing that

could compromise my position here if your promises turn out
to be little more than hot air masquerading as selium?"

"There is one thing. Warden Baset has set me the task of
sussing out the source of clearsky here on the island, and I am
certain I'm not the only one. If you were to be thrown into
tighter security – or executed – before rescue arrives, then that
would throw a spanner in things, wouldn't it? Can you cease
production for a while? Claim illness, or the requirement of
deeper research to your masters?"

"Hmm." He dragged his fingers through the tangled
whiskers of his scraggly grey beard. "I could, for a short time,
but there is the trouble of my supplies."

"Supplies?"

"Guards loyal to the empress slip in the raw ingredients
I need for my experiments and collect my letters to the
empress. One such transaction is scheduled to occur tomorrow
evening."

Ripka rubbed her temples with her thumbs. "Why this
shielding from Baset? Why does the empress not want him
in on your doings? Surely wider distribution through the
warden himself would allow you greater success in your...
research."

"Indeed. But she is not entirely satisfied with Baset's
loyalty. She fears that booze-bloated old man is taking bribes
from powers growing within the Scorched. Paranoid, no
doubt. The empress is forever seeing daggers in her shadow.
But, nevertheless, we have been sworn to keep our activities
secret from the warden, lest he sell off my research to another
bidder."

"Very well," Ripka said as she rose to her feet. She ached all
over, but held her head high, her back straight. She needed
her body language, her tone and her words, to all work
together. To convince these two that she was in charge. That
she alone knew the right path to take.

It was just too pits-cursed bad she hadn't a clue what the

best course of action was.

"If I may make a suggestion," Enard said as he rose alongside her. She inclined her head to him. "If the supply exchange must be made tomorrow, then allow us to make it. We will claim the Lady Kanaea has taken ill, and Master Bern is too busy tending to her to make the meeting himself. Surely with some parchment from you confirming the fact – they know your handwriting, yes? – there will not be too much trouble."

Nouli snorted. "And what would a couple of petty thieves know about making clandestine exchanges, hmm?"

Kisser actually laughed – a sharp, abrupt sound, as if she were trying to keep it back and choked on it instead. "Tall, dark, and useful here has the background to handle it. Valet for the Glasseaters, were you?"

He bowed a touch from the waist. "Something like that, lady."

"You'd never know by looking at him," Nouli said.

Ripka gave Enard the side-eye. "I believe that's the point."

"Indeed," Enard said, shifting his weight from one foot to the other, the only sign he'd had yet to show of being uncomfortable in talk of his long ago past.

"I'll give you this chance, Miss Leshe." Nouli flicked a wrist at them in dismissal. "If you botch even the smallest detail, you will have no agreement from me, understand? I cannot put my freedom, nor my neck, in the hands of an incompetent."

"I understand, Master Bern."

"Excellent. Allow Kanaea to see you back to your cells, she will debrief you on what is required along the way. I will have a letter sent to you by the midday meal – beg off sick for the morning shift, if you can."

Ripka thought of Kisser pretending stomach pangs the first time she'd shared a meal with the rest of the women and suppressed a smile. So that had been a meeting day, too. How often were they, truly? That had only been two days ago.

"Anything else?" Kisser asked, brows raised as she peeled herself off the wall and angled toward the door.

"Just one thing," Ripka mused, trailing her toward the exit. "Could you please inform Misol that there's no need to keep spying on me? I find her rather unsettling."

Kisser blinked at her. "Who?"

"Misol... The guard who minds the yellowhouse."

Kisser rolled a shoulder and swung open the door. "Never been there. Don't know what her trouble is. Come along now, we already strained our time frame and our guard escort is going to have his knackers wound right up his rear."

Ripka trailed Kisser out, scarcely listening to what the woman said as she briefed Enard on the arrangements for the exchange.

The yellowhouse had nothing to do with Nouli. With the clearsky.

So then, who was Misol? And what in the sweet skies were they doing out there?

CHAPTER 25

Detan grabbed Pelkaia's arm, saw Tibs do likewise for Coss, and ran like the fiery pits were opening up beneath him. He watched in fascinated horror as the realization of what Pelkaia was washed over the gathered watchers, watched the initial tinges of revulsion fade away to shock and anger.

It was easy to hate a thing once you'd learned to fear it.

"Make way!" Detan screamed, because he figured that was at least worth a shot. Watchers spent their lives listening for an authoritative bellow and, sure enough, a few stepped clear of his path on instinct, bafflement overriding fear, anger, and duty. He could have laughed – if it wouldn't have meant making himself vulnerable to do so.

Pelkaia wrested from his grip and slipped sideways, skimming past the reaching arms of a nearby watcher. Shock passed. They closed in upon the fleeing five, a wall of blue cutting off Detan's view of the dock – and the *Larkspur* – beyond.

"Hullo," Detan said, waving his fingertips with overwrought glee at the watcher who stood before him. He took a nervous step backward and his back thumped into Pelkaia. They'd been corralled into a sour little knot in the center of the room. Closer to the exit than they'd been when they'd started, sure, but as far as Detan was concerned that dock was as close to him as the Valathean isles were.

"Now, now," he spoke as if coaxing a startled child, patting the air before him with his hands, and let himself babble to give himself time to think. "I'm sure we can talk this through. There's no need to send a perfectly good sel-sensitive to their death, now is there? She'll be no menace to society all locked away on the Remnant, as a proper prisoner of the Fleet."

"The Fleet!" The watch-captain spearheaded his way through the nervous cluster. A dusting of spittle speckled his whiskers. "You really expect me to believe you're sands-cursed Fleeties after that? *Run!* I heard you clear as the skies are blue."

"I think you'll find the skies are quite black at the moment," he rambled, peering through gaps in the ring of watchers. Someone moved on the dock – Pelkaia's people? He had to keep the watchers talking long enough for Jeffin and his yokels to realize something had gone amiss.

"To the pits with the color of the sky! You and your gaggle of... of ... Who *are* you people?"

"I believe," Laella cut in, "we have already been introduced." She'd had time enough to calm herself and smooth her features back into something like the hard, authoritative mask she'd worn when she'd first walked through the door. Maybe she'd be good at this sort of thing someday after all.

"Are you challenging my commodore?" Detan threw in, just to snap the watch-captain's head back to him. He hadn't a clue if that sort of attitude was something a real Fleetie would put on, but it didn't matter. He had to keep the captain confused, keep him talking. Keep him from giving the order to clap them all in chains.

"Will you be silent!" the captain snapped at Detan and jerked his attention back to Laella. The girl stood straighter, thrusting her shoulders back as she crossed her arms over her ribs.

"You are in no position to give orders to my men. I apologize that this one overreacted; many would do the same in the face of such a creature."

The captain snorted. "Commodore Eradin of the *Mirror*, is it? We'll see. You'll all have to wait until we can get word back from Valathea confirming your identities. Men." He snapped his fingers twice in the air. "Show the 'Fleeties' to their new rooms on the top level, and secure that ship of theirs. Throw the doppel and her associate in a new cell until we can arrange an execution."

"This is unconscionable!" Laella stomped her foot in typical spoiled-aristocrat fashion and jabbed the captain in the chest with her finger. The watchers hesitated. Every soul on the Scorched knew not to move a muscle when an uppercrust was busy throwing a fit. Fits had a way of latching on to the slightest of movements. "You will *not* make me get caught in the monsoon!"

Outside, the sky gave a grumble of thunder as if to punctuate her point.

"Miss, if this is a misunderstanding, then I apologize. But we've gone beyond your schedule."

The watchers stepped toward their huddled group, reaching for batons and shackles alike. Sweat itched between Detan's shoulder blades. He couldn't think of a thing to say. At least, nothing that'd do any more good than getting him cuffed for speaking. He shuffled back as the watcher he'd waved to reached for his arm, pressing his back tight against Pelkaia's. A strange keening echoed from the direction of the dock, a mournful wail that sounded far away – as if his ears were stuffed with cotton.

Behind him, Pelkaia murmured, "Finally."

The doors to the dock burst inward on a mighty blast of wind, the keening growing and swelling until it was an all-out banshee wail. Detan flinched, ducking down as the front of the storm slammed into the gathered watchers. He shivered as he sensed the source of that wind.

Wasn't wind at all, that gust blowing the doors so wide they cracked their frames. A wave of selium washed over him, around him. He had a chance to take a breath before it enfolded him, filling every crevice. An unseen sensitive shifted the gas back to its natural hue. It glimmered and flashed like someone had taken an opal and turned it to smoke.

The selium displaced the air around them, fogged their eyes and tingled in their nostrils. Someone screamed, then a whole lotta someones were screaming. The first needles of panic probed at Detan's nerves and he shivered, ducking his head, as if he could cower away from the glittering shroud that wrapped him tip to toe.

Someone grabbed his wrist and he lashed out, panicked. His other wrist was grabbed and he stared into Tibs's calm, weathered face, saw the rangy bastard's lips moving but couldn't hear a word he was saying over the keening in his ears.

Tibs. Tibs is here and the watchers aren't grabbing me and this is our rescue and it's going to be all right just run – just fucking run.

He nodded to Tibs, letting him know his panic had settled, and parted his lips to find he could breathe. Whoever controlled the sel that covered them had pulled back, switched from an all-consuming front of fog to a whip-like storm. Lashes of brilliance tore through the air, separating the watchers from their prisoners, stirring up real wind and scattering the light.

The watchtower's oil lamps blinked out, one by one, leaving only the gleam of sel, beautiful in its endless anger. Detan reached out a hand, entranced by the shattered and coalescing rainbows flowing around him. He'd never seen it like this before, never seen it so whipped up and... and not *free*, not exactly – but he sensed a delight in it. As if, in this wild storm, it could release a little of its anger, a little of its frustration at being tamed – at not being allowed to rise up and up and kiss the sun.

Could the sel feel? He wondered, trailing fingers through a wisp that turned carnelian and malachite and broke across his skin in waves of topaz. Did it know what it was to be tamed?

Did it hate being caged like he did?

Did it want him to free it, even if it meant its destruction?

Tibs yanked Detan's wrists and he stumbled, remembering where he was, remembering he needed to run. He'd done a lot of that – of running. He was good at it. Better than he probably had a right to be.

Severed from communion with the selium, he ran through it without a thought. Wisps brushed against his clothes and skin as he plowed straight through. Watchers shied away from those ribbons as if they were poison, calling amongst themselves various words of reorganization. He heard, as if from a distance, the captain's whistle give its futile toots, trying to rally them against their terror.

Hopeless, really. Detan doubted the poor sods had ever seen selium up close, unless it was contained within the banal leather of buoyancy sacks. This was something beyond their ken, something out of old fairytales. Detan wouldn't be surprised if the poor launderers had an extra basket of watchers' trousers to clean tomorrow morning.

He staggered out the door after Tibs, broke through the storm of sel onto the strangely peaceful dock, bathed in plain moonlight instead of the restless, thrashing prism of selium.

The *Larkspur* reared before him, as glorious in its sleek lines as it had been that first night, so long ago, when it had loomed in the embracing arms of Thratia's dock. A fresh love for it swelled within him, choked him briefly. Tibs stalled as well, his eyes wide as if he were trying to drink in every glorious line of her.

On her smooth deck Jeffin stood, surrounded by a half dozen other sensitives Detan did not know, sweat sheening all their faces, dampening their tunics so that they plastered across their shoulders and chests. Every last drop of the selium used to disguise the *Larkspur*'s iconic beauty had been stripped away, manhandled by her small crew to disorient Pelkaia's captors.

A jolt of awe startled Detan. A small part of his mind worked the cost of all that precious gas, and what it would sell for on the black market, even as he marveled at the ship itself.

Pelkaia cuffed him on the back of the head. He jolted, spun around to tell her off, then noticed the watchers spilling onto the dock. A scant handful had mastered their fear long enough to break through the storm, but there would be more. With a grunt he sprinted toward the *Larkspur*'s gangplank, dragging a startled Tibs along behind him. They scrambled up together, fell panting side by side in a heap of silky-smooth ropes piled up against a cabin wall.

Laying on his back, shivering with remembrance of the whole experience, he watched Pelkaia stride up the gangplank after him, her first mate and young, brave Laella trotting at her heels.

"Bring it in!" she barked to her sweating, straining crew, and spun around to heave up the gangplank with her own hands.

The ship jerked as she hauled the plank in, slewing away from the dock by the unseen force of someone – no doubt Pelkaia – shoving on the selium hidden away in the ship's buoyancy sacks, clustering it to one side of the ship. A sloppy turn, but a decent enough fix to lurch them out of reach of watcher hands.

Groaning, Tibs hauled himself to his feet and offered a hand to Detan. He eyed it, wary.

"Get up, sirra. Work to be done."

"Ship's got a full crew," he grumbled.

"Little busy right now."

Detan took Tibs's hand and allowed himself to be hauled to his feet, every joint screaming in protest. The sensitives were arrayed against the *Larkspur*'s aft rail, hauling in the clouds of selium they'd used to frighten the watchers. Great snakes of it flowed out from the watchtower lobby, trailing after the ship like the tail of a shooting star. They were straining, all of them, and even Pelkaia had gone to join them. Every hand was needed to hold onto and reclaim the precious selium that hid their ship from prying eyes.

And not a single hand was left to see to the ship's tiller.

"Good ole-fashioned flying," Detan grinned at Tibs as he forced himself over to the captain's podium, working the cranks that angled the sails and set the gearboxes on the ship's great propellers spinning.

"Not for long," Tibs said, jerking his chin to starboard. Detan leaned from his heightened perch at the captain's podium, peering down at the dock they'd abandoned. The watchers piled onto the craft he'd spotted earlier, encouraged by the sweet prize of the *Larkspur*, and were lifting off below.

"Oh," Detan said, fingers going white on the wheel.

"Tie on!" Tibs barked, and reached for his anchor rope even as he latched one onto Detan's belt.

Muscles burning, breath stuttering, Detan threw his back into the crank of the *Larkspur*'s largest aft propeller, throttling them out and into the clouds – and toward the dark smudge of a storm appearing upon the horizon.

The watchers followed, chasing the starfall trail of selium Pelkaia's crew struggled to reel back in.

CHAPTER 26

When the cell doors were opened for the morning meal, Ripka's was left sealed. A few coded knocks against the wall she shared with Enard revealed that he had been left in place as well. After their neighbors were led down to breakfast, stale buns stuffed with stewed greens were shoved through the slots in both their doors.

Ripka ate the now familiar fare quickly, anxiety stirring her feet until she paced while she chewed, wearing a thin path in the dusty floor of her cell. Was the sealed door Kisser's doing, or Radu's? There was no way to be certain, and the question gnawed at her. She had expected to pretend to her guard that she was too ill to attend the morning meal and subsequent work shift, not to be left alone while the gears of the Remnant ground on without her.

As the bells rang out to call the convicts to their work, two slips of paper followed Ripka's roll through the slot in her door. She scooped them up, hungry for information. One was sealed with wax, Nouli's crest stamped into the dark-gold blob – his letter to the empress, no doubt. The one which she was not supposed to open, lest Nouli's contacts think something was amiss.

The other was folded over and sealed with a blob of guar

sap. She tore the page apart and peered at the sloppy hand, taking a moment to resolve the slanting letters into words.

You will be escorted to the drop by a guard of my choosing.
Ask no questions, speak only when spoken to. Do not fuck this
up.

Ah, Kisser must have written this. She crumpled the note and shoved it up her sleeve to dispose of later. Nouli's report she slipped into her pocket, careful not to disturb the elegant seal holding the paper's lips shut.

The information should have soothed her, but she continued her furtive pacing. What guard would Kisser choose, and how could she be certain that guard was loyal?

Why, if a guard must be used to explain Kisser's movements when she made these meetings, didn't they send the guard to make the exchange? If they were truly loyal, then there should be no need to risk other guards – or Radu himself – discovering a prisoner out of place.

It made no sense, and that made her skin crawl.

Kisser was not, so far as Ripka could tell, a sloppy woman. She must have her reasons for this method, but Ripka could not work out what they were.

When presented with an unanswerable question, Detan had said, *stall.*

Ripka grunted at the memory. Not, she supposed, the most useful advice – that man was unnaturally assured of his own invulnerability – but it was the only path she had to follow for the moment.

A thump sounded on her door, startling her out of her thoughts, and it swung inward. Hessan, her block's centerpoint guard, stood at her threshold, eyeing her with barely concealed disdain.

"Out," he ordered.

Swallowing a sharp retort, Ripka stepped out into the hall

and was startled to see Enard already waiting, a pensive crease to his brow. Kisser had implied that only one of them would make the exchange. Her stomach churned with a sudden pang of worry. Was this really Kisser's man – or another play of Radu's? There were too many unanswered questions in the air for her comfort.

"You have it?" Hessan asked.

Ripka arched an eyebrow, then realized he must mean Nouli's report. "Yes."

"Good. Follow me."

She fell into step alongside Enard, the silence between them thick with tension. There was little they could do now, save move with events and see what happened. To return to their cells would invite nothing but trouble, and to cry for help would do nothing but draw unwanted attention.

The weight of Kisser's letter was like a stone in her sleeve. She hated being so far out of control – so vulnerable to the whims of those she did not like, let alone trust. As she walked, she ran through her options.

She could disable Hessan, if it came to that. But what then? She could not shut herself back within her cell and pretend innocence. No doubt she'd be tossed to the sharks – and then what of her contact with Nouli? To betray Kisser, even in self-defense, would erase all hope of winning the man and his talents over to her side.

Ripka exhaled slowly, breathing out her worry. She'd promised Detan and Tibal she could recover Nouli. And though she knew they would not blame her, she knew as well that the man might be Hond Steading's greatest hope.

They passed through a door and out of the prison walls, onto the hard, rocky soil of the island. A bitter cold nipped her face, but she found she no longer trembled at the sea's chill touch. She'd always been an adaptable woman. If she hadn't been, she'd be bones beneath the sands of the Brown Wash by now.

Enard made a small sound in the back of his throat, unnoticed by the guard who stalked ahead of them. He tipped his head back, drawing her eye to the walk atop the prison dormitories, where a guard was always set to watch. The walk was empty. If it were not for the faint murmur of hundreds of voices concealed within those hugging wings of stone she could not have been sure the island was inhabited at all.

The paths wound closer to the sea. Low tide had slipped in, and the air was heavy with the decay of sea-plants and unfortunate creatures who had been abandoned to the sands as the tide retreated. Down a steep path, angling across the crumbled face of a fallen cliff, she spied a marshy pool tucked within the rocks, reeking of the reeds that dropped their seeds into it to molder.

She flicked her wrist, a subtle movement, and dropped Kisser's note into the pool. Committed, now, to whatever was to come, she felt a weight lift from her shoulders. Betrayal or no, she'd kept her word. She could only hope Kisser believed Ripka had a way off the island.

The path opened onto the rocky shore. Ripka took a moment to admire the endless freedom of the gleaming horizon. She would have that freedom again, someday soon. Once her task was finished.

The beach was a thumbprint on the chiseled shoreline. Scarcely fifty paces across, it looked as if an elder cliff had collapsed, leaving this crescent strip strewn with rough rocks.

The low level of the waters exposed a bit more ground, cluttered with strips of kelp dancing all over with the jump and scuttle of sandfleas. Into this temporary stretch of land a flier had dropped anchor. The craft boasted a single sail, its hull narrow and low with only a cursory attempt at a railing. A single propeller graced its aft, the lacquer to protect the wood from cloud mist chipped and peeling. Tibal would have had a fit to see a propeller in such disrepair.

A wiry man stood on deck, his thatch of dark hair shot all

through with grey. He crouched at an opening in the rail, hovering above a natty rope ladder, the bottom rung of which dragged in the damp sand. A pack rested beside his knee, good oilcloth bulging at the strapped seams. He wore no insignia nor uniform, but his appearance was not the puzzle that caught in the brambles of her mind.

A small ship, smaller than Detan's flier, could not cross the open sea to the Remnant.

Hessan whistled a strange bird cry. The man nodded in acknowledgement. They tromped across the uneven beach to the smoother sands the tide had given up, Ripka's shoes sucking in the muck.

The man jerked his chin toward them "Who're those two?"

Hessan looked at them as if he'd been reminded of an unsightly boil on his bottom. "The Lady's pets. She took ill and shoved them along in her place."

"Took ill for truth this time, eh?" The man had a soft, affable chuckle. "False words plant blighted seeds." Ripka started. That was an old Catari saying, supposedly outlawed with all other cultural accoutrements of the people Valathea had rolled over to take control of the Scorched and its precious firemounts. She shifted so that the sun was not in her eyes to get a better look at the man. He had the same branchbark hue to his skin as most on the Scorched did, but a smoothness to his cheekbones betrayed a stronger Catari heritage.

"Enough of that," Hessan said. "Do you have it?"

"Wouldn't be here if I didn't." With a casual kick he knocked the pack at his side to the sand. The guard cursed as he picked it up, brushing off the wet muck. "You have the results?"

"Here." Ripka stepped to the ladder and held Nouli's carefully sealed envelope up to the man. He eyed the distance between them, and smirked.

"Best come up a bit, now," he said.

She examined the frayed rope ladder, not relishing a

tumble into the sodden sand. "Can't you come down?"

The man's expression darkened, thunderclouds rearing in the smooth darkness of his eyes. "I will never set foot on this place."

Ripka bit her tongue, remembering Kisser's warning not to speak unless spoken to. Shunting aside curiosity, she braced herself as she eased one foot onto the first rung, leaned her weight against it, and then added the other. The man puffed out an annoyed breath.

"Don't have all day, lass."

"Clearly you're not rushing off to repair your ladder," she blurted before she could stop herself.

The man's brows shot up, the darkness in his eyes clearing as he barked a laugh. Tension fled her shoulders.

"There they are!" A male voice she did not know thundered across the bay.

The man above her cursed and leaned toward her, hand outstretched. For the barest of moments she thought he'd pull her on board, but he snatched the folded envelope from her hand and reared back, severing the rope ladder's connection to the deck with two quick swipes.

Her side slammed into the wet sand, the abandoned ladder crumpling atop her. She grunted, kicked out to regain her feet and staggered upright, ignoring the ache in her arm and side.

The flier slid out across the sea, the man cranking frantically at his propeller, the anchor left behind in a heap of rope. Ripka scowled after him, cursing his retreat. But then she saw the reason, and went very cold and very still.

Down the track six men in prison jumpsuits sauntered. One of them familiar to her even at a distance. The songbird's man, Oiler. The Glasseater who'd harangued Enard. She bristled as she watched the men work together without an order spoken, fanning out as they approached their target, cutting off all hope of escape. No guard accompanied them.

They had the easy stroll of the fearless.

"Leave us," Enard said, stepping forward so that he was in front of Ripka.

"Oh ho, now he wants nothing to do with us." Oiler grinned. His two canines had been filed down to knife-points, his lips twisted to one side by old scarring. As Enard spoke, stalled, she sized them up – decided she'd take the one to Oiler's right, first, as he was the most substantial of the lot. No doubt Enard would handle Oiler if it came to that.

Remove the largest boulders, and the rest of the rocks will fall.

"What are you doing outside of the walls without escort?" Hessan reached for his baton as he stepped forward to stand level with Enard.

Oiler held his hands out, palms up, and shrugged. "Work detail forgot to recall us. He was busy, ya know? It's a mighty distraction, having your ankles tied up by your ears. When we spotted those two missing, figured we better have a look 'round. This island can be dangerous, you know."

"I have asked you politely to leave," Enard said. Ripka heard steel in his voice she hadn't realized him capable of. "I will not ask again."

Oiler snorted. "Looks to me like we're the ones going to be doing the asking."

There was a subtle shift in their formation, orchestrated after a tilt of Oiler's head. The fan tightened toward the end closest to Hessan.

Whatever their reasons, the Glasseaters wanted the guard out of commission first. Hessan's hand drifted toward his collar, as if he were going to adjust it. She saw the line around his neck, then, the worn cord that held a brass whistle. Of course they wanted him out first. He was the only one of them who could call for help.

A scrawny Glasseater darted toward Hessan – but Ripka moved first. She swept in and shouldered Hessan aside, sending him sprawling. Shouts broke out all around her but she ignored them, focused on the arm's radius immediately around her, as she'd been trained.

The Glasseater barreled into her, sweeping her off her feet. She landed hard on her back, and rolled before the man could follow up with the kick he'd aimed at her ribs. He reached for her, but she scrabbled forward, fingertips tearing as she dug them into the sand to give herself purchase. Hessan lay just ahead, groaning. He rolled to-and-fro, a mass of kelp tangled with the thatch of his hair.

A hand closed around her ankle, jerked. She yelped as her arms went out from under her and smacked face-first into the rocky beach. Gravel and sand clogged her mouth, scratching her cheeks. Kicking back with her free foot a solid connection jarred her and then she was free. She fumbled with the thick cord around Hessan's neck, rifled through his loose shirt, fingers sliding over his sweat-slicked and hairy chest.

Her fingers brushed warm metal, closed round it.

Hands grabbed her by the hair, the jumpsuit, tore her away from Hessan and lifted her as if she were little more than a troublesome puppy. The cord bit deep into her palm, spilt crimson blood down her wrist, the searing pain of it overridden by her need to complete her task.

As the hands – too many to count – lifted her and hauled her back, she pressed the bloodied whistle to her lips and blew hard enough to set her eardrums ringing.

Valathean engineers did not mess about when it came to the effectiveness of their designs. The whistle had been crafted to be heard anywhere on the island, and before she could draw breath to blow again, the great brass alarm bells atop the prison's walls rang out.

Help was coming. They need only to survive.

She hit the ground, dropped, and grunted as her chest smacked against hard, jutting rock, her unprotected face scraped by rough gravel. Better than the Black Wash, at least.

Her fingers went numb, so tight was her grip on the whistle.

"Fucking bitch." Oiler growled and hawked spit. "Clear, boys."

"But–" one protested. The heavy thud of palm on cheek filled the air.

"Quiet. This place'll be swarming with guards soon and they won't all be friendly."

Wary of moving too quickly, lest she draw unwanted attention to herself, Ripka rolled over and scrabbled backward, crab-crawling as quietly as she could. The Glasseaters pulled back, clustering around Oiler who stood before Enard.

A narrow stream of blood trickled from the corner of Enard's lips. He stood with a slight hunch, but otherwise seemed whole.

"Remember this, Tender. There's only one way out. We'd rather have you back, but..." Oiler shrugged, both hands open to the skies, then spat at Enard's feet and whirled, striding back the way he'd come, his foul friends flowing after him.

Enard moved. He flowed like silk, like lightning. Before Ripka could register his target, Enard's fist held Oiler's hair, a well-aimed punch to the kidneys collapsed Oiler's knees. The ring-leader's body betrayed him, tense with pain and spasms, as Enard bent him backward, backward, over his knee and crouched down, drawing face to face with the crime-boss.

The Glasseaters rushed back to aid their leader. Ripka shoved ineffectually at the ground, trying to lever herself to her feet. She couldn't get to him before the Glasseaters closed ranks, but she could damn well try.

Enard whispered something in Oiler's ear.

"Stop," Oiler said. His men obeyed.

Oiler's body trembled, his heels slowly dragging through the sand as he verged on losing whatever slim footing he held despite being bent over Enard's knee like a human bridge. Sunlight glinted off bright rivulets of blood dripping from his cheek to the sand, turned his complexion a phantom shade of rose.

"You may have lost track of me," Enard said, voice raised for all on the beach to hear. "But I have not forgotten you. You in *particular*, Onrit."

He flinched. Enard smiled.

"Yes, I know your name. Father made all his sons learn the fine details of each Glasseater's life." Enard scooped a handful of gravel from the beach and placed one black stone on Oiler's cheek.

"This," he said, "is Marya. And this, Ledi." A grey stone followed onto the other cheek. Ripka's stomach sunk as tears mingled with the blood dripping from Oiler's cheeks. She didn't know who those names belonged to – but she knew what they meant to him. That was enough.

"If you come for me, or for my friends, again, I will come for them. Not you. Them. Am I understood?"

"Pits swallow you," Oiler rasped.

"Good." Enard stood in one fluid movement, dropping Oiler to the wet sand. He pinned the other Glasseaters with his gaze, and flicked the remaining handful of sand toward them. "Do not think for a moment I will not gather the names the rest of you hold dear."

They did not disgrace themselves by running, but they helped a dazed Oiler to his feet and hurried back down the path all the same.

Ripka felt as if she were witnessing something deeply private as Enard observed his old gang mates retreat up the crumbled slope. He seemed open to her, vulnerable in a way she couldn't quite place. Marya. Ledi. How long had he carried those names on the off chance he would need them as weapons? How many more weighed him down? Alone on the beach with him, Hessan their only witness, she wondered if she were any safer now than before the Glasseaters had arrived.

Enard shook himself and straightened his shoulders, the rigidity of his bearing chasing away his phantom grace. So that was how he'd hidden his talent for violence so long beneath her nose. Only then did he turn, and his brows shot up as he hurried toward her. She must have looked a mess, kissed all over with minor scrapes and cowering on the ground like some strange crab.

"Are you all right, captain?" he asked. Despite her reservations, she felt the weight he lent to the word captain like a balm – it was no nickname for him. He believed in her old station, even if she had left it far behind.

"It's all surface," she said as he helped her haul herself to her feet. She winced, examining the deep gouge left across the soft pad at the base of her thumb by the cord. "Well, except for that." She gave her fingers an experimental wiggle and hissed through her teeth from the pain. Still movable, so nothing vital had been severed, but she'd hurt for weeks due to it – if not full moon turns – and the threat of it festering was quite real. The guard hadn't struck her as the cleanest of folk.

"And you?"

Enard prodded his cheek and cringed. "A passing annoyance. Our brave escort?"

Ripka smirked at the serious way he pronounced brave, and knelt beside Hessan. He lay on his side, groaning softly, hands limp against the ground. With care she felt around his head with her good hand and found a knot forming near the base of his skull. She sighed. He must have struck his head against a stone when he fell and, based upon his current incoherent state, she guessed a mild concussion had occurred. Pity, that, but he would live. She doubted they would have lived if she hadn't gotten his whistle away from him.

Shouts sounded nearby. Guards rushed haphazardly down the path, cutlasses and batons both wavering in their hands. Ripka shook her head in disappointment. If one were to trip, they could knock the whole pack down. Someone was bound to get stabbed in that scenario.

"Step away!" A guard barked at her as he drew near. She frowned, thinking she recognized him, but all their faces were beginning to blur together for her. If she had had trouble keeping track of the individual members of her watch, she had no doubt Radu couldn't name even half his staff.

Raising her hands to show they were empty, save the whistle dangling from her wounded palm, she backed slowly from Hessan.

"He has a slight concussion," she explained. "I suggest you get him to the apothik. Correct teas will ease his disorientation."

"Be quiet." The guard gestured a few of his colleagues towards her. Peacocks, all of them. She wondered if any were Kisser's loyalists, and if they might have an idea of what Hessan was out here for.

The guards took her and Enard roughly in hand, and she suffered a poorly done pat-down before her wrists and ankles were clasped in shackles. She cringed as the cold metal closed over the wrist of her injured palm, even that small jostling causing her some agony.

"We were assaulted..." Some bastard cuffed her on the head.

"I said be quiet," the guard holding her bonds growled in her ear. "We can see well enough what you've done."

"I–" she took another thwack to the skull. Vision slewing, she blinked her sight clear. Enard stared straight at her. He gave a slight shake of the head, and she resigned herself to silence. They had allies to call upon, eventually, but these were not them. Whether they were Radu's, or neutral in the Remnant's power games, it was best to keep silent. He was right, though it grated at her. No explanation could smooth away the scene these guards had stumbled upon. No doubt they'd think she'd cut her hand trying to wrestle the whistle away from the fallen guard before he could call for assistance.

It was, she realized bitterly, precisely the decision she

would have come to under the circumstances. Her stomach dropped. Maybe these were Kisser's allies, after all. Maybe she'd set them up.

Captain Lankal picked his way down the path, his expression wrought with bright anger. He glanced to Enard, to Ripka. Took in the whole scene, and shook his head with disappointment. Ripka flinched, hanging her head despite herself.

"Captain," a guard said, and Ripka looked before she realized he was talking to Lankal. The guard held out the oilcloth pack, the top flipped open to reveal the contents. Pale, silvery grey bark in tight curls filled the interior. It was rather pretty, but Ripka could not place it. She doubted the source was native to the Scorched.

"I see," Lankal said, prodding at the contents with a finger. "Warden will want to see this."

The guard said, "This time of day, sir, the warden has meetings."

The way Lankal's expression darkened, Ripka realized the only regular meetings Radu held were with a bottle. He evaluated the angle of the sun, and nodded. "And I bet they've already begun. Very well. Take those two to an apothik, then throw them in the well for the night. And if either of you struggle, I'll have the other killed first. Clear?"

"Yes, sir," Ripka and Enard said in unison.

The captain looked a little surprised by their obedience. He took his hat off, ran his fingers through greying hair, then glanced back at the sack of curled bark. Disgust twisted his mouth. He shoved his hat back on with purpose.

Back up the unstable cliff side they were marched. Ripka's thoughts struggled as she tried to figure out a way to explain what had happened to Radu.

Whether Kisser had betrayed them or not, she required an explanation that would not, under any circumstances, reveal the presence of Nouli Bern.

CHAPTER 27

The *Larkspur*'s controls were familiar in his hands, the waxed wood stable and reassuring, just as it had been in the days after he'd first stolen the ship out from under Thratia's nose. It'd be smooth sailing, if Pelkaia hadn't gone and moved some of the rigging around. Blasted woman had a nasty habit of meddling with everything she touched.

Detan eyed a suspiciously small wheel to the lower right of the primary wheel, dyed a bright cherry red, and wondered what would happen if he gave it a twist.

"Best not," Tibs said. The twerp wasn't even looking Detan's way. He'd stationed himself at the navigator's podium, a smaller version of the captain's, and had his head down to fiddle with some contraption or another.

"How in the black did you–"

"How couldn't I?"

Detan rolled his eyes and snapped his attention back to the task at hand, doing his level best to ignore that tempting little wheel. Someone had gone and dyed the wood a cherry stain, the bright color drawing his eye even as he focused on the yaw of the ship. Couldn't see much of the horizon from the captain's podium, not with clouds sealing them in, but Tibs was fitted up with periscopes and signal flags. Of course, the crew who was supposed to speak with the navigator in semaphore were currently occupied recovering a fortune's worth of sel – so, really, he just had his periscopes.

Which should pits well be enough. If Tibs could spot Detan sneaking a sweetcake off a cart at a hundred paces, he had better be able to spot any new threat sneaking up on them. Tibs was sometimes worse than a mother dogging his heels.

"Mark course." Detan popped out one of the chock pegs inset into the podium that were designed to brace the handles of the primary wheel.

"Course?" Tibs's voice ratcheted high. "You find me some stars, I'll find you a course."

A cottony blanket of grey cloud scraped the sky above their sails, blotting out all hope of navigation. The soft glow of Petrastad's lights smeared the horizon to their aft, and nothing but empty blackness yawned to their fore. Below, all around, the black silk of the sea stretched. Endless and, without the stroke of the moon's light to give its sheen away, too easy by far to confuse with the horizon.

He swallowed, realizing the nightmare they'd been pushed into. Out over the open water, in the middle of the night, with a storm coalescing all around them, horizon blindness could settle in quick.

If he could get a drop of selium, he could let it go – watch it rise to be sure of their vertical axis – but all the ship's excess was tied up in the illusion the *Larkspur*'s crew was struggling to recover. The buoyancy sacks in the ship's belly should hold enough to keep them a touch above neutral, the ship's ability to climb reliant upon its propellers and the angle of its stabilizing.

If the watchers didn't back off, give them time to gather themselves and orient properly, there was a very real chance Detan would accidentally steer them straight into the sea. And in his very limited experience, there was no charming one's way out of a shark's mouth. Or hypothermia, for that matter.

"We're fucked."

"The thought had occurred to me," Tibs drawled.

"Climbing," Detan said, and reached down to crank the wheel that controlled the tilt of the lift propellers. He set it spinning, letting the masterful gear ratios do the heavy lifting for him, one hand on the wing's wheel to keep them as close to level as possible.

A narrow liquid level had been set into the top of the captain's podium, the air bubble within gleaming up at him as he stared it down, keeping the thing right smack in the middle of the central lines. He couldn't let the *Larkspur* yaw to one side or another – any subtle variation could set them on a course to the waves.

"Mark weather," Detan called back to Tibs, unwilling to peel his eyes from the level while they were ascending.

"Fuckin' soup."

Detan kept on climbing, sweat breaking across his brow as he stared down that bubble, not daring to breathe too hard lest he twitch the wings the wrong way. How high? If this ship had a barometer, he couldn't see it, and Tibs wasn't calling out the pressure as he would have if he'd had access to the right instruments. Wisps of cloud licked at his clothes, dampening him all over. Detan's ears popped.

"Tibs?"

"Thinning."

Clear air washed over his back, brushing away the thick moisture of cloud cover as the *Larkspur* heaved itself atop a wooly blanket of grey cloud. He locked the lift wheel into place and the ship jerked as it nosed down, almost stalling into an aft-slide.

He glanced up, expecting to see clear sky, but instead Pelkaia filled his view, her tired features pinched into a tight scowl. He'd have much rather come face to face with more nasty weather.

"Get off my podium."

Detan snorted, straining as he held the wheel straight under the buffeting of higher altitude winds. "You can captain this ship when you've got all the sel back." He called over his shoulder to Tibs, "Mark course already!"

"Working on it," Tibs's voice was strained, made thready by the wind whipping past his lips.

"This isn't your ship, Honding. Step aside and help the others."

"By the pits, Pelkaia, you think I'm enjoying this? You ever flown into a sea storm before?"

The twitch at the corner of her eye was the only answer he needed – no, she hadn't. Detan straightened, firmed his resolve not to let her take control of the wheel. An inexperienced pilot in this mess could send them all splashing down. And he'd just replaced his boots, too. It'd be a shame to ruin them in the salt water.

"I see you haven't. Well, I have, and I'll be damned if this is the right moment to teach you how to handle it. Thank your cursed stars I happened to be aboard, and go get your sel back. And don't come bitching to me if we lose the watchers before you succeed. My goal is getting us out of this alive and free. I don't care about your surplus."

Pelkaia opened her mouth to protest just as a gust struck the ship, throwing the mainsail hard to one side. Detan cursed and clutched at the wheel, bracing himself against the podium as he straightened the ship's sideways slew.

"You want to help? Get those sails down! And have everyone tie in. Things are gonna get rough."

She glared at him, but strode off anyway, her footsteps easy and comfortable over the bucking surface of the deck. Soon dark silhouettes moved across the deck, away from the aft where the struggle over the sel continued, spindly figures swinging up on the masts to bring the great sails down. He breathed a sigh of relief. One less thing to worry about.

A black bolt skittered across the deck, nicking the heel of

his fine new boots. He yelped, jumped forward enough to slam his chest into the wheel. The ship began to slide, but he straightened before the effect could be troublesome.

"What in the black–"

"Company to starboard," Tibs said.

The watchers' craft had caught up, pacing the *Larkspur*'s rail. It was a low-bellied thing, narrow enough to cut through the sky just as quick as its propellers could force it along. Selium shimmered all around it, twisted into strange, knotted shapes as the sensitives on board the *Larkspur* struggled to wrench it away from the three sensitives Detan had seen fixing the craft when they'd first arrived. All along the deck a string of watchers spread out like links in a chain, at least eight of the bastards, with blackened crossbows pointed straight at the *Larkspur*'s deck. And there wasn't a sensitive aboard the *Larkspur* willing to answer those crossbows with the ship's harpoons so long as the sel remained in jeopardy.

"You make a real nice target," Tibs mused.

Another bolt skittered across the deck near his feet. One thunked into the wood of the podium with a heavy twang. "Pits!" Detan hunched down in the three walls of the podium, struggling to keep his body hidden while still being able to exert enough leverage to work the great wheels.

"They've got a harpoon!" one of Pelkaia's crew yelled, voice sharp with panic above the howl of the storm-winds.

"Hold on!" Detan called back, praying to the clear skies that Pelkaia had got his message across to everyone to tie themselves in. Huddled as he was, the wheel was a bear to turn, but turn it he did, groaning and growling as he heaved the wheel to the larboard. The sleek ship responded immediately, tearing away from the watchers' vessel so quick Detan feared he'd roll them. Screams – mostly startled – popped up all around. He jerked the wheel straight and risked a glance over the top of the podium for the starboard side. The watcher craft was a good couple of hundred strides away, and although Pelkaia's crew was scattered like thrown sand all across the deck, they appeared to all be there.

"Whoo!" He grinned, popping up to his full height, and angled the ship for a gentler curve to take them away from the watcher craft. Soft, fat drops of rain began to pelt Detan's head, running down his hair and into his eyes. The shadow of the watchers' craft turned, following tight behind.

A damp Pelkaia marched toward him, the rain making the sel on her face shimmer as it plowed riverbeds through her illusion. It gave the effect of her skin cracking, as if she were leaking selium from within. Detan shivered.

"Blow it," she demanded, thrusting a finger toward the watchers' craft. Selium enveloped it – Pelkaia's surplus.

Hot sweat mingled with the cool rain on his neck. "No."

"No? No? Look at it! We've lost it. Blow the watchers, and we can reel in what's left."

Detan squinted, shading his eyes to keep the rain clear. The amorphous blob of pearlescent gas twisted at the edges closest to the *Larkspur*, connected to the main blob around the watcher craft by thready wisps. His little stunt had gotten them out of harpoon range, but it'd been too sudden – half the crew had lost their hold.

But he could still feel it, looming like the promise of a stiff drink in his mind.

"So you lost it. So what? I told you–"

"Sirra." There was a warning note in Tibs's voice so stern that both Detan and Pelkaia whipped around to look his way. "We've a problem."

Tibs pointed. Detan's gut nearly emptied itself on his new shoes. A great column of cloud, grey and bulbous and churning, loomed on the horizon. It speared up from the sea like a god's leg, its body crackled with streaks of lightning. The patchy clouds that spilt rain upon them reached out toward that swollen pillar, twisted into smears as they were pulled in under the force of the storm's updraft.

He'd seen columns like that before. Usually on the far horizon. Spears in the sky bidding him to go around. Had seen the bodies and ships of those who'd flown too close to them, too. Broken husks, cracked in so many pieces they looked as if they'd fallen down the rocky side of an endless canyon. Half-frozen and half-mashed.

Never had he seen one so close it filled his view, dwarfed his vision and his hope.

"What–" Pelkaia began, but he cut her off.

"That's a cloud suck. A god's tower. That's death."

"Captain!" Coss struggled toward them, the growing winds already swirling clockwise over them. "The watchers are gaining again."

Detan looked to the watchers, standing between them and Petrastad. Looked to the cloud suck, standing between him and Ripka. Made his choice.

"Right," he said, bracing himself, straightening his spine. "Pelkaia. Use what you've got left and block the watchers' view of us. Throw up a mirror of the cloud suck, right in their path if you can. We're going the long way around, and we don't want them following. We'll have enough problems without 'em on our heels."

"Just blow the cursed–"

He slammed a chock-plug in to brace the wheel and turned, grabbing the front of Pelkaia's shirt in one fist. She gasped, startled, as he jerked her forward to stare eye-to-eye with him.

"I said no."

"Think you can intimidate me, too? I'm not my crew, Honding. I know the make of you. Now blow that skies-cursed ship."

The crew went quiet, every last eye on the deck glued to Detan and their captain. He felt them all. Felt them probing at him, wondering. Wondering if he'd blow more than the watcher vessel, if Pelkaia pushed him just right. Wondering if they could bash his head in before he got the chance. Detan cleared a rough catch in his throat and lowered his voice to a raspy whisper. "No innocents."

"You think they are?"

"You think Ripka wasn't?"

She swallowed, catching his meaning. Watchers were just doing their jobs. Doing the best they could to keep their cities safe, never mind their masters.

"We clear?" he said.

"As these skies."

He released her. She spat at his feet. They stared at one another, nothing in all the world except Pelkaia's storm-grey eyes tinged with green, her skin of selium peeling in the rain, her thin lips twitching with all the foul words she held back. To put up a mirror to scare off the watchers would be to lose the sel involved in its making. That'd be it. The whole of their reserve. A fortune lost to the storm. To running. She knew it. He knew it. He didn't dare look anywhere but at her cold, hard stare.

Detan refused to say another word. Just stood steady, and waited for the crest of her anger to break. Her cheeks twitched. She reached up to drag her fingers through wet hair.

"Won't be any hiding the *Larkspur* after this," she said.

Detan turned his back on her, gripped the smooth controls of the ship he'd planned to steal all that time ago.

"Then I suggest you practice putting on Thratia's face."

She stomped off, Coss trudging at her heels. Detan shut them out of his mind. Shut the howl of the wind and the cursing of the crew away. Shuttered aside the cold on his skin and the weakness suffusing his bones. Damped the white ember of rage blossoming in his chest.

When he opened his eyes again he was centered, calm. Only Tibs's voice mattered now. Tibs's voice, and the feel of the wind.

Tibs marked a course, and Detan began to steer around the rising storm.

CHAPTER 28

The watchers were suicidal. Either that or so frothed with anger at having been played by a couple of conmen and a doppel that they couldn't see the danger. Didn't much matter the reason. It only mattered that, as Detan steered the bucking *Larkspur* through troubled winds, the watchers' inferior craft dogged their heels.

"Are they trying to get themselves killed?" he called to Tibs above the whip of the winds.

"Are we?"

Detan grimaced and re-squared his stance, gripping the wheel so hard his knuckles went white. Maybe he was as mad as the watchers, but at least Detan figured he had a good reason. His options were limited, after all. He either turned around and got himself arrested in Petrastad, or risked the storm to reach the Remnant. Neither path had a particularly sunny outlook. He told himself he was doing it for Ripka, New Chum, and the hope of Nouli. Told himself the risk was worth it, that it'd be all right in the end.

Didn't matter what he told himself. The storm was the storm, and every new gust threatened to cartwheel them through the clouds.

The cloud suck towered on his left, the mighty edifice of wind and rain and lightning indifferent to his struggles. Detan wrinkled his nose at it in defiance. Couldn't ever count on the weather to have any manners. The wheel gave a shiver, just to shake his nerves up some more, and the nose of the ship jerked upward.

Someone let out an undignified squeal. The podium shuddered as a deckhand rolled into it. The wheel jerked from Detan's hands and spun, slamming into a half-pulled chock peg. Wood cracked, split down the middle, shards scattered across the deck. He grabbed for the wheel but the ship swerved to larboard, dipping as the wheel forced the wings to bank.

His heels kissed the sky as his ass became acquainted with the deck. He swore, pain exploding in his backside, teeth jarred by the impact. Scrambling, slipping, he hauled himself half-upright and fumbled for the wheel. A gust rocked the ship, tossing him. He missed, grabbed the little cherry red wheel instead. It was tough, whoever had made it hadn't wanted it pulled without real effort, but Detan's weight hauled down on it as he scrambled to his feet, not realizing what he held.

The ship dropped. Hard.

"Close it off!" Tibs screeched. With a curse Detan grabbed the main wheel and yanked it over, setting the *Larkspur* straight again. He got his wits together enough to realize what he'd done and cranked the cherry wheel back until it wouldn't turn anymore. Too late to do much good. He'd purged one of the buoyancy sacks. A neat trick, if a sel-sensitive were prepared for it, ready to take control of the sel and push it out with enough force to speed the ship along. But none of them had been ready for it. And now the ship was sinking.

"Jettison!" he yelled loud as he could above the winds.

Crew scrambled. Barrels of water and coils of rope and sacks of cloth were heaved to the sea. The cabin doors were yanked open, every scrap of inessential materiel thrown to the yawning black. The ship settled into an unsteady neutral. Detan shook so hard he had to set a fresh chock in the wheel to keep from vibrating them into a turn. That was too damned close.

He rose to his toes and peered over the top of the podium. A wind-whipped deckhand staggered to his feet, looking like he'd kissed the wrong end of a porcupine.

"You all right?" Detan called above the winds.

The deckhand shook his head to clear it and prodded at his newly purpled cheek. "Whole enough." He tested the tie-line hooked to his belt that held him to the ship. "Still secured."

"Wonderful." Detan beamed at him. The deckhand beamed back. "Now don't touch my fucking podium again."

The deckhand blanched, cut an awkward head-bobbing bow, and scuttled back to whatever his position was.

"Good for the morale," Tibs drawled.

"When being charming will wiggle us away from this storm, then I'll put the manners back on."

Detan wound up the starboard propeller, hoping the extra propulsion would force them to turn despite the winds. He'd rather use the stabilizing wings to ease into the turn at a gentle bank – or, pits, even the sails – but with the winds gusting he didn't dare take the ship off a neutral attitude. If cloud cover washed over them again, he'd bet his new boots they'd be in the water before he could find the horizon again.

"West thirty degrees," Tibs called.

The propeller's gear wheel groaned in his hand as he heaved it around. Even the fine gear ratios of Valathean engineering had a hard time gaining traction against these winds. A gust rocked the starboard, swung up out of nowhere, and the ship slewed, drawing startled yelps all around.

Detan glanced up on instinct, and regretted it as soon as his vision cleared the podium's top. The *Larkspur*'s ponderous turn kept it level, but the deck was scattered with crew who'd been knocked over by the gust, dragging themselves back to their feet. A few crew had latched themselves into the auxiliary cranks on the propellers, adding their muscle to his when the wheel he controlled signaled them to heave-to. Their extra strength was, no doubt, the only thing standing between Detan's manipulations of the ship and the force of the storm winds.

The cloud suck loomed off the prow. Wasn't close enough for Detan to make out much detail, thank the clear skies, but it was close enough to make his skin crawl. Crackles of lightning tore through its heart, great swathes of grey-black cloud twisting around an eye bigger than the whole of Petrastad. He couldn't see the top of it, it reached so high. The whole of the massive system bled out into a smear of steely grey. No stars peaked through those clouds. His stomach clenched.

He'd heard stories of ships that got caught too near those towers. The currents were strong enough to sweep up anyone who wandered near. Sweep them up and smash them against the ceiling of the sky. What was left of those ships, if any remains were ever found, was scattered in unrecognizable bits in too large a radius to search, some of the wood frozen solid from the great heights. The corpses fared worse.

"We'll make it," Tibs said, as if he could hear the direction of Detan's thoughts. Maybe he wasn't full of shit. Already they'd banked far enough away from the great tower that the strength of the winds began to slip, to ebb. The wheel jerked less beneath his palms, the wings trembled only slightly. A gust of hail scattered the deck, bouncing off the hardened wood and bewildered crew. A thumbnail sized chunk of ice pinged off Detan's head and he yelped. Tibs chuckled.

"Shoulda brought a hat."

"Shouldn't have let a wiry scab make off with my hat."

"Ain't yours."

"Fits me just fine."

"If by fine you mean it looks clownish on that pinhead of yours, then sure."

"You dustswallower—" He cut himself off as a ripple of panic spread across the deck. Crew members who'd been attempting to recover the cloud of selium before they'd entered the storm crowded the larboard rail. Some held hands to their mouths in mute shock, others waved arms over the edge in direction.

Curious as a cat in a cave, he made sure all the wheels were chocked before scurrying over to join the crew at the rail. His tie-line trailed out behind him, growing taut as the captain wasn't meant to stray far from the podium when the skies were rough enough to require tying in. He made it to the rail, the rope tugging his belt behind him, leaving him open to a rather chilly gust down the backside.

Below, farther than he'd be comfortable jumping, the watcher craft was in trouble. It shimmied and slewed in the winds, the tattered remains of its sail whipping in all directions as the winds gusted up and over. Watchers scurried to and fro across the deck, not guided by a practiced hand, everyone trying to do whatever they felt was more pertinent in the moment. Detan winced. Any captain blind enough to lead a craft out into a storm like this without a prepared crew should lose his post, if they didn't lose their life for the error first.

He clenched the rail, leaning as far forward as his tie line would let him. The *Larkspur*'s presence – a stable shadow above the craft – was outright ignored by the watchers. They had bigger troubles than an empress's ransom in selium and a rogue doppel to capture.

The sel Pelkaia's sensitives had tried to reclaim drifted through the air, pearly shimmers blending with the clouds like oil slicks. Whatever cohesion had existed within the cloud was lost to the storm and the tug-of-war game Pelkaia's people had played with the watchers. Her crew continued on, trying to recapture what was left, but Detan knew it to be a lost cause. His strength may have been enough to gather it all up, but he wasn't about to take that chance.

"Looks bad." Tibs sidled up to Detan's side, his tie-line

pulling the back of his coat into a puffed-up tent.

"Don't think they'll make it back to Petrastad. Or the Remnant, if they can even find the heading."

"Don't think they need to."

Tibs jerked his chin to the west, and Detan squinted against the wind to see what he meant. Somewhere down there in the water was a darker splotch. Oblong and ragged, one of the smaller members of the Remnant Isles pockmarked the white-capped sea, the only refuge the watchers had to hope for this far from the coast. That spit of land, where the weather would keep on being rough and food would be scarce. Or the *Larkspur*.

He sighed. And those watchers were probably having such a pleasant evening until he sauntered into their tower. Detan surveyed the deck for the lean, familiar frame of Pelkaia. He spotted her near the main mast, inspecting the damage. Coss was hooked in beside her, coiling a rope.

"Ho, captain!"

She glanced up, saw him waving at her, and went right back to what she was doing. Stubborn woman. Ignoring the exhaustion turning his legs to jelly, he sauntered toward her, careful not to tangle his line, and stopped when he was close enough to lean his weight against the creaking mast.

"Pelly, our courageous leader. How about showing off a soft spot on that old heart of yours and bringing our new friends aboard? It's us or the water, I'm afraid, and I think they'd much rather be our prisoners than the sharks'."

"Leave them for the sharks. Maybe they'll get indigestion from my stolen selium."

Coss flinched, but kept his head down, fussing with a knot.

Detan lowered his voice and leaned forward, angling his body to cut off Pelkaia's view of the mast. "They're innocents."

"They would have killed me for my birthright. That strike you as innocent?"

"Ripka would have killed you, too."

"She changed."

"She had time to. Time you're not giving those boys in blue floundering below. You save them, maybe you might win some hearts. Or are you only out to spill blood in this war of yours?"

"I didn't start this war."

"Just because you didn't start this war doesn't mean you can't change how it's fought."

Coss's head jerked up and he stared at Detan like he was seeing him for the first time. Wasn't right to look at a soul like that, like you could see every bit of them exposed right out on the deck. It sent shivers straight down Detan's spine. Pelkaia pursed her lips and started to protest, but a cry from the rail overrode her words.

Detan abandoned them to their repairs and hurried back to the rail, flicking his tie-line behind him to keep from becoming entangled in one more thing. He could hear Pelkaia and Coss hurrying after him, but he ignored them. He peered over the edge, and his stomach sank.

The watcher craft was badly damaged, slewing in a slow spiral toward the sea. They'd turned it around enough that it might make it to the black mass of an island, but steerage was clearly out of their hands now. One end dipped precariously, the other reached toward the clouds. The watchers' cries were drowned out by the wind and the rain, but he could imagine them all the same. Could imagine their fear.

Sel leaked from a crack in the sinking end of the ship, the crew of Pelkaia's *Larkspur* dutifully reining in what little they could reach. Detan sucked his teeth, stiffened his spine. The watchers had tied in – he'd seen that truth for himself – and they were heading straight toward a small spit of land. Some would survive. Some would be in need of medical care. Care the crew of the *Larkspur* could provide.

Before Detan could act, Tibs turned tight on his heels and stalked to Pelkaia's side.

"We're landing," he said with a voice like calm winds. Like

iron. "We're going to help those people."

Her lip curled. "Those watchers."

"Last time I checked, watchers were people."

"Captain–" Coss said. She snapped a fist up to silence him.

Detan held his breath. He could see the tension in Tibs's shoulders, the tendons straining at the sides of his narrow neck, his fists held low and tight. Not a threat. Not exactly. You'd have to know Tibs well to see the anger building, the storm about to break.

"Captain," Detan said, forcing his voice to be chipper. Tibs didn't so much as twitch an eyebrow as Detan strolled over to his side and clapped a hand on his shoulder. "It has occurred to me that many of the solutions to your present predicaments may be found in coming to the aid of the watchers below."

She tipped her head, but her gaze remained locked tight on Tibs. "The solution to all my problems could be found in throwing you both off my ship."

"Ah, well. While your proposed solution offers a certain ruthless charm, allow me to recommend a less messy path."

Her hand raised in threat of a gesture. He swallowed, certain that if he allowed her to complete that motion she really would sentence them both to being tossed to the sharks.

"Hear him out," Coss said. Her arm froze mid-motion. She said nothing.

He cleared his throat. "It has occurred to me that the *Larkspur* is in need of weapons and selium. Both items sure to be aboard the watcher craft, though admittedly in lesser quantity now than when they set off upon their merry chase."

"Do you suppose I have forgotten why the *Larkspur* is in need of those things?"

"I'm supposing the why doesn't matter. The need is there. You have a solution to a problem."

Tibs said, "I suggest you take the Lord Honding's idea to heart."

"*Lord*?" Pelkaia said, but Coss slapped her on the back in

feign of comradely affection, and cupped his hands around his mouth.

Coss called to the watching crew, "Man stations! We're going down to that hunk of island to rebalance our scales!"

A hesitant cheer went up from the crew, a bit worse for their exhausted and water-logged state of being, but Detan wasn't one to quibble with their enthusiasm. He was busy trying to nudge Tibs away from his viper-glare showdown with Pelkaia, and desperately clamping down an urge to point out Coss had gone ahead and issued an order against his captain's wishes.

"Coss," Pelkaia said, finally relinquishing Tibs from her stare. "My quarters."

She strode off, Coss trailing her heels, and Detan let out a ragged, nervous laugh.

"Some ally we've got in our corner. I'd have rather made friends with a weaver-spider."

Tibs gave a slow, ponderous shake of his head, rain water and bits of ice slewing off the brim of his hat. "Knew what she was when we called for her."

"Thought we did, anyway." Detan sighed and shook out his hair with his fingers. "Too bad she didn't come with a convenient warning label, like our friend Commodore Throatslitter."

Tibs cocked a surly grin at him. "How does Captain Ruthless sound?"

"Bah. That's too on the nose, old chum. I'd prefer something truly sinister. Like Colonel Cuddles."

"Awful."

"See? Perfection."

Detan threw an arm around Tibs's shoulder and began to steer them back toward the captain's podium so that they could help with the ship's landing. There was no telling how long Pelkaia would be busy dressing-down poor Coss.

CHAPTER 29

Pelkaia held her tongue until the door to her cabin closed. She let her hand rest on the cold metal knob for a while, feeling the chill of the world through her fingertips. The rain and the wind were loud enough to drown out any shouting, but she didn't want to shout at Coss. The last thing she wanted to do was to piss the man off when he was already so clearly displeased with her. She took a breath, pushed her shoulders back, and turned to face him. She almost recoiled from the look in his eye.

"You gave an order I didn't issue," she said carefully. Not an accusation. Just raw facts.

He leaned back, putting distance between their bodies, and crossed his arms over his chest. The defiant lift to his chin would have been enough to piss her off on any normal day, but after Petrastad... She was too tired to be angry with him. And wanted, desperately, to know why he was angry with her. She was surprised to realize she wanted to fix that. To repair what she'd broken and beg amends.

"I gave the order you should have given. That's my job as first mate, isn't it? Interpreting the best course of action when you are otherwise unable to do so."

"I was right there. I was perfectly capable of making the call."

"The right call?"

She pursed her lips. "Yes."

"And that's where we disagree. Captain."

She kept her face a mask of placid calm, wishing to the blessed stars that she had some more sel with her to hide her real features. Having her true skin exposed to the air when she was otherwise vulnerable made her scalp prickle with anticipation of disaster. If only she had another face to hide under, then she could pretend a little longer that Coss was arguing with that person – not her.

"You disagree, you take it up with me in private. That was our deal."

"Doing so now, ain't I?"

Her fists clenched. "You know clear as the skies are blue what I mean. You knew I wouldn't have made that call. Knew it would have made me look weak to override you after you'd called it out."

"Maybe you need to look weaker."

"What in the fiery pits is that supposed to mean? I've a ship to command, a war to win. I've no room for weakness, especially not in front of my thrice-cursed crew."

"Is that what you're doing? Fighting a war?"

Her mouth gaped open. "Whose ship have you taken berth on, Coss? Where do you think you are? I've been fighting this war since I spilled Faud's blood in Aransa, and I won't stop until Thratia joins him in the dirt."

"That's just the problem, isn't it?"

"Gods," she muttered and pinched the bridge of her nose between two fingers. "For the love of a clear sky, explain what you're getting at. I'm too sandblasted tired to wiggle my way through your nonsense."

"Nonsense?" He snorted and shook his head. "Let me make the problem real clear for you, captain. You're fighting a war. Where's your army?"

"My crew–"

"Those aren't your soldiers!" She clapped her mouth shut from pure shock at his outburst. "Your crew out there, those souls you order about like they should know the meaning of military discipline. They're not soldiers. They never have been soldiers. They're deviant sensitives, yes, and some of their abilities may lean toward a military persuasion, but they're civilians, Pell. Skies above, they're *refugees*. You're shoving refugees in the path of the monster that's oppressed them and demanding they scream your battle cry. Demanding they draw blood, when half of them haven't slaughtered so much as a chicken before in their lives."

"I seem to recall you saying they were ready for this," she snapped. "I seem to recall you telling me to give them more rope, more freedom to get involved."

"I said they were ready to *save* their own people, ready to learn to carry arms in defense. I never said they were ready for this..." He grasped the air as if he could squeeze the words he wanted out of it. "This wholesale slaughter."

She sat hard on the bench before her vanity, and let her hands dangle between her knees. She stared at her hands, wondering when she'd gone from rearing dear Kel to spilling blood in his name. She clenched her fists.

"I never asked for this."

"Neither did they. This is your crusade, and it could be theirs, too, but you're pushing them too quickly. Expecting them to take up blades of battle right after setting down their damned cheese knives. That's not a group of killers you have out there. And that's a *good* thing. But you're scaring the salt out of them with all this let-the-watchers-die talk. Shit, Pell, some of them are people who just weeks before we picked them up would have happily gone to their local watch with any trouble in their lives. Petty thieving isn't murder. The two don't translate."

"It's Honding," she protested. "He's pushed things forward too quickly, didn't give me time to get them acclimated to the fight–"

"Honding's a catalyst, I won't deny it. But he's only showing off the cracks that were already there. It's not his fault the crew's shying from your fight."

"It's mine."

"Yes," Coss said, and the word weighed heavy in her heart. He knelt before the bench and reached out to take her clenched hands. With his big, scarred fingers he eased her fists open, smoothed out the taut and spasming muscles of her palms, then held her, gentle as could be. She dared to pick her head up, to look him in the eye. He smiled, and she felt a little lighter.

"Come on, captain. Let's get back out on deck and show them how strong that heart of yours can be."

"Lead the way," she said, and stood, hands still wrapped in his.

"I already did." He dropped her hand and gestured toward the door. "The rest is up to you."

CHAPTER 30

Pelkaia showed a deft hand at the captain's podium as she angled the ship toward the island, descent propellers heaving away to overcome the ship's natural tendency to stay on a neutral plane. Detan had declined the crew's offer to join them on the cranks for those particular propellers. He had, after all, a sore back from wrestling the ship through the storm and rather felt he deserved the rest.

He crowded the fore rail with a damp Tibs at his side as they dropped through the thick layer of cloud cover, following the faint wisps of selium leaking out from the watcher ship. Between cloud and rain and sleet, Detan's clothes and hair were plastered to his body, a permanent shell of cold. He crossed his arms to huddle against the wind, but didn't find the experience much better.

"Wish I had a hot whisky," Tibs said, mirroring Detan's hunkered posture.

"Wish I had a hot anything."

"We'll get a fire going on the island."

"So our benevolent captain can roast us over it?"

"You know what? I'd be all right with that about now."

The cloud peeled back and the island revealed itself. Little more than a thumbprint of land clinging to life amongst the waves, the rocky shore was dotted with wind-bent trees, clustering toward the center of the island in a great green mass. A narrow stretch of empty beach ringed the north end of the island, the only place large enough to anchor a ship the size of the *Larkspur* with any hint toward safety. Sure enough, the ship angled that way, even though the watcher craft was tangled up in the trees a good ways down the shore. Detan flinched, glancing away from the wreckage, and told himself the moans were the wind groaning through the trees.

The crew fired the anchor harpoons from the fore and aft, the ship jerking as the heavy bolts bit into the soil and held tight. Rope ladders were slung over the rail, the weary crew shimmying down them with what little medical supplies they had to spare strapped to their backs. Pelkaia's crew was in poor enough shape to care for themselves, let alone the crashed watchers. But this was the least they could do for their fellow men and women. And maybe, just maybe, they could convince a few watchers they weren't such monsters after all.

Stamping some semblance of warmth into his feet, Detan joined the crew at the ladders and dropped down to the rough rocks of the beach. His heels sunk in, squelching as he tromped across the sand. Hond Steading may have been a bit north and prone to a chill breeze on occasion, but Detan reckoned his bones weren't bred for this kind of cold, and the sticky mist clinging to him wasn't doing much to help the situation. Huffing breath into his hands to warm them up, he stomped circles on the beach as the rest of the crew spilled down the ladders. Jeffin stayed behind to work on repairs. Detan was grateful for that. The man's simple presence irked him.

Something dark and lean nestled in the curve of the northern stretch of beach. Detan squinted, brought a hand up to shield his eyes, then realized there wasn't any sun to shield them from.

"Hey, Tibs," he called. "You see that?"

Tibs tipped up the brim of his hat to see better. "Looks like a shed. Or a boat."

Detan snorted. "A real boat? Ridiculous."

"Either way, we're not alone on this island."

Essi wandered over to them and peered at the structure. "Who'd want anything to do with this anthill?"

Detan and Tibs exchanged a look. "Someone wanting close proximity to the Remnant," they said in unison.

Detan spun around and sought out Pelkaia, standing off to the side with Coss and Laella. He raised his voice to carry across the wind and distance. "Pelly, arm your people! We've got company on this pits-cursed island."

Pelkaia raised the cutlass she had been fitting into her weapons belt. "Had you expected us to charge in after the watchers without protection?" She eyed him pointedly. "Although it occurs to me that, despite best efforts to the contrary, we are substantially under-armed."

"Err, yes, of course. Carry on," he said and kicked at a clump of seaweed.

"Going to tell her about the key?" Tibs asked, drawing a curious glance from Essi.

"When she doesn't have something pointy in her hand, yes."

"What key?" Essi asked.

"The key to that mouth of yours."

She kicked sand over Detan's wet boots and stomped off to join the rest of the crew.

"You got a way with kids," Tibs said.

"I am a charmer."

"Didn't say it was a good way."

They tromped across the beach, joining the back fringe of Pelkaia's group, and followed the spearhead of her armed crewmembers along the rocky shore toward the last sighted location of the watcher craft. They didn't have far to walk.

The moans of pain reached them before the sight of the wreck did.

The airship had snagged in the treetops on its way down, spilling its crew in a heinous spiral across moss-covered boulders and the rocky shore. Tie-lines had snapped under the force of the crash. Those who escaped relatively unscathed were at work gathering their injured on softer ground, but Detan counted only three watchers on their feet. The rest were broken shades of themselves.

Detan had gone three steps before he noticed Tibs had halted. And then he realized his mistake in bringing Tibs here.

Watchers – men and women in uniform – strewn broken and weeping across the sands. The heady tang of iron-rich blood on the air, the eerie mist of selium escaping through the treetops. The twisted wooden wreckage. All things Tibs had seen before – *must* have seen before – in darker times when he served the empire. When he kept the machines of war breathing fire from above.

"Tibs, why don't you go back to the ship and keep an eye on Jeffin? With strangers on the island, wouldn't want the kid getting out of his depth."

It was a weak excuse, and they both knew it, but Tibs took it like a rope thrown to a drowning man. He nodded, gaze glued on the damaged bodies, and sucked at his teeth.

"Reckon that's a good idea."

Detan waited until Tibs was a good halfway back to the ship before he turned his attention to the damaged watchers. He cursed himself for a fool for dragging Tibs out here at all. He should have known what the scene would look like. Should have known it'd hit Tibs as hard as rounding a corner into a whitecoat party would hit Detan himself.

Pelkaia's cutlass was sheathed as she talked with the injured watch-captain, but Laella and Coss had their blades out. They held them low and at ease, but the threat was clear enough. Detan lingered behind the group and ignored their conversation. He had no stomach for the petty dance of threats they were playing.

A watcher woman lay on the sand not far from where he stood. She leaned against a dripping boulder, legs splayed out before her, swimming in pools of red. Her eyes were closed, but her chest rose and fell with ragged breath. She didn't appear strong enough to have pushed herself up on her own, which meant her fellow watchers had propped her up. And then left her to die.

Detan ambled over and sat on the sand beside her, ignoring the salty wet seeping through his backside. He was already wet enough, he could handle a little more discomfort to see this woman through to the endless night.

"Hi," he said. Her eyelids fluttered. "I'm Detan."

She tipped her head toward him, lolled it against the rock. One eyelid was swollen shut, the other half-open, but the eye behind it bright. Alert. He shifted in the sand so that she could see him without having to crane her head.

"Alli," she said. "Have you come to pick us off?"

"No." He shook his head. "We've come to help, if we can."

She swept him from his crossed legs to his ruffled hair with her one good eye. "I can't say we would have done the same for you."

"That's all right. I don't blame you."

"You should."

She coughed, her shoulders shaking. Detan waited until the fit had passed before he spoke again.

"You were just doing your job. Trying to keep Petrastad safe. I understand that more than you might think."

She chuckled. "Do you, now? I didn't realize you were an expert on municipal matters, though that explains the ease with which you infiltrated our tower."

He grimaced. "I don't mean to belittle what you do."

She waved him to silence. "No. No. But I meant to belittle you. I've heard that some people get calm when they're facing death. That they go into the dark with grace and dignity. Turns out I just get surly."

He thought of Ripka, standing on the roof of a jailhouse in Aransa, wearing a coat much like the one Alli wore. Thought of her lifting her chin, facing the Black Wash and her impending death with pride and calm. He'd admired her for that. He found he admired Alli, too.

"There's no good way to go," he said.

"I suppose there isn't."

She fell quiet for a while, her good eye gazing out to sea. Detan wondered if his presence was a comfort or a hindrance. If he were bleeding his last in the surf, he'd want someone there to witness it. To sit with him while his blood mingled with the salt and the world drew in to nothing all around him. But he worried that he might be imposing. That maybe she'd sent her watcher fellows away, and that's why she was all alone here. Could be she was only suffering his presence because she lacked the strength to tell him to get lost.

He shifted, making to rise and leave her to her peace, and her eye snapped open as far as it could. He stayed.

"I took this job for the money," she said.

"Isn't that why people take jobs?"

"Hah. You're as cynical as I was. No. Lucky for the two of us, it isn't. Some people don the blues because they want to help. They care. I came to, in time, but to start with... Well, my husband was a sel-miner, fell to bonewither earlier than most. Shuffles around the house like my grandpa used to, and he's only forty. There's the stipend for retired miners, but the good medicines... They cost."

"So you didn't take the job for the money."

"Maybe not. But don't mistake me, Detan, I've a taste for fruit pies the stipend just wasn't covering."

He laughed and rummaged through his trouser pocket. "It's no fruit pie," he said and pulled out a waxpaper-wrapped bar of sticky honey and crushed nuts. "And it's probably wet and salty, but here." He broke off a small corner and placed it on her tongue. She swished it around and smiled.

"Salt's a nice touch."

He took a bite and grimaced. "If you say so."

They sat in silence for a while, sharing the ration bar while the pool around her legs got darker and her skin grew paler. When the bar was finished, he scrubbed his hands in the wet sand and wiped them pointlessly against his Fleetman's coat. The sun sagged against the horizon, pink-crimson spears radiating through the sky. He looked away, not liking the color of the sky any more than he liked the color of Alli's face.

"It was the bonus pay that did it," she said.

He blinked. "Huh?"

"After Aransa fell. Every watcher district was promised a bonus for each deviant or rogue sensitive turned over to the empire. Petrastad never had many before, you know. We're not a sel-city, which is why my husband and I moved out here. Thought being away from the source might help. But the city always had its fringe, weak sensitives who escaped notice. The watch looked the other way until Valathea started offering a premium per head. That's why we chased you down. Whole ship full of rogue sensitives? It'd mean a fortune."

He closed his eyes as his stomach sunk. "I'm sorry."

"Don't be, Lord Honding."

He winced. "You knew?"

"I guessed. Detan's a common enough name, but the *Larkspur* is unmistakable. I hadn't seen it before today, you understand, but the description got around. Valathea wants you something bad, you know. They've been sending delegates to every city with a watch presence to distribute your likeness and warn us all to take you in upon sight. I don't know what you did, I doubt it's what they've told us, but..." She licked her lips, lapped up a bit of the honey left there. "They're hungry for you. Don't let them catch you."

"I've no intention of letting them."

"Good." She nodded firmly. "So that really is the *Larkspur*, then?"

He grinned. "Yes, it is. Beautiful, isn't she?"

"I've never seen anything like her. It's like a real, old ship sailing through the sky."

"I suppose that was the idea when Thratia commissioned her. Now Pelkaia's crew has to keep most of her lines masked so as to not give the game away."

"The game," she rolled the word across her tongue. "You and that crew really are picking up rogue sensitives all across the Scorched?"

"They do. I'm just aboard to call in a favor."

"And what might that be?"

He chuckled. "Nosy, aren't you?"

She winked at him with her good eye. "Who am I going to tell?"

"All right." He crossed his legs and leaned in closer. "Answer me this, then: what are they saying I did in Aransa?"

"Ooh," she whistled, a soft, thready sound. "Got that big of an ego, eh?"

"The biggest."

"Well, they claim you tried to set off the firemount there, and that Watch-captain Leshe died stopping you."

He snorted. "I'll tell her that. Not only will she be offended she's dead, she'll be doubly offended my sorry hide managed to pick her off."

"Your turn," Alli's voice dragged out into a rasp.

"I'm using the *Larkspur* to pick up a friend."

"Vague," she admonished.

"Captain Leshe herself. From the Remnant."

She tried to raise her brows at him and winced. "I would have heard if she were working there."

"She's not."

"Now *that's* interesting."

He held both hands toward the sky. "I aim to entertain, my dear."

"I almost wish I could live a day or two longer, just to see how you plan to get her out of there."

"I assure you, I can get up to all kinds of trouble in the time you have left."

Her head rolled against the boulder, angling her vision toward the crew working with her watcher brethren. "They're good people, the crew of the *Larkspur*?"

Detan licked his lips and eyed them. Pelkaia had reached some sort of agreement with the watch-captain and was helping him distribute the troops as it were, matching up her crew's skill sets with complementary sets from the watchers. She'd forgone a face of selium, leaving her Catari blood bare to all who looked at her. Sandy hair, the same color as Ripka's, fell around her cheeks in waves made frizzy by the rain and sea-winds. She looked harried, but focused. Determined to see this thing through, and to do it well. Detan smiled.

"They're getting better. Better than me, at any rate."

Alli's hand flexed in the sand, trembling from lack of strength. He took it without asking, held it between both of his and stroked the back with care. She didn't so much as glance his way. He suspected she'd run out of strength. He considered laying his sodden coat over her, but he knew full well her chill was coming from within. The warmest coat in the Scorched couldn't hold it back.

"I want you to do me a favor."

"Ask it."

"My husband, Rei. He has a sister in Salsana, north of here, with a little boy about twelve. He's started to show some sel-sense..."

"Strong?"

"Unusually."

He nodded and squeezed her hand. "If Captain Pelkaia won't get him out of there, I will."

She swallowed. When she spoke again a soft rattle hissed in her chest. "Lovely sunset today."

He freed one hand and reached to turn her head away from the crew, back toward the sinking sun. When his fingers curled around her chin, he found her skin cold and clammy. Her eyes, once turned toward the sun, were empty. Glazed with something like tears.

Detan folded her hand into her lap and arranged her with as much dignity as he could. He sat there awhile, holding vigil. Wondering why he couldn't feel her presence anymore, though her body sat cooling beside him. Nothing had changed, not really. If he ignored the stillness of her chest he could tell himself she'd speak again. That the growing emptiness beside him was nothing but his own fear.

He'd never been a religious man. Never prayed to the stars or the sky unless in jest or curse. Not even when his mother lay still beside him, the bonewither eating her up until there was nothing left but the same emptiness he felt now. The only comfort he'd ever wrapped himself in was the company of his friends, the sureness of his scheming. If Alli had religious beliefs, she hadn't mentioned them, and yet he felt like he should do something. Felt that there must be *something* one does to honor the end of a life.

Bel Grandon's throat, gaping red and pumping her life to the floor, filled his mind. He shivered. What had been done for her, after he'd leapt from Thratia's dock?

"Detan," Pelkaia's voice was soft, but he jumped all the same and glared up at her. "You'll freeze, sitting in the surf like that." She offered him her hand, reaching across Alli's body. He took it, pulled himself to his feet. Brushed sand from his pants and coat.

"The others?" he asked.

"Those who didn't die on impact are mostly whole. We may lose a few in the cold tonight, or to infection, and the broken bones are always a risk for future illness. But most should survive. Watch-captain Gisald is wary, but thankful to have our help. They've agreed not to pursue us once we get them on their way again. We've confiscated their weapons for the time being, though most are waterlogged. The selium remaining in their craft is sparse, but..."

Detan felt the sudden cold of the setting sun lance through him. "You will let them keep it to get home, Pelkaia. You will not take it for your ship."

She kicked at a seashell. "I agree with you. We'll camp on the beach for the night and move the injured watchers to the *Larkspur* in the morning. Then we can see about patching up their barge."

He nodded. "I'll go back and tell Tibs and the others, maybe grab a few extra rations and tarps."

"You do that."

Detan trudged off back down the beach, wishing he'd volunteered to stay behind and get the fire burning instead. His sodden clothes clung to him, felt like tiny knives of ice kissing his skin all over as the night winds swept in.

"Honding," Pelkaia called after him. "This was the right choice. Thank you."

He kept on walking, pretending he hadn't heard, and listened for the soft tread of her feet retreating back across the sands to rejoin her crew. Any other day he'd gloat. He'd dance around her scowling face and sing his own praises, insisting she should listen to him more often. But not today. Not with the chill of Alli's hand in his no different than the icy brush of the sea. He'd made the right choice insisting they come down here and help, he was sure of that.

He just wasn't sure he'd made any of the right choices leading up to that moment.

The more he played these games, the more he found doing things for good reasons wasn't enough. Dealing a blow to Thratia. Sparing a murderous doppel. Making off with a ship and then letting it go.

Convincing Ripka and New Chum that Nouli was Hond Steading's greatest hope.

He shoved his hands in his pockets and shivered, speeding his steps toward the *Larkspur* and Tibs. He'd feel better, he was sure, if he had Tibs nearby to explain what an idiot he'd been. It always sounded better when Tibs laid things out for him.

A strand of trees to his left rustled and he paused, expecting some weather-beaten local animal to make its presence known. Instead, a rangy looking man stepped from the trees and stood before him, a nice shiny crossbow leveled at Detan's chest.

Detan giggled. The man's eyebrows shot up.

"Something funny, boy?"

"Oh, it's just been one of those days." He held his hands up to either side to show they were empty, and was unsurprised when two other men slunk from the trees and patted him down for weapons.

"What are you doing on this island?" the man demanded when his fellows had declared Detan free of weapons.

"Would you believe vacationing?"

Someone clipped him in the back of the head and he sunk to one knee, head swimming. A hand grabbed the back of his collar and jerked him to his feet, touching the scar flesh of his family crest there. He grimaced as his collar was twisted askew so that his captor could get a better look.

"Got ourselves a Honding," a man said. The one with the crossbow smirked.

"Interesting. Walk, Honding. We're going to go have a chat with your friends."

His captor spun him around and shoved him forward, back toward the crew and the watchers. Detan tromped along, wondering if he'd ever be warm again.

CHAPTER 31

Lankal would not speak as he lowered Ripka and Enard into the well. His silence shamed her more than any words could, the grievous frown turning down his lips wounded her pride more than a sharp retort. Ripka knew that his disapproval should not bother her. Knew that he had only a partial view of what was happening on his island and her involvement with it. But she'd spent far too long struggling to gain the approval of authority figures not to be made uncomfortable by a kind captain's disappointment.

The wound in her hand hurt less than that silence.

Enard went down the well first while another harness was found for Ripka. It seemed that, despite the Remnant's fearsome reputation, the guards didn't often have reason to drop two people down the well for punishment at once. Or, at the very least, they rarely had two people they'd trust not to kill each other during their confinement.

She hadn't been able to grip the side of the well with both hands as she'd done before, her injured hand possessed no strength, so she'd dropped over the side, trusting to Lankal's ability to fit the harness properly. It dug into her ribs and armpits, but it held.

As her feet touched down in the dark, loamy soil, a couple

of waterskins and a few rolls of bread tumbled down after her. They bounced in the dirt. When Ripka felt the waterskin, she realized that, this time, they had been shorted. She supposed it didn't matter much. They'd try to spend most of the night sleeping, anyway.

Lankal and the guards who lowered them said nothing. They just left.

"So this is the well," Enard said. He ran a hand over the slick stones and pulled it away, rubbing grime between his fingers. "I've stayed in dirtier hostels."

"I think you'll find the room service leaves a lot to be desired." Crouching, she scooped up one of the hard-crusted rolls and flicked off dirt.

"I'm sorry you've had to enjoy the well's hospitality twice now."

"I'm sorry you've had to enjoy it at all. I don't reckon the night will be any easier than the day."

A low wind howled over the mouth of the well, sending a spiral of cold air and leaf debris down into their tiny prison. She shivered and sat, huddling up as she rested her back against the dank stone. Reluctantly, she gnawed on the roll. Enard joined her. She scooted away, putting darkness between them. They used more water than they should washing down the old bread, but she didn't care. She wasn't even sure they'd live past their meeting with Radu in the morning.

When they'd finished eating, he asked, "What is it?"

She pressed her back against the wall. "What do you mean?"

He sighed. "Interrogate me."

"What?"

"This well is three strides across, and you've never been further away. Ask. Whatever it is you need to, just... Ask."

Ripka licked her lips, and squinted across the small space between them. It had grown dark enough that she could not see his face, couldn't even begin to read the expression there, and so she closed her eyes, and listened to the subtle intonations of his voice instead.

"Marya. Ledi. Who are they?"

"They…" His voice caught. "They're Oiler's daughters. Twins."

"Are they known to the Glasseaters?"

"Not widely, no."

"How did you come by this knowledge?"

Hesitation. "Father had us follow all of the big bosses for a moon-turn. Oiler only visited them once during that time, but it was enough. I remembered."

"Why?"

"It was my job to."

"And would you make good on your threat?"

Fabric rustled as he flinched, but his answer was without hesitation. "No. Never. Those girls… I never told Father about them. But they were the only leverage I had today."

"And if they become your only leverage in the future?"

A sharp intake of breath. "Then I will be without leverage."

She chewed that over, wondering. Violence had come so easily to him – as it did to her – but she had been trained to restore peace, not to sow fear. How deep were his instincts, despite his wishes to change? If they ran as deep as hers, then they were a part of him, immutable. Breath, sinew, and bone.

"You seem wary of me still."

"I've seen men and women who've said they'd changed, Enard. Seen them swear up and down that they had a child now, a husband now, a new view of life. That this time things would be different. And I'd catch them up to the same nonsense in a week, or a month, and they'd make the same promises all over again. The trouble is, circumstances are never enough to push a person to change. Not even wanting to change is enough. You have to work for it, every day, every moment. So I'm not asking if you've changed, or if you're going to, I'm asking if you're ready to work for it. Every day. Forever."

"I have been trying to change since the day I saw the truth of what I was. I'm not going to stop now. Not for Oiler. Not for anyone."

She opened her eyes, and scooted back around to sit beside him.

"Thank you," he said.

"For what?"

"Believing me."

They sat in silence awhile, letting warmth gather between them as the wind whipped above the mouth of the well, driving a chill deep into Ripka's sore bones.

"What are we going to do?" she asked the dark.

Enard shrugged, sitting so close the motion jostled her shoulder. "Radu is too unstable to plan for, I'm afraid. We'll have to see how he reacts, and adjust from there."

"Think we can convince him we don't know who the clearsky dealer is?"

Enard's answer was a chuckle.

"Right then," she said.

Another gust rattled down the well, and she shivered. Enard hooked an arm around her shoulders and huddled her close. Their combined body heat fought off the cold. For now.

"Let me see your hand."

She extended it to him without question. He curled her fingers gently to hide the whip-stitched and oozing flesh away, then cradled it against the hard warmth of his chest.

"Don't tell me you can actually see in this hole," she said. "How's it look? The apothik said it probably wouldn't fester. Not a ringing endorsement."

"No, I can't see." She felt him shake his head. "But you should keep it off the ground and away from the walls to reduce chance of infection."

"When you'd get so clever?"

"I didn't have a choice."

She closed her eyes, nesting her head against his shoulder.

He hugged her harder and rubbed her upper arm.

"Tell me about her," she said.

"Who?"

"The woman." *The day you say you saw what you were.*

"Ah." A pause. Then, "It started with her younger brother. He wasn't even old enough to grow stubble yet. We were in Rinton, on the western coast."

"We?"

"The Glasseaters. They were expanding into that city, putting down roots. The brother got picked up by a boss to be a package boy, running errands on behalf of the Glasseaters. He was good, or so I heard. Quick and fearless. Didn't take bribes that didn't come from his masters, and was marked to move up the ranks as soon as he learned a few trade tricks.

"Then his sister found out. She was furious, I take it, though I never saw her act that way myself. They were on their own, you see. I never did find out what had happened to their parents. But the sister wanted good lives for them both, and didn't want her brother mixed up in anything illegal. I suppose she knew that if she asked the Glasseaters to lay off him, they'd only ramp up their conditioning of the boy. So she decided to play them."

"What was her name?"

"I never knew her real one, and she wouldn't want to be remembered for her false one. But she was an actress, and a fine one. She raided her company's costume trunk and decked herself out like the biggest, baddest of mercenaries. I remember the day she walked into my bar. Never seen anything like her. She looked like she'd just held up a whole Fleet caravan and hadn't broken a sweat. She swaggered up to an empty table, put her feet up on it, and ordered a whisky straight. My bosses were enamored with her, and she kept them entertained with stories of all her imaginary conquests.

"After a few days of her strolling in, drinking, and telling her stories, the bosses decided to offer her a job. They gave

her control of the west district, where her brother was errand-
boy. Her costume was so good that the kid didn't recognize
her. But he did grow upset when he noticed he was being
given easier assignments.

"So she gave him the bad ones. The nasty ones. The ones
where he'd see innocents hurt, blood spilt. The ones that
would give him nightmares. And when he came to her – his
sister, not his boss – one night and told her what he'd been
involved with, and how he wanted out, she showed him the
money she'd been putting away. Said they could run the next
week, she just had a few loose ends to tie up.

"I don't know how my boss found out, but he did. Probably
he looked into one of her stories and realized there weren't
any bones to it. But despite the fact she'd been a decent
enough boss herself, he felt he'd been made a fool of. He
wanted her to pay.

"I followed her. Found out where she really lived, what
she did. Saw the way she handled her district, deflecting
some of the nastier work. Saw she intended to bolt. When I
knocked on her apartment door one night while the boy was
out, she knew why I was there. Didn't even seem surprised.
She invited me in, made me tea. Told me everything. And as
she was confessing I knew... knew she was confessing to the
man she thought would be her death. I saw myself through
her. Saw how, if she could be brave in the face of what I'd
been raised to be, then so could I. I left, and told to my boss
she hadn't been in.

"I went back the next night. And the next. And..." He
cleared his throat, his chest grew hot against her hand. "Soon
I started leaving with the morning. By the end of the week I'd
given her a path to take out of Rinton, a path that'd be damn
hard to follow. One I wouldn't join her on.

"And then I went home. I packed my things. As far as the
Glasseaters were concerned, I vanished with that woman and
her brother. I left hints of my path, knowing they'd want

me more than her. Knowing they might just assume we'd traveled together. I knew they'd catch up with me eventually, but Aransa seemed safe enough until Thratia took over."

"That's why you left with Detan."

He chuckled, and she felt the sound as a low vibration deep in his chest. "Among other reasons, but yes. I'm sorry. I should have told you. I'd been foolish to think I wouldn't be recognized. Tibal should have come with you instead."

"I'd been foolish to think *I* wouldn't be recognized. And Detan needs Tibal. Could you imagine him without Tibal around?"

"I can, and I'm not sure I like the thought."

"Exactly." She paused. "I'm glad you came with me."

"Me, too," he said, and held her a little tighter.

CHAPTER 32

Their captors had the good manners to supply them all with a toasty, roaring fire. It was just too bad they were enjoying it in sodden coats with their wrists trussed up like they were ready to be roasted over the flames. Detan muttered and squirmed, drawing a sharp glare from the man he'd named Grumps, as their captors had declined to introduce themselves.

Grumps sat on an upturned log at one end of the fire. His companion who Detan thought of as Greybeard, sat opposite. The men who'd come at him with crossbows conferred somewhere in the strange forest.

He'd never seen such creepy trees before, with silver bark and leaves so dark green they appeared black. Someone had been tending to those trees, weeding around their roots and pruning the branches with care. Sacks of bark curls huddled near the roots of one tree, and strips of bark had been hung up to dry from a washing line strung between two branches. He eyed Greybeard, imagining him with a flower-embroidered gardening apron and a watering can of blood to feed his trees with.

Upon his return to Pelkaia's crew, he'd been dismayed to discover that they had nothing to answer for the well-oiled crossbows pointed in their direction. He'd expected, at the very least, the entertainment of a scuffle, but instead they'd put their blades down and lifted their hands to the air much as he had. No doubt they suspected they couldn't poke holes in the men before their assaulters got their shots off, but Detan had been disappointed by the rollover.

He was wet. He was tired. And he was incredibly sick of having to fight for every damned little thing.

But the watchers hadn't rolled on them, as he feared they would. They kept their lips clamped as tightly as Pelkaia's crew did, shrugging in faked ignorance when their captors pressed them for details on the *Larkspur*'s unique shape, and what kind of crew was left on board.

Pelkaia sat beside Detan, Coss directly across the fire from them, the sparking flames obscuring his face from view. She shifted, a touch more subtly than Detan had done, and he had to repress a sigh. She was clearly trying to communicate something to Coss, and doing it poorly. Which meant he had to cause a distraction, lest they all get beaten for her disturbance.

Trouble was, he had no idea how to go about causing a distraction that wouldn't get *him* hit. He eyed their two minders, ignoring Pelkaia's ineffective squirming, and decided to focus on Grumps. That one looked least likely to do his talking with his fists.

"Hey, Grumps," he called above the crack of the flame. Both of the guards looked his way.

"Quiet," Greybeard snapped.

Detan sighed and slumped, shifting his feet as if he had an itch he couldn't shake. Grumps and Greybeard kept an eye on him, but held their admonishments for the time being.

Pelkaia angled her wrists around her back and tried to flash a hand gesture down low by her hip. No way in the pits Coss was going to see that, not with the flames blaring bright in his eyes. Pelkaia should realize that.

An out of place shadow flitted over Coss's shoulder. Ah, so

the signal wasn't for Coss. Someone was out there, moving through the woods, and he had a real good feeling it wasn't the crossbowmen.

"I've got to use the little boy's tree," Detan said.

"Hold it," Grumps said.

"Not likely."

"Just take him," Greybeard said.

"You take him if you're so keen."

"Somebody take him," Pelkaia said. "Or I'll kill him if he wets himself sitting next to me."

"You're not killing anyone, missy."

"Sure about that?"

Greybeard stood, baited by her implicit challenge, and Detan had to keep himself from snorting at how easily the old bastard had been manipulated. Greybeard stroked the forward curve of his crossbow, the weapon resting against his shoulder. His walk had a slight stutter to it, some old injury giving his knee a twinge every time he stepped, but he carried himself easily as he approached Pelkaia, his smirk growing with every hitching step.

"Think you're tough, lady? All tied up like that?"

"I could take you drunk and stumbling, old man."

He spat at her feet. "You're not worth the time it'd take to strangle you."

"And yet you hobbled all the way over here to tell me that."

He lashed out, striking the side of her head with one flat palm. Her body jerked, shoulder slamming into Detan, and he stiffened his back to keep them both from toppling over. With a snorting laugh, she shook her head and grinned up at Greybeard. Detan winced. This level of escalation really wasn't what he was after.

"That's no way to treat a prisoner," Detan said, forcing his voice to calm gravitas. Greybeard snorted.

"Have I offended the lord's gentle sensibilities? Mercy me.

Was it this?" He spat at Pelkaia's feet again. "Or this?" he raised his hand to strike her once more.

"Easy," Grumps said.

"Aw, come on, we're allowed a little fun." He grinned with all four teeth. "We're simple servants of her highness, after all."

Detan's brows shot up. "You work for the empress?"

"Shut your mouth," Grumps said.

"Bah." Greybeard waved Pelkaia and Detan away with a flick of his hand. "Who cares what they hear? Once Tek takes their ship they won't be telling anyone about this, will they?"

What warmth the fire imparted to his tired skin fled in a flash. They were being held as potential hostages for Tibs and Jeffin. Nothing else. Which meant that the crew left aboard the *Larkspur* was unlikely to leave it. Whatever Tek concocted to lure them off the ship, Tibs would see through it in an instant. So they were on their own out here. Just Pelkaia, her tired crew, and a couple of pits-battered watchers. Maybe he hadn't seen anything important in that shadow after all.

Pelkaia stiffened beside him, more than likely coming to the same conclusion. Detan surveyed the state of the watchers. Across the fire, the captain looked hale enough, and by the glower shoving his slate brows down Detan guessed he'd figured out what their future looked like, too. The two watchers tied next to their captain were in a worse state, lolling against each other and generally having a hard time keeping their eyes open. A watcher on the other side of Pelkaia looked like she might be able to get to her feet, but that was about it.

The rest of the crew was exhausted, heads sagging. They may have had the greater numbers, but he doubted they could get the upper hand. If they'd had the strength, they would have fought back when their captors made them leave the most grievously injured of the watchers behind on the beach.

Greybeard shuffled back to his post, and while his back was turned Pelkaia met Detan's gaze. Her eyes were bloodshot, her temple swollen and purple, her lips tinged with blue from the cold. The sea had plastered her hair to her head, and the warmth of the fire had fluffed it out again. She looked like a wild thing. A creature risen straight out of the thick brush all around them. Wild or not, there was a question in her glance, a slight tip of the chin and raise of the brow that he recognized all too well: *ready?* she was asking him.

He shrugged. Whatever she had planned, he wasn't going to be *more* ready for it anytime soon.

"Coss," she said. Just that. Just his name. But that's all it took.

Detan's world turned inside out.

His ears popped, his head spun. Detan swayed, disoriented. People around him shouted things. He had no idea what they were.

"Honding. Focus." Pelkaia's voice was in his ear, her shoulder shoved up against his. He'd slumped into her, nestled his cheek against her collarbone. He jerked up, startled. What in the pits had Coss done?

Above the fire an amorphous blob distorted the air, a place of unreality as tall as his arm was long and wide as his waist. It shimmered, then split, each half hurtling toward Greybeard and Grumps respectively. Sel. Out of a dark, empty sky.

Greybeard drew his arm back, taking aim at Coss, ready to throw his knife. Detan's stomach lurched. It was them, or everyone else. Maybe all of the above, if he couldn't rein his strength in. Exhaustion swelled through him, threatened to drain away even the weapon of his anger. He breathed deep, watched Greybeard bring his hand back and cock his wrist as if from a faraway place, as if everything in the world were slow but Detan.

Coss slammed the sel blobs into Greybeard and Grumps. The blobs were too big. Detan'd burn them all.

Greybeard leaned forward, oblivious of the real threat behind him, and his hand angled as he prepared to throw. Coss could not move out of the way in time. Not trussed up like that. He was dead already, if Greybeard threw.

Detan let his anger go.

He was warm and he was wet again and he didn't know why. His ears rang, a soft tin hiss that wouldn't let him go. He shook his head, struggled to stand, swayed and put a hand down, realized his wrists had been freed. He blinked, saw grey smudges in his eyelids and blinked again. Pelkaia took his arm and eased him back down to a seat on a log. When did he get a log?

Her cheek was smattered with blood, her hair too, and she stared so hard into his eyes he squirmed from the pressure. "What happened?" he asked.

She opened her mouth, closed it, and shook her head. "You tell me."

Behind her, the watchers and crew members were cutting their bonds with Greybeard's knife, grime faces spattered with blood like it'd been coming down with the rain. He scowled, rubbed at his temples, and took his hands away to find them wet with blood too. He stared at his reddened fingers, at the speckled faces of the others. Realized with a sharp start why he didn't see Greybeard and Grumps anymore. So much sel. So little flesh.

The fire had blown out, but a single tree burned merrily enough, its silvery bark letting off a noxious, acrid smoke. Detan grimaced, reached to rub his sore eyes, and thought better of it.

"Find the other three," Pelkaia was giving orders to her crew. Orders the watchers appeared more than willing to follow. "Don't parley."

Determined nods all around. Of course. They wouldn't want word of this little display leaking out. Detan shivered and lowered his head into his hands, not caring that he smeared his face and hair with another's blood.

"Honding?" Pelkaia crouched before him, gripped both his wrists in her hands and moved his palms gently away from his face. They were alone now. There was real concern in her eyes, concern so motherly he almost laughed at it.

"I'm uninjured," he said. Not *all right*. Not *fine*. Just uninjured. She seemed to take his meaning, and nodded.

"How long?" she asked.

It took him awhile, but understanding came. "Aransa."

"The sky?" she pressed.

He swallowed, and nodded.

She sighed and shifted to sit next to him, keeping one hand locked around his forearm as if she were afraid he would blink out of existence if she let go.

"Tibs warned me," he said. "Warned me I was losing it."

"You think you're losing control?" She shook her head. "You're wrong."

"That little display not evidence enough for you?"

She pursed her lips, mulling something over. "Think. Think back. What's changed since Aransa? What really?"

"The sky. I set the sky on fire. It was too much. It..." He cleared his throat. "It opened a door."

"No."

"No? No? You're not in my head, Pelkaia, though pits know you're trying to be. You've no idea what I feel when I try to push it back. No idea how good it feels when I finally let go."

The rustling of leaves and the heavy thuds of a scuffle echoed back to them over the steady patter of the rain and the howl of the winds and the crackling of the burning tree. He wiped his bloodied hands on his knees and tried to ignore it all. Tried to bring his world in so that all that mattered was the warmth of the fire and Pelkaia's presence, a grounding weight at his side.

"Think harder," she said. "Burning the sky was something you've always been capable of. The Century Gates, your pipeline at the Hond Steading selium mines. They're all evidence of your ability, reaching back long before you ever set foot in Aransa. The sky is not what's changed you."

"Then why do my small uses spiral out of control? If I'm so unchanged, why does every attempt at deviant power I make go haywire?"

"I never said you were unchanged."

He scratched the inside of his elbow. "Then what? What the fuck is wrong with me?"

"Nothing's wrong, either. You still know all your calming techniques, all your meditations, don't you?"

"Yes," he said, thinking back to the small meditations that Pelkaia had taught him on the deck of the *Larkspur* during the days they were all licking their wounds from Aransa.

"You still have Tibal. You still have your freedom. You should be able to achieve the same level of control you had in the days before Aransa. So what changed you?"

He stared at his arm. The heat of the raw spot of skin he kept scratching radiated through his sleeve. "The injection."

"Yes. You saw, for a moment, what Coss sees when he uses his sel-sense. It's hard for him, he can't always see it. Can't always make it work. What you saw is the limit of his sense, taking the small particles eddying in the winds and condensing them together. He'll be aching for a week for that effort. But thanks to that injection, you've seen it now too."

"It wore off," he snapped. "I can't see what Coss sees."

"Anyone can tell rain is wet. Anyone can feel damp in a cloud. But it takes a special sense, an unnatural nudge, to feel the moisture in every breath. The tinge of water in the desert winds. It's there. It's always there. You saw sel's omnipresence. That's a hard vision to shake. I suspected, when you turned that tiny drop into more at Cracked Thorn, but–"

"I can't see it anymore," he insisted, and took a deep breath to push his anger aside. "When I reach for my sel-sense all I see is the sky as you see it, maybe even less refined. All those little lost particles, too small to fight the currents of air and rise upward, they're gone. I'm blind to them now."

"You don't need to see them to know they're there. You aren't losing control, Honding. You're getting stronger."

She pat his knee and stood, striding off into the forest in the direction the scuffle had sounded. There wasn't a care in the world in her stance, in the sway of her hips or the easy roll of her steps. Detan scowled after her, hating her for being at ease with the world when he was so torn up inside. He relaxed his face and shook his hands out. Harboring a grudge against Pelkaia for being happy wouldn't help anyone, least of all himself.

Probably he should have been worried about that silver-barked tree catching flame on the other side of the firepit, but he had a hard time rustling up any feeling aside from a vague sense of self-pity.

He lost track of time, sitting there letting the heavy mist in the air dilute the blood on his hands until nothing was left save a ruddy orange stain. He ignored the shouts in the trees, the scuffling and twang of bows nearby. Pelkaia's crew would win through the night, or they wouldn't. He'd deal with the consequences of either outcome when they came to find him.

A crunch of leaves nearby brought his head up, made him focus on reality once more. Tibs slipped through the trees, narrow as they were, and settled on the log beside Detan where Pelkaia had sat. His hat dangled from his hands. He spun it round and round by the brim between his fingers.

"Rough night," Tibs said.

"Had worse."

"Every night listening to you snore is worse."

Detan snorted, and Tibs clapped him on the back. "Everything's secure. Pelkaia's crew helped the watchers patch up their barge and they're going to go on their merry way in the morning. Don't much like the look of that repair job, blasted crew was all left thumbs slapping it together, but it should hold to Petrastad. Watch-captain said he'd tell his superiors back home they lost us in the storm."

"And us?"

"We'll spend the night here, and set out for the Remnant in the morning."

Detan looked up at the sky, at the stars turned into foggy blurs by the smeared clouds and angry winds. "Hope she's ready for us."

Tibs chuckled. "This is Ripka Leshe we're talking about. She'll probably be queen of the place by the time we get there, ordering Nouli to figure out some new contraption to make food distribution more fair and efficient while forcing New Chum to lead a team of inmates and guards alike in scrubbing the place from top to bottom."

"That's our girl." Detan snatched the hat from Tibs's fingers and plunked it on his too-wet head. He stood, scrubbing the last of the blood clean on his Fleetie coat, then chucked the coat into the remaining fire. It sparked, warming his cheeks. He brushed his hands together, wiping away his troubles with each stroke. Ripka waited. He was not going to let her down, no matter what strange poison had taken hold in his veins.

"Come along, old chum. Let's go see if we can rustle up some warm food and warmer blankets."

CHAPTER 33

The scuffle of the crew on deck dragged Detan from a dead sleep. He cracked an eyelid, regretted it as the morning sun lanced straight through to the back of his skull, and groaned. Someone elbowed him in the ribs and he grunted, flopping from his side to his back.

Tibs's head made a mighty fine sun block. Detan peeled both eyes open and wriggled his fingers and toes to be sure they all still worked. He seemed whole, more or less a few shreds of dignity.

"Morning, princess," Tibs drawled and dropped something round and light onto Detan's chest. It bounced off with a hollow whump.

"Morning yourself. Did you even bother pretending to sleep, or does the crew now suspect you of undead strength?"

Detan rolled himself to a seat as Tibs settled down on a crate beside him. They'd spent the night huddled up against one of the cabin walls, letting the eave above keep the rain off even as the wind pounded through their thin blankets. He rolled his wrists and shoulders, listening to the cold muscles and joints pop and creak.

Coss had taken pity on them and loaned Detan a new coat and Tibs a thicker blanket, but still the wind had bitten. Detan would have asked the crew to let him sleep on the floor of one of their cabins under any other circumstances, but the body language of all involved made it clear as a spring rain he wasn't wanted. Not even Essi had had so much as a smart remark for him. They were tolerating him, but just barely.

"I believe it's you they think came back from the dead, walking on board covered in blood like that."

"Mist got most of it off."

"Not nearly enough."

Detan fumbled until he found the stale bread roll Tibs had tossed him. It was soggy with mist, which did nothing for the flavor, but at least made him feel like he wasn't about to crack a tooth with every bite.

"I bet New Chum and Ripka are eating better than us," Detan muttered around a mushy mouthful.

Tibs snorted. "I bet rats are eating better than us. Haven't had a good meal since..." His eyes crossed.

"Um... Cracked Thorn?"

"Grass millet and stale beer don't count."

"Sweet skies, Tibs, I can't afford to please your refined palate."

"You can't afford to please a donkey's palate."

"I'd rather have an ass for company."

"You're in luck, sirra, you'll always have yourself."

That should have cheered him, Tibs calling him an ass always brightened his spirits, but still the bread tasted like ash in his mouth, the water stagnant and bitter. Heaviness dragged at him, a weight that had nothing at all to do with tired limbs and lack of sleep. A weight not even Tibs's cheery barbs could lift free. Detan thought about saying as much. Thought about asking Tibs to just let him cry his heart out on his shoulder. But he didn't even have the energy left for that much. He caught Tibs watching him through the corner of his eye and flicked his gaze away, studying the crew.

There weren't many aboard, just enough to make it look like the ship was staffed enough to avoid suspicion, and none of them looked like they were born to the jobs they worked. Well, except maybe Essi. That girl could shimmy up a mast pole like her favorite sweet was waiting on top.

Though the sky had calmed some, ragged hints of the storm remained. Great swathes of cloud smeared the sky with grey, and fog lay heavy over the island. Detan gave up any hope of ever being dry again.

If he craned his head just right, he could make out the last remnants of the cloud suck. A vortex of death lancing up from the far horizon. Where once that sight would have sent a spear of fear straight through him, it now gave him a tingle of pride. He cracked a grin up at Tibs.

"We're the best damned pilots on the Scorched, you know."

"Woulda been a sight easier if we'd had someone on hand to manipulate the sel."

Detan winced. "All that fear and power flying around? Couldn't risk it."

"Could learn to."

He scowled and jerked his coat off, wringing the water out even though the persistent mist would wet it all over again. "Been trying. Or has that escaped you?"

Tibs brought both hands up and dragged rangy fingers through his hair, making it stick up in all directions. Tiredness suffused his expression, and it wasn't just from the long night. Detan saw himself in a lot of those fine lines ringing his friend's eyes, and each one was a pick to the gut.

"Comes a time a man needs a tutor."

"And just how–?"

"You know how."

He could take a lot of abuse from Tibs. Expected it, for the most part. The man's easy criticisms had become the soothing background hum of Detan's life. But to be cut off like that, not allowed to finish one of his rambling rants? That stung.

"I'll talk to her," he muttered, and gave a pile of rope a desultory kick.

"See that you do."

Traitor, he wanted to say, but he knew Tibs was right. Knew it was time to reach out for help. The iron stains embedded in his fingernails told him as much. Even if it meant sticking his head in a viper's nest.

He found her standing side by side with Coss, staring down the storm that boiled across the sea. Though she must be weary, though every limb must weigh heavy with exhaustion, her back was straight, her hands clasped with care behind her as she canted her head toward Coss to hear whatever it was he had to say.

Pelkaia was strong, Detan reminded himself. Had nursed her pain for years, burned her spirit to a cinder seeking revenge and risen again from the ashes; proud, controlled. She was on course for a victory he could only allow himself to dream of. She could help him. She had to.

He let his footsteps be heard against the deck, and their conversation fell silent. Pelkaia half-turned, regarding him in profile for a long moment, then jerked her chin to beckon him. He felt a child, all of a sudden. Too small in his borrowed coat, too small on the back of the world. Just a speck of a man. For a moment he wondered what the point was. Why someone so small as a single soul thought anything they did, or didn't do, mattered at all. He swallowed. He'd never wanted to be a good man. Never particularly wanted to be a bad man, either. Just wanted to be left alone to serve his family and his home. Wasn't his fault he was burdened with his gift. Wasn't his fault he'd been broken over it.

"Morning, Honding," she said. He stood alongside her, pulled by her greeting. He couldn't bring himself to look at her, not yet, and so he stuck his gaze on the cloudhead they'd been watching and hung it there.

"Can I have a private word, captain?"

The very fact he'd used her title, and not some silly name, made her cock her head. He felt her curiosity like a cold rainfall, and forced himself to keep on staring out across the oil-dark waters.

"I'll leave you to it, then," Coss said. Detan heard him clap his captain on the shoulder before striding off. When his steps dissipated, a cold sweat beaded on the back of Detan's neck. Now that he had the chance, he wasn't sure he could force the words out. What would Tibs want him to say here? She knew what was happening to him, Pits below, it should be her coming to him with an offer to help.

"Well?" she asked, and some trick of the wind brought her perfume around to him – the same vanilla and haval spice blend she'd worn in Aransa. The one that'd given her away. It reminded him that he, too, had his own tricks to play. His own hand full of value.

Reminded him that once, he'd sat cross-legged on this very deck while she ran him through his paces, testing his control. He'd kept up, even though his back had still burned from setting the sky above Aransa alight. Maybe he wasn't so small.

"Long time ago, you said to come see you, when I was ready. Ready to fight."

"And are you?"

"No. But I want to be. I need your help, Pelkaia. I need you to teach me to control this new strength you say I've awakened." The words came out stilted, jumbled, his usual rambling and cajoling cut short by the rawness of his need. He didn't dare look at her.

After the silence had stretched on so long he feared he'd break down into a begging mess, she said, "Things have changed. My crew fears you."

He swallowed bile. "I know, and I'm sorry. I never meant to… Well, it doesn't matter what I meant, does it? Just that it was wrong of me. With your guidance, your lessons, it won't happen again. I swear it. Drug me until I'm docile, if you'd like. Tibs would be delighted, I'm sure." He tried out a nervous chuckle. She did not join him.

"I remember when I first saw you, card sharking at the Blasted Rock inn. I thought to myself: there he is, that Honding. The one the rumors swirl about. The man who lost his sel-sense in a mining accident – a fire – and disappeared into Valathea for a year, only to return a criminal. A homeless wanderer. A con man and, if the rumors were to be believed, worse. But I knew. I knew no amount of trauma could scare sel-sense from a body. If that were true, the Catari would have discovered it long ago. The stars know we tried."

Detan's mind whirled from her change in topic, struggling to find the meaning of her words. Struggling to find an angle he could use, a way to show her she could trust him aboard her ship, amongst her crew. "Your people tried to scare the sel-sense from themselves? Why?" he asked, to give himself more time to think.

"In special cases, yes. We knew of deviant abilities, of course – though we did not call them as such, they were normal variations to us. We named them: illusionist, mirrorworker, windsingers, painters for those who can shift sel to only one color. I never dreamed you were what you are. You're supposed to be extinct, Honding, did you know that?"

He snorted. "Certainly many have tried to make that a reality."

"Not *you* – your talent. By the time I was born your talent-brothers and sisters were already believed to be gone from the world. My people had tried everything to expunge the talent, you understand. But it could not be done. Your ability is too... volatile. Too dangerous. Do you know what we called your type?"

"No."

"Worldbreakers."

"A bit dramatic," he grated, gripping the rail.

"I thought so, at first. But we had stories. Folktales, I

thought, but they were grounded in history. Tales of your type banding together, overthrowing our leaders, wiping out rival tribes by bringing their local firemounts to roaring life. The Catari thought... *We* thought, that we'd purged your strain. But some must have escaped. Perhaps a distant ancestor of yours, fleeing north to the Valathean archipelago. Perhaps that is where your family got their sel-sense from, and why your great-grandparents were drawn to the Scorched. I cannot say for certain.

"I have taught my crew to call you a firebug, Honding, because I do not want them to know what you are capable of. I will not allow them to learn otherwise."

"I don't... I don't want to blow open any firemounts, Pelkaia. For pits' sake, I'm asking you to show me how to control it."

He felt her turn to regard him, but did not take his eyes from the blackened sky. "You're angry now, aren't you? Can feel it building?"

"Don't."

She sighed. Her hand alighted upon his shoulder and squeezed. "Leave, Honding."

"And go where? This ship—"

"I do not mean this ship. If you value your life, you will take your flier and flee the Scorched. Flee all of Valathea's puppets, flee any and every land touched by the use of selium. Go to the backwaters of the far north, or set out to the rumored western continent. And once you are there, and certain the land is dead around you, destroy the flier. Scatter its selium to the high winds. That is the only way."

"This is my home, sure as it is yours. How dare you—"

"Tell me: when was the last time you loved?"

"None of your pits-cursed business," he snapped.

"That long?"

He swayed, rage boiling within him, and was grateful for Pelkaia's hand gripping his shoulder, keeping him steady.

He breathed through his mouth, soothing his already frayed nerves. This was ridiculous. Why should he listen to what this woman had to say? Just because Tibs thought he needed help didn't mean he had to ask it of *her*. He could figure it out on his own. He'd been doing things that way most his life, anyway.

"Thank you for your time, captain." He turned to leave, but she dug her fingers into his shoulder and spun him around to face her. Eyes that were so like Ripka's bore into him, raking hot claws of guilt across his heart.

"You will not allow yourself to love, because you fear the strength of your anger if that love turns to hurt. No – don't protest. Just... Just listen to me. I will help you rescue Ripka and New Chum, I will help you return them safely to Petrastad. But it's not due to any tongue wagging of yours. I see two possible realities behind Captain Leshe's imprisonment. The first, that she and New Chum became entangled in some matter working against the empire and were arrested. The second, that they allowed themselves to be carted away to that horrible place for some other purpose.

"I don't care what the truth is. I have worn that woman's face, and in doing so worn her habits, her mannerisms. There is very little left in the world that I hold faith in, anymore. But I do believe in one thing: Ripka Leshe is a force for good. And I will not see her suffer, if I can help it. I owe that woman. The world owes that woman, too, they just don't know it yet.

"But after that, after I save her, you *must* flee, do you understand me? You walk too close to the line of your control as it is. I have my crew to care for, and you have your friends' safety to think of."

"Black skies take you." He shook her hand from his shoulder, then stormed back toward Tibs.

"Do not make me hunt you, Honding," she called.

He answered her with a raised finger.

CHAPTER 34

Though she had known it was likely that the warden would already be drunk, Ripka found the reality disappointing. His face was flush from the warmth of the rum he'd no doubt paid a premium to smuggle in from Petrastad. A premium covered by funds meant to keep the prison in working order. He leaned forward across his desk, arms spread wide and palms face down as if he were trying to keep it from spinning away. As Ripka and Enard were ushered through the door, he squinted, trying to place them. She stood at ease, hoping whatever state the bastard's mind was in was one she could work with.

"What's the meaning of this?" he slurred, cleared his throat and straightened his shoulders. "I did not ask to see these two."

Captain Lankal stepped forward. Ripka was pleased to see his disgust was no less facing down his drunken boss than it had been in discovering their stash of strange bark peelings. "Warden, sir, we are not certain of the specifics, but we believe we have interrupted an escape attempt. We discovered these two on the beach with Guard Hessan. They had been in a fight, as you can see, and Hessan was severely injured by a concussion. Luckily he managed to get to his whistle before these two could wrest it away from him and finish what they'd begun. And there was this with them."

He slung the oilcloth pack onto Radu's desk and pulled the top flap open. Radu leaned forward, half standing, to peer into the silvery collection of bark. He sniffed the air above it, and a dark scowl overtook his features.

"I see." He ran a hand through his hair and his dark locks stayed put, grease sealing every strand into place. "Leave me with them. Do not go far."

"Yes, warden."

Captain Lankal and the other guard left, leaving Ripka and Enard in chains before the warden. Tense, she waited, wondering what truth the muddled man's mind would decide upon – and if she would be given a chance to defend herself. He squinted at them once more, then nodded as if having reassured himself of whom he was speaking with.

"This is how you repay me, captain?" He waved a hand over the open mouth of the sack. "With treachery? With turning the very information I gave you against me?"

"I was in the process of investigating the clearsky chain of ownership when–"

"Enough!" He slapped an open palm upon his desk. "You think you're clever, eh? Think you're smarter than me?"

"I didn't–"

"Did I tell you to speak?"

Spittle flew from Radu's lips, tangling in his moustache. Ripka clenched her jaw to keep from speaking. This was not a rational man she was dealing with. She couldn't expect him to listen to what she had to say, and her attempts to persuade him seemed only to insult him – to make him angrier.

"I know your game," he said, and she felt a tingle of fear in her heart. Did he truly? Would Kisser have turned their secrets over to him? She could think of nothing that woman would have to gain from such an act. She could also not imagine Radu sussing out any truths under the roof of the prison he'd been given to manage, let alone her secreted agenda.

"Sir," Enard spoke in his smooth, placating voice. The picture of respect, the same tone she imagined he'd used with his Glasseater bosses. "I assure you that our intentions were for your benefit. To discover the smugglers to whom you set us to uncover, we—"

Radu's expression changed in a flash. His lip curled into a canid snarl as he grabbed a trinket holding down a stack of papers and threw it at Enard. Ripka winced as the weighted brass struck him with a heavy thump. Enard took the blow as if it were little more than water rolling down his back. With her own collection of bruises and aches from their previous scuffles, she suspected she wouldn't have been so stoic in the face of such an affront.

"Think you can talk your way out of this, do you?" Radu snapped.

"Warden," Ripka spoke to distract the man from his new quarry, "if you would tell us what it is you think us guilty of, then perhaps we could come to an understanding."

"An understanding? Are you so fool headed you think yourself in any position to negotiate?" He snort-laughed and slapped the bag of bark shavings, tumbling a few of the silvery curls to the top of his desk. "I know what this is, *captain*," he laid all the sarcasm his drunken mind could muster onto the word. "And now I know the shape of the viper secreted in my nest."

"You think me behind the new drug?" She cursed herself for not managing to keep the affront from her voice. Damn watcher pride.

"*Think? Think?* Do not pretend the matter is in question! My guards caught you with your arms full of the raw material. This, this sack of *shit*." He growled and shoved the bag away from him, spilling a few more curls, as if the very sight and scent of the resinous wood disgusted him. "I don't know what made you think you could get away with this.

Greed, more than likely. But playing both sides? I will not be deceived!"

"Warden." She struggled to keep her voice as calm as Enard's had been, struggled to push aside her desire to roll her eyes at this overwrought man and his paranoia. "The drug was in circulation within your prison long before I arrived here. How could I possibly be the source?"

"Source? Pah, I don't think so highly of you, girl. You are but a pawn. A poor one, at that. Who are you working for?" He grabbed the sack in one hand and shook it at her. "Where were you taking this, hmm? Who is your master?"

"I hadn't yet discovered who the parcel was to be brought to when your guards–"

"Lies!" He threw the satchel at them and it slapped against Ripka's chest. Plumes of silvery bark shavings arced into the air. She coughed as the bitter scent clouded around her, the slight musk of the bag clogging her breath. She swayed, already weak from the fight on the beach. Enard grabbed her arm to steady her.

"Sir?" Captain Lankal cracked the door, his brows raised in question. "Is everything all right?"

"These two serpents won't talk." Radu paced around his desk and kicked the fallen sack. "So we'll have to see just how precious that information is to them, won't we?"

"Sir?" Lankal asked, his expression drawn tight.

Ripka stared at the enraged warden, at his flush-red face and his clenched fists. His twisted shirt, and the crimson stains that had nothing at all to do with blood dotting his collar. How this man had lucked into his position here, minding the most valued prison in all of the Scorched, she could not say, but in that moment, watching the man's veins bulge and his lips crack as he drew them into a sneer, she resolved to see him removed from his position.

One way or another, she would see Radu Baset fallen from his post. By the distaste in Captain Lankal's eyes, she was certain the change would be a welcome one.

"You would be party to torture?" she asked Radu, her voice soft, made quiet by her attempt to sift the rage from her tone. He turned his wild gaze on her and hissed.

"Think you're precious, don't you, watch-captain?"

Lankal's head jerked back.

"I'm not that," she said. "Not anymore."

"No..." He cocked his head to one side, thinking. "But that doesn't much matter, does it?"

He grabbed the shoulder of her jumpsuit and stomped off, steering her back toward general population. Her heart hammered as he forced her along, the soft rustle of Enard's chains as he followed only a small comfort. Her time in the watch had given her some training to resist pain, but she knew well enough that even the sternest of souls would eventually crack under a well-applied knife.

Echoes of Detan crying out in the night, his dreams beset by memories of the torture he'd suffered in the name of experimentation at the hands of the whitecoats, came back to her all in a rush. He'd told her one night, when they'd drunk a bottle dry and sat staring at the stars as the sky he'd set alight burned around them, that he'd told the whitecoats everything. Anything. That he'd begun making up ridiculous stories about where his ability had come from to make them stop. Anything to make them stop.

Fear prickled her skin as Radu shoved her along the narrow hallways, expecting a door to open to strange instruments at any moment. Radu was addled by drink and lack of activity. She could overtake him, subconsciously had already predicted where best to strike to deal him the most pain. His kidney if she could reach it, an elbow to his alcohol-sore throat if she couldn't. The halls were narrow, and she was fleet of foot. If Enard could keep up, then... Then what?

Radu yanked a door open and fear overrode sense. She twisted away from his grip. Hands closed on her from behind and shoved, making her ankles tangle mid-twist. Staggering, she stumbled through the door, righted herself just before she would have fallen face-first onto hard stones.

Increased brightness stung her eyes and she closed off her stance. A cool breeze ruffled her hair, chilled the sweat at the nape of her neck.

A breeze. She forced herself to open her eyes fully. He'd thrown her through a side door into the rec yard. A dozen or so prisoners nearby watched her, all conversation cut short at the sign of this new entertainment. Radu smirked, propping his fists on his hips in an attempt to cut a commanding figure. He swayed slightly.

Captain Lankal herded Enard out after her and, his face a tightly reined mask, removed both of their shackles. Ripka rubbed her wrists, eyeing Radu warily.

"Lankal, see that these two are fed. I wouldn't want the *watch-captain* to miss her dinner due to our little chat." He waved at her. "Come and see me again when you have more to say."

He turned, and slammed the door shut behind him. It echoed in the growing silence.

Watch-captain. Little chat. Her stomach turned to ice as realization set in. Once the rumor spread... She was a dead woman.

"Captain Lankal?" He put a hand on her back and steered her toward the food line. He shook his head, lips pressed tight.

"Unless you're ready to give up your sources, there's nothing I can do."

"But I don't..." She clenched her jaw. She did, of course. She could give up Nouli and Kisser and... then what? Radu would find a way to kill her regardless, she was sure of that much.

"I know," Lankal said, placing her at the end of the food line. "I'm sorry."

He left them there, waiting for their meals. Unnatural

silence spread out around her as if she were a stone dropped
in calm water.

"Enard..." she whispered.

"I know," he said, and squeezed her shoulder. "I know."

The first rock thrown missed her. The second did not.

CHAPTER 35

A spark of pain pinged off her arm. Her cheek. She did not look in the direction of the stones. She kept her eyes forward, her back straight, shuffling along in the line that had slowed to a crawl. Those before her wanted their meals, but sensed the shifting tide of their fellow inmates' ire. She felt for them, despite her own pains. They didn't have anything to do with this. No matter what they'd done to end up in the Remnant, they were now tired from a long day of labor and seeking their suppers.

The line moved forward. Another ping. Another. She struggled not to flinch, to remain calm and serene while tension mounted all around her. Keeping her head forward, her gaze darted around the yard, marking knots of potential trouble, the direction of the shallow rain of stones. They were coming from her right, provided primarily from one woman. She didn't have to look directly to know the woman's face. It'd be the Glasseater songbird, hungry for revenge. Wanting to make something hurt as much as she did.

"Traitor!" The songbird's familiar voice screeched, and a murmur fluttered around her. Ripka was one away from the front of the line. Could see beads of sweat on the back of the neck of the man in front of her.

"Snitch!"

Ripka pressed her lips together, continued her covert survey of the rec yard. Where was Kisser? Honey, Forge, and Clink? Enard's presence at her back was a comfort, but a small one. She knew well their chances of breaking through this crowd if the whole population went feral.

Knew well that Radu would be just a touch too slow in issuing orders to subdue them. Would frown and sniff over her corpse, muttering about the unfortunate way in which the Remnant was understaffed.

If she died here, torn limb from limb or beaten pulpy, that sniveling rat of a warden would walk away from this with an excuse to hire more guards, more lackeys in his pocket. More grains to fall through his fingers as he pissed away the welfare of his charges for his own pleasure.

The man minding the food line handed her a tray, his hands trembling as he sensed the change in the crowd, their intense focus. They began to advance. She gripped the tray until her knuckles ached.

"She's no inmate!"

Radu didn't care if his people were harmed in the riot he'd kicked up.

"Sandrat!"

He only cared that the experiment being done on his charges didn't benefit him.

"Boot-licker!"

She'd be damned if she let Radu-fucking-Baset continue running this sordid little nest.

"*Blue coat!*"

"I look good in blue," she said to the confused man spooning her out a ladle of porridge.

Her shoulders jarred as she spun, slamming her food tray into the advancing songbird's face so hard her fingers went numb. Bone crunched, the songbird squawked, clutching her bloodied face with both hands. Porridge flew from the bowl, forming a gleaming, slimy arc in the sky. She watched it for a breath, feeling slowed, stuck in time, as the songbird crumpled under the force of her blow.

There – over the songbird's shoulder – the door to a dormitory half-opened, a faint shimmer in the air like heat off sand, the half-silhouetted face of Misol, her plush lips pulled back in a smirk.

Escape, or something else. Better than facing the foaming mob.

"Run!" In the moment before the group's shock at her abrupt attack fled, she flung her tray aside and grabbed Enard's wrist, yanked him in the direction of that half-opened door. He flew along beside her, no questions, no hesitation, just the patient patter of his feet over the filthy floor.

Her grip on Enard's wrist jerked and she pivoted around the tug, turning to see a man she didn't know reel back his fist, aiming another blow for Enard's already purple face. Dropping Enard's wrist she darted in toward the man's side, quick as a rockviper and just as unexpected, muscles singing as she swept the man's forward leg from under him. He went down, grunting. Enard vaulted over him, following the path she'd begun carving toward Misol.

The crowd's hesitation broke. They flowed around them, cutting off their route, circling, tightening, herding them toward the edge of the yard where directional options were fewer. Ripka slowed, hesitated, dug her heels in and refused to take a step back even as they pressed in closer. Enard flanked her right, his posture all assured calm, his hands held ready and low at his sides.

She examined the crowd; counting, estimating, watching the wariness in their faces, the tension in their arms. Who would swing first? Mobs like this didn't kick off all at once. They needed an instigator. She had to take that person down before they could get the crowd good and frothed.

Couldn't see her songbird, couldn't see the man who'd

hit Enard though she wasn't sure she'd recognize him.
Glasseaters? Yes – of course – but with their tattoos covered,
she couldn't pick them, and had no way of knowing which
amongst them would be the leader.

Who who who, she thought, trying to undercut the tide
before it broke and swamped her.

Through a break in the crowd, she saw Misol in the
doorway, her smirk faded to a tight scowl. The woman's
fingers drummed on the haft of her spear, anxious to put it to
use, but her legs stayed rooted. No rescue there, then. They
were on their own.

Which meant they were dead.

"This is all wrong," a soft, raspy voice said.

Ripka turned to a bulge in the crowd, watched the
tightening ring of inmates shift aside as a petite woman with
a mop of golden curls strode through. Honey. Ripka's gut
clenched. *No*, she wanted to yell. Didn't Honey see the tide
was against them? Couldn't she see this crowd was on the
brink of boiling and tearing everyone in its center to bits?

Honey strode through the crowd, their ranks parting as if
for a ship's sharp prow, and came to stand beside Ripka, a
little frown turning down the bow of her lips, almost a pout.

"Captain's my friend," she rasped, and turned a darkened
eye upon the crowd, sweeping them all up in it. Ripka was
shocked to see a few recoil from that glare. "Don't matter
what color she used to wear. She wears beige now." Honey
flicked the sleeve of Ripka's jumpsuit. "And I think it becomes
her."

Ripka stared at Honey in disbelief. It was the most she'd
ever heard the woman say all at once. The crowd shifted,
some of their ire fading in a strange mix of confusion and
fear – none of them understood what was happening here
anymore than Ripka did. She risked a glance toward Misol's
door and saw a shadow cast above the crowd – a cloud? No, it
was too regular. Trying to keep her glance subtle, she flicked

her gaze up to the dormitory balcony above and saw Forge and Clink maneuvering one of the trestle tables, preparing to drop it on the group below.

Ripka swallowed a lump. Willed herself not to look their way.

"She's a plant!" The songbird got back on her feet and shoved her way through the group. "A pitsdamned watch-*captain* here to rat us all out to the warden! You all saw them talking! Heads together like old pals!"

Honey cocked her head to the side, considering. "No," she said at last.

"No? No? We all saw!"

"Did you not hear me?" Honey's jaw went rigid. The songbird drew her head back, stunned by this dismissal. With deliberate care, Honey slipped her hand within her pocket and withdrew a meat cleaver, the metal polished bright, the wooden handle dark from use. Ripka stared at the gleaming stretch of steel, dumbfounded.

She turned it over, admiring the gleam with a loving eye, and pressed the flat of the blade to her lips. Resting the dull edge against her shoulder, she stared down the shuffling ring of would-be rioters.

"Captain's my friend."

To Ripka's shock, a few of the men and women crowding them broke ranks and ran. She swallowed. Who *was* this woman?

"Honey, you don't have to–"

"Shhh," she murmured, reaching without looking to press a finger against Ripka's lips. "Shhh."

"Fuck this," a woman said, and charged forward. Ripka slipped into a ready stance as the instigator broke the tension holding back the wave. The sounds of the crowd devolved into a meaningless roar as they charged, closing the circle. Enard's back pressed against hers, and still Honey stood apart at her side, holding the knife against her shoulder with a moue on her lips.

"I tried," Honey whispered.

The table launched from the balcony above, slamming into the crowd. Confusion erupted, knots of men and women turned on each other, a few unlucky souls buckled beneath the crush of the heavy wood. Shouts of rage and pain sounded all around. Ripka braced herself for the coming fight, lamenting that she would not have a chance to break through the path the table had carved her.

Honey began to sing.

It was a high, keening song, the language alien to Ripka's ears, the sound eerie and shrill enough to startle the advancing tide. Even Ripka took a step back, accidentally shoving Enard, unable to look away from Honey despite the advance of the crowd. Of her death.

Honey danced.

She twisted and pirouetted, nimble as a willow switch, snaking in between groups, bodies, the gleam of her blade catching the sun and sparkling while she sang and swayed. Sprays of blood arced into the air, painted crimson doorways in the sky.

Honey hewed a path with her song, and all around her joined a chorus of screams.

No time to waste. Ripka bolted for the path the table had carved, Enard tight on her heels. She ducked a fist, twisted away from someone reaching for her, vaulted over the twisted tangle of wood and limbs, scrambled across the shattered rubble. All the while that high song keened in her ears, sending gooseprickles down her spine. She knew that Honey danced at her side, saw the fans of blood unfurl themselves to the sky as her expert swipes of that too-sharp knife opened throats and hearts and lungs to the bright of day.

Inmates ran, screaming fear and wards against evil alike. Anyone of them could have tackled her. Anyone of them could have put a stop to the slaughter, if only they'd work together, if only they'd mob her. Ripka feared at any moment they'd be swamped, driven under a frantic press of bodies, but the moment never came. The terror of Honey's grace, the nightmare of her song, pushed them back. Paralyzed them.

Ripka tamped down her own fear, and fled. She was a practical woman. Survive now, vomit out your fear later. Impossibly, she stumbled through Misol's half-open door, shoulder slamming into the wall opposite, the cold stones a balm to her nerves, to her burning muscles. Enard stumbled in after her, then Honey leapt within. Misol slammed the door shut, plunging them into the faint light of a single oil lamp.

"Well," Misol said, regarding their panting, sweating, blood-spattered party. "It seems I can't leave you alone a moment."

"Honey..." Ripka gasped, trying to reclaim her breath, and forced herself to stand tall, to reach for the woman to see if she were injured.

"I'm all right," she said, her voice a fainter strain of rasp than usual.

"Your voice..."

She looked at the knife in her hand dripping crimson. "It's not good anymore, I know. I sang too much."

Ripka stared, knowing without asking that Honey never sang unless she had a knife in her hand.

"Charming," Misol drawled.

Ripka gathered herself. "Forge and Clink are on the level above, we've got to get them out before the other inmates find a way up to them."

Misol shook her head. "No time. This place is boiling, we gotta take our exit while we still can."

"But they–"

Honey pat her arm, making gentle shushing noises. "Don't worry, Captain. They've been here a long time. They'll be all right."

Ripka pressed her lips together. "Fine. But I will not let that favor go unreturned for long."

"Come on, let's get moving. Boss wants to see you," Misol said.

Ripka spat foamy blood. "I won't see that shit-sucking rat Radu–"

"He was never the boss here." She took the lantern in hand. "Try not to drop too much blood on the rugs."

"All right," Honey whispered, humming a soft, fairytale tune as they trailed after Misol's lantern in the dark.

CHAPTER 36

Detan stood beside Pelkaia with his wrists in chains, watching the so-called inescapable Remnant prison rise from the horizon before him. Despite his unease at what was to come, he allowed himself a small smirk. It was going to be a pleasure to ruin the reputation of the empire's finest prison.

Whatever they'd gone through – whatever tension thickened the short space between him and Pelkaia – was worth it to wrest Nouli from the empire's grip and rub their noses in their failure. Once this was done, he'd spread rumors and seeds of tavern songs all the way back across the Scorched to Hond Steading to rub the embarrassment deeper.

If he returned home. Pelkaia's words hung over him like a death shroud, clouding his mind and obscuring all future options. He'd have to tie the ends off on this scheme before he could get a clear head around what was going to happen next. He swallowed dry air, remembering the gleaming firemounts of his home city.

"Don't see it," Tibs grumbled. Detan started, peering into the curtain of mist that hung over the rocky island. Tibs was right. The signal they'd devised with Ripka had not yet been flown, or else it'd been taken down. There was no way to be certain what had happened, save that neither Ripka nor New

Chum had attempted to make any contact with them. Which meant they were still within those sheltering walls and hadn't yet found a path to communication with the outside world.

He shivered. Maybe the captain and the steward were comfortable being hemmed in, but Detan'd go mad by the second day if he'd been the one slinking around those halls. He could only hope his companions had had an easier time of completing their task than he had.

"Then we're going in blind," Detan said.

"Was to be expected."

"Not a lot of arts and crafts on the ole Remnant, eh?"

"I reckon not."

"Will you two," Pelkaia grated, "please explain yourselves?"

Detan locked eyes with Tibs and arched a brow. They still hadn't informed Pelkaia that their intention was to free Ripka, New Chum, and Nouli. He reckoned it'd be rude to spring an uninvited guest into the party, but Tibs gave a slight shake of the head, and Detan decided to listen to him for once. They didn't have the others safely in hand yet. There was no telling what Pelkaia would do if he explained his ulterior motive. Anyway, it was a right bit unsettling talking about anything at all with Pelkaia while she was strutting around wearing Thratia Ganal's face.

"We've got a system," Detan warmed to the half-lie, giving her a small shrug. "We signal if we're ready for intervention. Ripka'd run a flag up somewhere – special design, we'd know it if we saw it, and it ain't there."

"She knows you're coming?" Coss asked, not bothering to hide the incredulous lilt to his voice.

"How could she not?" There was more edge in his tone than Detan'd intended. He was trying to keep himself light, cheerful. The same man of rambling home and rambling tongue that'd first strolled onto the *Larkspur*, hoping the crew would forget his fireworks display and start laughing again. Hadn't seen so much as a smile since the cloud suck, but he kept on as best he could.

Still, the insinuation that Ripka and New Chum would expect him to abandon them rankled. What kind of flimsy sack did they think he was? He stifled a sigh. The rambling probably wasn't helping his case on that account. Hard people to charm, these crew members of the reborn *Larkspur*.

Wasn't his little snap that'd made the whole crew fall silent, though. Down below, the Remnant was in chaos. Smoke billowed up from what he assumed to be the rec yard, knots of men and women fighting or fucking or just generally shoving up against one another, he couldn't tell. Panicked guards scurried about the place, brandishing batons but quite clearly overwhelmed by the mess of it all.

Detan's smirk grew into a full-fledged grin, and a bubbling little chuckle escaped.

"What is it?" Pelkaia demanded.

"I'd bet my shorthairs Ripka had her hands in that hubbub."

"Not a bet anyone is wanting to take."

"Their loss."

Coss chuckled, covered it with a rough cough, and Detan could have kissed the man. Finally some pits-cursed levity. Tense people made him nervous. He'd found them to be prone to overreaction, and usually in his direction.

"Captain," Laella said, appearing at the rail with a pinched expression between her brows. "There's sel somewhere down there. A lot of it."

"I feel it," Pelkaia confirmed.

Detan was tempted to reach out to confirm the hidden lode with his own senses, but he refrained. He didn't need another accident on his head.

"Backup storage for refilling the transport ships?" he asked.

Pelkaia regarded him with one of Thratia's eyebrows arched. "Too large for that. Can you pinpoint it, Coss?"

He leaned against the railing, the muscles of his neck bulging as he focused his sense. After a moment, he grunted.

"Seems to be concentrated over there." He gestured to an empty stretch of tumbled-down stones and scrubby cypress trees.

"Interesting," Pelkaia mused.

Detan's skin crawled. Wasn't a thing there that could hide so much of the stuff, not even a half-hearted attempt at a gardener's shed. "Any chance it's an underground cache?"

"No," Coss said.

Well then. Someone had an awful lot of sel on the Remnant, and was able to use it to hide whatever it was they were storing the sel in. A few beads of sweat prickled between his shoulder blades, turning cold in the insistent ocean breeze. A doppel, perhaps. Or something else. Something new, like what Pelkaia had amassed on the *Larkspur*'s shining decks. Could be a special prison for rogue deviants, as the guards back in Petrastad had implied. Could be a trap.

No going back now, though. Not with Ripka and New Chum down there somewhere, waiting for him to swoop in and swoop out with them safely in his charge. Not like Pelkaia would have agreed to turn around, anyway. Not with the *Larkspur* bare to all who looked at her. No doubt the shifty woman was already planning how to wrest away the prison's selium supply so that she could use it to mask her ship.

As they drew near the island, the crew drifted away from the fore rail, taking over the piloting of the ship with their hands instead of their senses. It wouldn't do to let the whole of the prison know the *Larkspur* was manned by a couple handfuls of over-powered sensitives. Not yet, anyway.

Pelkaia turned her back to him, directing her crew with sharp hand signals. Tibs sidled close to him, voice low. "You ready for this?"

"You'll find me up for the most daring of feats, the most courageous of rescues, the–"

"Just try not to get anyone killed we don't want dead."

He sighed. "You've no sense of theater."

"You've no sense at all."

He grinned, relieved. Tibs wouldn't bother to insult him if he still had his mood in a dark knot over Detan's failure to win Pelkaia's tutelage. The ship shuddered as an upward gust of wind rocked the sails to one side, the crew overcorrecting without the ease of their sel-sense to guide the ship into port. Damn silly crew, gotten lazy through the use of their talents. Detan itched to scurry over to the captain's podium, Tibs at the nav, and guide the ship smooth as silk against the dock, but the chains around his wrists held him steady. He had a new role to play. One he'd spent far too many years avoiding.

Wary of the winds, the *Larkspur* slipped up alongside the Remnant's largest dock. He gave the tie-posts along the dock a wary eye. They looked far too flimsy to hold a ship as large as the *Larkspur*, but they'd have to do. At least their flimsy construction would make a speedy escape easier, if it came to that.

The roof was aswarm with guards. They rushed toward the dock with red-slapped cheeks and panicked expressions. A few of them hung back, casting nervous glances at the riot brewing in the rec yard below. They hadn't a clue what they were supposed to do now; see to the new vessel, or assist their comrades with their work. Good. Confusion within the ranks made a situation easier to manipulate.

"State your business!" A man with a few more stripes on his sleeve than his fellows barked up at the ship. The crew swung the gangplank around, and Pelkaia mounted it at an easy stroll. The guard's face paled. Apparently even the rats of the Remnant were familiar with Thratia's sharp visage. Hopefully not too familiar.

"I've brought your warden a present. Where is he?" Pelkaia's voice was so like Thratia's it made Detan's stomach swoop with nerves.

"I don't know…" he stammered, glancing toward the other guards who all rolled indifferent shoulders at him in

response. "The prison is on lockdown," he explained, seeing
the distasteful sneer curling Pelkaia's lip. "Inmates got it in
their head one of their own was an informant, some lady
blue coat, and went wild. Warden could be seeing to business
anywhere."

Ripka had been outed. He felt the reality of it like a slap,
like a stab to the heart. His breath quickened, desiring
nothing more than to bolt down the gangplank and out into
the fray, to fish Ripka out and whisk her away to safety. How
he'd manage that, he had no idea. He'd be more likely to get
himself killed than pull off any rescuing. But the urge was
there, distracting, sharpening the edge of his nerves.

"I see." Pelkaia sauntered down the gangplank. Coss gave
Detan and Tibs a nudge and, obedient as prisoners, they
shuffled down after her. "And where is this troublesome
woman?"

"Shit if I know," he said, his neck flushing after he realized
what he'd said. "I mean – down there, somewhere. If her
dorm guards are doing their jobs then they've locked her up
until this calms down."

Detan swallowed sour spit. He sincerely doubted her dorm
guards had done anything of the sort. Where would she go,
if pressed? Would New Chum be implicated along with her?
Would she even have the option of escape – or was she down
there now, fighting for her life?

He leaned forward to try and see over the roof's edge
and Coss gave him a sharp cuff on the back of the head. He
grunted, but held back a snappy retort. *You're a prisoner, don't
blow it.*

"Given that your establishment is so clearly out of control,
I must insist you bring the warden to me."

Keeping the *Larkspur* at her back, her escape route open.
A clever idea, if she truly meant to deposit Detan and Tibs
then be on her merry way. He considered that this might be
a double cross, that she might be entrusting the dangerous

"worldbreaker" to the containment of the empire's grandest prison.

But she wouldn't. She knew as well as he did that they would not keep him here. That it would be the Bone Tower for him – and a forging into a weapon only the empire could wield, whether he willed it or no. He'd plucked her out of the way of that fate once before. No matter her feelings toward him now, he knew she wouldn't leave him to that very fate.

He hoped.

"We don't know where–"

"Find. Him."

"Ma'am, you're going to have to wait–"

"Ma'am?" Pelkaia strode forward until she was a forearm's length from the guard. "Do you not know me?"

"Commodore Ganal." He cleared a hitch in his throat. "Forgive me, but, our resources are strained as it is. If you could wait here–"

"Enough. What sort of joke is the empire running here? My crew and I will help you secure your prison, and then we'll see to the warden."

The guard's throat bobbed as he swallowed whatever he wanted to say. "I'll take you to the warden's office."

He tried to make his tone stiff, firm, the voice of authority letting Thratia know just what was going to happen in this place that was under imperial control. Poor sap didn't realize the hesitant flicker of his gaze, the little twitch at the bow of his lips, gave away his certainty – that no matter that the prison was dissolving into chaos all around, the warden would be in his office. Possibly under lock and key, and maybe even hiding under his desk.

A glance passed among the other guards, a less subtle movement, something he was sure Pelkaia wouldn't miss. They were hesitant, but hopeful. Hopeful that Thratia Ganal would take control of this situation, and possibly control of their warden, and put things to rights.

Dissatisfaction amongst the ranks. Interesting.

"Very well." Pelkaia flicked her hand to indicate her impatience. "Take me to his office, then, but I will wait no more than a mark before I take this disastrous place under my arm if your warden decides not to pay me a visit."

"Find him," the guard snapped to his fellows, and gestured Pelkaia forward. "This way please, commodore."

Pelkaia held up a fist and circled it, indicating that all those not already required to come with her were to stay behind and look after the *Larkspur*. And be prepared to take off at the slimmest notice, no doubt. Detan would have much rather been among their number, but the lure of rescuing Ripka and New Chum urged him on.

Not much could be discerned from the drab interior of the Remnant. They were led down a narrow corridor, stone walls hemming them in all around. No decoration adorned the walls, though hints of graffiti of times past could be seen in half-chiseled gashes and the mangled remains of staining inks. Not even a rug cushioned the ground. Detan was beginning to loathe all municipal construction. A flair for comfort amongst his civic betters wouldn't have gone amiss.

After this was over, he resolved to lay around on silken pillows for *at least* a week. Or until Tibs kicked him off, at any rate.

He lost track of the twisting and turning of the hallways, each door with its odd number or jumble of letters a new mystery to him. He'd spent more than his fair amount of time behind bars installed by imperial hands, and yet he'd never seen anything like the stone bowels of the Remnant. He had no idea what those numbered doors meant – or where they'd lead to. Chances were quite good, he surmised, that he'd never, ever want the answers to that particular curiosity.

What went on behind the locked doors of a prison's inner sanctum wasn't anything he wanted to be acquainted with. He'd spent time enough in the whitecoats' company to satisfy any morbid curiosity a younger, stupider version of himself might have held toward the particularities of torture.

Not that his captors had ever set out to torture him. No, he'd just been a specimen. A thing to take apart and figure out how to put back together again. He never had found much comfort in that knowledge.

The guard knocked on a door with a bit more shine to its wood than the rest. Figured the king rat would squirrel away in the middle of his nest. Probably had stuck himself on the end of a twisted route in case a riot got loose in the building. Wouldn't want the inmates to have too easy a job finding their crummy warden.

The warden's office was a master class in disappointment in the Valathean system. Haphazard stacks of paper littered the floor, the desk. A bookshelf caked with dust leaned crazily against one wall, threatening to topple over at the slightest bump. Though the single window was thrown open to let in the ocean breeze, the sour tang of old wine and unwashed breath hung in the air. A hint of smoke, too, though Detan couldn't place the source. Certainly wasn't the cold hearth opposite the tottering bookshelf. He figured he'd rather spend his time in a cell than this rat hole. At least cells were sloshed down with water once a week. Musta been killing Ripka to stay in this disastrous place.

The warden himself sat hunched behind his desk, beady eyes screwed up tight and a tighter scowl on his lips.

"Commodore," he said, "I didn't expect to see you again so soon."

Well shit. Pelkaia scoffed, buying herself time to figure out a proper response, and Detan prayed to the clear skies that her acting skills hadn't grown rusty. He caught Tibs's eye and raised a brow, wondering if they should try to cause a distraction. The warden answered his question for him.

"I have had no progress in rooting out our imperial underminers, if that's what you're here about." The warden's voice was raw with defensiveness, and he shot an annoyed glance at the guard who'd led them to him. "Or didn't you notice I currently have my hands *quite* full? The inmates have been anxious, despite our efforts to keep them subdued. Mudleaf isn't enough to calm a nervous heart in these circumstances, despite your *insistence*. A mouse knows when it's caged next to a lion."

Detan's mind reeled. That was all very interesting – if completely without context to him. Thratia had a deal with the warden. Made sense. Thratia wanted the inmates calmed because... lions? Gods below the dunes, but he wished he could find Ripka and New Chum and ask them what in the pits was going on around here. Pitsdamn Thratia, that woman had longer fingers than a willow tree stretched on a torturer's rack.

"It's not your progress I'm here about," Pelkaia said, keeping her voice tight and clipped. A good move, that. Detan would give her a big ole round of applause if he wasn't playing the part of a docile prisoner. Though he was dying to find out what the agreement was between those two spiders, she didn't know enough to step out onto that particular stretch of quicksand, and they'd be in it up to their necks in no time if she tried.

"I see." The warden's pursed lips got even thinner. Detan caught himself wondering how a man wound up that tight could ever take a shit, then chased the thought away with a revolted shiver. Curiosity wasn't always a winning state of mind. "Have you brought two to add to your menagerie then?"

Silence all around. Detan stared straight ahead at the wall, not daring to catch anyone's eye lest he give away the fear racing through his veins like cold iron. Menagerie.

All that sel, in all that empty space. The guards' rumors... Didn't take a whole lot of thinking to draw some real stark conclusions from the facts at hand.

Pelkaia had to clear her throat to smooth a rasp from it. "Yes. Of course."

"Very well." The warden waved them off with a flick of his wrist. "Though I warn you again that this is madness. You won't find what you're looking for in my population, and the more freaks you drag out here the more wound up my cattle gets, even if they don't quite know what's making their skin itch." He glared out the window, lips hitching up in a curl of disgust. "Makes *my* skin itch."

He eyed Detan and Tibs then, as if seeing them for the first time. At least Detan no longer had to fake shock and horror at his current predicament. "Bringing them out here yourself, I bet these two are more dangerous than most."

"You could say that," Pelkaia said a little too quickly.

"Well, go on then. You know the way, and as you can see I've a lot on my hands at the moment."

"I require your man here to lead the way." Pelkaia tipped her chin toward the one who'd brought them this far. "With a riot happening, I'd like to keep someone to hand who knows all the pathways."

He snorted. "Forgot the path you picked already? Typical. Go, then. I'll send word when I've rooted out our little problem for good." The warden glanced at a strange, silvery curl of bark on his desk and his disgust returned anew. Did the man have a botany problem? Odd thing to be concerned about, with half your prison breaking anything they could get their hands on – heads not excluded.

As the guard led them out into the hall Pelkaia dropped back, hissing low against his ear. "Now what?"

"We've got to see it through. We've got to get them out."

"Might be more 'them' than we intended," Tibs murmured low enough for them to hear.

Detan shivered. What in the black skies was Thratia up to on this forsaken hunk of rock?

CHAPTER 37

Ripka marked the doors they passed, struggling to orient herself as Misol set a brisk pace through the labyrinthine corridors of the Remnant. Constructing the pathways so that they were difficult to follow helped stem the possibility of complete mutiny, but irritation at the prison's designers still rankled her. It was one thing to design against an uprising. This was madness. How the guards, untrained as they appeared to be, kept track of where they were at any given time baffled her. It was no wonder Noull had managed to hide out within their walls for so long.

Misol skirted the edges of the prison and by extension the rec yard at its heart. Each time they drew near an exterior-facing wall she could hear the muffled shouts and thumps and thuds of a riot spun out of control. Ripka cringed. She was the cause of that madness – never mind that Radu had set her up for it – and she'd walked out and left it to fester.

"There's nothing you could have done," Enard said.

"Am I so transparent?"

He quirked a tight smile. "I know you."

"Hush," Misol advised tartly. "It's not all friends running through these walls, understand?"

She did. The guard staff of the Remnant was split along

loyalties – Nouli had made that clear enough – and the division made it all but impossible for Radu to lead, even if he had been inclined to actually better the conditions of his charges.

Ripka stared hard at Misol's back. To whom did she answer? Not Radu, that was clear enough. And yet Misol's name had not so much as twitched an eyelid on neither Nouli nor Kisser, making her unlikely to owe her allegiance to the empire.

"Who–" Ripka began, but Misol waved a hand to shush her.

The next door opened to the bright sky. Ripka brought up a hand to shade her eyes. The sun wasn't as bright as it had been in Aransa, but after the innards of the Remnant it stung her eyes to tears all the same. Misol gave the area a perfunctory check, then took off at a sharp angle toward the yellowhouse. Ripka's skin tingled, sensing answers close at hand.

She probably should have been afraid, or at least wary, but the lure of solving a mystery was sunk too deep in her heart. She acknowledged the fear that should be there, and strode off after Misol. Honey hummed softly under her breath, swinging her arms in wide arcs at her side. Definitely should be afraid, she mused. And yet she wasn't. The end result of too much time spent roaming around with Detan, no doubt.

"Captain," Enard whispered, laying a hand on her shoulder. "Look."

He tipped his head to the side, and she stopped cold. Anchored to the roof of the prison's administrative building was the *Larkspur*.

Not some other ship, gussied up to resemble the infamous craft. Not swaddled in layers of obscuring selium, as Detan had postulated it would be.

The real thing. Whole, gleaming. Its accordion wings folded at its sides, its hull bearing a few scratches, but nothing to diminish its beauty. The *Larkspur*. Here.

Detan had come along after all, and they were nowhere near ready for him.

"Huh," Misol murmured. She stopped a few steps ahead, shifting the spear cradled against her shoulder as if it chaffed. "Looks like she got it back. Good. Didn't expect her so soon, though."

"You..." Ripka cleared a hitch from her throat. "...work for Thratia Ganal?"

Misol scoffed. "Not directly." She turned back toward the yellowhouse and set off again. "I'm just another worker bee in her hive."

And yet someone Radu feared. Ripka's mind drew connections between facts as if she were working a case back in Aransa. Misol worked for Thratia, and yet Radu deferred to her, sweated in her presence. The shimmer about the house. That same sheen she'd seen when Misol opened the door in the rec yard. Ripka's mind had been too crowded with fear and pain to realize what it meant. What Misol'd used to signal her. Not a trick of the eyes, then. Not her desperation making her hallucinate.

Doppel.

The word clotted on her tongue, her skin itched with the desire to flee. Something was amiss here. Something she hadn't counted on. Something Detan and the others were walking into, right now, all unknowing. She shared a look with Enard, could see worry crinkling the corners of his eyes.

"You'll be safe enough here," Misol said and reached out to open the door to the yellowhouse.

Ripka didn't want this mystery solved any more. She knew enough to know she should run. Run like the pits were opening up beneath her. But she walked through the door anyway, trailing Enard and Honey in her wake.

Dust swirled in the sunlight filtering through half-shuttered windows, gleaming like fairy dust. Like sel.

And a woman in a long, white, coat turned to smile at her.

"Good evening, Captain Leshe. This is an unexpected pleasure."

The voice was older, deepened by the lengthening of the girl's throat as she'd grown. Grown tall and thin, though the hint of hips pushed at the rectangle her coat was trying to make her into. The girl – she must be thirteen or fourteen, now – wore her chestnut hair up high on the back of her head, wisps escaping to give her a harried look. The look of a young woman who worked hard, long hours. Ripka had no doubt of that. She'd only met her once, and briefly, but that girl's name was burned into her mind. Seared there by the fear Detan's voice had carried when he'd spoken it.

"The pleasure's mine, Aella Ward," she lied, hoping to keep things congenial until she could find her footing again.

They locked gazes, smiling at one another with all their teeth. Misol didn't seem to notice the tension.

"You know her?" Misol said. "She's the one I was telling you about. The one that could see the strangeness in the house and kept coming back to it."

"Ah," Aella clucked her tongue against her teeth. "I am afraid you were mistaken, Misol. Captain Leshe's keen perception is well known to me, but I am *quite* certain she does not possess sel sense of any kind."

Ripka suppressed a flinch, understanding the ice in Aella's tone. It'd been Callia's mistake, Aella's adopted mother, to assume Ripka possessed sel sense. To presume that she could make Ripka ill with it, and that presumption had allowed Ripka to crack her over the head with a wrench. Ripka never had found out if the woman had survived that encounter. Ripka'd left her breathing, but that was all she knew for certain. When Detan had told her later what they'd done to him... Breathing might have been more than she deserved.

"Why are you here, Aella?"

The girl smiled, showing some of the youth hidden in the roundness of her cheeks. "I could ask the same of you, Leshe. I know you well enough to know you did nothing so untoward as to actually deserve that costume you're wearing."

Before Ripka could respond, a soft ruffling of cloth drew her attention. The sound emitted from behind a broad desk, and the soft hiss of chainlinks followed.

"Ah, she's awake." Aella turned toward the desk and held one hand out low. "Come say hello to our guest."

A dark grey hand slipped into Aella's, its fingers knobby with bulging knuckles and thick veins. Misol glanced away, fidgeting with the leather wrap on her spearshaft. Ripka braced herself. Anything that could unsettle the doppel was bound to be poor news for her.

A rickety woman half crawled, hunched over and trembling in a robe of sky blue silk, from behind the desk. Steel-grey hair fell over the sides of her face, hiding her expression, and the knobs of her spine poked up against the fabric that covered her. She straightened herself as best she could, little more than a stunted hunch, and peered at Ripka through fringed bangs.

Ripka's breath caught.

"Callia?"

The withered woman made a soft sound and cocked her head to the side. Ripka tried to keep the shock – the revulsion – off her face, but knew she did not succeed. "What... What happened to her?

Aella rolled a small shoulder and gave Callia's hand a gentle squeeze. A length of glittering chain passed from Callia's hand into Aella's, its terminus somewhere amongst Callia's shaggy hair. "Her mind was damaged by your blow. Halfway through our journey across the Darkling Sea she mixed up her medicines and poisoned herself. Such a tragedy. I did not know enough to ensure her survival, so we raced back to the Scorched and threw ourselves upon Thratia's generosity."

"I see," Ripka said, gut clenching. "And I suppose your shifting allegiance is a result of admiration for Thratia's... generosity."

Aella beamed at her. "I knew you'd understand. How could I return to my old masters after Thratia went out of her way so? She did all she could, but I could not return Callia to Valathea in this state. It would shame her. And so here we remain, doing what work we may."

Ripka could almost see Aella's triumph, burning bright behind too-sharp eyes. Ripka knew damned well Callia would have received no trumpeted glory upon her return to Valathea. Her failure to capture both Detan and Pelkaia would have ruined her standing within the order of the whitecoats and, by proxy, undermine Aella.

Ripka wondered how long Aella had waited before switching her adopted mother's medicines for poison. How long she'd pretended to be distraught before hitting upon the "sudden" inspiration to turn back to Aransa and throw herself at Thratia's feet.

There were plenty of cities between the Darkling Sea and Aransa. Plenty of apothiks skipped over so that she could ask Thratia directly for aid. Ripka wondered if that were the point. If having sought help at a coastal city would have left Callia too hale, too willing to point a finger Aella's way.

"Thratia is capable of mercy, when so moved to it," Ripka said, hoping her tone implied agreement with Aella's actions. She needed to get out of here. Needed to grab Nouli by the scruff and run as quick as she could toward the *Larkspur*.

"Speaking of," Misol said, and Ripka almost screamed just to cause a distraction. She should have thought to drag the conversation away from all mention of Thratia. "The *Larkspur* has put in over by Radu's office. We should get a visit from the commodore shortly."

Aella's icy gaze snapped to Ripka and froze, holding her, hunger burning behind her too-small pupils. Ripka forced herself to keep her face smooth, impassive, but knew that forced calm would tell Aella as much as full-on panic would.

"Is it now?" the girl asked Misol, but did not so much as

glance away from Ripka. "You're certain it's the *Larkspur*?"

"No mistaking a ship like that." Misol grabbed Ripka's shoulder and started to steer her around. "I'll take this lot back to their cells, then. Don't want the commodore finding any normals kicking around here, eh?"

"I think not." Aella's voice was a crisp slap.

Misol froze. "No?"

"No."

Misol shrugged and dropped Ripka's shoulder. "Whatever suits you."

Aella cradled Callia's chin in one hand. "Go and fetch us some wine." Her words were tight, precise. She placed the other end of Callia's leash back into her hand and waved her off. The skeletal woman shuffled away toward a door at the end of the room, surprisingly quick and smooth of movement for one so worn.

Ripka forced herself to keep a small, ambivalent smile on her face as Aella turned back to her. The girl beamed. "I can't *wait* to welcome our new guests."

CHAPTER 38

Detan and his motley entourage were led through the twisting corridors of the Remnant and out into the open air. Cold wind raised prickles over his skin. He tried to convince himself that all those prickles were due to the chill. Wasn't fear at all. Not for Detan Honding. But he'd never been very good at convincing himself of anything at all.

They followed a narrow, packed dirt path through scrub trees and a few rows of carefully tended crops. Great heads of wheat and corn bowed to the winds rolling in off the sea. He couldn't help but be a little jealous of the variety of foods the inmates had access too. He hadn't had a good roasted cob of corn in *years*, not since his auntie had some flown in for his twelfth year celebration. Wasn't much arable land out by Hond Steading proper. Most of their food came from the coastal farming towns a day's flight to the north. Yet another way Thratia could cripple Hond Steading.

Detan forced himself to focus. He was here for New Chum and Ripka, sure, but he was here for his auntie, too. Here for her whole city, and that meant seeing this straight through to the end. No running, no failing. He had to get all his happy charges, plus one Nouli Bern, bundled up safe on the *Larkspur* and make like a monsoon wind for the mainland.

Right, he told himself. He'd been in worse spots. And, sure as the pits were black, he couldn't allow himself to panic. Not now, not with that great looming mass of selium they were approaching calling out to him on the periphery of his senses.

A small, yellowstone house sat at the end of their chosen path, right smack in the shadow of that giant sheet of sel. He couldn't see the gas, but he could sense its presence above – ominous, looming. As if it were watching him and daring him every step he took. Daring him to reach for it. To mold together with it. To release its potential.

He stared at the house ahead, refusing to so much as glance at the false, pleasant blue of the sky above. Pelkaia rolled her shoulders uncomfortably, twitched at the ends of the bandana that hid her hair. Sweat stained the collar of her tunic.

"Ugly little place," Tibs remarked, snapping him out of his mounting anxiety.

"Saying you want to move in?"

"Naw. I think it'd suit you better."

"Quiet," Pelkaia-Thratia said, because she couldn't be seen letting her prisoners chat out their fear right under her nose. He was grateful she let them slip in what little they got. Tibs's barbs always gave him a sense of calm. Of normalcy.

Of home.

Every step forward he wanted to dig his heels in and refuse. But he was committed, there was no turning back even if he did lose his nerve. When the guard leading them down the path flung open the house's door, he'd like to think he didn't flinch. He did, of course, but he'd like to think he didn't.

The faint light in the room wouldn't let him see what he was walking into, so he strode in blind, keeping his head up and a stupid, hopefully disarming smile plastered on his face as he followed Pelkaia-Thratia into the dim room. Light bled across the floor from poorly pulled shutters, illuminating floating dust motes.

His eyes adjusted. His smile disappeared.

"My my," Aella said, cocking her small head to the side as she regarded Pelkaia. "What an unexpected delight, commodore." The slight emphasis she placed on "commodore" made Detan's blood run cold. She knew. Of course she knew. And she could dash the facade away, if she so chose. The crook of his elbow burned from her nearness.

Tension gathered in the room, knotted and clotted up just like his anger did when it was preparing to rear its head. He saw the withered creature huddled by Aella's side, wine carafe clutched in skeletal fingers. Saw New Chum, standing alongside some woman with a spear, face a mass of placid geniality. Saw Ripka, skies bless her, standing between him and Aella, her bruised fists held low, a golden-haired woman with a knife at her side looking just as ready to fight. But no Nouli. Not yet. Ripka's mouth moved. She thought better of whatever she'd been going to say and closed it.

He ignored their bruises. Their bloodied lips and black eyes. The filth and blood staining their jumpsuits. If he didn't... Well, it was just better that he saved that information to give due consideration later. When there wasn't a vaporous cloud calling his name above his head.

"Right," he said and clapped his hands together, donning his smile like a mask. "It is such a pleasure to see what a lovely young woman you've grown into, Aella! Though I must confess I do not believe white becomes you."

He strolled round the room as he spoke, drawing everyone's eyes, trying to keep them looking, guessing, trying to figure out how he was going to salvage this mess.

"And you, Callia." He paused before the withered woman, pointedly ignoring the thin silver chain hanging from a collar around her neck. A perverse shock of pleasure rocked him, made his smile genuine. "You look as lovely without as you are within."

"Enough." Aella's voice lacked the snap of her predecessor's, but her exasperation was just as cutting. "Misol, secure the building."

The lanky woman with the spear shot Pelkaia-Thratia a wary glance, but shrugged and angled for a doorway. Going for assistance, Detan realized. Going to gather up all her sister spears and hem them in with pointy edges. Pelkaia's fists clenched and unclenched at her sides, a hatred deeper than anything Detan'd ever felt burning bright behind her borrowed eyes.

He had Ripka, New Chum, Pelkaia, and Coss. Tibs, too, could be handy with a wrench if pressed to it. Aella was outnumbered now. She wouldn't be again. There would be no other opportunity.

"You are such a thoughtful host." Detan sidled up to Callia and took the wine carafe from her trembling fingers. With a flourish he plucked a cup from the neat desk and began to pour.

"Tell me," he said, keeping his gaze on Aella, not daring to look at either Ripka or New Chum lest he give away his intent. "Do you have my package?"

"I can collect it in a moment," Ripka answered, crisp and efficient, while Aella's eyebrows knotted in confusion.

Ah. Well then. What she needed was a distraction. He was good at those. It was cleaning up the mess afterward that'd always proved his problem.

"Be a dear and fetch it, hmm?"

He dashed the cup of wine in Aella's smug little face.

CHAPTER 39

A good plan, Detan had taught her, functioned on three founding principles: it must be followed, it must be trusted, and it must be thrown straight out the window when it inevitably goes to the pits.

She ran like her ass was on fire, only vaguely aware of the shouts behind her. Detan knew what he was doing. He must. She just had to get Nouli. If he proved reluctant, then she'd knock him on the head and drag him out. If Kisser was in her way, she'd knock her on the head and drag her out, too.

She brushed past the woman who must be Pelkaia, skin crawling all the same as she touched the likeness of Thratia. Honey darted in front of her, blonde mop of hair glowing in the sunlight as she flung the door open. The three of them spilled out into the breezy day, the weather cool and pleasant and bright, cheerfully ignorant of all Ripka's plans evaporating before her eyes. Her heels skidded in the dirt outside the yellowhouse's door. Enard grabbed her arm, steadying her.

His expression was calm, controlled. Willing to do whatever needed doing next. Would have made her a fine deputy, had circumstances turned out very differently.

"What now?" he asked.

Shouts and clangs and grunts sounded behind her. She

pretended not to notice. Detan had given her a task. She knew how to perform her duty.

"We need Nouli."

"Kisser's uncle?" Honey asked.

"You know him?"

She toyed with the ends of her hair, gaze tracking some sea bird as if it were the most fascinating thing in all the world. She was bored, Ripka realized. Bored and looking for some new challenge – or more than likely for someone new to kill. "Met him once. Don't know where he is."

Ripka eyed the path back to the prison, laying a map in her mind over what she saw. They weren't far from where Nouli's workshop *should* be, but then, there was no telling what would happen if they re-entered those hallways. They could get lost. They could be captured. And while Honey was itching for another bloodbath, Ripka had no stomach for it.

Enard cleared his throat.

"I'm thinking," she snapped.

"Had you, perhaps, considered the grate against the wall?" His tone was gentle, but still held a rebuke. She'd been too tangled up in the strange doors and labyrinthine pathways. She'd let the complexity of the situation blind her, when the solution was so simple. Nouli's venting window had been covered with a grate, a rather obvious addition to any stone wall. They just had to find it.

"Clockwise or counter?" she asked.

"I've always been fond of widdershins." Enard grinned down at her, his sweat-slicked hair swooped over to one side. She would have chuckled if she weren't so very aware of the shouts of battle behind her.

"Let's go."

They cut across the fields, ignoring the possibility of detection from above. Things were moving too quickly, and she could hear hints of the riot raging within the prison's choking arms. The guards would, hopefully, be too busy to pay the fields any mind. And if they weren't – well, Honey was more than willing to deal with them.

Each time they passed a window that could not be Nouli's, a lump of dread hardened in Ripka's heart. How long had they been away from the yellowhouse, from whatever nightmare battle raged within? She had no doubt that Pelkaia could handle herself in a fight, and that lackey of hers had stood with the stance of one who'd seen one too many rows, but Detan and Tibs weren't prepared for this. She wondered how much sel Aella had tucked away in that house, and just how angry and scared Detan might actually be, and forced herself to move faster.

"Captain," Enard said from somewhere behind her, the question in his voice strained by lack of breath. She paused halfway up a hill, and was shocked to realize how far ahead she'd run. Enard and Honey approached the base of the hill, their faces red from exertion.

"What?" she asked, voice thready from lack of air.

"Look around."

The hill she stood atop was one of a handful arranged to form a narrow valley in the fields. There was nothing natural about their placement. The humps were too regular, the spacing almost perfect. And while the contents of the valley could not be seen from anywhere below the hills – and what inmate ever had reason to climb them? – the crop was obvious to her now. Hip-high shrubs laden with dark, black-brown leaves bowed in the wind, the sun making their glossy foliage gleam like an oil slick. Though the valley funneled most of the wind out toward the sea, Ripka could scent the sun-warmed leaves. The sticky tar aroma of mudleaf.

So here was Radu's cash crop, carefully tended alongside the food crops. She had never been so desirous of a flint to strike in all her life.

"Oh," was all Honey said as she came to stand alongside her.

As the scent of the mudleaf plants wafted up to her, Ripka recalled with sudden clarity the faint aroma of mudleaf in Nouli's laboratory, and she choked back a laugh. Of course he wasn't a user of that rival drug. He'd never risk slowing his already damaged mind. No, he'd just had his workshop placed near the one place the fewest inmates on the Remnant would be allowed to go.

She scanned the wall with renewed intent, and there, near enough to the end of the row of hills that it was nearly covered by the mounded soil, gleamed a faint hint of metal.

"Gotcha," she said, grinning, and jogged down the side of the hill, struggling to keep her jelly-tired knees under control. Just a little while longer, and then she could throw herself down to rest on the deck of the *Larkspur*. They were so, so close.

Brown-black smears of sticky nectar clung to her arms and legs as she waded through the rows of mudleaf shrub. She hesitated before the grate, breathing deep of the sea-damp air, waiting to be sure she caught no hint of the poisons Nouli brewed within wafting out at her. When she was certain the vent was clear, she felt along the edge of the grate, fingers dragging over the rough metal, until she found the hook that held it in place. Shoddy workmanship, but all the better for her purposes.

With Enard's help she levered the grate free and threw it to the dirt, then peered carefully within. The room was faintly lit, the ruddy glow of cheap beeswax candles behind dusty glass the only source of light in the room.

"Nouli?" she whispered.

A soft rattling echoed from within. Nouli's head appeared above his table, his face sallow and pinched with worry and suspicion.

"Captain, is it? Thought you buggered off with my supplies."

"Our task was betrayed, I'm afraid. To the Glasseaters."

Nouli hissed through his teeth, darting an uneasy glance at

the door. "You'd better come in."

"Can't you come out?"

He glanced pointedly at the window, then at the width of his chest, and Ripka sighed. There was no way he could squeeze through. They'd have to take him out through the prison proper, and that meant risking detection.

"Honey," she said as she levered herself up to crawl through the window. "You don't have to help us with this. You could sneak back into general pop, maybe even all the way to your cell–"

"I'm coming," she said, and though her voice was as soft as always there was no room for argument in it.

After what felt like a good half-mark of cursing and squeezing and scraping, they were all three through the vent, forming a half-circle around Nouli and his cluttered table.

"We must go now," Ripka insisted. Nouli clutched a satchel bulging with papers tight to his chest.

"My niece..."

"We were sold out to the Glasseaters. Kanaea Bern is the only one who could have done this." She hated to cut to the point so, but there was no time for this. They had to flee, *now*.

"She wouldn't!"

"Unless it was you, there is no other possibility."

He sucked his lips and shifted his weight, then pushed his spectacles up his nose and nodded to himself. "I do not like it, but I believe you. She has been acting... strange... lately. I fear she is more and more her father's child every day. A gambler, that one. Obsessed with risk. I see no other solution to the evidence before us."

Ripka sighed with relief. It was a pleasure to convince a mind as loving of evidence as her own. "Good. Do you know any shorter paths out of this place? We must avoid detection at all costs, and make it to the sparrow's nest, where our escape ship is docked."

Nouli barked a frantic laugh. "Impossible. There are less

used ways, but with the prison in chaos there's no way to know where the guards will be. Never mind any rabid inmates running amok."

Ripka forced herself to relax her jaw. "Very well. Then we will do our best. Be quick and be quiet, do not speak unless—"

The workshop door flung open. Silhouetted in the brighter light of well-tended oil lanterns stood Kisser, flanked by two tough looking men who wore guard's uniforms. Ripka reached instinctively for her cutlass, cursed and grabbed for one of the crates Nouli used for chairs instead.

"You two," Kisser said, "are terrible at dying." She advanced into the small room, thugs in tow.

CHAPTER 40

"Hold them." Aella ordered no one in particular as she wiped wine from her eyes with the back of her wrist. Detan danced back a step and waved the clay jug through the air as if it were as deadly as a sword. Aella snorted.

"Try not to embarrass yourself too much, Honding."

"Bit late for that, don't you think?"

"Was too late before we ever met."

Tibs chuckled.

"Traitor," Detan said

"She's not wrong."

"*Honding.*" Pelkaia's voice cut through his rising mood like the *Larkspur*'s prow through a storm, and he winced. Wonderful. In one stupid word – never mind that it was his name – she'd encapsulated all her annoyance, all her questioning. Though he kept his gaze snapped on Aella he could practically see Pelkaia with her arms crossed, foot tapping out an impatient staccato as she waited for him to come up with some way to *fix* this. He looked at the wine carafe, at the maroon dribble snaking down its side, and tried to ignore the sound of nice military boots stomping through the halls, surrounding them.

"Err."

"As entertaining as you are, I'm afraid I've rather had enough of this." Aella tipped her chin toward the doorway behind her, and through it spilled a half-dozen guards looking like they'd had their lunch interrupted. One even had a smear of oil and vinegar at the corner of her lips. Didn't hamper her ability to point a crossbow at him, however.

Despite her obedience, the salad eater looked a touch confused. She squinted at Pelkaia-Thratia. "Begging your pardon, mistress, but the commodore...?"

"Oh, *that*." Aella held out a hand and clenched a fist. Detan felt nothing, he had his sel sense reined in tight, but Pelkaia staggered to one side. Coss barely got a hand out in time to hold her upright, and her face melted clear off, leaving the sand-dune cheeks she'd been born with.

"There. That's better. Now, say hello to our latest additions," Aella said, and there was a soft muttering amongst her people.

"Don't look keen on it," the woman with the spear said.

"Are you still here, Misol? Go and collect the other two," Aella said.

Misol rolled her eyes and strolled out the door. Detan found himself wishing he could tag along with her. "If it pleases you, Aella, I'd be happy to retrieve my wayward companions–"

"You're not getting out of my sight. Nor you and your friend, Pelkaia."

"Who *is* this girl?" Coss asked.

"Just another collector." Aella flashed Coss a smile.

"Enslaver, is more like it," Pelkaia's voice was a soft growl. "Did you come here for Ripka's list as well?"

Detan and Tibs exchanged a nervous glance. In all the commotion, he'd forgotten to let Pelkaia know that Ripka harbored no such thing.

Aella's brows shot up. "List? Never mind – I will discover the truth of that soon enough. If you must know, I'm here looking for our ilk."

As Aella's six guards spread out, Detan shifted his weight

and cast a glance at Tibs, who only shrugged. No ideas there, either. The room was small, the door behind him of average size, but the windows were quite large, if partially shuttered. His mind raced, grasping for a solution while Pelkaia and Aella postured like overfeathered cockerels.

"In a prison?" Pelkaia scoffed. "It suits you."

Aella's smile was small and coy. "You'd be amazed how many deviants find themselves on the wrong side of imperial law without being caught out for what they are. Most have more tact than you, after all."

He let the truth of Aella's words settle in his bones and cringed. Their six new friends were deviants, then, and he had no particular way to know their type. Despite Pelkaia's assurances that his line was rare, he could be surrounded by six people just as jumpy and prone to making things go boom as he was. He didn't even like being surrounded by himself at any given time.

And there was that blanket of sel, hiding away the whole of the house. So close, drifting above... Beads of sweat crested his brow, memories of how elated he'd been in Aransa when he'd finally let loose. At how calm he'd been in the days after, his anger burnt up with the boiling of the sky.

"You *really* don't want me in here right now." He angled himself straight at Aella, stared at her until the strength of his gaze made her look away from Pelkaia.

She rolled her eyes. "You are no challenge for me."

Emptiness washed over him like a shroud, and for a moment he felt bereft, desolate. And then positively cheery, a refreshing weight off his shoulders. A shudder of relief stretched through him. His arm didn't even itch anymore. "Oh, that's nice."

"Do be quiet."

"Never been very good at that."

"I am aware."

Pelkaia's hand darted out, gathering the selium that had

escaped her face in one outstretched hand. Aella scowled, and Detan's awareness of the cloud above all their heads came crashing back as Pelkaia's globule floated free once more. He staggered, nausea threatening to rise. Tibs grabbed his shoulder to hold him steady.

"You can only shut down one of us at a time, then," Pelkaia said, and though he couldn't see it her smirk was palpable.

Aella sighed and gestured toward her arrayed guards. "And yet you are hopelessly outnumbered. Please, do not debase yourselves by attempting to fight. You are welcome here, could even come to be treasured here. I can offer you knowledge and training beyond whatever small truths you've been forced to scrape together."

"Knowledge earned with a whitecoat's scalpel," Detan snapped.

She inclined her head to him. "Yes. My methods, however, are not that of my adopted mother and her colleagues."

"The way you treat your mother tells me all I need to know about your methods."

"And you disagree with my treatment?"

Detan winced. From the little smile quirking the corners of her lips he could tell she'd seen his momentary pleasure at Callia's pain. "She deserves punishment, not cruelty."

"I do not see the distinction."

"Then we will never be in agreement."

"You will change your mind in due time. Kneel, all of you. I'm afraid chains are necessary until I can come to trust you all." Aella flashed a truly pleased smile. "Though I hope they will not be needed long."

"Begging your pardon," Tibs drawled, "but it occurs to me to mention that I'm a square peg in your round hole."

Detan stifled a frantic giggle.

"Guilt by association, I'm afraid, Tibal. Now kneel."

The six stepped forward. Detan took an involuntary step back, hands held palms-out toward them. "Hold on a tick, we were just starting to get friendly, I'm not ready for you to bring the ropes out yet."

Pelkaia said, "Coss, now."

Vertigo washed over him. The room shifted, the atmosphere thickened, as if the whole of reality were bunching up, dragged toward the pinprick of stability that was Coss. Tibs's fingers dug into Detan's shoulder, minute sparks of pain grounding him, keeping him upright. He gasped for air like a starved fish and bent over his knees as sparks of white light encroached upon his vision.

The world around him lit, nacreous brilliance falling like a curtain, cutting him off from all those around him. Sel. All the tiny bits of it drifting through the air. All the miniscule intrusions it made upon their world every day, too small to be noticed or made use of, brought to brilliant flaring life.

For the barest of moments terror shook him. He was transplaced, pushed back to that terrible moment a year ago when Callia had thrust a needle in his arm and allowed him to see the truth of what he saw now – and what he'd done with it. The heady control as he fine-tuned his power and shattered the table beneath his back. Pelkaia had said he was capable of harnessing that finesse still. Had seemed certain of the fact.

Black skies, but he wanted that power *back*.

The glittering tore away from his eyes, coalescing around Pelkaia, and perverse jealousy shot through him – how dare she strip his treasure from him. How dare she command that which was *his* birthright. Coss dripped sweat, his narrow face slack with effort.

Detan's ears popped. All the sel pulled away from him, a receding tide that he wanted to wash him away. Someone screamed, and the sel began to splinter – to fling outward from Coss as if it were broken glass. Detan reached out for it, fingers trembling. Tibs shook him, punched his arm. He hardly felt it.

He pushed out, stripped the sel away from whoever held it with the force of his will, slammed it against those shuttered windows, and let loose.

His ears rang. His eyes filled with grit and his mouth felt stuffed with wool. He lay on his side, Tibs blanketed over him, a burning ache in his legs and a dull throb racing from his head down to his toes. Blackness encroached upon his vision and then he was standing, Tibs grabbing him by the collar, jerking him along as if he were a marionette. Dust filled the air, acrid, choking. He coughed and spluttered and they heaved themselves over the stone rubble of the wall, out into the cold breeze and the annoyingly cheerful sunlight.

Somehow he gained control of his feet and staggered alongside Tibs to the other side of the rubble. He expected to feel light, free of his burdens, as he had after Aransa.

And yet hunger still consumed him.

"Not your best plan." Tibs brushed chalk-white dust from his coat and slapped his hat against his thigh. Somehow the ties had torn off his wrists during the blast, leaving rashy smears across his skin. A thin trickle of blood leaked from his temple. Detan looked away, stomach clenching. It was all he could do to ignore the siren call of the sheet of sel blanketing the building. Whatever Coss had condensed from the air, the raw mass of Aella's defensive measures remained. He suspected, though the memory was hazy, that it'd been Aella's ability that cut him short before he made use of that thick cloud.

Great bells rang out, clanging from atop the towers of the Remnant's five buildings.

"Desperate times." He tried to keep his voice light, but it creaked over the dusty dryness in his throat and his grin was limp.

Pelkaia staggered out behind them, Coss's arm thrown around her shoulders to keep her upright. Detan looked away from the anger in her eyes, tried to stifle the firestorm of guilt building in his chest. He'd been careless, as usual. Throwing around his power to suit his need. Could have been a load-bearing wall, he realized. Could have brought the whole thing down on their heads.

"Sirra," Tibs said, and the use of his nickname brought his head up sharp. Tibs was frowning at him, the blood from his temple having found a smeared path through the stubble on his chin. "Still with me?"

"More or less," he grated, looking around at the disaster he'd wrought. Stone groaned, the ominous, grating sound loud to his ears even above the peel of the Remnant's alarm bells. The whole windowed face of the yellowstone house was blown clear off, the rectangular shape of Aella's desk the only stick of furniture left standing, its presence made ridiculous by its normalcy.

Through the drifting clouds of dust, figures began to stir. He was a little disgusted with himself as relief washed over him. They were his enemies. He should crow victory at their defeat, be angered that they still lived. But he didn't want them dead, not really. Didn't want any more blood on his hands. He glanced to Tibs, to the guilty smear down the side of his head, then sharply away. Too late for clean hands.

Pelkaia and Coss stumbled up alongside them, and they all knelt down behind the false shield of the rubble he'd wrought, praying to the sweet skies Aella hadn't spotted them yet.

"What now?" Pelkaia hissed, all business, not willing to delve into a finger-pointing match until they were safely away and she could take her time clobbering him.

Behind them, the Remnant's doors began to disgorge a stream of disheveled, confused guards. Detan dared to hope the distraction was at least enough to give Ripka a clearer path to safety.

"I suggest you put the mean face back on," he said.

"Why bother? She can yank it away at any moment, blasted girl has grown too strong."

Detan caught Coss's eye. The rumpled man's brows shot up as understanding passed between them. Coss nodded.

"Not," Detan said, "if we can keep her busy, and hope Ripka can get the *Larkspur* pointed our way in a hurry."

"Bad plan," Tibs said.

"Only one I got."

"Honding," Aella's voice rang out, sing-song, through the dust and destruction, "you've been a very naughty boy."

He gathered himself, and stood to face his fears.

CHAPTER 41

Ripka took a step backward, giving ground to Kisser and her guards. They herded her back until her thighs pressed against the low, thick edge of Nouli's worktable. Honey lingered to her left, fingers tapping against her hip to some internal song. She had to diffuse this, quickly. Before it grew into a bloodbath they couldn't escape drowning in.

"He wants out," Ripka said, tipping her head toward Nouli without taking her gaze from Kisser. "See? All packed and ready to go. Wants to take you with him. We can do that. I can get you out of here, Kanaea. Back to the mainland."

She snorted and kicked a crate out of her path. "You think I want to stay here forever?"

"You didn't sell us out?"

"To the sand munchers? I might have whispered in their ear. But make no mistake, I want off this rock as much as you do, lil' Miss Leshe. I've just got my own methods, my own loyalties, and you're not on that list."

"Loyalty?" Nouli clutched his bag to his chest, cheeks red. "You lecture on loyalty, child? Child of my sister? What do you know of it save that you scorned it?"

"Whoa," Ripka held her hands out to Nouli and Kanaea, standing sideways between them. In the corner of her eye

Enard slipped to the side, angling himself nearer the biggest of Kanaea's pet guards. "I don't know what blood's gone sour between you two, but I know it's not Nouli running around with the Glasseaters." She jerked her chin at the two bruisers.

Kanaea snorted. "You think these men are Glasseaters? Are you crazy? Those rats are taking cheese from Radu's hand, not mine. Not the empire's. We all know it. Been traipsing around here like they own the place, getting freedoms no one else has to go tend their mudleaf crops. Radu thinks the inmates don't notice, but they do. Guards do, too." She tipped her head to the man standing closest to Enard. "That's why they help us – help the *empire*–" her lip curled over the word, "because good men and women don't want to bend knee to Radu and his scheming."

"And yet you set them on us," Ripka snapped.

She rolled her eyes. "Poorly, it seems. Thought those dogs had more teeth."

"You sold them out!" The satchel squeaked in Nouli's grip.

"Yes, Uncle, I did. For your own good."

The guard nearest Enard stepped forward. Enard caught her eye, a question, and she gave a slight shake of the head. Best not escalate the situation until they had no choice. Nouli was a frail man, addled by age and addiction both. And she still held out hope of taking Kanaea and her chemical genius with them. If not for the saving of Hond Steading, then at the very least to keep her out of Valathea's hands.

"Master Bern," the guard said, "is it true that these two have devised a way for you to escape the Remnant?"

"Yes. These people, they've brought a way."

"A way that is *rapidly* losing viability," Ripka said, trying hard not to glance at the window she'd crawled through and think of the confrontation brewing in her wake. "We must go, now. If you both do want to leave, then–"

"I can leave whenever I want," Kisser said. "The empress may want Uncle on lockdown, but no one cares what his sweet niece is up to. Not even Warden Baset would hold me here if I requested it. I'm just not ready yet. I don't need *you*."

"And would Radu let you walk if he knew about this?" Ripka waved a hand over Nouli's worktable. "He's hunting the source of Nouli's experiments. It's only a matter of time until he has you both hung for dipping into his profits."

"Profits?" Nouli's voice was tight, barely restrained. "You told me the subjects were addicts seeking temporary relief from their suffering. You said nothing about *profits*!"

Kisser spit and jerked her head to one of the guards at her side. "Protection doesn't come cheap, Uncle, and I couldn't let Radu know what you were up to until we had solid footing, not with the way Thratia has him wrapped around her fingers. The stuff *works*. My leaks via the guards into Petrastad are proof enough of that. We could make a fortune, selling it on both sides of the war. Me to the empire, and Radu to Thratia. Think of the gold. We could rebuild the Bern estates anew. You could rebuild your library." Her eyes shone with genuine, if sickening passion. Ripka looked away, unable to stomach the stark fanaticism in her face.

"You mean this? Truly?" Nouli asked, his voice firm, even. Ripka admired him for that.

"You've earned it! This exile is a farce and everyone knows it. We need only the grains to restore you to your proper place."

"To restore the Berns to their proper place," he echoed.

"Yes!" Her fists clenched over her chest and she leaned toward him. Hopeful, vulnerable.

"No," Nouli said.

"What—"

He kicked the leg of his table, a practiced jab, and the whole workstation collapsed in a rain of broken glass and spilt chemicals. Ripka jumped away as the many-colored fluids began to pool together. To fume wisps of cobalt smoke.

"Idiot!" Kisser hissed. "Honey, restrain that one." She

flicked a hand at Ripka and advanced upon her uncle. Nouli stepped backward, hesitant, his eyes glued upon the swirling puddles of his concoctions. Sweat sheened his brow, and Ripka realized he was waiting for something she didn't want to wait around to see.

Honey didn't say a word to Kisser. She slipped forward, smooth as a viper, stuck her knife in the neck of the guard closest to her, humming a soft tune as she danced away from his crumpling, spasming body.

Kisser whirled toward her once-accomplice, eyes wide. Honey grabbed her hair, yanked so that she bent over backwards and fell hard to the ground. The other guard turned toward them. Nouli's eyes bulged.

"Get out!" Ripka barked, leaping over the felled guard and Kisser to grab Nouli's arm and haul him out into the hall. Shouts and stomps and curses echoed behind her but she pushed on, shoving Nouli ahead, praying to the blue skies he knew where he was going.

A concussive whump sounded against the stone wall, the ground shaking as rivers of mortar streamed from cracks between the stones. She stumbled, fell to one knee. Enard was beside her in an instant, pulling her back to her feet, urging her forward while Honey sang a lullaby to herself somewhere behind them in the hall.

"Was that–" she began, but Nouli cut her off, shaking his head so hard sweat flew off him. "Wasn't mine, not yet, hurry."

Enard mouthed, "Lord Honding."

She shivered and forced herself to run on, praying all over again that Detan and the others were safe. That whatever that was, he'd been in control of it.

Light fingers brushed the back of her neck and she almost jumped clear out of her skin. She whirled to find Honey pressed up close against Enard. "May I lead? The way behind is clear."

Ripka looked back down the narrow stone hall, and saw no sign of pursuit. "How?"

"I closed the door." Honey hummed.

The great wooden beam, used to keep Nouli tucked safely away.

"You locked them in?" Nouli demanded.

"Yes?" Honey cocked her head to the side, not understanding the horror writ upon his face.

A soft hiss echoed from down the hall, rising in pitch until it became a wail. Human voices joined the screaming, indistinguishable from the roar of the chemical firestorm Nouli had set off. Someone pounded upon the door, heavy, pleading thunks that echoed down the hall, and then the great brass alarm bells of the Remnant drowned them out. Nausea gripped Ripka. She swallowed bitter bile.

"Nouli – I... I'm so sorry."

His expression hardened, his shoulders straightened. "She did this to herself." He shuffled away, turning his back on his niece's cries. Honey took the lead, and Ripka was happy to let her do it. She'd had enough of blood. Of suffering. Kisser may have betrayed them all, but that only earned her a place in a cell. Not a molten, screaming death.

The hissing shuffle of chainmail echoed ahead. Ripka tensed, preparing for a fight, and edged in front of Nouli. He may know the way better than she, but he was no use in a fight that didn't involve rhetoric. He grunted, squeezing himself against the wall to let her pass, but by the time she'd gained the position Honey had done her work. She stood in the crossway of two halls, blood dribbling from the tip of her blade, humming a gentle tune and swaying as the man at her feet spasmed and choked on his own blood.

Ripka cleared her throat, then felt perversely guilty that she could do so while the man at her feet could not. "Which way?" she asked no one in particular.

"Left," Nouli answered, voice cracking. He cleared it. "To

the stairs at the end, then up and right. You'll find servants' stairs at the end of that hall. If you need guidance, ask, otherwise..." He glanced at the guard, now grown still, and swallowed. Ripka caught Enard's eye over his shoulder and he nodded. Enard would guard the rear, Honey would be their spearpoint, and Ripka would shield Nouli from any more trauma, if at all possible. It would work. It had to. It could not be *that* far to the roof. Enard relieved the guard's body of a cutlass. No one commented.

Honey started off, humming softer now as to not draw attention, and Ripka wished she'd go ahead and sing already. Any sound would be better than the suffocating silence of the stone walls, the frantic thundering of her heart, and the ragged breath of her companions. Detan damn well better hurry with that ship, for she was not certain they could make another stand if it came to it.

She wished they could pass through the halls like shadows, slipping through the dark corners of the prison unseen. Instead, they stumbled and shuffled and dragged themselves creaking and groaning and swearing at the occasional stubbed toe. Nouli whispered course corrections in her ear when necessary, Honey's bright hair bobbed before her like a light. Like a ghost lantern leading her into the deepest dark.

At last they came across a ladder and Honey shimmied up the rungs without effort, throwing open the top hatch to spill cloud-greyed light down upon them. Ripka hesitated, remembering with a sense of foreboding the last time she'd climbed a ladder to a sun drenched roof in Aransa. That should have been her death, but she'd cheated it. She'd cheat it again, if it came to that.

Muscles burning in protest, she slung herself up after Honey and scrambled onto the dusty tiles of the roof. Her heels rang out against hard ceramic. It made sense, the part of her that gathered details and analyzed them thought wearily. Ceramic was light. She'd seen plenty of stone roofs collapse in the poorer districts of Aransa. Roofs thrown up by people who didn't have the grains for ceramic, or the ability to weave sawgrass thatch.

She blinked, letting her eyes adjust while the others scrambled up behind her, and froze. Three guards stood at the edge of the roof, their backs to them, looking down on the mess that was the rec yard riot. Honey put a finger to her lips: *shhh*.

Motioning for Nouli to be still, Ripka crept after Honey. Enard's shadow stretched out before her, each step she took crunching over the slight grit of the roof louder than any alarm bell to her ears. But the great brass bells continued to sound, drowning their advance in the thunder of their voices. Halfway there... a third...

The bells fell silent. Honey's heel clicked against the baked tiles. One of the guards began to turn – Ripka lunged. Her world dissolved into shouting and grunting as she leapt on the back of the nearest guard, wrapped her elbows around his neck and squeezed. Honey took up her song. Enard swore somewhere distant.

Her vision swam as the guard jerked side to side, shaking her like a dog shakes its wet coat, jamming his thumbs up under her arms and wrenching, prying, clawing til her skin bled and she was roaring in his ear to stop, it was safer for him to faint. Honey's song wouldn't find him then. He staggered, swayed, the world pitched up and she saw nothing but blue as the backs of his thighs hit the low wall hemming in the roof. Her stomach dropped. The guard lurched, unconsciousness taking him at the most inopportune of moments.

Heavy hands grabbed her upper arm, the side of her jumpsuit, and yanked. She let go of the guard, swore as he tumbled over the roof without her.

"Thanks," she said, panting, and forced herself to stand, rubbery though her legs were.

"I'm afraid we've begun a bigger problem." Enard, stoic as ever, peered over the edge of the roof. Ripka forced herself to the edge, though her stomach protested at being too near the height that'd almost taken her life.

The guard's body splayed in the rec yard, limbs twisted askew, a dark stain spreading out around him. He'd drawn other guards like flies, and they pointed toward the roof, shouting. Ripka grimaced and stepped back. They'd be swarmed in moments.

"How many entrances?" she asked, then realized no one would know. "Find them all!" She put some command into her voice, because at least that made her feel like she might know what she was doing.

Honey, Enard, and Nouli scrambled, searching the square roof for hidden doors, while she grabbed the heel of the guard Honey had, apparently, stabbed in the kidney, and hauled his corpse over to the trap door they'd come through. The other guard lay beside him, neck twisted. Ripka told herself Enard hadn't had a choice. None of them had.

She stacked the corpses on top of the trap door and brushed her hands off as Enard trotted up to her.

"Well?"

"Only the one entrance, and an empty docking post, captain."

She almost laughed with giddy relief. "Good. The guards' weight should slow anyone coming through down."

"Not for long," Nouli said, staring at the door, his tanned face wan and sallow in the clear light of day. Poor bastard had probably never seen so much blood up close before.

"It'll be enough," she said, not believing it, and then reached down to peel the baton and cutlass from a fallen guard's body. After a second's thought, she took the coat too.

"You cold?" Honey rasped, her voice all motherly concern.

"Hardly. Come on, we gotta hang this from the dock post so Honding can find us."

"Won't he see the battle?"

Ripka grimaced. "I'm hoping he'll get here first."

Thudding pounded below the trapdoor, crushing her hopes as soon as she'd spoken them.

CHAPTER 42

Dust-coated figures emerged from the wreckage. For a moment his skin prickled, thinking he'd made ghosts of them all. But they wiped their faces with the backs of their hands, clearing away the stone powder, and fumbled for weapons that he knew would soon be pointed his direction. Aella advanced, the hunched form of Callia shuffling along beside her.

I am going to fight. The realization shuddered through him, and he swallowed bile. Not really. Not in truth. Just a few misdirections, nothing to do anyone real harm. He hoped.

"Hold, Aella," he said, trying to force some iron into his voice. Trying to remember he was a lord, for better or ill, and if it weren't for the singular fact that he was a wanted man he would outrank this girl.

She paused, but appeared to have done so only to brush more debris from her clothing. "I'm happy to wait for the regular guards to come along and take you in hand, if that's what you want, but I suspect they'll be rougher with you than my people."

He wiped sweat from his forehead and glanced over his shoulder. The guards weren't far, a line of ants advancing on a freshly discovered carcass. Not much time to prepare.

Not much time at all.

"We're walking out of here, kiddo. Or did you miss the implication of my little demonstration?" He held his hand out, palm open, as if preparing to gesture her way and funnel his power into the sel hovering above the house. He felt ridiculous, like a clown capering for a bored noble, but he kept his face stern and his back straight. He'd playacted a lot of things in his time. Pretending he had control of himself was just another mask to don.

To his relief, Aella's thin brows pinched and she squinted at him, looking genuinely consternated for a moment. "You expect me to believe you intended that?"

He resisted a nervous urge to lick his lips. "Wasn't an accident I blew the wall no one was standing against, was it?" It was pure dumb luck, flailing in his panic, but he couldn't let her know that. Couldn't let her see how close he'd come to tearing them all to itty bits.

"I don't believe you, Honding."

"Ready," Pelkaia said. He nearly jumped out of his skin when he saw her wearing Thratia's face, just as pristine as it had been when they'd walked off the gangplank. She turned her back on Aella and marched toward the approaching guards, affecting all of Thratia's confident swagger despite the dust and dirt clinging to her clothes. The side of her cheek began to smear. To twitch.

"Coss," he prompted.

The first mate jumped and reached toward Aella and her cohort, condensing a sliver of selium out of the air near the ground, precisely in the middle of their two groups. Detan grit his teeth, struggling for all he was worth to ignore the layer floating above the house, and snapped his fingers.

The sliver went up in flames, throwing rocks and dirt in all directions. He grinned like a madman as Aella yelped and jumped backward. His power sapped away from him in an instant as Aella shifted her focus.

"You there," Pelkaia yelled. Detan resisted an urge to look. He hated having a bunch of swords at his back, but he'd hate having Aella there even worse. "Assist me in humanely securing these prisoners. Obviously the Remnant is not capable of housing more dangerous threats."

Blue skies, but he was lucky Pelkaia was a quick thinker. Disgrace Aella's abilities *and* get them all off this horrible hunk of rock? He dared to hope the ploy just might work.

"I think not," Aella said, taking a step forward. Detan held a threatening hand toward her and she rolled her eyes. "You're shut down, Honding."

"And you're out of line," Pelkaia snapped. "Guards, apprehend this child and her people as well. I expect a full inquiry to be performed upon this little project."

"But, it's your project, commodore," one of the guards stammered.

Aella smirked. "That is not Commodore Ganal."

Detan's power rushed back to him, dizzying, but Tibs was there to prop him up as he swayed. Coss saw him stagger and reached out, condensing a walnut-sized chunk of sel from the air a bare three strides from Aella. Detan blew it without hesitation. The girl swore and stopped hard, jerking her skirt smooth. With a scowl she flicked a wrist at Detan and his power retreated once more. Tibs abandoned him to hold up Coss, who looked green about the throat and poured sweat like he was single-handedly attempting to drown out the desert.

"You cannot keep this up!" Aella shouted at him.

"Don't push me then," he growled, surprised by the raw anger in his own voice. She was right. He'd lose control, or Coss would faint dead away, and either way they were royally fucked. Pelkaia's true face would be revealed. Those working for Aella would hem them in completely.

He shot a glare at one of Aella's deviants, and the woman stopped hard in her slow encircling, but he knew it wouldn't last. They were roped in. They had no idea what Aella's cohort's capabilities were.

They were going to die here, or be captured.

Detan spared a hopeful glance at the sky, and saw no familiar shadow bobbing toward him. He sighed. Not so lucky this time, then.

"Honding." Pelkaia's voice was a soft growl. "Remove these traitors."

She turned back to him, the guards that'd spilled from the Remnant arrayed around her like a fading crescent moon, her false face stern and her borrowed chin tilted up in defiance. She knew it, too. She must know they were screwed – and this was the only option she saw. The only one he could see, too.

Eliminate the one who could reveal their lies to the guards. Eliminate those loyal to her. Eliminate every other soul who was hiding in that cracked-open yellow house, injured or otherwise cowering with fear. A few had trickled out from the broken building. He could see them only in silhouette, the sun setting behind the house's back, hunched over in the scrub or sitting under trees. Their heads were collectively turned toward their leader and the half-dozen men and women who were, apparently, meant to be their protectors.

And that layer of sel hanging above them, soft as a cloud, called his name.

"*Honding*," Pelkaia said again.

Coss swayed in Tibs's grip, face gone white as a sheet. Too much strain. Coss had never trained for this. Detan wasn't even sure if he could have been trained for it. The man would be bedridden for weeks as things stood, Detan knew what it was to use yourself up like that. Knew, too, how relieved he'd felt the first time he'd emptied all his power. The first time he'd burned the world just to spite it.

Worldbreaker.

He shuddered, feeling as nauseous as Coss looked. Blood

dripped from Tibs's chin, splashed across Coss's bent forehead. Tibs's ropey muscles strained, his eyes bloodshot and his wrists rubbed raw and angry. Tibs looked at him like he wanted him to do something, but Detan didn't know what. Looked at him like he feared him – feared whatever he would do. Feared there'd be no coming back from it.

And there was Aella, a smug smile on her rounded lips, her arms crossed loose and easy as her loyalists continued to fan out around them all, tucking them into a neat little trap. Just a matter of time, and then she'd have them all in hand. For Thratia. For the woman who was preparing to march on his family's city. He could be done with her. Wipe out Thratia's secret weapon before it ever got pointed his auntie's way.

Anger constricted his chest, the layer above sang to him, the boiling of his blood harmonizing with it. Heat radiated from his injection site. As if his blood knew the choice he'd been given and was hungry for his answer. The eyes of the injured watched him. Tibs's words rushed back to him: *This plan ain't what we do. So you best figure out another way.*

Detan picked another option.

"I apologize," he lied, eyes locked on Aella because he daren't look at Tibs. "I will come freely with you, Aella. There is no need for us to take up anymore of the commodore's time. Please see to it that her ship is refilled with the selium it needs to cross the sea safely."

"What?" Tibs blurted.

Aella's eyes narrowed. She took a hesitant step forward. Detan didn't think Coss could condense sel again even if he'd wanted to.

"And if I decide I would prefer you all to stay?"

He cocked his head to the side and allowed his gaze to drift upward, to the layer they all knew was there, his palm angling just a touch. He said nothing. Let the ease in his shoulders and the serene mask plastered across his face communicate his intent. If Aella deigned to take them all into her clutches, he would do it. And, oddly, he did not think she was capable of stopping him.

"Very well," she said eventually. "And the other prisoner?"

Tibs. Detan's heart ached. "I see no reason why the commodore's custody would not be sufficient."

"Sirra," Tibs said in the same tone he always used when he thought Detan had come up with a particularly idiotic idea. Detan said nothing, turned to look at Pelkaia instead, to be sure she understood his intent. Her false face was twisted with disgust.

"Very well." Aella flicked a hand and her cohort moved forward. "My people will see the others back to their ship to be certain of their... safe return."

"Detan?" Tibs's voice cut. Pain weighted him down, threatened to crush the breath from his chest. That slight plaintive note in Tibs's tone was worse than a slap. Worse than anything. But he had to keep his head up. Had to keep himself together.

This was the way. The only way any one of them could walk off this island without wading through a pool of blood first. And maybe, just maybe, he might be able to work some chaos from within Aella's world. It would be the hardest game he ever played, but he could make her trust him. Make her think he was her man in mind and body. Had to, if he was going to wring any good out of this.

"We'll be back for you," Tibs said, too loud as he struggled to help Coss away. Aella'd heard. She must have. He winced, knowing what he must do. Knowing the rift he'd have to carve to drag Aella to his side. To make certain Tibs didn't get himself killed coming back for him. He made his face a mask of angry stone, and faced Tibs.

He couldn't look him in the eye. Had to stare at a point just above his head. But Aella wouldn't be able to tell that, and Tibs wouldn't see the difference. He always missed the finer points when he was truly hurting. And Detan meant to hurt.

He forced his voice to calm indifference and said, "Don't bother."

Tibs froze. "You don't mean that."

"I've accepted Aella's offer of knowledge. We're done. *Go.*" He flicked his wrist, the dismissive gesture of a noble to a servant. Tibs drew back as if he'd been struck.

"You don't have to do this," he insisted, voice harsh. "We can find another trade. Another way–"

"This isn't a trade!" Detan forced himself to his full height. Forced himself to cut the air with his hands as he spoke. Funneled all his anger at being caught in this trap into his voice, and redirected it at Tibs. "You wanted me to seek help? Well I fucking have!"

"Not from her."

"Then from who? Pelkaia has made it clear as a spring sky she doesn't want me on her ship. You don't have a lick of sel-sense in that whip-thin brain, and there ain't another sensitive with the knowledge I need in the whole of the Scorched. Unless you'd rather I throw myself straight on the steps of the Bone Tower?"

"We can find someone else, anyone!"

Aella said, "Gentlemen, please–"

"Shut the fuck up!" they said in unison.

Detan clenched his fists, breath heaving. The rubble strewn all around him felt close, choking. This had to cut. Deep.

"What good are you to me? You can't even stand seeing a bunch of blue-coats bleeding on a beach. These years, you've only grown weaker, while I've grown stronger. Leave! There's nothing more I need from you." His voice rasped. He couldn't help it.

"Need? Need?" Tibs's wild brows drew down into an angry crease. He loosed Coss, lunged at Detan, gnarled hands outstretched to grab his shirt, face blossomed all over with red blooms of rage.

One of Aella's goons got an arm around Tibs, hauled him

back out of strike range. Detan bit his cheek until it bled to keep from calling out. To keep from blubbering apologies until they were both weeping. Aella let him stay like that, numb and staring, until his companions disappeared within the walls of the Remnant.

Tibs did not look back.

Aella's hand lighted upon his shoulder. He was proud of himself for not flinching.

"If Ripka's still here, you best let her go before I lose my pits-cursed mind."

"I'll release her and your other friend. This trade is worth that much." Her fingers curled into his shoulder, a perverse mirror of Tibs's earlier support. He bowed his head. He could not help it.

"Come now. Let's find you a room, and some food. We have much to discuss."

He followed Aella into what was left of the yellow house, the shadow of the *Larkspur* boring a condemning hole into his back with every step.

CHAPTER 43

Each time the trapdoor was struck, the corpses piled on it jerked and twitched. They had to shove them back onto it, keeping the weight centered, keeping their boots on top of the door to hold it down. The door jumped again, jarring Ripka's teeth. She flexed her fist on the cutlass she'd stolen and scowled.

"Where in the pits is that idiot?"

"The Lord Honding is rarely late," Enard drolled, pushing a flopped-over arm back into the pile with the edge of his cutlass.

"Rarely on time, is more like."

"As you say, captain."

"Is he really a lord?" Honey asked, her glassy eyes wide. Ripka snorted.

"In name only."

"Little more than a scoundrel, my dear," Nouli added.

And yet they were all waiting for him. Hoping for him to come and save them as soon as he could. They searched the skies, but did not speak.

The trapdoor thumped again. Honey shrieked and leapt back, taking her weight off her corner of the door, hopping around like her foot was on fire.

"What in the–"

"They stabbed my foot!" She rocked back and sat hard on her rump, holding up the sole of her boot for all to see. A neat two-inch gash opened it, blood seeping out to the baked tiles. As one, they stepped back from the trapdoor.

"Can you stand?" Ripka moved to offer her a hand up. Honey's expression had gone dark. She glared at the trapdoor like it'd stolen her lunch money and called her mother a whore.

"Let them in," she said.

"No."

"Please?" she turned wide eyes and pouting lips on Ripka. Ripka stifled a laugh, thrusting her hand toward her once more.

"You'll see 'em soon enough. Now get up, if you can."

Honey hobbled to her feet, favoring her bleeding foot. The dribbles she tracked across the tiles weren't enough to be worrisome, she wasn't going to bleed out before either rescue or doom befell them. Still, she was hurting. Slowed. The best of them in a fight, Ripka had no doubt of that, incapacitated. If that door gave way before the *Larkspur* arrived, they were in for a world of hurt.

"Wish they'd stuck me instead," Nouli muttered, and Ripka found she agreed.

"No sense in dwelling on it. Keep the bodies centered as best you can, no one put a bit of themselves on that door if you can help it."

They clustered back around the door, sweating, fidgeting, poking corpses back into place each time they shifted. The sun bore down on them. Ripka spat to curse the sea for denying her its icy bite right when she actually wanted it. She understood now why the old sailors cursed the water as much as they worshipped it. Fickle bitch, indeed.

"Captain," Enard said. Something in his voice made her shrink within herself. Whatever he had to say, she didn't want to hear it.

"Yes?" she asked anyway.

"It appears our pursuers have diversified."

"What are you talking about?"

He pointed with his cutlass, his form perfect despite his exhaustion. She followed the line of his blade to a roof across the rec yard. A handful of guards were rigging up a flier, getting it ready to set out toward their empty docking post. Her stomach fell. There was no cover here – not from sight, and not from crossbows. They couldn't hide, and they couldn't go down – who knew how many jackals were waiting to tear them apart past the door.

"Fucking Honding." She kicked a corpse, but it didn't make her feel any better.

The trapdoor jerked, one corner lifting, and a gauntleted hand shot through. Before she could think she kicked it, swore as bright motes of pain exploded in the corners of her eyes. Wood groaned, the others piled their weight on. But the guards had leverage, now. It wasn't enough.

The first one through fell to Enard's cutlass, throat opened to grin at the sky as his head tipped back and he fell down the ladder. From the thumps and shouts he'd taken a few behind him with him, but it was only a temporary reprieve. Bottleneck or not, they'd be swarmed in moments.

She hooked her aching foot under the flung-open trapdoor and struggled to heave it back closed. Nouli helped, huffing and puffing as he shoved at the blood-sodden wood. They got it to the apex, shoved it down, and it bounced right back up.

The head of a door-breaking ram crashed through. Where they'd dug the thing up, she had no idea, its paint was peeling and its irons rusted – but it shattered the door all the same, wrenched the hinges free with squeals. She staggered back from the explosion of splinters, as did everyone else. Just what the guards had wanted.

"Close the neck!" she snapped, but it was too late. One

was up, two. They couldn't fell them both before the others poured through. Their advantage was lost.

"Behind me," she ordered Nouli, and sliced down a woman who closed on her, chopping her like she was wood, trying not to think of the friends and families and passions she was destroying with every strike. Watch-captain Leshe, killing guards like they were sent for slaughter. Her stomach boiled with shame, but she dug her heels in, stood her ground. They'd kill her for this. No one saw a trial who felled a body in a uniform with their fellows around.

She figured she deserved it.

Somewhere on the other side of the swarm boiling up through the broken door Enard's roar of effort turned into a screech of pain. She winced, letting the man facing her get inside her guard with her fear. He scored a cut on her arm and she hardly felt it as he pressed the advantage, shoving her back into Nouli, turning a clipped duel into a shoving, grunting match that was likely to end up on the ground. Someone always died when a fight like this went to the floor. She was tired. Worn out. Ripka steeled herself, hoping they'd let Nouli live in the end.

Someone screamed, and it wasn't from pain or anger or death, it was a shriek of pure, raw, fright. A shadow flickered over the melee and other shrieks joined in, the guards breaking, scattering. Ripka staggered back, dumbfounded as her partner squirreled away from her, Nouli's hand on her back the only thing that kept her on her feet.

Through the sky twisted a massive beast, a serpent wrought of silver and cloud, its writhing body undulating above their heads as its great maw snapped down, breathing crystals of ice.

Ripka froze, momentarily stunned. A thing of legends, a creature out of fairy tales... Like a doppel. Or, she recalled, an illusionist. Frantic, she searched the sky, saw a gleam of pearlescence by the dock. Pelkaia. Had to be.

"To the dock!" She grabbed Nouli's wrist and ran.

Steps pounded after her, she didn't know whose, prayed it was Enard and Honey but didn't dare turn her head to be certain. Nouli huffed along beside her, not questioning, not even as she tore full speed across the spit of wood and stone that stretched out into open sky. She saw the gleam again. Thought there was something like a smirk in it.

Death by blade, or by falling. Either way she was destined to die. Might as well risk it.

Her boots hit the last board of the dock. Nouli screamed. She leapt.

Hardwood slapped her feet, her knees. She crumpled, landing hard, awkwardly as she couldn't see her goal. Nouli splayed away from her, rolling like some flicked larva. Someone grabbed her arms and hoisted her up, dragged her out of the way and dropped her back to the deck where she lay on her back, arms wide, staring at the blue sky and its slight gleam.

"Knew you'd see it." Pelkaia stood above her, sweating, ruffled, but smirking. Ripka never thought she'd be pleased to see that smirk.

"The others—"

Pelkaia cocked her head, smiled. "Arrive now."

Honey and Enard leapt through the air, appearing out of nowhere, arms windmilling and eyes wide with horror as they tumbled to the deck. Enard was bleeding, seeping his life out his side, and Pelkaia's crew rushed him, bundling him up so quick she began to doubt she'd ever seen him in the first place. Honey crawled over and flopped down beside her, smiling.

"You jumped," Ripka said, realizing that neither Honey nor Enard could have known what they were leaping toward.

"He said it was all right. Said the captain wouldn't ever lead us astray."

Honey trailed her fingers through Ripka's hair, and she

didn't know whether she wanted to laugh or cry from relief. Pelkaia helped her back to her feet and snapped for one of her crew to come see to Honey's wounds.

"Need an apothik?" Pelkaia raised her brows at the weeping wound on Ripka's arm.

She looked at it, almost startled it was still there, and shook her head. "In a moment. I want to watch this place fade away."

"As you like. Aft rail will have the best vantage." And then Pelkaia was gone, shouting orders as if it were the most natural thing in the world.

Ripka limped her way to the aft rail. Tibal lingered there, his back hunched, his arms hanging over the rail with his hat in his hands as he worked the brim around. She came up beside him, eased her weight against the railing, and watched the mist roll back from the Remnant as the *Larkspur* changed course for the Scorched.

"Long time," she said, after the silence had grown too wide.

"Mmhm," he said.

She fidgeted with the frayed hems of her sleeves. Didn't he have anything to say to her after all of this? After all she'd been through on behalf of their mutual scheme?

"Where's Honding?"

He spat over the rail, shoved his hat on, and stomped off back toward the cabins. Ungrateful man. No matter what spat had brewed between Tibs and Detan this time, he could at least answer her with words instead of bodily fluids. Ripka stared out across the fading Remnant, too choked with questions to give voice to any particular one.

CHAPTER 44

Aella had given Detan a room to share with the man he'd been chained to when Callia'd held him captive, because she'd thought it was funny. Old friends reunited, but this time free of locks, she'd said, winking, and he'd wanted to vomit all over her pretty little slippers to show her what he thought of that particular notion.

But he'd smiled, and made nice with the old man, and told himself again and again this was the best course. He was doing this for a reason. Not just for his own control, but for his Aunt, for Ripka, and... and Tibs, too, if he'd ever come around to believing a word he said again.

Even with the layer of sel gone to hide the *Larkspur*, he'd grown too anxious beneath that low, stone roof, craving nothing but the sky and the stars and the wind above his head. And so he'd left, wending his way across the island, testing the length of his new leash. Aella'd let him wander all the way down to the shore, to a crumbling cliffside with a scrap of a wall left from what had once been a lookout post, and didn't send anyone looking for him.

She wasn't worried about him. That galled him more than anything.

He leaned against the wall, rested his arms over the top

of it, and stared at the sky until his eyes watered. Not tears. Not exactly. He'd have plenty of time for those, later. This was something like penance. A taste of the pain he knew he deserved for what he'd said to Tibs. A taste of the pain for never getting the chance to say what he wanted to Ripka.

He stared, and his eyes dried out, and they watered again. The cold seeped into his knees, his chest. If he merged with the stone, joined with rock and myth as a statue grown here on the island, he wouldn't have minded. Then maybe someone might take pleasure from his life someday, reading the fairytale of the Remnant's stone man. Or a dog would come along and piss on his leg.

He shook his head. Ripka would whip him bloody for being so melancholy. He had to gather himself. To get ready to fight a war of a different flavor than Pelkaia desired.

Aella stepped behind him, a waif of a shadow thrown over his shoulder. Small as she was, that shadow felt heavy across his back.

"This is a long way from the yellowhouse," she said.

"Wanted to see how far you'd let me go. How far that trust of yours extended."

"You presume I trust you, Honding?"

He traced the path the *Larkspur* had taken away from him, clinging to the faint evidence of its passage in the smearing of the clouds, and allowed himself a tight smile.

"You presume your trust matters?"

She scoffed and stepped beside him, laying her hands on the crumbling stone top of the wall. "You are in my power now. Even you must see that."

His laugh started out as a low rasp, then mounted to a raving roar. He knew he must sound mad – wondered if indeed he had finally cracked – but found little point in caring. When his laughter had subsided to hiccupping chuckles, he wiped the wet from the corners of his eyes and faced her. Her small face was slack, eyes wide with surprise.

She would never believe he had been turned, not really. Would never believe he'd constrained his spirit, bent himself to another's will. And so if he could not fake docility, he would have to fake madness. Flaunt arrogance. It was not so far a stretch.

"I have knelt for greater masters than you, and risen whole," he said, voice rising as he warmed to the task. "I have stood in the mouth of a firemount constrained by my greatest fear and still, *still* I stole from you everything I sought to take. Even now I stand before you beaten, and yet you cannot see behind the captivity – cannot see that while you crow your triumph I have stolen the most valuable mind in all the world from beneath your stunted nose."

"What do you mea–"

"Be quiet! Your ignorance does not compel me, nor do your threats. I have been trading my freedom for victory the whole of my sorry life. Gloat, if you will. Toast with your cursed sycophants and send glowing words back home to your master. But do not, not for a single beat of your blackening heart, think you ever hold *power* over me. Your triumph is temporary. I have stolen the sky from you and yours, stolen the bread from your mouths and the heart-knot of your scheming. Do you think I cannot take a city from you? A continent? A future?"

She ruffed her hair with her fingers, and his heart panged with how young she looked. "Your honesty endangers you, Honding."

"Oh, Aella. I will be honest with you. And still I will win."

"You are without your friends here, be reasonable."

"Tell me, do you truly believe that my being without my friends makes you *safer*?"

She was quiet for a while, staring at the clouds through which the *Larkspur* had left. Though her cheeks were still rounded with youth, and her build slight and willowy, she held her experiences around her shoulders like a cloak.

Wrapped herself in the cruel details of her past. When she spoke again her voice was quiet, smooth. It was the most honest tone he'd yet to hear from her.

"I will not crow victory at you, as you say. Instead, I will ask you a single question, Lord Honding." Her hand disappeared within the folds of her white coat. She pulled something small, something gleaming, from her pocket. It clinked as she set it on the top of the stretch of wall between them. She pulled her hand away.

A single syringe lay on the grey stone. Its steel tip glinted in the faint starlight. The smoky-red liquid within shimmered, swirling with its own currents. He'd know it anywhere. The same fluid that Callia had injected him with in Aransa, opening him up to greater power and greater shame. The same fluid that would, if Callia were to be believed, enslave him to be near selium at all times. A leash, tied to his blood. One that'd been tugging at him, quietly, since he'd first tasted it near on a year ago now.

He licked his lips, and could not take his eyes from it.

"This is your price. This is what it costs, to learn from me without imprisonment."

"That wasn't a question," he rasped.

She lifted the syringe. Held it poised. Ready. Extended her hand for his arm. "Some questions do not require words."

Detan Honding knelt.

ACKNOWLEDGMENTS

While the mad rush of drafting a novel is an inherently solitary act, this story wouldn't exist without the advice and support of a great many wonderful people.

First and foremost, thank you to my long-time writing group, Earl T Roske, EA Foley, and Trish Henry, for your always insightful critiques. And, of course, for suffering my caffeine-hyped ramblings about plot, characterization, and worldbuilding.

Thank you to my Secret Agent, Sam Morgan, and the whole JABberwocky team for backing up this crazy thing that's become my writing career.

Thank you to Marc Gascoigne, Phil Jourdan, Michael R Underwood, Penny Reeve, and the Angry Robot team for all your support and insight.

Thank you to Jay Swanson, whose drawings of cats on airships never fail to buoy my spirits.

Thank you to all the wonderful authors who have offered me their support and advice over this last year. There are just too many to list. Your generous spirits and immeasurable talents are what keep the genre community going strong.

Thank you, too, to all the bookstores and wonderful booksellers who have hosted me.

And of course, thank you to Joey Hewitt. I wouldn't be half so sane without him.

Last but not least, thank you to you. That's right, *you*, dear reader, for allowing me to spin you a tale. I hope you'll stick with me for many more to come.

ABOUT THE AUTHOR

Megan E O'Keefe lives in the Bay Area of California and makes soap for a living. (It's only a little like *Fight Club*.) She has worked in arts management and graphic design, and spends her free time tinkering with anything she can get her hands on. Megan was a first place winner in the Writers of the Future competition, volume 30.

meganokeefe.com • *twitter.com/MeganofBlushie*

PREVIOUSLY...

Available in
paperback and ebook from
disreputable merchants across the city.

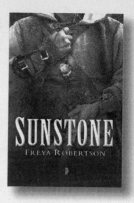

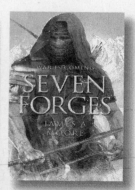

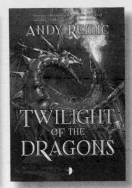

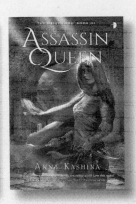
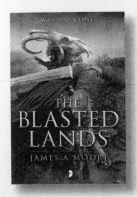
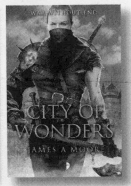
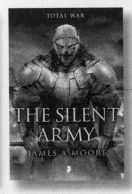